Born in Scotland, made in Bradford sums up **LIZ MISTRY**'s life. Over thirty years ago she moved from a small village in West Lothian to Yorkshire to get her teaching degree. Once here, Liz fell in love with three things: curries, the rich cultural diversity of the city . . . and her Indian husband (not necessarily in this order). Now thirty years, three children, two cats (Winky and Scumpy) and a huge extended family later, Liz uses her experiences of living and working in the inner city to flavour her writing. Her gritty crime fiction police procedural novels set in Bradford embrace the city she describes as 'Warm, Rich and Fearless', whilst exploring the darkness that lurks beneath.

Also by Liz Mistry

End Game

LIZ MISTRY

ONE PLACE. MANY STORIES

HQ
An imprint of HarperCollins*Publishers* Ltd
1 London Bridge Street
London SE1 9GF

www.harpercollins.co.uk

HarperCollins*Publishers*
Macken House, 39/40 Mayor Street Upper,
Dublin 1 D01 C9W8
Ireland

This paperback edition 2023

1

First published in Great Britain by
HQ, an imprint of HarperCollins*Publishers* Ltd 2023

ISBN: 9780008532529

MIX
Paper | Supporting
responsible forestry
FSC™ C007454

Printed and bound in Great Britain by
CPI Group (UK) Ltd, Melksham, SN12 6TR

To everyone struggling at the moment
who feels their voices are unheard

'Silence is the most powerful scream' Anon

Silence is the most powerful scream. Anon.

Prologue

Then: Marnie

It is the hottest day of the summer yet. That shimmering heat idling just above the grass. Even in my shorts and strappy T-shirt, just looking at it makes me feel sticky and tired. I want to laze under the massive spreading oak tree with my colouring books. Just sit quietly, with my own thoughts. Starting high school after the summer holidays preys on my mind. Such a big step. Such a massive change. I'll be leaving my friends behind because, despite my arguments, they've decided the local comprehensive school isn't good enough for me. I don't get it. If it's good enough for my friends then why isn't it good enough for me? Do Mum and Dad think I deserve more than Alice or Fiona? That feels wrong to me.

Anyway, this was day five of my war against the parents. I'd tried arguing, I'd tried pleading and nothing had worked. Today I was trying silence. The only problem is my annoying little sister Jilly. Why can't she just find something to do that doesn't involve annoying me? God she is soooo lame. Sooooo annoying. There she is trundling out the back door, a plastic bag filled with picnic stuff hanging off her wrist and a smile as wide as one of those arches on the viaduct we'd visited the other week. I edge my way round the foot of the tree till I am out of view of the kitchen window and tuck my legs out of sight.

'Marnie. Marnie. I know you're there. I saw you crawl behind the tree. I've brought snacks.'

Aw shut up, Jilly. The heat is making me mardy and Jilly always brings out the worst in me. She's always there. If she isn't harping on at me about something, she's following me and my pals around like a stupid collie dog desperate for a pat. I hate her sometimes. Sometimes I really, really hate her.

'I know today's your "not speaking to anyone day", but you still got to eat, Marn. I've got ice lollies.'

The ice lollies are tempting. Little dribbles of sweat are trickling down my front and soaking into my new bra – my first bra. I stick my boobs out and study them – two fried eggs underneath a padded egg cosy. I don't really need one yet, but Mum had insisted I should wear one before I went to high school – **all the girls will be wearing them, Marnie – you don't want to stand out, do you?**

Even the memory of her words pisses me off. Who the hell is she to tell me to fit in? If I went to the comp in Baildon with everyone else, there'd be no need to fit in, would there? **Why can't she see that?** *Alice and Fiona don't care if I wear a bloody bra or not. I wiggle my shoulders and study my boobs some more. I actually quite like wearing it. Maybe I just don't want to admit that I'm growing up. Starting my periods was bad enough, but sprouting boobies is a step too far. Although they're only small, they still jiggle when I run and that makes them rub against my T-shirt when I play football. At least the bra stops that from happening.*

That's another thing. There's no football at the posh new school – well not for the girls anyway – probably not ladylike enough for them. They know how much I love playing football. They know how good I am at it. If I went to Baildon High, I'd get a place on the team, no probs. Now where am I supposed to play? **You can take up a new sport, Marnie. Find something**

else you like doing – maybe hockey or volleyball? *I don't want to play bloody hockey or bloody stupid volleyball. I* **want** *to play football. That's what I want to play. Tears well in my eyes and I brush them away before Jilly comes into sight again.*

A shadow blocks the sun from me and there she is, all smiles and eagerness as she flops down beside me cross-legged. 'Come on, Marnie. Have a lolly. You don't need to speak, but you can have a lolly.'

Her face is all puckered up – her forehead all covered in lines and her lips are all wobbly, like she doesn't know what to do for the best. I know she's worried about me. I take pity on her and without smiling, I hold out my hand and she slaps the ice-cold, already-melting lolly onto my palm and then sidles right up to me and leans against the tree, her legs straight out in front of her.

'Jilly, Jilly. I can see you out there. Your legs are sticking out from behind the tree. Have you seen Marnie? She's got a dentist's appointment in a bit.' Mum's voice penetrates the space between the kitchen window and the tree at the bottom of the garden with no bother. Jilly looks at me and shrugs. 'Sorry, Marn. Should've kept my legs crossed.'

Still in silent mode I grab her hand as she gets to her feet and place my fingers near my lips, making a locking sign. Jilly smiles. 'I won't tell her where you are, sis. Course I won't. I'll go back up before she comes down here looking for you herself. You keep the snacks. There's Oreos and Irn-Bru and crisps in the bag.'

For some reason Jilly bends down and kisses the top of my head, the scent of her strawberry shampoo tickling my nostrils. 'Don't let the Beep Beeps get you down, Marn. Don't ever let the Beep Beeps win.'

The incongruousness of her words makes my lips twitch. Her use of Beep Beeps instead of bastards is just soooo Jilly and I have an urge to whisper **I love you, Jills,** *but I don't. Her words strengthen my resolve to remain silent. Jilly's never kissed me on the head like that before and I don't know why she's done it now. But it feels good.*

Like we're a team. Like, all of a sudden, my annoying little sister has grown up. Then it hits me. She'll miss me when I go to high school. She'll miss seeing me in the playground or walking beside me to school. Things are going to change for her too, not just for me. Why didn't I realise that before? I'm the worst big sister ever. I smile at her and wink and she skips back up the garden, her skinny legs all angles and knobbles.

With Mum's voice fading away I close my eyes and suck on my lolly, savouring its orangey tang. Even with Jilly covering for me, Mum will find me eventually. Course she will. She's nothing if not relentless, my mum. I sigh as the last slush of ice slides down my throat, giving me brain freeze. For now, though, I can savour the quiet. I hadn't realised being silent would be so hard. Never realised before how often I used my voice – how many words spluttered out of my mouth. The strain of swallowing my words was hard. All through breakfast, she'd bombarded me with questions, then threats, then angry words, but I'd held firm. But who knew how long that would last?

As a dark cloud dims the colours behind my eyelids and the warmth of the sun dissipates, I shiver, sensing the shadow looming over me. Unsure whether Jilly has come back or whether my mum has found me I pretend not to know anyone is there. They'll speak soon enough. Jilly can't stay quiet for longer than two seconds and as for my mum, she'll be fuming by now.

But, nobody speaks. The silence thickens and I wonder if maybe Mum is playing me at my own game. That's when rough hands grab me by my shoulders and haul me to my feet. Sweat and stale smoke pervade my nostrils as I struggle against those calloused fingers that are digging into my skin. I could open my eyes. I could break my silence. I could scream. But I don't. I've no idea why I don't. I just don't – I can't. My heart hammers so hard and a gush of something dark and scary fills my head. I can't even swallow. The sticky orangey lolly taste clags up my mouth, like superglue sticking my tongue to the roof of my mouth. I want to struggle. I know I should, but my legs and arms won't move. Like the rigid sticks of Whitby rock we'd bought at the seaside, they won't bend. I try to force my fingers into fists so I can lash out and make him let go, but nothing happens.

The dark in my head makes me dizzy and, eyes still closed, I sway and my mouth fills with vomit as his hands move to my waist and haul me off my feet into the air. The movement makes me swallow my own sick and my eyes fill with tears as it burns my throat. As he lifts me through the air, I tighten my eyes even more, hoping that he'll throw me on the grass and run away. But no, instead he hoists me up until I land belly first over his shoulder. That's when I take a peek. Bouncing along on his back, his legs marching beneath me, I see the lush green of my lawn turn into cobbles and I know he is taking me out of my garden and onto the cobbled path leading to the car park on the edge of the moors.

Why does no one stop him? I lift my head, hoping to see Mr Grayson our nosy old neighbour walking his dog, or even the paperboy with the spots and the weird piercings, but nobody is about. On we go, over the car park pebbles, little wisps of dust whipped up by his boots as he marches on. Then, with his wheezing breath in my ear, the bleep of a car unlocking sounds, followed by the creak of a door opening and moments later I am thrown onto a hard surface, the impact robbing me of my breath as, blinded by the sun, I blink up at him.

Again, I open my mouth to scream, but again no sound comes out. I am in the boot of a car and silent. As he looms over me, his features warped by rippling rays, that's how I stay: silent. No voice, soundless. To be silent is the only control I have left. As I wet myself, I vow I won't speak again. Not till I can whisper the words to my sister that I should have spoken earlier. **I love you, Jills.** My heart hammers so loud I think it will burst and all I can do is look at him as tears trickle down my cheeks. He grins. The scar on his cheek moves like a writhing snake as he leans over me. It is only then that I see he has something in his hand. As his ugly face comes closer,

I try to scramble backwards away from him. He laughs – all loud and nasty – and pinches my arm.

The prick when it comes nips and my eyelids flutter as he slams the boot shut. All at once I am in a dark space where all sights and sounds are cut off. And then there is nothing . . .

Chapter 1

DI Nikki Parekh would have missed the entrance if she hadn't caught sight of the round mirror reflecting in her headlights on the opposite side of the road, indicating a concealed drive, as she crept along in her Touran. DS Sajid Malik was beside her, clutching his seatbelt as if that would protect him should Nikki misjudge one of the tight bends in the rural lane and send them plummeting into a ditch or through one of the dry-stone walls that bordered fields. 'Relax, Saj. This is it. You can stop panicking now.'

Sajid, released his grip on the belt but continued to sit rigidly beside her. 'You're a bloody menace, Nik, you know that?'

Nikki grinned. Saj hated being a passenger, which was fine by Nikki most of the time because his Jaguar was infinitely more comfortable than her vehicle. However, shock horror, his precious Jag had developed a fault that caused the windows to keep going up and down at random. Thus, it was in the garage till tomorrow morning and Sajid was forced to slum it with Nikki in her car. Nikki had quite enjoyed riding with Saj when the windows played up – not because she enjoyed being unexpectedly hit by driving rain or wind, but because of Sajid's reaction to the indignity of it. He'd taken it as a personal affront – as if the car had developed the electrical fault solely to inconvenience him.

Because his reaction had been so extreme, Nikki had taken great delight in recording the entire event, starting with the beetroot bloom that had suffused his face, encompassing the darkening frown that had pulled his brows over his eyes and ending with the diatribe of swearing that erupted every time the window swished up or down.

Of course, he hadn't been best pleased when she'd shared the recording in the team's WhatsApp group – but hey-ho, that was life and, despite being reduced to travelling in the Parekhmobile, he seemed to have forgiven her. One glance at his face had her reconsidering her earlier assessment because Sajid's glower was enough to curdle milk still in the cow's udder.

She guided the car onto the drive and slowed right down to navigate the bends that swept unendingly before them. 'Come on, Saj. It was only a joke.'

'You didn't have to share it though, did you?'

He had a point. She didn't *have* to share it; however, she'd really, really wanted to. 'I'm sorry. Mates again?'

Before Saj could reply, Nikki slammed her foot on the brakes sending Sajid pitching forward, grabbing for the dashboard as he attempted to brace himself. 'For fu . . .'

'Now, now, now, Saj. No need to swear. Look.'

In front of them a massive house dominated a parking circle with an ornate fountain in the centre. Even in the murky dark, the glow from strategically placed lights highlighted the picturesque feature. Nikki opened the driver's window and the tinkling of the fountain filtered through. Parked all around the fountain were police cars and CSI vans with uniformed officers dotted around setting up the outer cordon. Crime scene tape, secured in place across the front of the house – which was really a mansion – by metal stakes, fluttered against the breeze.

'Crap, the first responders should have secured a wider cordon. All these vehicles will have obscured any possible tyre tracks or signs of entry to the house.' Her gaze moved from the officers busily trying to expand the tape around the circumference of the house to the sweeping stairs that led up to the huge arched front door. 'We're talking serious money here, Saj. Serious dosh.'

Saj cracked his door open and stepped from the vehicle, his eyes scanning the scene before them, his head shaking from side to side as if in awe that someone could actually live in such a dwelling. 'What exactly did Ahad tell you, Nik?'

She shrugged. 'Not a lot. Gave me the address and told me to get over here as senior investigating officer for a home invasion with fatalities. Didn't even say who called it in, so you know as much as I do.'

She joined her partner on the overcrowded drive, pulled her coat collar up against the drizzle and approached the officer holding the crime scene log. 'DI Nikki Parekh and DS Malik. I'm taking over as SIO on this one. Okay to go in?'

After signing in, she and Sajid suited up and made their way under the tape and up the massive sandstone slabs that led to the entrance. As she walked, her eyes scanned the scene, trying to get a feel for what might have gone down inside. 'Bloody hell, Saj, check this out. Who needs a door that tall? It's massive – like over eight feet tall *and* it's double the width of my front door. I mean are they giants or something?'

After pushing the door open, she saw that the CSIs had already placed metal treads for them to follow. This was not the sort of property Nikki was usually called to and the chill that had made its way into the building with the coming and going of police and paramedics gave the old building a slightly eerie feel. It wasn't just its obvious grandeur; it was the sheer opulence of it. Nikki was more at home in inner-city terraced houses or working-class ex-metro estates. Here, she had to work hard to resist feeling out of her depth. It shouldn't matter where the crime scene was, or how rich the victims had been, but this was surreal and the only frame of reference Nikki had was when she'd visited

Harewood House in Leeds or some other stately home. She'd never attended one where someone *actually* lived – or in this case – died. She grimaced at the thought.

The owners were clearly more than just "well off" and in this rural Bradford village, there was normally little need for CID presence. Nikki couldn't recall ever being called out to this area for a suspicious death in all her ten years of being a detective. Oxenhope folk didn't usually commit murder and the sorts of crimes usually perpetrated here were robberies, which of course Nikki's team didn't deal with. 'You reckon this is a burglary gone wrong, Saj?'

Beside her Sajid peered at the spacious hallway with its panelled wood walls, strategic lighting and shiny floor, and shrugged. 'Could be, but I doubt DCI Ahad would send us if that was the case. It's usually D Team who liaises with robbery when that happens. Farah will know.' He stepped forward and did a slow turn, shaking his head as he rotated. 'This hallway's bigger than mine and Langley's entire flat, Nik.'

Nikki smiled. Sajid's flat was one of the designer ones built in Bradford's historic Lister Mills to appeal to millennials with spare cash and it was a far cry from Nikki's own much-loved, but well-worn inner-city terraced home. Whilst Nikki was more Primani, Sajid aspired to be more Gucci and Vuitton, so this sort of wealth would definitely blow his mind.

As DC Farah Anwar approached, Nikki studied her face. Anwar was one of the calmest, most unflappable officers on Nikki's team, yet judging by her pallor and the rigid way she held herself, the scene had affected her. 'You okay, Farah?'

After exhaling, long and slow, Anwar nodded. 'Not one of the easiest scenes to view, boss, but I'm fine. Victims are the Salinger family; mum – Patricia, Dad – George, kids – Jason aged sixteen and Karen, aged eighteen. It's tragic. Just bloody tragic what's been done to them.'

Affected by the distress that was evident in Anwar's slumped

12

shoulders and tight lips, Nikki shuddered. Anwar was a solid officer and not much fazed her. Whatever had happened here in the Salinger house would not be pleasant. How could it be? The mere thought of an entire family being annihilated in their own home sent icy tingles up her spine. The idea that someone could have no compunction in either snuffing out an entire family during a burglary, or could hate a family so much they would murder all of them was inconceivable. However, Nikki had seen so many soul-destroying things during murder investigations that she realised that sometimes the inconceivable became a harsh reality.

The Salinger family like any other would have secrets. Of course, some of them would be irrelevant to Nikki's investigation into who had killed them, but some of them would hold a clue to who had committed this barbarous act. Even the most diabolical killers had a motive or a reason for committing their crimes – albeit sometimes a distorted one based on fantasy. Nikki hoped that the perpetrator of this crime had a more prosaic motive, because those at least were usually a little easier to untangle. 'Who called it in, Farah?'

Farah rolled one shoulder as if to dislodge an unpleasant thought and grimaced. 'It was an anonymous tip-off. Female voice said they wanted to report an attack and gave this address. They then hung up. The responding officers arrived twenty minutes after the 999 call and found the front door ajar. They entered the property and found the scene.'

An anonymous call . . . that was strange. 'Where did the call come from?' Even as Nikki asked her next question she knew what the answer would be. And Farah soon confirmed her suspicions.

'The landline.'

Okaaay, so twenty minutes prior to the police arriving someone in this house had been alive. It remained to be seen whether that person was a suspect or a witness. It was time now to view where the murders had happened, so that the victims could be transported to the morgue. 'Want to walk us through it?'

Anwar's eyes flitted to the open front door behind Nikki as if she'd prefer to escape through that than to walk her bosses through the scene, but she straightened her shoulders and gave an abrupt nod. 'Okay. This way.' She paused. 'It's not pleasant and. Well you'll see – it's very confusing.'

As Nikki and Sajid trailed after Anwar down a long chessboard marbled hallway, with dainty highly polished tables on which sat alabaster statuettes of women in various ballet dance poses, Nikki soaked up the essence of the family who had lived here. *How the other half lives – or dies.* The thought made Nikki exhale. Whilst many of the victims her team found justice for were from poorer families and marginalised groups, the wealth of these victims would have no impact on how Nikki progressed the investigation. Whilst they would receive no preferential treatment – Nikki gave her all to whatever investigation she led – they would definitely have all the skill, energy and resources at her disposal until she found their killer or killers.

Along the wall, the theme of alabaster dancing women was echoed in paintings and photographs. Nikki paused at one of the photographs. Although the dancing female figure was the focus of this particular image, before her – as if part of her audience – stood an older man and a younger male and female. The photographer had captured a moment of pure joy with the ballerina in mid jump, her movement graceful and fluid, her smile, in profile, iridescent, as if she could not be happier. The expressions of the spectators facing her reflected pride and total immersion in the older woman's delight. The dancer – presumably the woman of the house – was probably in her late forties, as was the older man – who Nikki presumed to be Mr Salinger. The two younger figures were their children, both of whom appeared to be in their late teens or early twenties.

As she absorbed the vitality that shone from the photograph,

14

Nikki realised that these people were probably the murdered victims. She took a moment longer to make sure that their images in life were firmly embedded in her mind, and then she turned and followed Farah and Sajid through a doorway to the right.

Chapter 2

It was worse than Nikki had expected and as confusing as Anwar had indicated. A Monopoly board, set for five players, lay in the middle of the mahogany dining table. Judging by the street cards, dice and Monopoly money scattered over the floor near each of the five seats, some with blood spatters on them, others with splodges of blood, which to a blood spatter analyst would tell its own story – the game had been in mid swing when the killer struck.

Still following the CSI treads, Nikki moved closer, but maintained a distance from the bodies. She wanted to take in the scene in its entirety before homing in on the specifics of the victims' positions and suchlike. 'Five players?'

DC Anwar, nodded. 'Exactly. That's only one of the things that's confusing.'

Nikki's eyes moved from the discarded board game to the four lifeless figures slouched in various poses around the dining table, each apparently killed by knife wounds, and saw what Farah meant. Five players, but only four bodies and, as far as Nikki could see, no weapon. 'The killer took the weapon?'

'It's not been found yet.'

Perhaps they'd be lucky and it would be found in the grounds of the house – not that there was any guarantee that it would offer up any forensically useful information if they did find it. A fifth person had been in this room at the time of the attack on the Salingers, which made that person either the killer or a witness. Who was this mysterious fifth person? Hopefully fingerprints would reveal that little mystery. Chances were, it was someone the family were familiar with – who settles down for a game of Monopoly with a stranger? So – family member, friend of the parents or friends or partner of one of the kids? Or none of the above? Nikki shrugged. It was too early to be sure and there was no certainty that the fifth person was also the killer.

Still focused on the empty chair – the only one with no corresponding dead body, Nikki frowned and tried to make sense of what she saw. This chair had, by the look of it, been pushed back from the table with some force and had toppled onto the floor, which might indicate a hasty, startled movement. Perhaps an argument had broken out among the players. However, either of the victims on each side of the chair may have toppled it as they struggled. The order of events was very murky. If this unidentified person was the killer, had they brought the weapon with them to the Salingers' home and used it to kill all four in a frenzied premeditated knife attack? Or had they found one on the premises and used it? Had this person jumped to their feet, toppling their chair in the process and lunged with deadly intent at the people with whom they were relaxing? That seemed unlikely, but in Nikki's experience "unlikely" wasn't always definite.

Besides, could a single killer wielding a knife kill all four victims? Had the mysterious player had an accomplice or indeed had a burglar panicked and lashed out at the family. If that was the case, then where was the other person? Perhaps they too had been injured during the attack – but they'd have to wait for all the blood analyses tests to come back before they knew that.

If the fifth player was the killer, what had motivated them? An argument over a board game seemed extreme, but stranger things had happened. Perhaps an argument blew up about something that had been brewing for ages? But it all seemed strange to Nikki. Why settle into a game if your intention beforehand was to kill? To lull your prey into a false sense of security? Whatever had prompted the attack, the absence of both the weapon and the fifth person was troubling. Perhaps the missing player was a witness who had escaped the killer. If so where had they gone and had it been them who made the call to emergency services? If they'd sought safety elsewhere then wouldn't they have heard from them? Or, had they been pursued and were now lying injured or dead somewhere nearby?

It was, as Farah said, all very confusing. 'Have the uniformed officers span out and check the grounds and into the woods. I don't care how late it is, I want neighbours roused and their outhouses and gardens searched. Maybe there's another victim out there and if so we need to find them.'

Content that she'd gained as much information as she could from studying the empty chair, Nikki's eyes wandered round the periphery of the room. Ornately decorated, the area, gleamed with rich burgundy paintwork, carefully angled lighting pointing at various artworks and pristine matching furniture. It spoke of understated wealth, whilst the entire house was the opposite of understated. Compared to Nikki's home with its jumble of well-used, well-loved furniture, the only artwork on display being photos of her, Marcus and the kids on various outings, Sunni's elaborate and abstract drawings of *Dr Who* characters and the Rubster's perfectly proportioned caricatures of friends and family, the Salingers' home was orderly. Despite lacking the loving chaos of Nikki's, it could not be accused of being cold and imposing. This was a family home too, just a more organised, less frenetic one than Nikki's.

However, the homeliness of the Salingers' abode was forever marred by the blood spatter glistening in pools on the real wood floor and the spray drops stretched up the walls indicating that the killer had struck repeatedly, sending droplets flying with

18

each thrusting movement. No doubt the forensic blood spatter analysis would confirm this. By the actions of someone earlier this evening, the Salingers' lives had been snuffed out and this home had been transformed into a murder scene. What a tragic waste of life.

From Nikki's analysis of the crime scene, George Salinger was the first victim. He was still in position on his chair, slumped forward with numerous wounds to the side of his neck and back. *Taken by surprise, no time to defend himself?* As Nikki studied the remaining victims she shook her head. 'This doesn't add up, Saj. You see it?'

'Yep. If Mr Salinger was killed first, then the others had time to react. Why have they hardly moved from their places round the table?'

Nikki eased round the periphery of the room, her eyes drinking up every clue they could. She'd be able to study the crime scene photos and videos at her leisure later, but she'd only get one chance to see everything in situ. 'The boy – Jason – was the next one. Look, he's slumped by the side of his chair as if he was going to assist his dad. See how his body's angled towards Mr Salinger?' Nikki once more shook her head. If Jason saw his dad being stabbed by a knife-wielding attacker, his expected response would be to either have jumped to his feet and closed the distance between himself and his dad in an attempt to help him or confront the attacker, or to run in the opposite direction to escape.

This boy had done neither. It looked like he'd attempted to get up to assist his dad because his chair was pushed slightly back from the table. He was facing his attacker but was struck by a debilitating blow that stretched from the front of his neck to the side and, judging by the blood loss, it had penetrated his jugular casting arterial spray up and over the board. The lad's response times were all wrong.

'Why the delay in his movement from the chair?' Nikki wafted her hand at the other two victims 'Why did none of them respond very quickly?'

Sajid had moved round the table. 'Well, Mrs Salinger's ankle's in a cast, so perhaps that explains why she's barely moved.' He shrugged. 'As for the others – maybe their fight-or-flight responses were delayed. Maybe they were so surprised by the attack that they just froze.'

Nikki was unconvinced by Sajid's arguments so far, but he was still theorising. 'Maybe there was more than one attacker. I mean that might explain it.'

But Nikki was focused on the fifth chair. The chair where the person playing had bought Bond Street and Fenchurch Station. 'Who sat here? Who was the other person playing this game?' She turned to DC Anwar. 'They searched the house on arrival?'

'Yeah. They'd cleared the entire property before I arrived.'

Nikki nodded and turned her attention back to the board game. 'This is all very weird. You don't break out a game of Monopoly with a stranger, do you? I mean it's a game you play with people you know, isn't it? In our house Monopoly can last for hours. God, I remember one Christmas, largely because of Marcus's machinations, it dragged on for over three days. We couldn't use the kitchen table and it became very competitive and tensions ran high.'

Sajid, who was prowling the room using the tracks laid out by the CSIs snorted. 'You're not suggesting the game itself was the motivation for this, are you?' He moved his arm around to encompass the entire horrific scene.

'No, no. Course not. It's just weird. Whoever the fifth person is, they sat round this table and now four people are dead. We need that ID sharpish. Whether or not they're our killer, they must know something, and we need to know who they are and what they know. What about security footage? A house like this will have security all over the shop. Anything that tells us who their visitor was?'

'We're having trouble accessing the system. It's password-protected, but we've contacted the security firm and hopefully, in the circumstances they'll bypass the need for a warrant and allow us access quickly.'

Nikki's gaze finally came to rest on the daughter: Karen Salinger. She studied the way she was slumped over the table, her chair still tucked tight to the table edge and her head angled to the side. She could almost have been sleeping – if not for the blood-drenched strands of hair draped around the gaping neck wound. Again, the knife wound seemed to have hit her jugular and incapacitated her quickly. Her arms hung to either side of her body and the only evidence of blood on her fingers was the gloopy drips that trailed from the wound to her fingertips before dropping onto the carpet. Her palms were clear of blood, which indicated that she'd made no attempt to staunch the wound to her neck.

After witnessing first her dad and then her brother being stabbed repeatedly, Nikki would have expected Karen to either try to escape or defend herself. 'Who the hell is this fucking fifth player?' Nikki turned to Anwar. 'Get the fingerprints processed ASAP, hound the security firm till they release the home security recordings and get the footage analysed pronto. Also get uniforms trawling friends and relatives.'

Her gut clenched, releasing an entourage of angry maggots squirming in her belly, warning her that this case was going to be complicated. It was always like this. It was a sort of heads up for her to prepare herself physically and mentally for being fully immersed in a complicated investigation for a long and draining period of time. This was her first official case as detective inspector *and* senior investigating officer, and she'd no intention of messing it up. This entire scene was atypical and at present they didn't have enough information on the family. It was time to order her team to uncover every secret held by each member of the Salinger family. She looked at Farah. 'What's his job? Where does his money come from? What does his wife do? I need to know everything about them.'

Gracie Fells, the crime scene manager, approached. 'Can we start bagging evidence in here now?'

Nikki hesitated. She appreciated that Fells had her job to do and that getting the evidence analysed forensically was important, but she shook her head. 'Sorry, Gracie. I think this scene warrants being seen by the pathologist in person. You'll have to wait till he's happy to let you take over. I want to nail down the choreography of the attack and Langley's our best chance of doing that.'

Fells's lips tightened, but Nikki ignored her reaction. They were rebuilding their professional relationship after a disagreement a while back, but Nikki stuck to her guns. 'Can you contact Langley? See if he can get here quickly? I really want his take on how everything went down.'

Chapter 3

I spy with my little eye something beginning with B . . . Betrayal.

When I find out what they've done, red-hot rage floods through me and incandescent fury possesses me. Shards of orange and yellow lightning streaks slice through my eyes and into my brain. My hands clench into fists and as I stride about the room, I want to land one into each of their faces. Ungrateful, disrespectful little creatures. After all I'd done for them, they repay my kindness with this. Scarface had given them instructions – clear instructions. They knew the score. Knew all too well what was a stake and what was expected of them – they were to disappear. But look what they've caused. So much chaos.

How fucking dare they? How fucking dare they indeed?

As I prowl around my home, I visualise having all of this taken from me. Visualise losing everything I've worked so hard to preserve over the years. We should have been more cautious. It's not like this is the first time we've released the petals in the wind. I overestimated our control over them. I should have anticipated that they might rebel, but after so long, it just didn't seem likely. Especially not with her little friend to take care of.

My breath fights to escape my lungs and I massage my chest,

till the sensation of drowning eases, before recommencing my stalking. I have to work out a strategy. One that will allow me to maintain the upper hand.

Thank God, Scarface was there. Thank God or I'd be down the station already. Thank fuck he sorted out the situation, took control. He'd questioned my decision to let them go, but I'd ignored him. It had worked before. Countless times. None of the others – bar one, had ever caused any problems and let's face it we had no real option.

I slam my fist into the palm of the opposite hand, still wishing it was one or other of their pitiful, ingratiating faces. What have you done? I hadn't expected this, hadn't planned for it and am not sure how to deal with it. I pause. And focus my mind. I have a meeting soon and when the others arrive, I'll have to be in control. No room for emotion, no room for anything. They must never suspect my involvement in any of this.

The burner phone I keep hidden in my locked bottom drawer rings, and I take a few slow breaths before answering with a single barked word. 'Update.'

By the time the voice on the other end of the phone has updated me, some of the tension has left my shoulders. 'You on top of things?'

Scarface pauses. I can almost hear the cogs in his brain whirr into action. He's always been analytical in his responses. Always weighing up the pros and cons of his replies. 'Work in progress I'm afraid. Need to keep our eye on the police activity, but I think all bases have been covered.' His husky laugh grated against my ears. 'Don't worry. I'll sort it.'

Of course he will. He always does. That's his speciality – sorting things for me. I perch on the edge of my sofa, pour myself a whisky and think through all the information I have at hand. Then, I smile. I have the perfect scapegoat at my disposal and with that scapegoat comes an ever-brightening glimmer of hope for my continued survival. If I'm clever and cover my tracks, I can make this entire debacle work in my favour. I take a mouthful of the single malt and savour it on my tongue before enjoying the slow burn as it flows smoothly down my throat.

I spy with my little eye something beginning with V . . . Victim.

A laugh builds in my throat and releases along with my words into the empty room. Once more my intelligence and caution will pay off. My victim is no match for me. She'll never see me coming.

Chapter 4

As Nikki paced up and down outside the Salinger property, the fine drizzle of rain, matching her mood, became a persistent shower. She'd been desperate to escape the confines of the house, imagining that she could smell the coppery blood even in the hallway and sense the property's life light stuttering to extinction. She welcomed the freshness the rain brought as she waited for the pathologist, Dr Langley Campbell, to arrive. As well as being the pathologist, Langley was also Sajid's fiancé and he and Nikki were friends. She trusted him implicitly and was eager to hear what he made of the scene. *Come on, Langley, get a move on.*

Nikki had learned that the property had been in the Salinger family for over fifty years and somehow the entire building seemed to be in mourning following the tragedy that had unfolded there earlier. Anwar had called in her sidekick, DC Liam Williams, and between them, they'd managed to contact George Salinger's business partner, Derek Bland. Nikki would visit him when she was done here. To give him his due, Bland had been cooperative and informative when they'd spoken. He'd agreed to wait for Nikki's visit no matter how late it was. On the phone he'd seemed devastated by the news and Nikki was keen to assess the depth of his grief for herself.

Williams having contacted Salinger's personal assistant, Alicia Harper, was now en route to their offices in Leeds where he hoped to gain access to Mr Salinger's electronic diary as well as interview the PA regarding any possible business conflicts. Nikki would take an initial statement from Derek Bland later and compare whatever information she got with that gained by Williams.

Neither George nor Patricia Salinger had living parents and, although Patricia had a sister currently living in Canada, George was an only child and his only relative was a much younger cousin, currently backpacking in Mexico. Sajid had settled himself in a small room adjoining the library and was in the process of trying to contact the sister and cousin.

Nikki's peeked her head through the door of the Salinger library and couldn't help pausing for a moment to scan the neat bookshelves filled from top to toe with books. She'd always considered that her kids owned lots of books and Marcus was an avid reader, but their random bookshelves, dotted in corners throughout her home, were put to shame by the grandeur of the Salinger library. On closer inspection though, Nikki noticed that none of these books bore the thumb-eared, well-used look of a much-loved and often-read book – unlike those in her house, which her three children and latterly Isaac had spent precious hours reading and rereading.

Her initial phone call with Salinger's business partner and the PA had intimated that the Salingers had a small group of close friends, many business contacts and were popular. Neither could offer any insight into people who might bear the couple a grudge. Nikki had discovered that Mrs Salinger, a trained ballerina who once performed with the Northern Ballet in Manchester, was now retired and had recently, during a horse-riding accident, broken her ankle, which explained the cast on her leg. She was a patron of various charities, all of which would have to be followed up on. The boy, sixteen-year-old Jason, was just short of his seventeenth birthday and attended Bradford Grammar school, whilst his sister Karen was studying politics at Cambridge University. *Oh, how the other half lived.*

With her own daughter, Charlie, currently in sixth form, with a view of attending Nottingham Trent to study criminology and law, Nikki was well aware how difficult the whole process was. Not only was Charlie putting in the hours studying, determined to meet the grades required of her, Nikki and Marcus were reassessing their financial situation because putting a child through university wasn't easy for middle- and working-class parents. Thankfully, when her mum died, Nikki had earmarked most of her inheritance for her kids' futures. She turned and studied the building behind her. With its ornate staircase and imposing towering stature, Nikki considered how very different the lives of the people who had once thrived in that home were to her own life. No money worries for them – well none that they knew about, so far. Everything looked hunky-dory, but Nikki knew that appearances could be deceptive.

As she returned to her pacing, Nikki mentally ticked off the actions she would order the following day: a deep delve into the family's financials; as much background as they could find on family, friends and acquaintances; a visit to the lad's school and the girl's university – Anwar and Williams would do the first – both fledgling detectives were excellent interviewers. Their empathy and lack of arrogance generally helped people open up to them. Nikki hoped that would be the case this time, because so far, the two people they'd spoken to and who appeared to know the Salingers well had provided no clues as to motive. For the latter and in the interests of expediency she'd enlist help from Cambridge police for now. She could always travel there should the need arise later, but right now, she needed to focus her attention locally.

She blew a sodden strand of hair that had come loose off her face and wiped away the residual dampness as she considered possible motives for the crime. The circumstances of the murders bothered Nikki. With the house being in the sticks, the likelihood of a random act of violence was remote and the possibility of a burglary gone wrong seemed even less likely. The fact that the many valuable and easily tradeable items had remained in situ put the kybosh on the burglary gone wrong theory. Her trawl of the rest of the premises had revealed gold and diamond jewellery cast aside carelessly on both Karen Salinger and her mum's dressers. No, burglary didn't sit well with Nikki as a motive, but she needed more – much more – if she was to get to the bottom of this tragedy.

As she waited, her mind kept flicking to the tableau of Mrs Salinger dancing in the professional photos in the hallway – so elegant and refined – and the awed expressions on her family's faces. That photo encompassed the essence of the Salingers and it was a difficult one to nudge from her mind. Of course, photos were staged to portray a particular message – to give a specific image. Nobody was likely to give photos of a huffy, argumentative, discordant family pride of place, were they? Perhaps, like the entire house, everything was carefully choreographed to create a fictional image – that of a united, solid, loving family.

Nikki tried to imagine replacing the photos that were dotted around her home, with more polished versions and smiled. The one of Sunni sticking his tongue out would be gone, as would the one with Charlie glaring at the camera, arms folded over her chest and a jingle bell hat on her head. The one with Ruby, head thrown back in glee because Sunni had farted whilst everyone else was holding their noses wouldn't have made the Salinger "cut" either. But those were the photos that made Nikki's heart sing. The ones that, whenever they caught her eye, brought a smile to her lips. Nikki would have to be careful not to credit those beautiful dancing images with more significance than they deserved.

Intermittently, Nikki kicked the step with the toe of her Doc

Martens. She wanted to really let go with the kicking – to really hammer her foot against the slabs – but there were too many CSIs and officers around, so she contented herself with this low-level anxiety-busting measure and a couple of surreptitious twangs of the rubber band round her wrist.

After her ordeal at the hands of her depraved father earlier in the year, Nikki had been advised to see a psychologist. She'd laughed at her boss when he'd suggested it and, knowing her history with her previous psychologist, DCI Ahad had backed off with the proviso that she reconsider if things got too much for her. Instead of reconsidering, Nikki and Marcus had invested in a punchbag, which they'd installed in the cellar of their Listerhills home. They took turns to release their pent-up rage and emotions on the punchbag. It felt good when she did it and she'd found she needed the rubber band less often. Still she wasn't quite ready to divest herself of a method she'd used for years in stressful times. As she waited for Langley's arrival, she wished she had the punchbag at her disposal right now.

The headlights of a vehicle wending its way up the winding drive had her dashing down the concrete steps, so that when Langley's Jag – one very similar to Sajid's – pulled up, she practically wrenched the handle of the door in her impatience to drag him in to the crime scene. A lumbering officer approached and thrust the crime scene log at the pathologist for him to sign. When Nikki approached, the officer yawned and stepped back, leaving Nikki to grab a pristine overall as she approached the pathologist.

'Hi, Nik, you . . . ?'

But Nikki shook her head and thrust a white crime scene suit at him. 'No time for chitchat, Lang – I need your input. Suit up and follow me.'

Langley rolled his eyes at the lumbering officer who, standing slightly behind Nikki, grimaced in a "you're on your own" manner, and ambled away. As Langley tried to contain the twitch of his lips, Nikki frowned and glowered at him. 'Something funny, Campbell?'

One leg through the hole in the suit and the other halfway in, Langley shook his head, with unnecessary enthusiasm. 'No, Nikki, absolutely not. Nothing funny here. Not a damn thing.'

He yanked the suit up and over his shoulders, thrust his arms in and pulled the hood over his blond hair for good measure. 'I'm all yours. Lead the way.'

Nikki spun round and marched back up the stairs, pausing only to cover her feet with new bootees. 'The CSIs are all but done here, but I'm taking no chances.'

As they walked down the hallway, Langley grabbed her arm lightly. 'You want to tell me what prompted you to call me in? You're usually happy with me viewing the video and stills of the scene. What makes this one different?'

Nikki exhaled. 'I'm just not sure. It just seems . . .' she bit her lip and twanged her elastic band '. . . off. I just wanted to be certain. Sorry for hauling you—'

'Not another word, Nik. I know you wouldn't drag me out here if you didn't think it necessary. Let's go and see what I can add to your investigation.'

Once inside the dining room, where the bodies remained in situ, Langley did exactly what Nikki and Saj had done ninety minutes earlier and stood on a CSI tread by the door, observing the room in its entirety. 'Wow.'

Beside him, Nikki only nodded. There was nothing to add. After a minute or so, Langley moved closer to the table and studied the scene. His eyes missed nothing as he scanned the disrupted Monopoly board, the blood spatters on the walls, the pools of blood on the floor, the positions of each of the victims' and that damning empty fifth chair toppled over with no sign of its inhabitant. 'I see what you mean, Nik. One person couldn't have done this on their own unless the four victims were subdued or compliant in some way, which makes things complicated. If the fifth person killed the other four on their own, there would have been more evidence of a struggle, more movement to defend the first victim – who, incidentally, appears to be the older male – the dad?' He quirked an eyebrow at Nikki and when she nodded, continued, 'Surely, even if the dad was incapacitated, the other three would have been able to subdue, or at least have tried to subdue the killer. I see no evidence of a struggle. Each of them clearly moved from their seats, but only a little – not far enough, or with enough speed to indicate they went to Dad's assistance. It's odd.'

He continued circling the victims, kneeling occasionally for a closer look of their wounds. 'I can't say for certain till the PM, but I suspect we may find that the same weapon – a long, probably non-serrated knife – possibly a kitchen knife caused all of these lacerations.' He glanced at Nikki. 'I wouldn't be surprised to discover that most of these wounds were delivered post-mortem.'

'So, a frenzied – possibly disorganised attack?'

He nodded and recommenced his assessment. 'Possibly, or alternately it could be staged to look that way.'

Still pondering the question of the Salingers' lack of reaction, Nikki asked, 'Would you say that the victims were each killed by the first wound?'

Langley paused and looked up at her. 'That's possible, but I won't know till the PM. I get that you're curious about the lack of response from the victims – the lack of movement – but many things could contribute to that. Maybe the killer threatened them in some way. Perhaps they were drunk or in shock or believed that if they complied they would be saved, or they were drugged or . . .' He wafted his hand in the air, indicating that there were countless other possibilities.

Nikki remained silent, allowing him the time to process the scene in peace and watching his every move. He prowled round, his brow furrowed as he glanced first at one chair then another. Unable to contain her questions any longer, Nikki cleared her throat. 'Could there have been more than one killer?'

'Hmm, if there was more than one killer, then all of the above remains true. This scene is impossible to analyse without a postmortem and the lab results from the CSIs.' He turned to Gracie Fells who was waiting by the door so as to give the pathologist space to work. 'I need all the glasses and their contents analysed and expedited please. We need to start ruling things out or in, rather than all this conjecture and guesswork.'

Nikki nodded. 'You suspect the drinks were drugged?'

But Langley was reluctant to commit himself. 'I've already told you it's a possibility, Nik, but you can't expect me to give definitive answers when there are so many alternative scenarios to consider. Which brings me to my next request . . .' He grimaced. 'I want to bring in a blood spatter analyst and a 3D laser technology operator. I want to reconstruct this entire scene using all the data at our disposal. It might blow your budget, but . . . ?' He shrugged. 'You asked for my expert opinion and that's what I think. It's the only way you'll get an accurate reconstruction of the crime scene.'

Nikki's cheeks puffed out as she exhaled. Budgets were becoming increasingly constricted and this would be expensive, but she had faith in Langley's judgement and, if he thought it necessary, then she'd justify it as an essential expense. They needed to know exactly how these murders had progressed. 'We'll foot the bill. I'll get DCI Ahad to authorise it.'

Although Langley nodded, his attention was still focused on the scene before them. 'I'll stay here till the reconstruction has been done. After that, I'll give the okay for the bodies to be transported to the morgue. I'll PM them tomorrow, but I can't start till late morning and with there being four of them to do, it'll take hours. I'll let you know precise times later. I have a feeling nothing is going to be simple with your investigation.'

As she left Langley to it, Nikki rolled her shoulders. Tension radiated across her upper back and a slight throb at her temple warned of a prelude to one of her ghastly headaches. The sooner she took a painkiller, the better. But for now, she had to collect Sajid so they could go and interview Derek Bland. She would not be sad to leave this particular crime scene behind.

Chapter 5

Derek Bland lived in what Nikki could only describe as an ultra-modern bachelor flat in Leeds. Despite the lateness of the hour, Bland – a smooth, well-muscled man in his late forties with salt and pepper hair and designer stubble – was fully dressed in chinos and a contrasting polo shirt. He bustled Nikki and Saj along a lilac-coloured hallway with a line of precisely positioned framed photos, each one depicting him shaking hands with some well-known dignitary or other; a shrine to his achievements that greeted every guest as they entered his penthouse. Nikki recognised a few of them: Richard Branson, the now disgraced Tory MP Boris Johnson, Prince Charles – and as she cast a sideways glance at Sajid, he smirked and rolled his eyes. This in your face "I am" show impressed neither of them, but it did give insight into the mind-set of the man they were about to speak with.

On the drive over, Sajid had googled Derek Bland and discovered he was the child of alcoholic parents. Against the odds he'd managed to gain a scholarship to Oxford University where he'd met his future business partner George Salinger, son of a Yorkshire Conservative peer with family money behind him. The unlikely friendship between two such disparate characters had intrigued Nikki; however, seeing this ode to the moneyed and influential in society, she now had a bit more of a handle on what made George Bland tick. He'd made his money by having the right friends, working hard and making wise decisions, and he wasn't about to let anyone forget just how influential he was.

Unlike Salinger, who had no need to justify his place in society, Bland clearly felt the need to underline the credentials that enabled him to inhabit the world in which he currently lived. Was this a possible motive? Had Derek Bland been the fifth player at the table at the Salingers' house? Perhaps an inferiority complex had driven a rift between the two best friends and business partners? She'd already decided to request his fingerprints, purely to eliminate them from the crime scene. Now, she looked forward to ascertaining his reaction when faced by the request. Although, the presence of his prints in his friend's home wasn't necessarily a smoking gun. It all depended on where they were found. They had retrieved fingerprints from the fifth person's glass, chair and the table around them, so if those matched Bland's the investigation would be a short one. On the other hand, if he was a frequent visitor to the Salinger home a healthy spread of his prints would be expected.

However, something told her Derek Bland wasn't their killer. Perhaps it was his anguished expression or maybe his eagerness to assist them, neither of which, she realised, were foolproof reasons to clear someone of the crime. On the contrary, often the people who displayed the most grief, or who were most eager to help, were the guilty party. In this case though, Nikki wondered if a combination of their old boys' fraternity and Bland's reliance on Salinger to pave the way through the upper-class hierarchy, would make it unlikely for Bland to kill his business partner. Besides, killing George Salinger was one thing, annihilating the entire family was something else entirely.

She stored her initial thoughts away for further perusal later on and prepared to keep an open mind as the three of them entered a plush living room, tastefully decorated in masculine greens with contrasting amber-coloured scatter cushions that weren't so much "scattered" as precisely placed, atop a cream sofa. *Who the hell had scatter cushions?* She risked another glance at Saj, then smiled inwardly at the way his eyes darted all over the room. She was sure he was making mental notes of the interior design and, too late, she realised she did know someone who owned scatter cushions – Saj. She shook her head. In her house the well-used living room cushions were truly scattered – normally after Sunni and Rubster had engaged in one of their pillow fights – *and* they were definitely the worse for wear.

'I can't believe this has happened. Can't get my head round this. George, Trish and the kids *gone*? God, Trish and George were the best parents ever. Such a close family, and now this . . .' He directed them to sit on the opulent sofa and stood opposite them, looking around his home as if unsure what to do with himself.

Wary that the sofa might trap her in its padded embrace, Nikki perched on the very edge of the couch whilst Saj, with no such consideration, dropped into its depths. When Nikki realised the seat was well upholstered and hadn't ensnared her partner, she leaned back and marvelled at how comfortably it supported her. It was a proper Goldilocks sofa – not too hard and not too soft – just right.

'We're really sorry for your loss, Mr Bland, but at this stage in the investigation time is of the essence and anything you might know could be vital to discovering who did this.'

With his fingers linked in his lap, Derek Bland, perched on the edge of the armchair as if the nervous energy that made his leg bob up and down might make him take off and speed walk round the room at a moment's notice. Nikki understood that feeling. It was one she'd encountered often since the death of her mother and the death last year of her cousin. That pent-up agitation that might blow at any moment if the release valve wasn't turned on. Hopefully Derek Bland could find his own way of coping with the tragedy that had so unexpectedly touched his life.

'So, they really are all dead? All of them? George, Patricia *and* the kids? Even the kids? Even Karen? I don't understand why she was even home. If she'd been at university she'd still be . . .' He jammed his fist against his mouth, jumped up and, breathing heavily, completed a circuit of his spacious living room.

Nikki allowed him the time to decompress. He was dealing with a lot and they'd get more information from him if they treated him gently. He slammed his left fist into the sage green wall, leaving a smudge of blood and a dent in the plaster. As small green flakes drifted to the floor, like leaves, Nikki nodded at Sajid who got up and went to the kitchen to find ice. Nikki understood the urge to punch a wall. Hell, she'd been self-harming as a coping mechanism for years and the release that followed these actions was intense relief. It was the guilt that descended afterwards that messed you up. With no judgement in her tone, Nikki asked, 'Do you feel better for having done that? Often the release of adrenaline can make it a little easier to focus.'

Bland nodded and in silence returned to his chair. When Saj returned with a bag of frozen peas wrapped in a tea towel, he glanced at his bloody knuckles, grimaced and wrapped the peas around his hand. 'I'm sorry. I'm not usually prone to that sort of behaviour. It's all been such a shock, but I'm ready now.'

Nikki doubted that. He might think he was ready, but he wouldn't be – not for a long while. However, she had a job to do, so she leaned forward and began. 'You said you were surprised Karen was home for the weekend. Was that so strange? Didn't she visit often?'

Bland smiled. 'Karen took to university life like the proverbial duck to water – or teenager to freedom. She didn't come back regularly – last time was Christmas, I believe.' He paused, his brow furrowed, and then he clicked his fingers. 'Tell a lie, she came home for a family meal out for Patricia's birthday in February, but she wasn't going to be returning to Bradford over the summer. She'd already sorted out a flat for the holidays.'

38

He grimaced. 'Karen was luckier than many students, in that money was no object for her. No student dives with peeling wallpaper and damp stains for her. No, George bought her a flat outright and she was going to charge a subsidised rent from her friends to finance her "expenses". He emphasised the last word and then laughed. 'She always had plenty of money, did Karen, and George and Patricia indulged her every whim, which I suppose wasn't entirely surprising, considering.'

Considering what? Nikki's interest was piqued, but she opted to catch up on that later. For now, she had a far more important question to ask.

'Would you have expected George to tell you his daughter was visiting for the weekend?'

'Of course. Normally, he'd have invited me for family tea. I've no idea why he kept quiet about her visit, unless she sprung it on them and just turned up unexpectedly.'

'Had she done that before?'

Bland shrugged. 'No, as I mentioned earlier, Karen was living her best life in Cambridge and didn't look back. She was reluctant to visit even at Christmas or for Trish's birthday. Both occasions were flying visits.'

'Could she have been in some sort of trouble?'

Derek's guffaw was so loud it almost rattled the crystal decanter in his drink's cabinet. 'God no. If she was in trouble, it would have been me she contacted, not her parents. Both Karen and Jason knew better than to worry their parents about crap going on in their lives.'

Nikki frowned. What would make the Salinger kids not want to worry their parents? George's account so far indicated that they allowed their daughter her freedom, but that didn't mean that his perceptions were accurate. Maybe Karen kept secrets to avoid conflict. From personal experience Nikki knew that teenagers often tried to protect their parents – especially if the parents were vulnerable. Recently, Nikki's own daughter, Charlie, had absorbed a lot of Nikki's mental anguish and tried to cope on her own. It had taken a real effort on Nikki and Marcus's part to rectify the situation. What had caused this sort of reaction in the Salinger household? Was one of the parents ill? So many questions flooded into Nikki's mind, but she'd pace herself and follow the threads Bland was revealing here and now, although her first consideration had to be finding out the identity of the fifth player. She raised an eyebrow indicting Sajid should continue.

In his usual smiley, "I'm not threatening" way, Saj caught Bland's eye. 'Would Karen have brought a guest to meet her parents? A university friend? A boyfriend? A girlfriend?'

Bland stared at Sajid as he processed the question, then a small frown appeared at the bridge of his nose. 'Was someone else there? Was someone else killed?'

Nikki took over. 'No, Mr Bland. Only the four Salingers were killed. However, they were discovered in the dining room around the table where a Monopoly board had been set out for five players and five glasses were on the table.'

She left the words to hang there curious to see how Bland would interpret them. Eyes narrowed, Bland glared at them. 'They were playing fucking Monopoly with the person who killed them? Is that what you're telling me? The person who killed them sat at their dining room table playing a fucking board game and *then* killed them?'

'That's only one avenue we're exploring, Mr Bland. However, we do need to identify the fifth player and any suggestions you could offer would be helpful.'

He shook his head, scraped his uninjured hand over his stubble and flung himself back in the chair. 'I've no idea. No fucking idea. I thought I knew them. I *did* know them.' He closed his eyes, and as if speaking to himself said, 'Why didn't they invite me? That's just so weird.'

The pain in his voice wrung Nikki's heart. Here was a man who at face value wanted desperately to help them, but who

40

didn't know how. He glanced at the two detectives. 'I'm useless. I just can't begin to think who they'd have invited to spend time with without mentioning it to me. We were pretty much in each other's pockets most of the time. Playing Monopoly was a family thing for them. I, as the kids' godfather, often joined them, but nobody else – they weren't close with anyone else – not like they were with me.'

'What about a godmother? Would she have joined them?' Giving voice to the word "godmother" even in such circumstances conjured up images of fairies and wands and Cinderella. Nikki had never had a godmother, fairy or otherwise, looking out for her and she supposed her small network of friends – Saj, Langley her old boss Archie Hegley, Ali, her new boss Zain Ahad and her sister Anika – were unofficial godparents to her kids, although Nikki didn't place a lot of store in the "god" element of her motley crew of friends' parenting skills.

Bland waved a dismissive hand. 'No, that's Trish's sister and she's in Canada. No way it could be her.'

Okay, that was a mystery that perhaps the CSIs would be able to solve. Perhaps there would be an indication of the fifth visitor's identity on one of the Salingers' electronic devices or in their diaries. 'Okay, let's think of possible enemies then. Can you think of anyone who might have had a grudge against the Salingers, no matter how small?'

For a moment Nikki was sure Bland was going to pass over the question with a blasé denial, but when he did respond, her ears pricked up. Having potential suspects gave an investigation direction and they needed direction right now.

'Well, that charity Trish volunteered for was pretty toxic. Imagine WAGS with all their competitive bitchiness and triple it and you'd about hit the mark. No idea why she put up with it. It caused her more stress than any other part of her life; still, she insisted on continuing her patronage. The bloody thing was filled with middle-aged women bored enough to need something to fill their lives between the detoxes, yoga and golf, but not bored enough to actually work for a living.'

He scowled and paused before tutting. 'Look, I'm giving entirely the wrong impression of it. The Yorkshire Children's Cancer Trust is a really excellent project that does some fantastic work in improving the quality of life for kids whose childhoods have been blighted by this disease, and Trish most definitely *wasn't* one of the women I've just described. In fact, there was a dedicated core of Trojans who worked hard to keep the trust viable. It's the others – the hangers-on – I was referring to, not Trish. Trish was talented and until the accident, her ballet and work with the Northern Ballet in Leeds kept her pretty busy. The trust was her passion though. She really put her heart and soul into it. Spent time with the children and their families. She was really hands-on and well respected among the trust patrons. A lot of the others, though, were just feeding their own egos and brought their own brand of narcissism.'

'Okay, so could she have had a dispute with someone from the charity? Made an enemy there?'

Bland rubbed his eyes as if that would make him think better, and his shoulders slumped. He exhaled then met Nikki's gaze. 'I hate dragging up private stuff about my best friends but . . .' he shrugged '. . . how can I not? How can I conceal information in these circumstances?'

He raked the fingers of one hand through his hair, making it stand up like snowcaps on a ski slope, and he tutted before speaking. 'Trish was having an affair. Some bloke she met through her charitable work, I believe. George and the kids knew about it because his wife turned up at the house over Christmas, yelling and screeching at Trish, with him on her coat tails trying to diffuse the situation It was a . . . fraught time for everyone. The kids were disgusted and angry. George was heartbroken and Trish was ashamed. They spent time – George and Trish – trying to sort through it. They agreed that they'd been through too much as a couple – as a family – to throw it away on her misguided actions. They were working through it. They really were.'

Bland's pleading eyes made Nikki wonder just *who* he was trying to convince. Information about an affair conjured up a myriad of possibilities – had the scorned wife taken her revenge? Or perhaps her children or one of her relatives? Or had the discarded man been infuriated enough to annihilate an entire family? Had the affair really ended or was Trish going to leave her family? As Bland bit his lower lip, his eyes flitted around the room, landing anywhere but on Nikki or Saj. She wondered what he wasn't telling them.

It struck her as strange that Mr Salinger wouldn't have confided in his best friend about the identity of the man his wife was having an affair with, particularly when Bland had been at such pains to paint a picture with him as a key player in a close-knit family. If it hadn't been for the fact that George Salinger had died first, and Trish Salinger was incapacitated by her ankle injury, Nikki might have reconsidered the murder-suicide option, but that was out of the question. Either scenario might explain it, but neither explained the presence of the fifth person and now she felt that Bland was being deliberately obstructive, which was at odds with his earlier demeanour 'We need a name, Mr Bland. Who was Patricia Salinger having an affair with? We need to eliminate both him and his wife from our inquiries.'

Silence filled the room as Nikki studied the man in front of her. Was that a smile that flashed across his face, or a grimace at her insistence on him naming the person with whom his dead friend's wife had an affair? His expression changed so quickly Nikki couldn't be certain either way. 'Come on, Mr Bland. We can't afford to waste time. If you can identify the couple who turned up at the Salinger home at Christmas, you should tell us.' She hardened her voice and leaned towards him. 'Now, Mr Bland.'

'Shit. This is crap. I don't . . . I really don't . . .' Then after a deep breath he spat a name into the room. 'Sukhjit. Sukhjit – he's

CEO of Kholi Kanna Enterprises – one of Yorkshire's most well-reputed producers of Indian sauces and curries. He wouldn't have killed them.' Bland paused. 'Fuck – *she'd* be more likely to kill them than Sukhi – the wife I mean – Ashleigh Kholi. Toxic cow, she is.'

It was fascinating that Bland chose to side with Sukhjit Kholi over his wife who'd been betrayed. In her experience it was often the women who were blamed for luring husbands away from their wives, yet Bland appeared to place little blame on Patricia or on the man she'd betrayed his best friend with, which made her wonder why Bland, and possibly George Salinger, appeared to nurture more animosity towards Kholi's wife than on Kholi himself. She wondered how Mrs Kholi felt about this. Her husband had betrayed her, she'd been upset enough to create a scene, and yet it seemed that Bland's sympathies lay with the dead wife and Sukhjit Kholi. Was Ashleigh Kholi's despair and anger sufficient to drive her to kill the entire Salinger family?

Nikki's head throbbed as she tried to make sense of the limited information they had. For the moment, it looked very much like the fifth player had killed the Salingers and taken the weapon with them. Could that have been Ashleigh Kholi or Sukhjit Kholi or even Derek Bland?

Nikki couldn't wait to receive Langley's final report on the cause and possible order of death so she could compare it to the crime scene, and the blood spatter analysts' reports. Something just didn't sit right with this entire scene. Nikki chose to reserve judgement on that. By Bland's own admission, Kholi's wife had every right to feel aggrieved, but in the space of the interview, their suspect list had already expanded by two. 'Okay, so there's clear animosity between the Kholis and the Salingers. Don't suppose you know how the Kholi marriage fared in the aftermath?'

Now that he had something other than the death of his friends to focus on, Bland relaxed and rubbed his fingers over his stubble before replying. 'You'd best get this confirmed as it's only really rumour and gossip that I've picked up from my PA. The Kholi marriage hit the skids after Ashleigh's meltdown. Rumour has it she slashed the tyres on his Jaguar and scraped a knife across the paintwork. Even heard that she scraped the word bastard onto the bonnet.' His lips twitched as if appreciating the drama of it all. 'See, I told you she was a mad cow! Who *does* that sort of damage to a state-of-the-art Jag?'

Nikki risked a glance at Sajid and was forced to swallow her grin as he shook his head as if mourning the death of a close relative rather than cosmetic damage to an inanimate object. *Men and their damn cars! Thank God Marcus isn't like that!* Privately Nikki thought that Sukhjit Kholi got off lightly, for she'd have been tempted to do something a little more physical than that. 'Maybe someone who has been betrayed and is hurting?'

'Yeah, but . . . it's a Jag.' Bland's voice took on the tone of a man used to ignoring human emotion – cold and assertive. As he added, 'A bloody, Jag, yes?'

Nikki's shrug was dismissive as she moved the interview on. 'What about business enemies – disgruntled employees, competitors, that sort of thing?'

Bland's demeanour changed. As he sat up straighter, his eyes found a point somewhere above Nikki's left shoulder to focus on and his reply was rushed. 'No, no, nothing like that. We run a happy ship. No complaints, no business issues.'

Eyes narrowing, Nikki wondered what business secrets Derek Bland wanted to divert them from finding out. Sensing she was onto something, she pushed harder, hoping he'd reveal something under pressure. 'So, you've no objections of us conducting interviews with your staff at your business address tomorrow . . .' Head to one side, she smiled allowing the insincerity of her smile to be visible. 'Often staff are much more attuned to the, shall we say, undercurrents of a business than the owners. That's what we find anyway, isn't it, DS Malik?'

Sajid's eyes were pinned on Bland, a tug of a frown at his brow confirming his boss's statement. 'Of course. I couldn't begin to count how many times we've gained pertinent information from interviewing business employees.'

Is it my imagination or did Bland's face lose a little bit of colour then? Pushing home her advantage, Nikki's insincere smile deepened. 'And, it would be good if you gave us access to your financials too. Who knows what possible motives our forensic accountant might be able to tease out with a sweep of your accounts.'

A flash of something indefinable darkened Bland's eyes, but before he could respond, Nikki – jaw aching from maintaining her grin – continued in a gush. 'Not that we're expecting to find any irregularities – I mean, why would we? But we wouldn't be doing our job if we weren't thorough, would we?'

Bland cleared his throat and got to his feet. 'I think I need you to leave now. This has all been too much for me and I really don't feel very well.' When his hand brushed over his stubble this time, there was a definite tremor.

So much for not concealing information. Nikki nodded and injected sympathy into her tone. 'Oh of course, Mr Bland. This must be so hard for you.'

She got to her feet, followed by Sajid, as Bland moved towards the door ready to escort them off the premises, but Nikki and Saj stayed put. 'You did say you'd help us in any way you could. I mean this is the murder of your two best friends and their children – your godchildren – we're talking about. Surely, you can give us the necessary permissions so we can hit the ground running tomorrow.'

'I . . . I . . . You need to allow me grieving time, Inspector. I'll consult with my solicitor in the morning and let you know.'

Noting the steely expression on his face, Nikki nodded and followed him towards the door. 'Well, just in case, we'll get a request in for a warrant, Mr Bland. Best to be ahead of the game. Don't want delays in the investigation now, do we?'

As they neared the door, Nikki remembered something from earlier in their conversation with Derek Bland and just before she stepped out of the flat, she turned in a Columbo-type moment. 'One last thing . . . You referred earlier to the family having been through so much already. Could you elaborate on that?'

A long slow sigh left Bland's lips and his grip on edge of the door tightened. His eyes closed for a moment and he swallowed a couple of times before responding. 'When Karen and Jason were very small, their older sister, Winnie, was abducted. She was only eleven. We never got her back. That was twelve years ago. It took them a long time to recover . . .' He shrugged and said, 'Sometimes, I wonder if they ever did.'

The man before her slumped against the door. He'd reached his limit for the night and Nikki was content to leave him with his grief for now. They could re-interview him tomorrow, but for now, she felt they'd extracted a lot of information from him. They had viable leads to follow and, whilst he slept, Nikki and her team would sift through what they'd learned. Nikki felt the weight of tiredness across her shoulders as she and Saj made their way back to her car.

'Fuck!' said Sajid, wrapping his overcoat around him, as he got into the passenger seat of Nikki's car.

He didn't expand on his expletive, but Nikki assumed that, for a change, he wasn't swearing about the sticky wrappers in the footwell. Nikki understood exactly what he meant. Although they'd gained a lot of insight into the Salinger family dynamics, added a few people to their suspect list, teased out a few viable investigative strands and been pole-axed by the shocking information that the Salingers had an abducted daughter who had never been found, the investigation seemed as wide open and cumbersome as it had when they'd first entered the Salinger residence just before midnight. A glance at her watch told her it was nearly 4 a.m. and she knew that she needed to grab some sleep because they were in for a long day ahead.

As she engaged the clutch and set off through the sleet, a shiver that was nothing to do with the cold shuddered up her spine.

She had a bad feeling about this investigation and was keen to get a head start on it. But, for now, she needed to rest and let her subconscious mind absorb the overload of information in peace if she was to be any use tomorrow. However, there was nothing to stop a few night-shift officers working overnight to gather together as much information on the Salingers' daughter's abduction *and* on George Salinger's business dealings as well as background on Trish Salinger and the Kholis. Hopefully by the time she returned to Trafalgar House after a couple of hours' snatched sleep, the picture would be clearer.

Chapter 6

Then: Marnie

*It's so quiet in here, and dark. So dark — or is that just because I'm too scared to open my eyes? I'm on a bed. It stinks of piss and vomit and sweat and all sorts of filth and for a blissful second, I think I'm dreaming. Then it all floods back to me. This is no dream — it's a nightmare. A daytime, **real** nightmare and as the memories rush through me it feels like I'm drowning in them. I can't breathe, can't move as terror holds me strapped to a mucky bed and nobody knows where I am. My head feels all fuzzy. My mouth is dry and a weird taste lingers there. I want to drink water, to wash my mouth out, but I'm scared to open my eyes. My arm hurts where Scarface injected me. I realise now that whatever drug was in the syringe put me to sleep and it's that realisation that punches me in the gut. I've no idea how long I've been unconscious — hours, days, weeks?*

The hammering of my heart bruises my ribs and reverberates like a woodpecker drilling into my skull. That's when, for the first time, I wish I was dead. My head's filled with cotton wool and I try to snatch the thoughts that are hidden there, but they won't come.

My brain's gone numb, like it can't work properly, and I feel like my body is floating above me, watching what's happening to me, but not really part of it.

I've not opened my eyes yet. I don't want to see where I am. The smell is bad enough; seeing where they've taken me can only be worse. But . . . I have to know. I have to prepare myself. I know the sorts of things people like Scarface do to girls like me. They speak about it in school. My mum's always on about it, telling Jilly and me not to friend people online who we don't know in real life. Just didn't expect someone to snatch me from my back garden. With my heart still hammering, I hold my breath and listen. I don't know who else is in this room with me. There're so many things I don't know about where I am, and so many more I'm not quite ready to find out. It's hard to hear anything over the muffled beat in my head, but finally, I'm satisfied that I must be alone.

Half expecting to be met with total blackness, I open my eyes. At first, relief that there's a dull lightbulb swinging from a cable in the centre of the room sweeps through me. I've never liked the dark – Mum still leaves the hallway light on for me. When I scan the room, I half wish there was no light because now there's no avoiding the horror of my situation. The walls are mostly red brick covered with random blobs of yellowing cement. Trickles of water meander over them and there are mucky pools of water on the cement floor. Fuzzy patches of mould dot the cracked ceiling and worm their way over the glistening bricks. It's like the cellar at home. I shiver. I hate the cellar and we rarely go down there and now I'm locked in one. Opposite me is a wooden door with a keyhole and I don't need to try it to know I'm locked in.

I look down at where I'm lying and realise it isn't an actual bed. It's just a thin mattress thrown on the floor against the back wall with a mucky-looking sheet covering me. Despite feeling dizzy, I struggle into a sitting position and lean against the wall, but only for a moment as the slimy surface chills me. If I wasn't so nauseous I'd get up and explore, maybe try the door, but I suspect that I might faint if I try to stand, so instead I crawl around looking for a way out, but can't find one. Not that I expected to. I've read all the books about this sort of thing. Seen all the films.

My chest is all wheezy and I know it's the mould that's causing it. There's nothing else in the room except for a bucket and a plastic bag. It's a tiny space with solid walls and a door to the right and a small window high on the wall opposite. The room's been painted white, and a single uncovered bulb hangs from the ceiling. I know what the bucket's there for, so I go to snatch the bag, hoping it contains food, for despite the stench and despite my fear, I'm starving. Thank God it does – a Morrisons' meal deal. Tuna wrap, bottle of water and crisps. I unwrap the sandwich, but the mere smell of the tuna has me rolling forward to the bucket where I vomit till tears trail down my cheeks, dribbling off the end of my chin. I crawl back to the mattress, pull the sheet up to my chin and rinse my mouth with the water.

With my head pounding and my throat aching, I lie on my back and allow my eyes to drift round the ceiling, trying to force the fuzziness out of my head. It's then that I see the cameras. One in each corner. Small enough to have escaped my attention if I hadn't been lying on my back. The thought of someone watching me as I crawled about on the cold floor, as I vomited, as I tried to find a way out sends a jolt of something red hot through my cotton-wool brain. It takes me a moment, but when I realise it's anger, I feel comforted, that I've not given up. It's then I concentrate on focusing on what I know.

In my mind I create a tick list. Number one: I was abducted from my back garden by a man with a scar. As flashes of memory hit me, I swallow hard and grip the sheet tightly between my fingers. **Stay in control, Marnie! Stay in control.** It's then that I hear Jilly's sweet voice. **Don't let the Beep Beeps get you down, Marn. Don't ever let the Beep Beeps win.** It's like she's right there beside me, grinning at me, twirling her hair round her finger, releasing the scent of strawberries into the air as she does so. I inhale deeply and then cough when, instead of summer fruits, the only smell invading my nostrils is mildew and piss. I almost let the tears flow, but I hear her voice again, soft and sweet. **Don't let the Beep Beeps get you down, Marn. Don't ever let the Beep Beeps win.**

She's right, isn't she. Of course, she is. Beautiful, smart, funny Jilly is right. I won't let the Beep Beeps get me down. I'll beat them. All I have to do is think. Scarface must have known he'd find me in the garden or around the house. He must have been watching me – for days, maybe weeks. Another thought strikes. What if he'd been watching both Jilly and me? What if he'd taken Jilly instead of me? My hand trembles as I pull at my hair. That thought doesn't bear thinking about, so I wrap it up in the cotton wool and push it to the back of my mind.

The more I think about things though, the more likely it seems that Scarface taking me was planned. But why? My heart accelerates as I realise there are only a few reasons for taking a young girl and none of them are very good. The best one would be that they were after money, but the main point against that is that my folks don't have loads of money. Yes, we're well off, but we're not millionaires, so I shelve that idea. Maybe someone has a grudge against my parents – again I shelve that. Yes, they're annoying, but not abduct-your-daughter-level annoying. Which leaves me with the one option I really don't want to consider – perverts. I've talked about perverts and creepy men with Alice and Fiona and the thought of what Scarface might do to me strikes me cold.

So, number two, I need to escape. Need to get out of here. But how? The door's locked, there's no windows, so I've got two options. One, I fight Scarface next time he comes in – but that doesn't seem like a good plan. He's huge, so I'd have no chance against him. The only other choice is to pretend to give in to him and keep an eye open for an escape route. If I want to get back to Jilly, then I need to stay alive and making him think I'm compliant might be the best way to do that. I don't want to, but oh, how I wish I was with Jilly again, so I'll do whatever it takes. I wish I was chattering to her, a thousand and one to the dozen. My silent treatment towards my family seems stupid now. Thoughtless and selfish and really, really stupid.

I swallow and open my mouth to yell. Maybe someone else is here. Maybe I can scream for help. Then I shake my head. Who am I kidding. There's no one to hear me scream. I decide there and then that I'll use my silence as a way of feeling in control. I'll save my words, my precious words for when I'm back with my family. Back with Jilly.

The days pass – long and cold and smelly and hateful – and I try to keep count of them. I can't remember how long I've been here when he wakes me – maybe day eighteen or nineteen? All I know is that it's dark and my head aches. This alongside the weird taste in my mouth makes me wonder if the water or food he gives me is drugged. I try to get my head round what's happening to me, but it's too much for my brain to cope with, so I shut those thoughts down and instead I close my eyes and think about my sister.

The image I hold in my head of her is so vivid I can almost feel her sliding her small hand into mine, her fingers sticky with sweat or sweeties or something I don't want to think about – she's always such a mucky pup. That's what Mum calls her anyway. But I need to hold on to that. It's the only thing helping me get through the days. Chatting to her makes me forget the other things. But I don't care how sticky her hand is. Right now, I want nothing more than to link arms with her and head to the park. I'd happily push her on the roundabout or the swings for hours and hours and hours if it meant I didn't need to stay here any longer. She's stroking my hair, whispering to me in her sweet lisping voice, and as she repeats the same phrase over and over again – **Don't let the Beep Beeps get you down, Marn. Don't ever let the Beep Beeps win. Don't let the Beep Beeps get you down, Marn. Don't ever let the Beep Beeps win.**

*I know that she'll always be with me, even when I can't see her or feel her or hear her. She'll still be there, inside me – a part of me – and I repeat my silent promise to her. 'I won't utter another word till I'm back with you, Jilly. Not one more word. I promise. And I won't let the Beep Beeps get me down. Not **ever**.'*

The image of Jilly fades, but the last thing to leave is the scent of her strawberry shampoo, which lingers only a second more, before the stench of filth floods my nostrils. How long have I been here? How long have I been out of it? Hours, days, weeks? The thought of it being weeks makes my heart hammer against my chest and I can feel it all the way down to my toes. I push myself into a sitting position and what I see when I glance down at my body chills me.

Gone are my shorts and strappy T-shirt and, in their place, I'm wearing a frilly dress and white ankle socks. I stare at the socks for a moment and then run my hand over the fabric of the dress and a shudder grips me, making my entire body convulse. Someone – probably Scarface – removed my clothes whilst I was sleeping and if he did that, then what else might he have done? Did he look at me? Touch me? As the thought sinks in, little imaginary people pound on the inside of my skull, their minuscule hammers hitting harder and harder as they try to break through the bone, their knocking becoming more and more frenzied as my breathing speeds up and my chest goes tight and feels fit to burst open.

My eyes flit round the room, looking for something – anything – to focus on, and still their insistent drumming becomes wilder and faster and more staccato, like a blade slicing through my brain. I spot the dull, yellow lightbulb swinging ever so slightly above and I replace its tarnished orb with an image of Jilly. She's smiling at me. Her dimples are deep in her cheeks and her eyes filled with love. The hammering recedes – just a little – but enough to release the tension on my chest and I can breathe again.

My hands fly up to my face and catch the tears that spring to my eyes as the realisation of what he's done to me hits. He's dressed

54

me up like a puppet – a real human plaything. A doll – a living doll – like in that stupid old song my mum used to sing to me and Jilly when we were toddlers. It's only when I rub my tears away that I see the streaks on my skin. Red and black and pink ones on the back of my hand. He's put make-up on me.

In that instant, I realise my fate is sealed and it's then that I hear footsteps approaching the door. I jump to my feet, my frantic eyes flitting round for an escape route, but the cold realisation that there **is** no escape for me, makes me flop back onto the mattress, like a puppet with its strings cut. Outside the door, every sound is magnified as the footsteps get nearer. Then they halt. A key jangles in the lock, taking an interminable time to turn, then the door opens, almost as if by a ghostly hand. I'm holding my breath now, my eyes fixed on the entrance as Scarface walks in, his BO adding to the claustrophobic stench of filth that dominates the small room.

'Up.'

The single word demands compliance as he glares at me, his snakelike scar taunting me. But, my legs are too weak to hold me. They're shaking and I just can't move. No matter how demanding he looks, how scared of him, I am, I have lost the power to stand up.

'Up!' He steps forward as he barks the word at me and I flinch.

Still looking at him, I try to get to my feet, but I only make it to my knees before he's there hauling me up, shaking me till every bone in my body rattles and more tears spring into my eyes. I blink them away. From nowhere, I hear Jilly's voice. **'Don't let the Beep Beeps get you down, Marn. Don't ever let the Beep Beeps win.'**

I raise my chin to meet Scarface's gaze, willing all the hatred I feel to flash out of my eyes and burn him. Don't know if it's my imagination or not, but I'm almost certain he flinches, then he's grabbing my hair and yanking me forward. 'You gonna do what you're told, bitch?'

I reach up and try to pull his hand away from my hair, but he's too strong. He shakes me and my hair is wrenched in clumps from my scalp. Still I remain silent although inside my head I'm repeating Jilly's words like a mantra. **Don't let the Beep Beeps get you down, Marn. Don't ever let the Beep Beeps win.**

His wheezing breath slows and his grip loosens. The stinging in my scalp is raw and hot, but the bittersweet sense of release when his grip lessens comes just in time. He glares at me, and I bow my head. My thoughts are all over the place, but I realise that until I can escape, I have to preserve myself. No matter what happens next, I have to stay alive. **Don't let the Beep Beeps get you down, Marn. Don't ever let the Beep Beeps win.**

The only way to beat them is by staying alive. There and then, I silently repeat my promise to Jilly. To get home and to tell her I love her, no matter what I have to do. I will survive this. I will escape.

Scarface lowers his head and glowers at me. 'You better fucking answer me, bitch. You gonna behave?'

Inside I'm screaming no, but he doesn't need to know that. So, I nod.

'That's more like it. Now come on. I've got a treat for you. But you better behave, right.'

Again, I nod and when his grip moves to my upper arm, I allow him to guide me from the room. As I walk down the corridor, our footsteps echoing in the cavernous space, I notice row upon row of locked doors just like the one leading to my room. **Are there other kids behind those doors?** The thought that perhaps I'm not alone down here sparks a glimmer of hope in my belly. If I make it back to the cell, I'll call out to them. Perhaps together we'll be able to devise a plan. This thought comforts me as I trudge along beside him.

I stare straight ahead, not daring to consider where he's leading me and what will happen to me when I reach my destination. Instead I drink in every nugget of information I can. I count the doors – six on each side of the passageway – each one has a heavy metal key protruding from the keyhole. All, except mine, that is. Scarface

56

pocketed the key to my cell when he entered and my previous hope that perhaps I'm not alone down here evaporates. If there were prisoners behind those doors too, then the keys wouldn't be in the lock. **He'd** have them.

We traipse up a flight of stairs, then another and, as we reach the third floor, the dankness of the cellar far below is replaced by the sweet smell of furniture polish, fresh flowers and air fresheners. These hallways are filled with gleaming furniture and the walls are covered with dark paintings of old men or bright paintings of fields filled with flowers and sunlight and water. The last flight of stairs leads to another corridor with doors that are ajar.

I peek in as we pass and my heart plummets to my tummy. Bedrooms. I know what that means. My overprotective parents have warned me often enough about bad men who like young girls. Maybe they weren't too overprotective after all. Maybe they should have been more protective. Maybe they should have locked me and Jilly in, covered every entrance to our beautiful home with security, every wall with barbed wire, every gate with digital locks and all sorts.

My feet trail and Scarface glares at me, his grip on my arm tightening as he lurches forward and almost throws me through one of the open doors. 'This is Lily,' he says.

For a second, I wonder who the hell Lily is, then I realise he means me. I'm too scared to react though, because inside stands a man. A smiling man with buck teeth and a pot belly. He's older than my dad and as his eyes rake over my body, I see the colour flushing into his cheeks. Then, he nods to Scarface who leaves the room.

I almost try to make my escape – to run after him, because all at once, Scarface seems so much less threatening than Buckteeth, but before I can, Buckteeth reaches out and runs his hand over my hair, then down my doll dress, before moving back up to my face. His touch sends shards of glass up my spine as he traces those scaly fishlike fingers over my cheeks.

'You've been crying, Lily.'

He raises one finger to his mouth and sucks on it. 'I can taste your tears.' He smiles and moves past me before he closes the door and all I can hear is Jilly's sweet voice. **Don't let the Beep Beeps get you down, Marn. Don't ever let the Beep Beeps win.**

Chapter 7

The sound of raised voices echoing upstairs from the kitchen woke Nikki up the next morning. Groggy from only a few hours of fitful sleep and with the throb of a tension headache pulsing at her temple, she almost pulled the covers up over her head and rolled over to snatch a few more minutes of peace and quiet before heading down to sort out whatever furore was kicking off between Sunni and Ruby this time. Only the knowledge that if the kids were already up and awake enough to fight with each other, then she'd wakened later than she'd wanted to.

With only a vague memory of rolling through the door after dropping Sajid off climbing the stairs on autopilot, before falling into bed and snuggling up to Marcus's warm body, the memory of the scene in the Salingers' home in Oxenhope was luridly fresh in Nikki's mind this morning. That wasn't a crime scene she'd forget in a hurry. Which was all the more reason to forgo a few extra snatched minutes in bed and get going.

As the voices from downstairs increased in volume, Nikki smirked, glad of the normality check and, bracing herself against the chill air, thrust her duvet off and slid her legs over the edge of the bed. Stretching her foot to find the slippers Marcus had considerately placed next to the bed, she rubbed her eyes, trying to dislodge the grittiness that made them feel heavy. She'd barely located one slipper when her bedroom door was thrust open and Sunni stormed in, followed by the sound of Ruby pounding upstairs. 'Mum, Rubster's being a cow-bag and I'm fed up with it. She's a bitch! A bloody damn bitch. Why does she get the last pop tart? Why does she?'

Nikki blinked a couple of times. She wasn't aware that they had any pop tarts in the house and she was pretty sure it wasn't something Marcus routinely bought. So, she was more interested in who'd smuggled them into the house and how they'd smuggled them past Marcus, who was always trying to encourage healthy eating, than in deciding how to mollify her youngest child. Before she had a chance to ask where the tarts had come from, Ruby stomped in, elbowing the door so hard that it crashed against the wall, making Nikki flinch as the sound reverberated in her already fragile head.

'You're a sneaky little snitch, Sunni. If you'd have kept your big trap shut, we could have shared it. Now you've gone and announced to the world that I managed to get pop tarts past Marcus and she'll tell him.'

So that's where they came from? Ruby, school uniform on, hair brushed and dark eyes flashing at her brother as she pointed a careless thumb in her mum's direction, was flushed. 'I was looking forward to it too. I saved it till today because this is his early shift at work. Now it's all spoiled.'

Exhaling a breath, Ruby flopped down onto the bed beside Nikki, her lips turned down demonstrating quite clearly that eating a pop tart was the only thing that would *ever* cheer her up again.

This was too much drama for Nikki to deal with, besides which, she quite fancied a pop tart herself. A sugar rush would be just the thing to get her moving after her limited sleep. Her eyes roamed from her middle child to her youngest and a wave of love so sharp she almost gasped out loud swept over her. They were her life and she wondered just how the Salingers had coped all those years after having their child abducted. How had it changed them? Had they become bitter and twisted? Had they clung on to their remaining two children, clipping their wings and restricting their activity? Nikki's eldest daughter Charlie had been abducted a few years ago. It had been only for a few hours, but that had been bad enough. How would she have coped if Charlie had never been found? How would she and Marcus have managed to continue living without knowing the fate of their child?

As she spotted Sunni's lip tremble, she jumped to her feet. Life was too damn short to argue about a bloody pop tart. 'Okay, you two. How about this? We cut the pop tart in three and . . .' she looked around the room and reduced her voice to a whisper, as if she expected Marcus might magically appear in the bedroom, 'we share the last of the Frosties, which I hid on the top of the cupboards. How's that for a compro . . . ?'

But Ruby and Sunni had dived out of the room and thundered downstairs with a 'You're the best mum ever,' from Ruby and a 'Yippee,' from Sunni, resonating around the room.

Charlie, her eldest daughter, slunk into the room, shaking her head. 'You're too soft on them, Mum.'

Nikki pushed herself off the bed, with a wistful glance at where her sleeping body had warmed the sheet, and stretched. 'You won't tell Marcus, will you?'

Charlie snorted. 'You really think Marccy doesn't know about the Frosties *or* the pop tarts? Don't be daft – if he'd really not wanted you lot to have them, he'd have confiscated them, wouldn't he?'

Nikki paused and thought about that for a second. Charlie was right. Marcus knew everything that went on in this household, so if the Frosties were where she'd left them, then it was because he knew she sometimes needed a sugar rush. 'When the hell did you get so smart, Charlie?'

Charlie rolled her eyes and moved over to drop a kiss on her mum's head. 'Well, I didn't inherit my smarts from you now, did I?'

As Nikki went to ruffle her hair, she pranced out of her reach, and with a 'I'm off. Maz is picking me up and dropping me at school, okay?'

Charlie's relationship with Nikki's friend Ali's son, Maz, was as strong as ever and it seemed to make her happy, so Nikki was happy too. She yawned and headed for the bathroom saying, 'Tell him hi. I got called out last night and it's a bad one, so I won't be around much. Be good if you and Maz hung out here a bit and helped Marcus with the others.'

About to open the bathroom door, Nikki paused, a frown drawing her brows together. 'Shit! Where's Isaac? I was supposed to . . .'

But Charlie interrupted her. 'Don't worry, Marcus dropped him at work.' And with a careless wave, she was off, thundering downstairs and yelling a loud farewell to her siblings who still seemed to be arguing in the kitchen.

Nikki took a moment to wonder when her kids had grown up so much. Sunni would be starting high school in September, Charlie was set to go to university and the Rubster would be making her GCSE choices soon. As for Isaac, her sort-of-adopted son – well he was happy working in the Lazy Bites Café near Trafalgar House. Despite missing her mum with a vengeance, Nikki felt for once her life was on track. No imminent threats, no fear, no danger – life was good. So why then did she always find it so hard not to worry? She shrugged and stepped into the shower. It was the nature of the job, that was all – that and residual trauma from her childhood.

Chapter 8

Trafalgar House was boiling when Nikki entered it via the officers' entrance at the back of the building. *When the hell are they going to get the heating fixed?* Rivulets of sweat formed almost instantly on her brow and all at once her outdoor apparel seemed to swaddle her, making her chest tighten and her breath hitch. As she marched towards the lifts, she struggled to undo her coat buttons with one hand while trying to unwrap her scarf with the other. The sensation of drowning in sweat threatened to prompt a panic attack. Marcus had given the coat and scarf to her for Christmas and she loved them. Loved that they were different from her old black leather jacket – more frivolous. Nikki was trying to introduce "frivolous" to her life more often these days, but at this precise moment, she could cheerfully have strangled Marcus. Not that her current situation was his fault and she knew she was being unreasonable; still, Marcus would understand how wrestling with her clothing in the middle of Trafalgar House in an attempt to offset another embarrassing meltdown would affect her.

From nowhere, firm hands gripped her scarf and began to unwind it from her neck, freeing her hand to work on her buttons. As she looked up into Sajid's calm face, her breathing eased and words tumbled from her lips as her breathing steadied. 'Too bloody hot, Saj.'

Still holding her scarf, Sajid stretched past her and pressed the lift button. 'It'll be fixed by the summer and by then the air con will break and we'll be freezing our arses in the middle of a heatwave.'

Together they stepped into the lift and as Sajid piled her scarf on top of the coat she now carried folded over her arms, Nikki wondered how the hell, no matter what the conditions, Sajid always managed to look so unflappable. Underneath his long coat, which he was now shrugging out of, he wore a suit – probably some designer make that Nikki had never heard of – with a tie that, more than likely, matched his socks. Nikki made a mental note to surreptitiously check that out later on when he wouldn't notice. But what really made her smile was the matching hand-kerchief triangle peeking out of his breast pocket. 'You going to a wedding, or something?'

'Har de har, har, har. That wasn't funny the first hundred times you said it and it's still not funny now.' He winked at her. 'You need to work on some new jokes, boss.'

He was right. Her joke hadn't been funny, but what *was* funny was the little splodge of jam on Sajid's lapel. A better friend would point it out to him. A better friend would offer the haggard old tissue that lurked in her jeans pocket. A better friend wouldn't rejoice in his lack of perfection. Instead, Nikki chose to relish the rare occasion when her partner began the day with a less than pristine presentation.

Her phone buzzed and a glance at the screen told her it was from her detective constable, Farah Anwar, telling her they were all present and correct ready for the briefing.

'We're up,' she said, stepping from the lift on their floor and marching ahead of Sajid towards the incident room. Although she'd stepped into the detective inspector job at the start of their previous big investigation, and despite having been senior investigating officer many times before, Nikki was keen to prove herself in her new role. When it had been thrust upon her after her previous boss, DCI Archie Hegley, had retired, she'd not had time to think too deeply about it. Now with some time having elapsed, she was eager to crack on.

She thrust open the door and saw that Farah and Liam Williams, the other detective constable attached to her team, had already made inroads into adding information to the crime boards that were positioned at the front of the room. Various uniformed officers, some at the end of their shift and some waiting to start theirs, and Gracie Fells, the crime scene manager who'd been in charge of processing the Salingers' home, sat on chairs and behind desks working on computer terminals. Farah, Liam and some of the uniformed officers had positioned four crime-scene boards at the front of the room. At the top of each was an image of one of the victims with their name and date of birth scrawled underneath. Overnight, each board had been filling up with details regarding the personal circumstances of each victim and more. A fifth board sat off to the side. It had a huge question mark in red in the middle with a circle drawn round it, and various points regarding the fifth game night guest were scribbled around it.

After dropping her coat and bag at her usual desk, Nikki strode to the front of the room and cleared her throat. 'All right, I notice all the information from the crime scene is up to date on the boards and also in the file marked – "Operation Chalice" on your tablets. You're all familiar with the crime scene through the photos already uploaded and if you're not, you need to make yourself au fait with them. DS Malik and I spoke with George Salinger's business partner last night and our report is also in the file – again familiarise yourself with it because that interview provided the focus for many of the actions completed overnight by the night shift and will form part of our investigation moving forward, particularly the bombshell that, twelve years ago, the Salingers' eldest daughter, Winnie, was abducted and has never been found. We can't discard that incident as possible motivation for the Salingers' murders, along with the reported affair between Mrs Salinger and Sukhjit Kholi, plus his wife's behaviour over Christmas when she rolled up at the Salingers' home. DC Williams spoke with George Salinger's PA and managed to access his diary – he'll report on that later – whilst DC Anwar coordinated information from the crime scene itself and she too will report on that later. This briefing will take a while, so I'm going to start with the officers going off shift.'

Nikki looked round the room and identified the officer she wanted to report back first. 'So first off, PC Dosanjh, what did you find out about Winnie's abduction?'

An older officer with bags under his eyes and sweat marks under his armpits got up. After clearing his throat loudly, he positioned himself with his feet apart and his hands folded into the small of his back, and with his gaze pinned somewhere towards the back wall, he addressed the room without referring to notes. Harry Dosanjh was an experienced officer who had chosen to remain a constable despite seeing many younger officers move up the ranks. Nikki had worked with him before and valued his input.

'Twelve years ago, the Salingers' eldest daughter, Winnie, disappeared from a family and friends' picnic, after wandering away from her friends who were playing hide-and-seek in Croft Woods in Silsden. She was eleven years old at the time and, because the gathering was crowded and the kids were playing together away from the adults, nobody was entirely sure when she went missing. It wasn't till the end of the picnic when the parents were gathering their offspring together that they couldn't find her. They searched the surrounding woods before reporting her missing.'

Dosanjh paused, rocked on his feet for a second and then continued. 'Winnie Salinger's file is in the Operation Chalice folder, but I'll summarise it here. Basically, there were no reports of strangers or unidentified adults in the area. No substantiated sightings of Winnie after her disappearance, no ransom note and her clothes and belongings were never recovered. Everyone at the picnic was alibied by the other attendees, so although the investigation team scrutinised the families within an inch of their lives, nothing broke. Basically, all inquiries ended in a whole load of nos – no sightings, no clues, no motive, no nothing. After a while the investigation was designated an open, but inactive one.'

'I was still at school at the time, but I don't remember anything about this.' Saj shook his head with a frown. 'You'd think I'd remember an unresolved child abduction investigation hitting the newspaper headlines.'

Dosanjh nipped the bridge of his nose between his thumb and forefinger and tried to suppress a yawn. His tone when he replied was flat and unemotional, but his lips had tightened, leaving nobody in any doubt that Dosanjh was pissed off by what he'd discovered overnight. 'That's mainly because the kid had run off three times before. Got as far as London on one occasion, I believe. Seems that the general feeling was that something was "off" with the parents, which caused her to run away.'

He snorted. 'None of that was substantiated, despite extensive probing into all aspects of their lives. Judging by the press reports, interest dwindled away in the months after the disappearance and public sympathy fizzled out along with the investigation.' He glared at Saj. 'She were only a kid. They should've done more, like.'

'Shit.' Nikki couldn't help herself. 'You're right, Harry. She was only a kid for God's sake. How can the investigation just have ground to a halt?'

'Well, maybe your old mentor can tell you more, boss. Archie Hegley was the SIO on this one and if my memory serves, he wasn't too happy about winding the investigation down either. You should speak to him about it.'

To say that Nikki was shocked was an understatement. The Archie she knew would never have allowed an investigation into a missing child to fall by the wayside. There was something else at play here and there was only one way to find out more about it. She'd have to speak to Archie. 'I'll do that, Harry.'

She paused, then: 'When was the last time the Winnie Salinger file was accessed?'

Harry's face broke into a huge smile. 'Well, that was fairly recently. Last year in fact and . . .' he paused, looking round the room for dramatic effect '. . . it was DCI Hegley who looked at it.'

Well, *that* was interesting. Nikki inhaled and nodded her thanks to Harry as she sent off a text to Archie asking him to meet her for coffee. 'Now, who was collating information on the Salinger family members?'

A young constable with a deep voice, and a smile that threatened to eclipse the room, stood. 'PC Gemma Gregson, ma'am . . .' She flushed and her eyes drifted towards Liam Williams, as she corrected herself. 'I mean, boss.'

Nikki winked at Williams to let him know she appreciated his giving the new officer the heads up on her preferred form of address, then smiled at PC Gregson for her to continue.

'I've nothing much to add about Winnie Salinger, boss. PC Dosanjh has covered that. As for the others, well most of it is in the file really. The kids – Karen and Jason – seemed well-adjusted, high-achieving kids who spent a lot of quality time with their parents. Their social media accounts . . .' again she blushed and looked at Nikki '. . . I hope it was okay to go into them – they didn't have high privacy settings so I could access quite a lot of information through that.'

'Good work, Gregson. That's just the sort of initiative we like to see.' Beside her Nikki could sense Sajid smiling. A few years ago, he'd have been the one doing the "touchy-feely stuff", but Nikki had learned a lot from working with him and, although it would never be second nature to her like it was to Sajid, she was getting better at it. Besides, the PC's flushed face was a visible reminder that the young woman lacked confidence.

Gregson pulled her shoulders back and although her flush deepened, she recommenced her report with new confidence. 'Basically, both Jason and Karen posted loads of photos from family holidays over the past few years – clearly, they're well off – the Alps, the French Riviera, India, Singapore, Japan. They went all over with their parents and, if Facebook and Instagram are to be believed, they all got on well. On Karen's account, the frequency of family photos has dwindled and been replaced by more recent ones of her and her student friends, doing all sorts of fun stuff from pub crawls to bowling to escape rooms – she's at university in Cambridge and seems to be living the life. She'd tagged her friends and I've started looking into her three best friends from uni, who also happen to be her flatmates.'

'Well done. Farah will arrange for an officer from Cambridge to do the initial interview with them later on today and if necessary we'll send someone down to follow up on anything they discover. What about Jason? Anything pop on his social media account?'

'Not really. He was still at school – enjoyed various sports from rugby to football to cricket. Had a couple of best mates who are also involved in the same sort of clubs. No obvious love interest that I could see.'

Nikki looked at the day duty officers. 'Right, two of you need to head over to the school after briefing and speak to his teachers and his mates. Check out alibis for all day yesterday and into the evening.'

Two PCs volunteered and Nikki nodded. 'Okay, Gregson, the parents?'

'Nothing much from social media – just typical sort of parent stuff – awkward comments, likes and love hearts on their kids' posts, but not much other activity. Mrs Salinger was a tutor at Leeds College of Ballet, or Northern Ballet as it's called now, but because of her accident was currently on sick leave. She was involved in Yorkshire Children's Cancer Trust and apparently was campaigning for the chairmanship of the charity.' Gregson paused, her eyes blazing and her entire body looking like it was about to explode. 'Guess who her opponent was in the upcoming election?'

Nikki started to shake her head and then something clicked . . . 'You're kidding. You're not telling me Ashleigh Kholi was standing against her?'

But Gregson was already nodding. 'Yes, just those two . . . reading between the lines of their campaign strategies, it wasn't a friendly a race, either.'

'I bet it wasn't.' Nikki looked at Saj. 'Soon as we're done here, you and I will pay Mrs Kholi a little visit and . . .' She frowned. 'What other information do we have on the Kholis? Do we have an address – or should I say addresses for them? I believe they've split. Anything else we need to know before we speak with them?'

DC Williams stood up. 'Mrs Kholi has filed for divorce and . . .' he nodded to Gregson '. . . like her chairperson's campaign, the divorce looks set to be acrimonious. They've no kids to fight over, but they do have a few properties – one in the south of France, a penthouse in London and a villa in Goa as well as the substantial portfolio Mr Kholi owns. At present he's renting a property on the outskirts of York whilst his wife lives in the family home in Holme-on-Spalding-Moor. Nothing popped up on a cursory sweep, but information is still coming in. If you don't mind, I'd like to interview him. I think Farah and I would be able to lull him into a false sense of security at this stage. Make him think because of our rank that he's not too high up the priority list.'

Unlike Gregson, Williams's usual flush was absent and Nikki appreciated his new-found confidence. Besides which, she suspected that Liam was right . . . Mr Kholi might be less on his guard with younger, lower-ranking officers and reveal something inadvertently, whereas Ashleigh Kholi, as the betrayed wife, would be more inclined to dish the dirt on her husband and hopefully her sense of grievance might make her indiscreet. Nikki didn't rate Mr Kholi's chances when facing Williams with his dogged perseverance or Anwar with her incisive ability to cut through the crap. 'Have at it, you two.'

Conscious that the first twenty-four hours in an investigation were crucial, Nikki was keen to get everyone off and doing stuff. The various strands made the investigation seem unwieldy at present. They should be focusing on the fifth guest but with no clues as to that person's identity, they had to cast a wide net until the forensics came in and hopefully narrowed that down. Nikki was forced to collate as much information as possible from a wide variety of sources until they could tease loose a viable thread. This was going to be heavy on footwork for the foreseeable future and Nikki was eager to get forensic analysis back from the lab and Langley Campbell's reports on all four victims.

'Come on, Saj. We've a disgruntled wife to interview.'

Sajid, who was scrubbing at the splodge of jam on his lapel with a tissue supplied by Farah, glared at her. 'You bloody well knew that was there, didn't you?'

Eyebrows raised, Nikki shook her head and raised her right hand, with three fingers in the air, palm outwards. 'Girl Guides promise I didn't,' she said and then promptly turned round to reveal her left hand with its crossed fingers, behind her back.

As Farah chortled, Saj mumbled about not letting her in his Jaguar, which he had retrieved from the garage first thing.

Chapter 9

Saj, moaning that his leg muscles were sore after being in Nikki's car the previous day, and now that his car was fully operational again, insisted that they drive to Holme-on-Spalding-Moor in his Jag and Nikki was happy with that. After all, Saj's car had heated seats.

Much as she might have preferred to take the scenic route, Nikki was happy when Saj opted for the more direct route on the M62. Time was of the essence and Nikki had to get back to meet Archie at 1 p.m.; however, she relished the time to chat with Saj about what they'd discovered so far.

'Don't know about you, Saj, but I feel really uneasy about this case. The mystery fifth Monopoly player sets my nerves on edge.' She paused, shuffled in her seat, savouring the warmth of the heated leather in the small of her back. It was almost enough to send her into a doze, but fortunately her mind was buzzing. 'It's more bloody Cluedo than Monopoly if you ask me. Unknown killer in the dining room with the knife! They should have been playing Cluedo.'

Nikki delivered the last sentence in complete seriousness. Still Sajid smiled. Nikki caught the look and frowned. 'Don't see what there is to smile about. A family of four knifed to death and a missing board game player. It's not a smiling matter, is it?'

She turned her attention to the passing scenery. 'I woke up this morning feeling like we'd amassed a tonne of information, but not a sodding viable lead.' She shuffled in her seat, trying to get the heat focused right in the small of her back. 'It doesn't feel like this is going to be the end somehow . . . or even the bloody start.'

Saj took a moment to overtake a transit van before replying. 'I get what you mean. There're too many moving parts. Derek Bland's hiding something from us and although he was keen to shift the spotlight onto Kholi and his wife, we don't know enough about the family's history, Salinger's business relations, his wife's life outside the charity, the son's friendship groups or what Karen was getting up to in Cambridge.'

Nikki drummed her fingers on her thigh and exhaled. 'In and among all the information we do have, there's so much more we still need to uncover. I wonder what, if anything, the Salingers' financial records will throw up. Has Bland been doing the dirty on his friend? He's in a prime position to siphon off funds if he wants and as a trusted family friend, Salinger seems to have given him free rein over the money side of things.'

The pair drove on in silence, each engrossed in their own thoughts, until Saj broke the silence. 'That business with the missing daughter's a bit strange isn't it? I mean, for there to be so little press coverage of it and for it to get put on the back burner like that. It's odd.'

The same thoughts had been going through Nikki's mind. 'Yes, the fact that Archie looked at the investigation so recently tells me he's got something worth sharing about it.' She shrugged. 'Not that we have any indication at this stage that Winnie Salinger's abduction is in any way linked to the murder of the rest of her family. Still . . .'

'Yeah, still . . .'

She leaned back, resting her head on the headrest, and closed her eyes, allowing the warmth of the car to lull her into a sort of half doze as Sajid put on his easy listening Spotify playlist.

Sometimes when she allowed her mind to drift like this, the pertinent points of the investigation drifted to the front. Of course, on other occasions, the jumble of ideas refused to untangle themselves and Nikki suspected that today would be one of those days. After a while, when none of her abstract thoughts would consolidate into a definite concept, she opened her eyes and shifted sideways so she could see Sajid's profile. Maybe what she needed was a complete distraction for five minutes. Something to focus on that was nothing to do with the case. 'How're the wedding plans coming on?'

Saj grimaced and rolled his eyes. 'They're bloody not. Langley is being impossible. Completely impossible about it all. Every time I mention colour coordinating our outfits with the napkins and flowers, or trying to pin him down on numbers, he becomes evasive and . . .' he risked a glance at Nikki '. . . I suspect he's over-invited.'

Nikki, in her role as Sajid's best woman, nodded in what she hoped was a sympathetic way, whilst trying to conceal her amusement. She didn't succeed.

'For God's sake, Nikki. You're supposed to have my bloody back, you know?' He tutted and sent a frown in her direction before focusing on the road ahead. 'I just want things to be right. Not too much to ask is it?'

Nikki reached out and squeezed his arm. 'Course it's not too much to ask. But, you know Langley will be happy with whatever colour scheme you choose. All he wants is to get married to *you*. He's not bothered about . . .'

'But that's just it, Nik. *He* might not be bothered about it, but *I* am. It's *my* thing, you know. I never had much control over shit when I was growing up. Never had money for nice things, wasn't allowed to choose things just for me. All I got was hand-me-downs from my cousins and by the time they got to me, they were pretty shoddy.' His mouth curled up at the memory, his hands tightening on the steering wheel. 'So—'

That single word said so much. Sajid, like Nikki herself, hadn't had an easy childhood. Apart from all the racist crap at school, he'd always been the odd one out and now that he was finally able to choose his own partner, his own clothes, his own lifestyle, he wanted to make his wedding perfect. Nikki understood his feelings in a way that Langley, his fiancé, perhaps never would. Most of the people attending the wedding on Sajid's side would be his friends and colleagues. There were only a couple from his own family who'd accepted the invite and Nikki had seen first-hand how hurt he'd been when the invite sent to his parents had been returned unopened. By contrast, Langley had a huge and very supportive family who'd embraced Sajid like one of their own. Still, it must hurt Sajid not to have his own parents by his side, supporting him – hell – just bloody loving him.

'I get what you're saying, Saj, and so does Langley.'

When Sajid snorted, she backtracked. 'Well, okay, I know he finds it hard to understand how horrid your childhood was and your mixed feelings about your family. But he loves you and he wants your wedding to be perfect. He's told me that. He knows you enjoy all that matching ties and socks and stuff, so he's happy for you to arrange all that. He knows you're better at that than he is.'

She bit her lip, wondering if she should continue, but then realising that pep-talking the groom was her responsibility, she cuffed his shoulder lightly. 'You're being a bloody diva, Malik. Langley's organised the venue, the registrar, the DJ, the cake, the . . .'

She paused trying to remember the other things Langley had told her about, but came up short. 'Well, other stuff too, and all you're doing is the bloody colour scheme. Just do it. I'll help, if you want.'

At Sajid's appalled expression she laughed out loud. 'Okay, well maybe I won't help with that, but Ruby can. She's got an eye for that sort of thing.'

'Okay, I'll text the Rubster later.'

'Good. Now while we're on the subject. Have you ever thought that Langley's inviting the people who share his love for you and who genuinely want to celebrate your marriage is because he wants to make up for your parents being complete bastards about this?'

Sajid's mouth fell open into a surprised O. 'I'm being a dick aren't I?'

Nikki started to shake her head, then smiled. 'Actually, yes, you are. But, it's only to be expected – you're nervous and all emotional and in loooove. It'll pass.'

Chapter 10

I spy with my little eye something beginning with M . . .
Or maybe it's L.

Yes "L" for Lily has a better ring to it!

The only way I can relax is by sifting through my archive as I wait for news. The time for recriminations has passed and all I can do now is relive the good times as I wait to be updated. I've got to keep my head together. I stop the recording for a moment, savouring the scene on the screen, before zooming in to see her face more clearly.

I reach for the play button and settle back in my armchair, allowing the Dolby stereo sound to sizzle around me as I watch how Lily responded to her first hours of captivity. You can tell a lot about their personalities by their initial responses. Whether they'll succumb easily or whether they'll need longer and more, shall we say, persuasion, to adjust. I enjoy watching them, assessing their potential and spotting in hindsight little ways I could refine things. I had a sweet feeling about this one and for a while, she'd lived up to every expectation. So much so that she'd confirmed my theory that the harder they are to break, the more useful they become and the better they acquiesce in the end.

Of course, my strategy is well-tested. Lily wasn't the first, nor will she be the last. Over the last few years, I've honed the procedure from the point where Scarface activates the process by snatching them, to the carefully devised programme that teaches them the benefits of being a team player. It's a strategy designed to whittle away their sense of self, their belief that they might be rescued and ultimately results in their succumbing to their new lives. Ultimately, the carrot and stick method works remarkably well. The little psychological games created with the sole point of making them off balance and therefore dependent on our goodwill has a ninety-nine per cent success rate.

As Lily finally plucks up the courage to unscrunch her eyes and assess her situation, I ponder how she became one of the majority who succumbed to her situation with good grace. I hoped she'd conform, because I was certain she would be popular with my clients. Watching her feistiness give way to despair and then to renewed determination over the course of the recording intrigued me – it still does. When Scarface told me she refused to speak I saw it as a challenge. My research indicated she was more than capable of vocalising her thoughts. I smile, recalling at least two occasions during my "in the wild" observation periods when I witnessed her being extremely vocal to her mum – in fact, almost objectionably so. I would have definitely employed the stick at that point followed by the carrot after she'd been allowed to stew in her punishment for a while. However, her rather too "right on", conciliatory mum had borne her daughter's abuse with remark-able fortitude. That was the woman's first mistake.

Still, the silence was unexpected. Intriguingly unexpected. I remember wondering if it would be permanent. In so many ways, I hoped so. I suspected, even then, that billing her as "a silent girl" would be her USP. I was sure my clients would appreciate something a little bit quirky and if so, my investment in her would be one of my more profitable enterprises – a welcome addition to my portfolio and one with long-term prospects.

I hit pause and sigh. It was so good whilst it lasted . . . My fingers tighten on the controls as I consider how much trouble she and her mate are causing me now.

To steady myself, I rewind to when she's crawling round, exploring the room. The after effects of the drug we gave them often left them dizzy and a bit wobbly on their feet. She was the first one to crawl though. Most of them curl into a ball, cry like babies for their mummies and wait till Scarface returns. Not my little Lily though. Watching her, so desperate, so alone, so . . . decimated releases endorphins to my brain. I can feel them surging through my bloodstream, the effect of the chemicals as good as a dose of heroin as my nerve endings begin to tingle, my blood bubbles and my smile widens when she vomits into the piss bucket. She was at her lowest ebb. I zoom onto her face as she struggles back to her mattress. Even through the recording, her defeat is palpable . . . but . . . wait for it . . . wait for it . . . Ah, yes here it comes, that flutter of a smile – just a momentary movement, but it still gives me pleasure, for it is *that* smile that first told me she had reserves of fortitude, deep inside her. The ability to find something – a lifeline to cling to even in her darkest hours. I rewind and play the flicker again and again and again.

If only I knew what elicited that smile. If only I knew what grain of hope lingered inside her fragile little mind – then I could have nurtured it. Used it to my own advantage.

I allow the recording to continue, pleased with the reminder of all I've achieved over the years. This is what entrepreneurship is all about. Spotting a gap in the market and filling it. Who cares if it's a dark market? Who cares if it's not mainstream? Who cares if I can't share my successes publicly? The fact that it's lucrative is enough for me. It has to be. It's my business and it's flourishing.

I dismiss the spark of annoyance that my skills have gone uncelebrated. That I work under the blanket of anonymity, unlike those toffs, born to succeed even though their skill set is inferior to mine. Idiots, the lot of them. Self-assured, pompous idiots, yet I'm the one who's made it. Made it against the odds. Made it despite the obstacles. I thrust these poisonous thoughts away. They are beholden to me. All of them who use my services are beholden to me and the fact that they don't even realise who they're beholden to or how much they are at my mercy makes up for everything else. Their time will come, as will mine.

For now, though, I fast-forward the recording until . . .

I spy with my little eye something beginning with D . . .
D for Doll

And doesn't she look sublime, this little living doll of mine? Unbidden, the old Cliff Richard song springs to mind. I rub my hands together, humming it with more enthusiasm than skill. Not sure this was quite what Mr Nice Guy Richards intended when he'd come up with this one, but it works for me. She really was a doll. The virgin-white frilly frock suits her and with her hair spread out like a halo around her sleeping head, she looks almost angelic on the screen.

When she stirs on the screen, I pan in, determined not to miss the expressions that I've seen so many times before as they flit across her face in rapid succession. With bated breath, I watch, savouring every moment. I could rewind and watch this delicious scene again and again at my leisure. Registering her panic, her fear for the very first time when she realises what we've done to her is oh so special. I lean forward, lick my lips and wait.

And there it is . . . the puzzlement signalled by a very slight "moue" on her lips. Her eyebrows pucker as she remembers where she is. That's followed by a dry swallow and her pink tongue flashes out as she licks her lips. She's thirsty from the drugs we'd given her. Next the frown deepens and ugly lines trail across her brow as her hand drifts up to her temple. Poor thing's got a headache.

I'm holding my breath big time now. The next bit is the best part. And . . . here it comes . . . Here it comes. Oh, delightful, absolutely delightful. Look at those emotions flashing over her face. She may not speak this little one, but with emotional responses like these, she hardly needs to. I always sensed that my little Lily is going to be very special. Very special indeed.

Her eyes move down her body and she realises we've changed her clothes. I can barely contain my joy at seeing her reactions. The horror that momentarily mars her precious features. Her hands follow her eyes as her fingers pluck at the fabric of the dress. She scrambles up the bed as if she can escape the frilly fabric before, curling up into a ball at the top of the mattress, she sobs – her tears trailing the carefully applied make-up down her cheeks.

By the time Scarface arrives to escort her from the room, little Lily is cowed. I'm content with her promise and as he escorts her from her cell, Living Doll morphs into Jessie J's Price Tag. I smile and do a little skip round the room. She's wrong, is Ms J. It *is* all about the money.

Chapter 11

As they drove into the quaint village that was Holme-on-Spalding-Moor, Nikki was enchanted and her mood lifted. Filled with quaint houses, with perfect gardens and a beautiful well-tended church, the village looked as different from Nikki's own home in Bradford as it was possible to be. Driving through the main street, adhering to the 20 mph speed limit, Sajid sighed. 'How the other half lives, eh? Not a mosque or a temple in sight.'

Leaving the village and entering an area of country roads bordered by hedges over which rain-drenched fields could be seen, Sajid progressed towards their destination. When they finally arrived at the turning, set off the road, which led to the Kholi house, Nikki was unsurprised by the grandeur of the estate. She'd checked the Kholi couple's net worth before leaving Trafalgar House and discovered that Sukhjit Kholi was the third richest man in Yorkshire – coming in after George Salinger who was second. As they waited to be admitted through the automated security gates, Nikki considered what she would do if she had even half the amount of money at her disposal that the woman they were about to interview had. Probably buy Marcus a new truck and take the kids on holiday to Centre Parcs. Other than that, she wasn't entirely sure.

When the gates slid silently inwards, Saj edged forward, peering up the drive towards a home that looked like something from *Brideshead Revisited*. Though not as big as the Salingers' home, Nikki appreciated that with it being situated in this rural area with a York postcode, it would be worth a lot more.

As Saj pulled up beside a Mercedes boasting the private number plate ASHKHO, Nikki giggled and pointed. 'Typical rich folk not realising the plate read more like ASSHOLE than ASHKHO.'

Saj laughed and then nodded towards the door that had just swung open, revealing a woman in her early forties. Ashleigh Kholi was stunning – in a plasticky sort of way, was Nikki's private thought – and the cost of her outfit would probably have covered Nikki's mortgage for a year. Whilst Nikki and Saj got out of the car and walked up the steps towards the woman, she turned and re-entered the house with 'Don't forget to wipe your feet' her only greeting.

So, it's going to be like that is it? Nikki's eyes narrowed as she exchanged a glance with Sajid. No way would she allow the older woman to get away with *that* attitude for long. Ashleigh Kholi may well have money and a big house and a pretty crappy personalised number plate, but she definitely lacked manners. Entering the hallway first, Nikki held the woman's gaze as she scrupulously wiped her feet on the coir doormat pretentiously emblazoned with WELCOME TO THE KHOLIS.

As she continued to wipe her feet, Ashleigh Kholi finally tutted. 'For goodness' sake, I think they're clean enough, don't you?' She paused and the mask slipped from her face revealing – instead of the haughty, unapproachable bitch from moments earlier – a fragile woman, struggling to cope with life. 'I'm sorry I came across so abruptly. It's just . . .' She wafted a hand in the air. 'Everything is so crap at the moment and I've had to be so careful – with the press, with Sukhi's lawyers, with the women at the Yorkshire Children's Cancer Trust and now this. I bet I'm the number-one suspect.' Her voice hitched and her chest heaved. 'It's taken quite a toll on me.'

It was only with her extended speech that Nikki picked up her broad Yorkshire accent and, seeing her eyes flashing so uncertainly between her and Sajid, Nikki felt like a cow. She stepped forward, hand outstretched, holding her ID and with a reassuring smile on her face. 'Look, let's start over again, shall we. We're not here to make you uncomfortable or intimidate you. We just have to follow due process and our investigations have inevitably led us here. I'm DI Nikki Parekh and this is DS Sajid Malik. As you know, we're here about the tragic death of the Salinger family last night.'

When, Ashleigh nodded, her hand fluttering up to tug at the gold cross around her neck, Nikki stepped closer. 'Let's sit down and we'll get this done as quickly and painlessly as possible.'

With a deep, grounding breath, Ashleigh Kholi straightened and an uncertain smile flicked across her face. 'Come on, we'll go into my hobby room. It's by far the warmest room in this mausoleum.'

Mausoleum? Well that is telling. They followed her into a room with a desk that stood with its back to the side wall, allowing anyone sitting behind it to glance through the wide bi-folding doors, which offered a view over a small patio and into the extensive back gardens. Not visible from the front of the Kholi home, the carefully cultivated gardens housed a wide array of plants and shrubs in a variety of flowerbeds, strategically dotted through winding paths that ended with an ornate, Indian-influenced gazebo at the bottom. A small cosy seating area had been created in front of a fire, which although at first glance looked like a real coal fire, was actually a high-quality imitation one. Ashleigh took one of the single chairs whilst Nikki sat closest to her on the two-seater sofa with Sajid electing to sit next to Mrs Kholi on a matching armchair.

In order to make things easier for Mrs Kholi, Nikki dispensed with pussyfooting around. 'We already know about your husband's affair with Patricia Salinger, Mrs Kholi, and we're also aware of the incident over Christmas at the Salinger home. Can you tell us about that?'

'Call me Ashleigh please. Hearing his name just makes everything feel so much worse. Oh, it was such a stupid thing to do. It really was.' Ashleigh closed her eyes and banged the heel of her hand against her forehead before meeting Nikki's gaze. 'I'd only just found out that Sukhi was cheating on me. He'd stupidly left the gift he'd bought for *her* in his briefcase and when I found it, all beautifully wrapped and dedicated to *Trish, the most perfect woman I have ever met*, my heart just splintered. Right there and then in the middle of his study, my heart shattered into a trillion pieces.'

Nikki allowed the silence to grow as a raft of emotions played across Ashleigh's face. The older woman was right back in that room, holding that gift with its treacherous message and Nikki felt like a voyeur as she watched her relive that traumatic experience. Ashleigh raised her head and despite her trembling lip and the shimmer of tears in her eyes, she continued. 'I'd had no idea. I thought we were solid. Solid and in love. We'd been through so much together you see, me and Sukhi. All the miscarriages, all the fruitless rounds of IVF, all the wasted years trying for something that was never going to happen and being hammered down every time we failed. The single thing that kept us going—' she laughed, the sound raw and hollow in the near-silent room '—or so I thought anyway, was our indestructible commitment and love for each other.'

This time her laugh carried an edge that sliced through her anguish with a razor-sharp point, making the transition from despair to anger more noticeable. 'He fooled me. *She* fooled me. Between them, they made me the laughing stock. All my friends had known what was going on. Every time Patricia Salinger spoke to me at our fund-raising events, her false compliments, her insincere smiles, her machinations to steal my husband because hers was so damn . . .'

A whoosh of air left her lungs and she fell backwards into the cushions and stopped. For a while, Nikki waited, thinking she'd resume her narrative but after two minutes, when the silence continued, Nikki prepared to speak. However, Ashleigh shook her head. 'No, let me finish.'

She clutched again at her cross, sliding it back and forth over its chain, the noise grating on Nikki's nerves, but Ashleigh seemed oblivious. 'At the time, I didn't realise what she was doing. But afterwards, when I'd had a chance to think about it, to look at everything with fresh eyes, I realised that Patricia Salinger and her husband are psychopaths. True, emotionless psychopaths whose main motivation is playing games for their own amusement at the expense of others.'

Games? Nikki thought about that. Was that what had led to the Salinger family's death? Had they played the wrong game and made an enemy that would exact the ultimate revenge? Nikki looked at Ashleigh Kholi sitting so pale and still, the light from the flames flickering over her face as she described the woman who'd had an affair with her husband as a psychopath. Perhaps, Ashleigh Kholi was the psychopath. Perhaps it was the woman sitting opposite her whose mind was so warped with hurt and grief that she could take the lives of four people. On the other hand, the report into the Salingers' abducted child Winnie had initially flagged up concerns about the family and the dad in particular. This was so hard. They needed the forensic reports back. They needed to identify the fifth person in that house and they needed to start eliminating their suspects. 'Where were you over the weekend, Mrs Kholi?'

Ashleigh's smile was hardly there at all. 'You're right to ask me that. I understand. But I'm afraid you'll be disappointed with my answer. I was here. All weekend I was here. On Saturday, I drank myself blind drunk and on Sunday I spent the day recovering. No visitors, no witnesses, nothing except an empty vodka bottle and a packet of paracetamol to corroborate my alibi.'

'Well, that's unfortunate, Ashleigh. It would have been good to be able to confirm your whereabouts, but perhaps you'd consent to DNA and fingerprint tests to eliminate you from our inquiries?'

As if her shoulders could barely hold her head up, Ashleigh's head flopped forward. Her fingers massaged each of her temples. 'Anything. Anything. I just want this nightmare over with. I had reason to want revenge on Trish Salinger, but I'd never have hurt her kids. Never.'

Shortly afterwards, Nikki and Saj left her house promising to send a couple of officers to take a fuller statement and to take the DNA samples. As he started the engine, Saj looked up at the door as it swung closed locking Ashleigh Kholi back inside her mausoleum. 'That poor woman. You could almost smell the hurt wafting off her, couldn't you?'

Nikki was also focused on the closing door, but her head was too full of contradicting thoughts to commit to excluding Ashleigh as a suspect. 'A woman scorned and all that, Saj. We can't be certain that Ashleigh's innocent, but at least she's happy to give the samples. Now all we need is the DNA from the crime scene to compare them to.' She slotted her seatbelt in place as Sajid reversed and headed back down the drive. 'What do you reckon about her psychopath accusation?'

'Hmm, that's a big accusation to make. Just not sure. Not sure at all on that one.'

Nikki slammed the flat of her hand on the dashboard. 'Damn, what I really wanted to do was to gain some clarity through that interview but Ashleigh Kholi has just succeeded in muddying the damn waters even more.'

Sajid frowned. 'Oi, watch the dash, Nik. It's sensitive, you know.'

But Nikki's mind was elsewhere in a room with four dead bodies, a Monopoly board and a table with five settings on it. 'None of this makes sense, Saj. Not one bloody iota of it.'

Chapter 12

DC Liam Williams pulled into the staff car park at Sukhjit Kholi's Leeds offices. A stone's throw away from the Royal Armouries and tucked between some of the designer penthouses, this was a prime location. After parking, Liam peered through his rain-spattered window at the three-storey building and released a long low whistle. Kholi Kanna Enterprises had offices in both York and Doncaster and if they were anything like this one, Kholi's business, despite Covid, appeared to be booming. 'Someone's raking it in.'

When Farah didn't respond, he dragged his eyes away from the sleek structure with its tinted glass windows and, frowning, glanced at her. Farah had been distracted and a bit tetchy for the past week – which just wasn't like her. Yes, she could be sarcastic on occasion, but she wasn't usually moody or mean. 'You okay, Farah?'

Farah stuffed a ginger nut biscuit into her mouth and nodded, but didn't quite meet his eye. Liam's frown deepened. She looked wan and her skin had a shiny hue to it. Was she fighting a fever or was it something worse than that? Unsure whether to probe more deeply, he sighed. He'd known that the odds were stacked against his and Farah's relationship working out. Her parents wouldn't be keen on her being in a relationship with someone before marriage and the fact that he was white compounded that. His family wouldn't be any better, with his racist brothers and a dad who'd voted for Brexit to "keep the Pakis out". He hadn't expected it to be easy, but he liked Farah. Liked her a lot and was prepared to divorce himself from his family completely if it meant he could be with her. He tapped the steering wheel, wishing he had the guts to just ask her what was going on.

With a sigh, he opened the door and stepped out into the rain, reflecting that the weather echoed the current mood. Farah got out and shoved a ginger nut between her teeth as she struggled to open her brolly. Liam strode round the car, took the brolly from her and opened it with a flourish, while Farah shrugged and grinned at him as she munched her way through the biscuit. 'Thanks.'

Liam studied her for a moment, as the rain dripped from the umbrella spokes. Her smile faded from her lips and a small frown appeared over the bridge of her nose. 'What? Stop looking at me like that.'

Her voice had an edge to it. A tone Liam hadn't heard her use with him before. 'You sure you're okay, Farah? You seem . . .' He allowed the sentence to fade away, unsure how to end it without annoying her more than he already appeared to have.

'For God's sake, Liam.' Her words were almost hissed at him. 'We're at work. Let's focus on the job in hand.'

And with no more ado, she strode off into the rain leaving Williams to trail behind her towards the offices. *What's got into her? Why is she being such a bloody cow?* He shook the brolly at the entrance and glared at her as she entered the whirly automatic door and slowly rotated into the building. Under his breath, he gave himself a talking-to. This was too important an interview for him to mess up. This was *his* chance to show Nikki that he could do it. 'Come on, Liam, get your head in the game and forget about the personal crap. This is more important.'

Shoulders pulled back, he entered the glass rotating doors and joined Farah in front of the front desk where she was standing, her body angled towards him, her arms folded across her middle and an apologetic smile on her lips. He ignored her, strode up to the desk with his warrant card out and addressed the tall, suited man who was engulfed in a mist of an expensive-smelling aftershave; one that Liam couldn't identify, but he thought one of his sisters might have given him the same one for Christmas. 'DCs Williams and Anwar here to speak with Mr Kholi.'

The man looked at their IDs, his lips curling in distaste as his eyes raked over them.

'I'm not sure Mr Kholi will have time for . . .' He circled his hand in the air leaving the words "the likes of you" unspoken.

Williams resisted the temptation to snarl at him and instead, he made a point of looking at the man's name tag, which was on the same deep green background as the business sign outside the door, before injecting his tone with sarcasm. 'Nigel, I think you'll find that Mr Kholi is expecting us, so maybe just point us in his direction; there's a good man.'

Nigel straightened his shoulders, his lips curling even more, and opened his mouth, no doubt to respond in the negative. However, the lift doors to the left of the reception area swished open and a middle-aged man in an understated grey suit with a red tie exited. On seeing the two officers by the desk, his face broke into a smile and he extended his hand.

'Hallo, I'm Sukhjit Kholi and I presume you are the officers who want to chat to me about the awful thing that happened at George and Trish's house.'

As he spoke the smile faded from his face and after exchanging a brief handshake with both Anwar and Williams his forehead puckered. 'Dreadful business. Absolutely dreadful. I'm still trying to get my head round it.'

He turned to Nigel behind the desk, whose face was now transformed into a mask of civility. 'Thanks, Nige. I've got this. Can you bring some drinks for us? We'll be in my office.' He quirked his head to one side and addressed the detectives. 'Coffee, tea – we've got some fantastic herbal teas – all sourced from fair trade tea plantations in India.'

Before Williams could refuse, Anwar stepped forward 'Oh, how lovely. Do you have a ginger tea?'

Sukhjit Kholi raised an eyebrow at Nigel who responded with a 'Yes of course. I'll bring one up for you.'

All trace of his earlier rudeness gone, he smiled at Williams, although Liam noticed the smile didn't quite meet the receptionist's eyes. 'And for you, sir?'

Past experience of the hazards of being out and about with a bladder full of coffee had taught Liam to avoid accepting well-meaning offers of refreshments, but in this instance, if it would inconvenience the snotty receptionist Liam was happy to make an exception. 'Lovely, Nigel. *So* kind of you. Mine's a coffee, white and two sugars please.'

That settled Kholi led them back to the lift and as they ascended to the top floor, Williams ran through in his mind the information he hoped to gain from this meeting. The first thing he wanted to do was establish Kholi's alibi. Then he'd move on, in light of his affair with Mrs Salinger, to discuss Kholi's relationship with both the older victims – Patricia and George Salinger. He needed to establish how the affair had impacted his business dealings with the husband, and how it had affected Kholi's relationship with his own wife. He hoped to get a sense of how Kholi viewed his estranged wife's attitude to the Salingers. Although Williams knew Farah would have his back, he didn't want her to take over. This was his chance to prove himself and, besides, he was still miffed with her earlier attitude. No way did he want to rely on her. Not this time.

Sukhjit Kohli's office was almost as big as the incident room back at Trafalgar House and as they walked in behind their host, Williams's feet sunk deep into the carpet. It was like walking on chiffon – not that Williams knew exactly what walking on chiffon would be like, but . . . *How the other half live.*

Kholi gestured for them to take the two chairs positioned directly in front of his oversized heavy mahogany desk. Within arm's reach of each of the chairs was a small very shiny coffee table with coasters placed strategically on top, whilst a larger one sat in before the chairs. Williams wondered if the affable man who'd greeted them downstairs was actually a little more manipulative than his earlier greeting had suggested. Had he positioned them before him like kids in a head teacher's office deliberately? Williams smiled. He remembered Nikki telling him that such displays of power by an interviewee could, in actual fact, play into the interviewer's hands. Let Kholi think he had one up on them, then when he was lulled into a false sense of security, it was time to – as Nikki said – "Do an Annie Wilkes and nobble the bastard with a question they don't expect." Over his time on Nikki's team, Liam had gained numerous pithily delivered words of wisdom from his boss and he'd carefully stored each piece away, recognising them for the gems of advice, hard learned by an officer struggling to find her place and authority in a police and society that was still filled with prejudice.

In this case, Williams reckoned his accent, job and youth could be considered to be a disadvantage when pitted against Kholi's posh upper-class English accent with only a trace of India weaved through it, his posh clothes, his money and the massive obstacle, in the form of a carpentered chunk of glossy wood that was placed between them.

Another one of Nikki's gems of wisdom was that if a suspect needed to place an obstacle between them, during an initial fact-seeking interview, then they were probably hiding something.

Williams hid his determination to get to the bottom of Kholi's behaviour, behind a neutrally respectful expression.

As they waited for the refreshments, Williams pushed ahead with his own web of deceit. 'Wow, Mr Kholi. What a beautiful office. We're not used to this sort of style are we, Farah?'

Liam, wide-eyed, glanced at his partner, who catching on to

his intent, shook her head in a mockingly indulgent way that wasn't lost on the businessman. 'Oh, Liam. Don't be such a pleb. Mr Kholi doesn't have time for this, do you?'

Kholi's smile widened, as he leaned back and crossed his legs. 'Of course, I want to help our boys and girls in blue. Who wouldn't?'

Inwardly, Williams flinched at the "boys and girls" jibe. How dare he! How dare the pompous git trivialise them to child status. It took all his willpower to maintain his smile, but made him more determined to come away from this meeting with something important. Something that might direct them to a viable investigative strand.

Meanwhile, Kholi's smile died away. He paused, bowed his head and rearranged some of the paperwork sitting before him on his desk, before saying in a voice that broke before he'd finished speaking. 'The Salingers' deaths are tragic. Truly tragic.'

It was impossible for Williams to work out if the man's emotions were genuine although he supposed it likely that Kholi's affair with Patricia Salinger made his grief more likely. Even if he hadn't *loved* the woman, the very fact of their shared intimacy must impact on him. Williams risked a glance at Farah. Even if Farah split up with him, he'd still grieve if she died – still miss her, still be in shock. The mere thought of Farah's death kicked him like a mule, deep in his chest. No way was he going to think about that.

Kholi raised his eyes and looked straight at Williams as if sensing a chink in the younger man's armour. One that he would use to probe for more information. 'Don't suppose you can tell me exactly what happened can you? I mean, I'm presuming it was a murder-suicide – that's what they call it in the American series, isn't it? Murder-suicide.'

Williams was saved from responding immediately by a quiet knock at the door, followed by the entry of a woman, in heels so high he wondered how she stayed upright. Despite his heavy sigh as she clip-clopped over the floor, Kholi waved her forward and summoned a smile that didn't quite meet his eyes.

'Coffee for your guests, Mr Kholi.' The woman, walking with admirable steadiness, deposited the tray onto the larger table, before transferring a shiny silver filter coffeepot and coffee mug for Williams onto his smaller table and a matching teapot with china cup and saucer onto Farah's. A plate piled high with an aromatic variety of Kholi's Kanna brand samosas and chutney accompaniments was positioned with side plates and cloth napkins on the larger table.

'Help yourself to samosas.' The woman gestured towards the perfectly fried, steaming pastries, then nodded to Kholi, before exiting.

With Anwar almost diving on the teapot, Williams rubbed his stomach. 'I'm afraid the samosas will be wasted on me, Mr Kholi. I've already eaten.'

He leaned over, pressed the filter down and poured his coffee before adding a touch of milk and sugar from the matching jug and bowl . . . 'You not having anything, sir?'

Kholi wafted the suggestion away with a grin. 'I have so many of these, I sometimes get fed up with them. I'll get Sandra to pack them up for you to take with you when you leave. I'm sure your colleagues will appreciate them.'

He quirked his head to one side. 'Unless of course you only eat doughnuts?' Laughing at his own joke, Kholi stood up and wandered round to the front of his desk where he perched, his legs crossed at the ankles before him. 'Now, you were telling me about this awful murder-suicide.'

Williams sipped his coffee, released an appreciative sigh and smiled. 'Actually, we're not at liberty to share the details of the crime scene with the general public, sir.'

Kholi pouted. 'I'm not sure I'd class myself as the general public. I was a close business associate of George Salinger.'

Williams took another sip before placing his mug on the

nearest coaster. 'Yes, I had heard that. But, you were also a *close* acquaintance of Patricia Salinger, weren't you?'

Williams smiled and quirked an eyebrow, enjoying the momentary tension that appeared on Mr Kholi's jaw at the emphasis on "close" and if he hadn't been watching for it, he might have missed the narrowing of his eyes.

'Yes, well, Trish and my ex-wife both serve on the board of a well-known charity – the Yorkshire Children's Cancer Trust.' He circled his hand in front of him dismissively. 'Of course, I've come across her at social events over the years.'

Williams smiled as his first Annie Wilkes moment approached. 'And possibly also in the bedroom?'

A flush spread across Kholi's cheeks, and his eyes darkened before he ran his fingers through his hair and gave a short laugh. 'Ah, so someone's been tittle-tattling, I see.'

'Hmm, not sure I'd call it "tittle-tattling", Mr Kholi. We are, after all, investigating the deaths of four people and naturally we have compiled a list of . . .' He paused and glanced at Anwar. 'What would you call them, DC Anwar?'

Still sipping her tea, Anwar took a moment to consider. 'Suspects? I don't think suspects is too strong a word, do you? Besides, our boss – DI Parekh – already interviewed your wife this morning and got all the information about your affair from her.'

Taking up the baton, Williams nodded. 'Yes, I reckon suspects is about right. I mean we don't want to be remiss in our investigation.' He shrugged. 'Can't leave any stone unturned, now can we, Mr Kholi? Especially after what your ex-wife shared with us.'

That was a pitch in the dark because Williams had no idea what Ashleigh Kholi had shared with Nikki. In fact, he wasn't even sure they'd completed that interview; still, if it rattled something loose from Kholi then it would be a bonus.

Kholi pushed himself away from the desk and returned to his seat behind it, his earlier benign expression becoming more thunderous by the second. With more force than was necessary, Kholi reached over and swung the Newton's cradle on his desk, causing the metal balls to crash together like rolling thunder. Williams didn't miss the significance of both actions. *Putting a barrier between us again, are you, Mr Kholi, **and** showing your temper?*

'I sincerely hope, you're not suggesting I had anything to do with the Salingers' deaths?'

With the sound of the balls fading to a gentle swish, Williams splayed his hands before him. 'Look, Mr Kholi, we can dance around this or you can answer our questions as fully as you are able, then we can leave you to get on with your work. Let's start with where you were yesterday between say midday and midnight?'

With Dr Campbell citing time of death as probably less than six hours prior to his examination of the bodies at the crime scene, they'd opted to ask for alibis covering that period.

As Kholi's eyes darkened, the hint of an Indian accent became stronger. 'This is preposterous. You can't possibly suspect me of any wrongdoing.'

Good cop Farah leaned forward. 'Look, Mr Kholi. My colleague may be being a tad inflammatory, but we *are* investigating the violent deaths of a family whom you knew. So, just tell us where you were, and hopefully someone can corroborate that, and we can move on.'

Kholi glared at Williams his fingers tapping the surface of his desk, as if he could release, through his fingertips, the anger that held his shoulders taut and his lips tight. 'I was home alone, okay? In my York flat, if you must know. Nobody can confirm I was there all day, but we do have a concierge who can confirm I arrived home at around 11 a.m. I'd just returned from a trip to India and was jet-lagged. I went straight to bed and didn't surface again until this morning at around sixish, when I left to drive here. I suppose you could check the security footage to confirm my arrival and departure times.' He glared at Williams. 'That enough for you?'

Anwar retrieved her tablet from the side of the chair where she'd slotted it earlier and made a note on it. 'Thank you, Mr Kholi. That's very helpful. We'll check that out.'

'So—' Williams returned Kholi's glare with a stern one of his own. 'Back to Mrs Salinger. We already know that you and she had an affair and that it supposedly ended at Christmas time when your wife turned up at the Salinger home and confronted her.'

'No bloody supposedly about it, Detective. After Ashleigh's appalling conduct at Christmas, we were aghast that our affair had been so insensitively exposed. Trish's children witnessed Ashleigh's meltdown, for goodness' sake. It just wasn't on. Ashleigh's behaviour was deplorable, and her erratic actions then resulted in me filing for divorce. She was becoming increasingly out of control.'

The sneering way Kholi spoke of his ex-wife didn't sit well with Williams. The woman must have been hurt, humiliated, broken by his betrayal and yet he appeared to have no sympathy at all for his ex-wife's feelings. Okay, perhaps turning up at the Salinger home at Christmas, in front of her family, wasn't her finest hour, but he could understand her anger.

'What about the Salingers? How did they react?'

'Mine and Trish's fling had already ended – amicably, I might add, long before then. Months before in fact. My ex-wife got drunk at Christmas, made a fool of herself and upset Karen and Jason. No amount of promising could convince her that the affair had ended. She was just another irrational woman, showing herself, and me, up.'

As Farah opened her mouth to respond, Liam jumped in. Judging by her heightened colour, Farah was about to do more than an Annie Wilkes on Sukhjit Kholi. 'So, your business dealings with Mr Salinger weren't affected by this? I mean he didn't cancel any contracts or anything like that? Bad-mouth you to other clients or business associates?'

Kholi tutted and swung his chair from side to side. Now his increased colour matched Farah's. 'Of course he didn't.

Why would he? Our business deals were very lucrative and, as I said before, the affair ended amicably and George was aware of it before my ex-wife's unfortunate display at Christmas. We'd all moved on. The only one who hadn't was my ex-wife.'

Williams shrugged and pursed his lips, deliberately giving the impression that he was sceptical of Kholi's narrative of his relationship with the Salingers. 'We have a digital team assessing all communications from the Salingers' personal and business devices. So hopefully your account of how things were between you, will be verified very soon.'

Kholis eyes darted between Anwar and Williams and the finger tapping intensified. 'Well of course my communications with Trish will confirm what I've told you.' He paused, the tapping pausing momentarily before recommencing. 'But surely that doesn't apply to the kids' devices too. For God's sake, don't they deserve some privacy in death? Besides, I'd have thought it was quite clear that George flipped and killed them all and then himself. He's had mental health issues before you know. Two breakdowns that I know of.'

'Hmm.' Liam took his time in forming his next words. 'That's a few times now that you've mentioned murder-suicide as the Salinger family's cause of death. It's almost like you're trying to push us in a particular direction. Almost like you were there.'

Kholi jumped up, his breath coming in laboured gasps as he glared at them. 'Right. I've had enough. I've tried to help as best I can, but you two seem to be wilfully misinterpreting my concern and grief over the death of four people I cared about. If you need anything more from me, I suggest you contact my solicitors.'

He picked up a business card from a tray on his desk and flipped it through the air to land at Williams's feet. 'This interview is now terminated. I'll get someone to escort you from the premises.'

Anwar stood up, her mouth curled into a snarl. *So much for good cop.* 'No need for that, Mr Kholi. We've taken enough of your time. We can find our own way out. Thank you for your cooperation.'

Liam stood and followed Farah to the door, but waited till she'd opened it and was stepping through before delivering his sucker punch. 'Of course, Mr Kholi. You won't be leaving the country, will you? We'll probably need to speak with you again soon. Perhaps next time it'll be at Trafalgar House.'

Anwar and Williams didn't discuss their chat with Sukhjit Kholi until they'd left the building and were ensconced back in their car, the rain still hammering on the windscreen and grey clouds skittling across the sky with the promise of a thunderstorm to follow.

'So?' Liam switched on the engine and turned the heating up. 'What do you make of that?

Farah grinned, all trace of her earlier snippiness gone. 'Guy's a dick, isn't he? Trying to intimidate us and he's got a temper – did you see the way he whanged that executive toy thing on his desk. Definite anger management issues. I hate blokes like that.' She ran her fingers through her hair, sending raindrops dripping onto the dashboard. 'You did good there, Liam. Really good.'

'Did you notice his reaction to the kids' devices being checked? What was all that about?'

Farah bit her lip as she considered the point. 'Not sure. It was weird. He seemed more concerned about us violating Jason and Karen's privacy, than us checking for evidence of a breakdown in business relations with George Salinger. Maybe one or other of the kids sent off a few nasty messages to him after what happened at Christmas. Couldn't blame them if they had. Anyway, I reckon we ask the tech team to focus on the kids' devices as well as Salinger and Kholi's business interactions. Who knows? Maybe their issues with their mum and Kholi's affair weren't resolved fully. Maybe they were still pissed off about it and blaming Kholi. Maybe that's the motive we're looking for.'

'Or maybe he and Patricia Salinger were still at it, but being more careful. Maybe one or other of the kids found out about it and decided to intervene.'

He snicked his seatbelt in place, checked that Farah was belted up and pulled out of their parking place, ready to head back to Bradford and hoping that he'd got enough from Kholi to satisfy the boss.

Chapter 13

I'm furious and although I've implemented a plan that will keep the jackals at bay for now, I'm not sure I'll be able to maintain a cool demeanour. I need to though, because too much is at stake and everything rests on my performance over the next few days. Which is why I've locked myself in here, blinds closed and with strict instructions not to be disturbed. Scarface reckons I'm obsessed with her, but he's wrong. I just find reliving her particular journey therapeutic. I flick the switch and she's there on my screen.

I spy with my little eye, something beginning with B . . . Broken.

As I say the words aloud, a smile dances over my lips. As I study her again from the recording, I wonder what she's thinking. She's a feisty one. Watch her as she stuffs her fist into her mouth to stop the sobs. See how she shuts her eyes. It's almost as if she's taken herself off to a fun park somewhere or the seaside. Maybe, in her mind, she's eating ice cream on a hot summer's day in Scarborough. She might not speak, this little one, but that doesn't mean she's weak. Far from it I suspect.

It's a shame I've got a meeting to attend because I could watch this recording of her for hours. It's quite refreshing to see her so dignified compared to some of the others – no yelling or uncomely sobbing for little Lily. Oh no, she's something else. I remember ordering Scarface to proceed to the rewards stage – part one.

His laugh had been full of glee. Even after so long he still loves all these little stages because he knows that the sooner we start a rewards phase, the sooner we'll progress to the punishment one. It's a long established, tried and tested method. Carrot and stick, that's what it's all about, carrot and stick. Keep them on their toes. Lull them into a false sense of security, spoil them, make them begin to believe nothing bad will ever happen to them again and then, make something bad happen, followed swiftly by something even worse. It's a learning process after all. It's about teaching them to put things into perspective. If they endure the short periods of unpleasantness, then we reward them.

On screen, the door to her cell opens and I see her flinch as Scarface walks in. A pulse in her neck flutters like a sparrow's heartbeat as she scrambles her way to the top of the mattress. When she sees what Scarface is carrying, she frowns, her lip trembles and, when I zoom in, I see her nostrils quiver. In anticipation I lean closer to the screen as he places the tray of food, covered by a metal dome, on the mattress in front of her and then extracts the brand-new jeans and T-shirt from the plastic bag hanging off his wrist. And places them at the very foot of the mattress. When he leaves the room, she hesitates, licking her lips and casting glances towards the door. She reaches out and then snatches her hand back as if the dome is too hot for her to touch. I smile. Outside the cell Scarface watches her on his phone. He's waiting for just the right moment.

She reaches out again and this time, grips the handle of the metal cover and just as she begins to raise it, Scarface pushes the door open again and enters carting a basin of steaming water. She drops the cover, sending it clattering over the plate of food and wide-eyed stares at him, bracing herself for a punishment. But Scarface smiles.

Not his usual nasty smile, but the one I trained him to use. It took him ages to perfect it.

'Here, get washed, before you eat.' He places the basin of water on the floor beside the mattress and drops the towel that's draped round his neck on the floor beside it. 'Get clean, then eat. No arguments, eh?'

When he's gone and the door is locked, Lily runs her fingers over her eyes. She's tempted by the food, but she's also tempted by the water and clean clothes. I wait, wondering which option she'll go for and, even though I've seen this scene before, when she complies with Scarface's instructions and drapes the towel round her before washing herself with the soap and flannel in the basin, I'm almost disappointed. I'd expected her to be so hungry now that she'd dive into the fry-up. I smile remembering that sinking feeling in my gut when I'd realised that I'd overestimated the fight in her. But that didn't matter now – I've had loads of other opportunities for punishing her over the years. So many more, and with that thought in mind, I fast-forward again.

I spy with my little eye something beginning with C . . . Compliance.

I enjoy revisiting this. The way she lies there limp and pale makes me smile. Defeated, with no fight left. Things were progressing well with Lily at this stage. Every day she was becoming more and more compliant. Learning to accept things – and her little bouts of rebelliousness are becoming less and less frequent.

I allow my finger to trail down the paused screen where her face, eyes closed, is so clear. I wonder what she was thinking about. She's not sleeping. No one can sleep that much. She's taken herself into another dimension just like all the others did before her. Still, I'd have liked to be privy to her thoughts. That was the one flaw in this method – no matter how often I scrutinise these recordings, how much I study their micro-expressions, I could never really tell what was going on in their heads. I'll never truly understand at what point their minds fracture and accept that they have no power over their bodies or what happens to them. I'd love to see where their minds take them in these rare moments of solitude – if it's into the depths of despair – a living hell – or if they soar high above the sky seeking to escape their earthly bodies.

How whimsical is that? Perhaps they don't think at all. Perhaps our conditioning leaves them without the ability to think beyond their next reward or punishment.

She still jolts when Scarface enters the cell and her lips still tremble, so I know she's not completely broken – that her defeat isn't absolute – not yet anyway. She still recognises her own vulnerability. Still fears punishment and still craves the rewards.

In a low voice, I repeat the caption at the bottom of the screen: 'I spy with my little eye, something beginning with C . . . Compliance.'

I punch the air as I yell the word out loud, rejoicing in the success of the programme. 'Compliance!'

But it's what comes next that really pleases me. My cheeks flush with the excitement of it all. The next part is the very best part. I forward the recording. Stop! There it is!

I spy with my little eye something beginning with C . . . Controlled!

I fist-bump the air, my grin fit to split my face in half. Day one hundred and three – a full *thirty* days sooner than my previous protégé – and Lily progressed to the next stage. Despite her unwillingness to talk, she surpassed my expectations and she was popular with the clients – well apart from the few who got a tad frustrated with her and left a mark.

I frown at that memory. It's written into their contract that we do not allow our goods to be beaten or marked in any way. If they desire a service that provides disposable goods, then they should look elsewhere. Unlike some of the businesses out there, mine is bespoke – providing high-quality, well-trained goods in a secure setting for the enjoyment of our clients. None of the nasty, conveyor-belt services some of the competition provides. Our procurement and training methods are second to none, which is why we can be so choosy with our clientele. We believe in longevity, which is why I spent so many years devising and refining our carefully constructed programme and recruiting my loyal staff. I laugh – loyalty is only half the equation. Money, greed, desire to dominate all play a part in their compliance. On the whole, I give them what they want, but they are well aware that they are beholden to me. That's how our franchise works.

Take Auntie Lee-Lee for example. She has been with me since the start. When I was looking for a reliable person to deal with the produce she was the obvious choice. Her ability to blend in with people from all walks of life, her ability to live a double life and show no chinks in her façade of respectability. Her ability to be in the spotlight, yet not reveal her narcissism – her desire to be in control, to manipulate, to reel in sources and clients and demand their respect make her indispensable. Well almost indispensable – nobody is truly indispensable, are they?

Chapter 14

Ex DCI Archie Hegley sat in the Waterstones café and glared into his coffee mug as if it had committed an offence of the highest magnitude. The phone call from Nikki had come out of the blue and had dragged up things he'd much rather forget. Then, the paper headlines hit and a heavy weight had descended on him. They say every officer has a case that floors them. A case that remains unsolved but that preys on their mind; torturing them in their sleep, grabbing them by the throat when they least expect it and generally tainting every successful arrest with the persistent "what if" questions. He wanted it clear in his head for when he talked to Nikki, so he allowed his mind to drift back to that day twelve years ago when instead of being a DCI he was a lowly DI.

Normally, after the sweet, sweaty warmth of the previous day, the cooler air and the wispy threat of rain that fanned his face would have pleased DI Archie Hegley. Not today though. His hand rasped over the stubble on his chin as he squinted into the sky at the rising dawn. The smell of his own perspiration clung to him, mocking his failure. All around the shaded woods with the first dappling diamonds of dawn breaking through the greenery, other officers stood in similar deflated stances. Shoulders slumped, red-rimmed eyes, the air of defeat heavy in every movement they made.

Archie turned a complete circle on the spot, his eyes probing the dark and dingy nooks and crannies of the forest, dreading what he might spot, dreading that he'd spot nothing. Only yesterday, this area had rung with the sounds of children's laughter as they played tig or created a made-up adventure game that would exhaust them so much they'd fall into their parents' arms at the end of the day. Their sun-kissed skin, rosy cheeks, sleepy smiles and flickering eyelids testament to their day of hard play.

However, instead of being bundled into air-conned vehicles, with promises of a story before bed, the children's tear-streaked cheeks and trembling lips told a different story. The parents' pinched lips, deep frowns and worried glances were testament to the horror of what had happened. Not that anyone seemed to be entirely sure what had happened; not the kids, not the adults. Only the woods held the secret of where little Winnie Salinger had disappeared to and they were resolutely silent.

The thought of that little girl, barely eleven years old, alone and scared in the woods weighed heavy in his heart. The alternative scenario – that she was no longer in the woods, but had been abducted weighed even heavier. All night, he and his dedicated band of officers alongside volunteers from the local community had trawled through the woods as dusk moved from deep darkness and alien sounds to the rising light of dawn. Police dogs and their handlers had been deployed and yet, despite their calls, despite their persistence, they'd found no sign of Winnie. Torn between the imminent need to find her if she was alone and hurt in the woods and the persistent thought that, should this prove to be an abduction rather than a lost child, all these people traipsing over the area were compromising any existing forensic evidence that could be there, Archie felt on the back foot.

Of course, the media lurked like hyenas, stalking the periphery of the search area, snapping photos and grabbing anyone they thought *might provide a soundbite whilst their colleagues, equally dedicated to snatching the scoop, hung out at the gates of the Salinger home, ready to pounce on any family or friend who entered or left the vast family property. Unhelpful and largely unsubstantiated hints of child abuse, neglect, paedophile rings and the child Lolita were dropped like cannons in newsfeeds and social media.*

With a glare in their direction, Archie swallowed hard, trying to dislodge the lump in his throat that reminded him they'd already used up twelve of the twenty-four hours that were crucial in such investigations. Heart heavy, he turned to leave Fogarty Woods, knowing that he'd never again view them as a benign and welcoming place, and trudged back to his car. It was time now to look at other options in more detail. Of course he'd set a team of officers to scroll through the Salingers' history and that of the other parents at the friends and family picnic. Archie believed in covering all his bases. Now, it was time though to move things up a gear.

The sound of a child crying in the shop below brought Archie back to the present. He exhaled and rubbed his hand over his near-bald head. The familiar block of ice was lodged in his gut like pernicious frostbite, freezing his insides black and sending sharp prickles through his chest. He rubbed his chest with his fist and tried to slow his breathing. For a long time, Archie had been plagued with thoughts of Winnie Salinger's fate. Perhaps now, with the death of the rest of her family, he was about to find out her fate too.

Chapter 15

It had been a few weeks since Nikki had last seen Archie. His new security business had morphed into a PI and security business almost overnight and they were both so busy with their respective jobs that they had only managed snatched phone conversations and the occasional text recently.

Having decided to chat with Archie on her own, she'd asked Sajid to drop her off on Thornton Road before heading back to Trafalgar House and now, as she walked through City Park, towards the old Wool Exchange building that now housed Bradford Waterstones bookstore, she felt her shoulders loosen and the tautness in her neck fade.

She'd been in the car for too long and even a short walk was paying dividends. Although, as she pulled her scarf up over her mouth against the icy afternoon air, she knew that it wasn't only being confined to a car for two hours that had her muscles clamming up on her. It was this case. On the way back from Ashleigh Kholi's house she'd flicked through the various forensic reports that were coming in in dribs and drabs. So far most of the prints lifted by the CSIs matched those of the Salinger family, a few matched with George Bland, but that was to be expected because he freely admitted to spending a lot of time at the house.

The prints on the fifth glass and around the area where their unidentified player had sat didn't match anyone on the IDENT1 or CODIS system, so, until they managed to match those prints or DNA with one of their suspects, they were no further forward.

There was no evidence of attempts to eradicate prints at the scene, so either their killer wore gloves or it was indeed some weird and wonderful murder-suicide that subverted all the expert opinion so far. Nikki "humphed" out loud, startling a man walking past. But she barely registered his startled expression or the way he widened the gap between them, so intent was she on thinking through all the information they'd gained since being called to the crime scene.

They were still waiting to discover if there was any as yet unidentified DNA mixed in with the blood spatter. So far, all the labs would commit to was that most of the blood seemed to come from the four Salingers, but they wouldn't commit to either the absence or presence of blood from another individual. The blood spatter was still being assessed and because of the crossover of spray from the various inflicted injuries, it was taking longer than usual to analyse. Each spatter pattern had to be matched to a victim and because there were so many injuries this was a time-consuming process, even with the use of the techy crime scene programme Langley had insisted they use.

With no evidence of forced access to the home it seemed likely their killer had been invited, but that didn't mean that an intruder hadn't gained entry through some ruse or other. The maid had confirmed that the family often left doors unlocked when they were at home. She really hoped that Archie would be able to point her in a new direction – one that would edge the investigation forward, for Nikki was all too aware that time was slipping through her fingertips, like grains of sand on a Whitby beach.

As she reached the top of the stairs leading into the Waterstones café, she marvelled once again at the grandeur of the Gothic building that had once been the old Wool Exchange. With its domed roof and arched stained glass windows, the building always made Nikki think of old black and white films with bats and belfries. She glanced around and spotted Archie sitting at a table for two near the banister that looked over the bookshop below. Archie, like Nikki, was a people-watcher, a trait directly attributed to their jobs. She took a moment to study him. He'd slipped off his coat revealing a bright orange jumper, with turquoise shirt collars peeping over the top. He looked slimmer than last time she'd seen him. Slimmer and less wrinkled – more relaxed as if his new job, which necessitated a fair amount of activity agreed with him. Although she missed his dour Scottish humour and his "proverbials" at work, Nikki didn't grudge him his retirement. Not that he'd actually retired. He was busier now than he had been before, but at least he was on the front line and not stuck rotting away behind a desk at Trafalgar House.

Approaching him, she smiled. 'Archie, you need a refill?'

Her old boss started, clearly having been in another world, and looked down at his empty mug before looking up at Nikki, a wide smile stretching across his face, lighting up his previous moody expression. 'Och yer here, Parekh. I was just about to order a wee snack. It's been a while since breakfast. A cheese and onion toastie maybe.'

He rubbed his hand across his tummy and sighed. 'I maybe shouldn't, but what the "proverbials" I'll have a slice of that beetroot and courgette cake with the frosted icing on top and a chai latte too.'

Nikki grinned. Some things never changed. Archie still had a sweet tooth and despite his heart condition, Nikki was happy to indulge him without comment because he'd lost so much weight. So, with a 'be right back', she approached the counter and peered into the glass cabinet, before opting for a slab of coffee and walnut cake to accompany her cheese and ham toastie, leaving Archie to continue his people-watching. Back at the table, waiting for their food and drinks to arrive, they spent a few moments catching up.

'How's Marcus and the kids?'

Archie paid Marcus cash in hand for surveillance work occasionally, so Nikki knew he'd seen her other half quite recently. 'Marcus is great. And the kids.' She remembered that morning's contretemps between Sunni and Ruby and added: 'On the whole anyway. Saj sends his love.'

Archie slapped his palm on the table top, making the condiments rattle and causing a couple on the next table to glance over. 'I miss that lad, you know. How's his wedding plans going? You got his stag do sorted?'

Nikki opened her mouth to respond and then clipped it shut again. Her eyes widened as the words "stag do" sunk in. 'What do you mean, stag do? I don't have to organise that do I? Nah . . . that's not . . .'

Archie tutted. 'For God's sake, Parekh. Are you the lad's best woman or not?'

Sensing defeat, Nikki nodded.

'Well then, the stag do is *your* responsibility so get your finger out and get one organised. And—' he glared at her '—I expect an invite.'

Shit, shit, shitty shit shit. Stag do? A wave of panic caught in her chest for a moment then cleared as she came up with a plan. She held up one finger, grabbed her phone and opened WhatsApp. Selecting the family group, The Parekhists, she started typing.

HELP! EMERGENCY! We need to organise Saj's stag do . . . ! 😆

Within seconds, the first reply came in from Charlie, followed swiftly by Isaac.

Charlie: *Eh . . . what do you mean WE? You're his best woman . . . You're on your own with this one. Also, that's a deer not a stag. Also, you don't need to type the word when you use the emoji* 😄

112

Isaac: *Can we go swimming?*

Fuck's sake! Couldn't any of them come up with a decent idea? Then, just as her panic felt bound to overtake her completely, Marcus responded.

Marcus: *Don't worry. We'll work something out. Love you* 😉

Panic dissipating, Nikki took a deep breath. She so wanted to do a good job for Sajid, but when she'd agreed to be best woman for his and Langley's wedding, she hadn't really understood what would be expected of her. Now, the jobs were piling up and she was ashamed to admit she'd not managed to tick one off her list. Good job Marcus had her back. However, this wasn't the time to think about Sajid's wedding plans. So, she pulled her chair close and leaned over the table. Although the café was quiet, she didn't want to risk anyone overhearing them. 'I need to talk with you about one of your old cases, boss.'

Archie dragged his eyes away from the activity below and, his brow scrunched into a frown, he nodded. 'Aye, I saw the papers this morning and wondered if that's why you wanted to meet up.' His brow smoothed as he winked at her. 'And I was right, wasn't I?'

But Nikki was thinking about Archie's earlier words. 'It's hit the press? Already?'

With a shrug, Archie leaned back allowing the waiter to deposit their order on the table before replying. 'They always manage to ferret out the proverbials, don't they? Bastards, that's what they are, the lot of them.' He started to fiddle with his phone and then turned it so Nikki could see. The headline from *The Bradford Chronicle* glared out at her, taunting her and sending a flash of annoyance up her spine.

TRAGEDY HITS LOCAL FAMILY FOR THE SECOND TIME!

THE QUESTION IS, WILL POLICE DO RIGHT BY THE SALINGERS THIS TIME?

Rage momentarily blinded Nikki. She hadn't given the press office permission to leak the identity of the victims. The only people her team had informed were those they needed to interview as a matter of urgency: Derek Bland, George Salinger's PA, the Kholis and the kids' respective educational institutions. So, how had the press got an identity so soon and, more to the point, how had they raked up the tragedy from the Salingers' past so quickly? She flashed back to their morning briefing where PC Dosanjh had first informed them about Winnie Salinger's abduction. Had someone on the wider team leaked to the press?

She scanned the first couple of paragraphs, which included a rehash of the limited information the press office had been authorised to release to media outlets with the added embellishment of lurid speculation and accusations of police incompetency surrounding the twelve-year-old unsolved disappearance of the Salingers' eldest daughter. Why did they have to be so damn provocative? She looked at the by-line and exhaled, taking the opportunity to twang her elastic bands a few times to calm her mounting anger. The article was the work of Lisa Kane, a journalist Nikki had encountered on more than one occasion. She might have guessed. There was no love lost between the two, but after Kane had outed Sajid, Nikki had hoped that their paths wouldn't cross again. Seems she'd been optimistic. However, what concerned her more was that Kane must have a source inside Trafalgar House, in order to have information not yet released to the press.

'You don't want to read the full article, Nik. It'll get yer gander up,' said Archie snatching his mobile back and shoving it in his pocket before Nikki could scroll down to the end of the piece. 'She's toxic, but just keep your head down, let Ahad deal with the flak and focus on the investigation.'

Archie was right. Of course he was. Still the ball of fire wedged in her gut wasn't likely to die out anytime soon. She wouldn't read the article, but that didn't mean she wouldn't hear what was in it. Everyone would be talking about it and by the time she got back to Trafalgar House she could expect to be greeted by the hyenas camped out on the doorstep of the station. Worse than that though, the bastards would invade the café where Isaac worked, and she doubted that Lisa Kane would have the decency not to pump the lad for information and gossip about Nikki. But she couldn't worry about that now.

She took a bite of her toastie, followed by a slurp of coffee and spoke through the mouthful. 'You gonna tell me the stuff that wasn't in the official file about Winnie Salinger's disappearance?'

Archie lifted one half of his toastie to his mouth, took a huge bite and chewed with his eyes closed as if that was the only way to get the full toastie experience. Nikki was happy to enjoy the rest of her sandwich as she waited. Archie was a team player and although he wasn't part of Nikki's team anymore, he would still back it. She was confident he'd share whatever insights he had and if there was a link between Winnie's disappearance twelve years ago and her family's murder yesterday, then Archie would help. The victims always came first with Archie – that was one of the things that bonded him and Nikki so closely. That and the fact that he'd also become a bit of a father figure to her from the day she first met him on the job.

His Adam's apple bulged as he swallowed and then he washed the remnants of his food down with a glug of chai. Wiping his fingers on a napkin, he studied Nikki, head on one side. 'Ah can do better than that. Ah can give you my unofficial Winnie Salinger file. I'll bring it to yours later on, but for now, ask away.'

As he pulled the slab of maroon-coloured cake towards him and began to demolish it, Nikki considered what she wanted to discuss first. So far, she'd interviewed two possible suspects in the Salinger family killing – Derek Bland and Ashleigh Kholi – and each had offered vastly different viewpoints on the family. Well aware that Derek Bland was biased in favour of the Salingers because of his close relationship with the family and that Ashleigh Kholi was equally prejudiced against them because of her husband's affair with Patricia Salinger, Nikki was desperate to discover Archie's take on the parents. 'Tell me your impressions of George and Patricia Salinger.'

Archie put down his fork, wiped the napkin across his mouth removing the frosting moustache that had moments earlier covered his upper lip. His eyes twinkled as he leaned back and considered her request. 'Weeell, Parekh. That *is* a conundrum.'

His glance danced over the lower floor of the bookshop where a frazzled dad with two very young crying children in a double buggy tried to manoeuvre through the crime fiction section towards the main door. One of the children had pulled their leg up and kicked off their blanket, which had then tangled round the wheels making it almost impossible for the dad, who hadn't noticed, to steer the pram without knocking into the book tables advertising best-seller books. In response to the drama below, Archie smiled. Then he turned back to Nikki, the smile dying from his lips. 'You've got to remember that it was under exceptional circumstances that I first met the Salingers. I mean, how does a parent behave when faced with the disappearance and possible abduction of their child? There's no rule book for that sort of scenario is there? Still—'

Rather than interrupt his flow, Nikki remained silent until Archie was ready to continue. 'Ah was an experienced DI at the time, you know? Ah'd been senior investigating officer on similar cases before, but . . .' he threw his soiled napkin onto the table '. . . the dad – George Salinger's reaction felt odd tae me . . . off, you know?'

Although she didn't fully understand what Archie meant, Nikki nodded and he continued.

'But then again so did that Derek Bland. I got bad vibes from him too. He was always hanging around the Salingers, "offering support". Archie used his fingers to make bunny ears, then grunted. 'They were a weird little trio. I had suspicions they were some sort of ménage à trois, but couldn't find anything to confirm that. Bland was ever-present and took over the reins of the business till George got himself back on his feet.' He snorted. 'That didn't take long, mind you. Other parents in similar circumstances were usually angry or distraught or veered from one emotion to another. Most can't get their heads round doing normal things. The Salingers though were . . .' He shrugged. 'I don't know. Cold maybe? Detached? Emotionless? Of course, we all gave them the benefit o' the doubt, put it doon tae the shock at the time and worked roond it, but . . .'

Nikki's thoughts flashed back to Ashleigh Kholi's assertion that the Salingers were psychopaths. Is this what she meant? At the time she'd taken it with a pinch of salt, particularly when Derek Bland had described them as loving parents and a close family. But, here was Archie, whose judgement she trusted implicitly, casting doubt on the Salingers . . . and on Bland too. Of course, the files from the investigation into Winnie's disappearance had hinted that there had been some doubt over Winnie's parents at the time. Doubts that further investigation had purportedly discredited. 'Come on, boss. It's me you're talking to – can't you be more specific?'

All trace of his earlier unconcerned "I'm loving retirement" persona evaporated as he looked at her. 'Look, all ah can say here and noo is that most of us thocht there was something odd about the Salinger family, but, well—' He shrugged again, his mouth screwed up into an angry pout. 'We were told to back off them. Then no matter how hard we looked, the investigation didn't turn up any viable leads. In the end, pressure was exerted to close up the investigation and put it down to a pre-pubescent troubled girl running away despite her loving family's best efforts to support her through her increasingly erratic behaviour.'

'But you don't believe that . . . ?'

117

Archie shook his head and pulled what was left of his cake towards him. 'No. I didnae believe that, but, I'm no' going to discuss it here.' He looked around as if suspecting that the frazzled mum with a toddler in a high chair three tables across was recording every word they said. 'Walls have ears, Nikki, hen. Walls have ears.'

For a moment, Nikki let his words sink in. In the space of the hour they'd been together, Archie had morphed from a carefree, "I'm going to enjoy my cake and toastie", living the retired life ex-police officer, to a slumped in his chair angry man with demons draining the blood from his face, leaving him ashen. Gone was the vibrant man she'd surreptitiously observed on entering the café and in his place was her ex-boss looking more troubled than she'd ever seen him.

Prickles piano-keyed over the nape of her neck and she felt as if she was being watched. The cold dread that she'd been free from since Downey died took on new life and she found herself scanning first the café, and then the ground floor of the bookshop. Nothing was amiss. She stretched her hand over the table and gripped his forearm and, as she leaned closer to him, she glanced round, before speaking in an urgent, yet whispered voice. 'You're talking about more than just pressure to close a case, aren't you? You're talking about something more insidious – pressure from the higher echelons of the police and beyond – politicians, economic advisers, business bigwigs. Am I right?'

If she'd blinked, she would have missed Archie's nod. He held her gaze, his voice equally subdued. 'I'll come to yours with my file tonight and we'll thrash through everything. Okay?'

She hesitated, then nodded and stood up, but Archie grabbed her hand. 'Watch your back, Nikki. I have a bad feeling about this one.'

Chapter 16

After leaving Waterstones, Nikki nipped into the Marks and Spencer's in the Broadway shopping mall and grabbed a few of their buckets of mini sweet treats to take in to the team – who didn't love a rocky road or a millionaire's shortbread? Experience, and Sajid's insistence, had told her that small gestures like these kept the team in good spirits and made them more willing to go the extra ten miles. She reckoned she might need to garner as much goodwill as possible before this case was over. Her mind flashed back to the violence of the crime scene she'd been at only a few hours ago and something raw and rotting squirmed in her gut, leaving a horrid taste in her mouth – this murder would require her team to put in long hours.

The busy Broadway mall irked her. Too many people going about their business, laughing and joking with not a care in the world, whilst her thoughts were centred on a tableau of a Monopoly board set with five places, but only four bodies and the metallic stench of fresh blood, needlessly spilled. As she jostled her way outdoors, the skies opened releasing a deluge of rain that bounced off the pavement, sending shoppers scurrying into the shopping centre or huddled together in shop doorways. Nikki pulled her hood over her head and stepped out into the rain, her mind filled with both the information that Archie had given her regarding the Salingers' eldest daughter and the strange pressure exerted on the police to close the case, as well as the meeting in York with Sukhjit Kholi's ex-wife, Ashleigh.

Moments after entering City Park, the rain subsided, although grey clouds still drifted across the sky, aided and abetted by the rising wind. Nikki tried to unravel the information at her disposal. Was Archie's information a dead end? An unfortunate occurrence from the Salingers' past that had no bearing on their deaths? Or was something more sinister afoot? Then, there was Patricia Salinger's affair with Sukhjit Kholi and Ashleigh's reaction to it.

The photographs on the Salingers' wall taunted Nikki. Was the closeness and love that Nikki had sensed when looking at the images all fake? A veil of deceit? A web of misdirection? Thinking of the framed images dotted around the Salinger home made Nikki realise that none of them were of the older missing daughter. Was that strange? Nikki couldn't imagine ever erasing any of her children from her life if they'd gone missing. Surely, it was more normal to keep the memory alive through the few snapshots they had left of their shared time together. Perhaps it was too painful for them? Perhaps it was morbid and upsetting for the parents. Maybe it would have stopped them from moving on with their lives with their surviving children. Who was to say that well-thumbed and treasured photo albums, filled with poignant memories of their eldest child wouldn't be uncovered by the crime scene investigators?

As she strolled, heedless of her rapidly soaking coat and the way her boots leaked, her mind was fully focused on the investigation. So, when the notification of a text message, followed almost immediately by her phone ringing interrupted her thoughts, she jumped. A glance at her phone told her it was Sajid and she grinned. Probably wanting her to hurry up so he could scoff the cakes she'd promised to bring. 'Hey Saj, you okay?'

'We've got a problem, Nik, and the bloody Dark Knight's on the warpath. It's bloody arctic in here. You need to get back.'

The smile that flitted across Nikki's lips at her partner referring to their boss as the Dark Knight, faded. Her heart thrummed in her chest and her stomach cramped for a mere second. 'You telling me there's been another one? Another murder?'

Sajid's frustration drifted into her ear and she imagined him, in his shirt sleeves, face flushed and hair spiked by him running his fingers through it in response to whatever crisis was unfolding in Trafalgar House. 'No, not another murder.' He paused and exhaled. 'Thank God. But it's nearly as bloody bad. That fucking Lisa Kane's been up to her old tricks again.'

'Yeah, I know. Archie showed me the article. Bloody cow questioning whether we're up to the task with her "Will the police do right by the Salingers this time?" jibe.'

'Not that one, Nik. *The Chronicle* has updated their feed with a new article by Kane. It's personal and vicious. I've sent you a link. Have a look at it and then get yourself back here pronto, before Ahad has a fit.'

Personal? Shit, what exactly had that poisonous cow written this time? The heavens chose that moment to send a booming rumble of thunder over Bradford, followed by a lightning flash, and Nikki shuddered. Whilst she didn't mind the rain, she disliked thunderstorms intensely. Was this an omen? But Nikki had no time for superstition, so she swatted the thought away and picked up speed as she strode through puddles towards the taxi rank behind City Hall. 'Okay. I'm on my way.'

Once in the taxi, she opened up the text from Sajid and pressed the link. When the headline came up – *Newly promoted Detective Inspector Nikki Parekh eating cake with her ex-boss whilst a family of four lie dead in the morgue and their killer still to be identified* – she growled under her breath. Kane was pure venom, but why was she focusing her attention on Nikki when there was so much more pertinent stuff she could be reporting about the murders?

To the side of the provocative headline was an ultra-clear image of her and Archie eating cake in Waterstones.

If Lisa Kane had been nearby, Nikki was sure she'd have noticed her. Of course, her previous photographer was rotting in Wakefield prison, courtesy of Nikki, so it was likely she had a new photographer – one Nikki didn't know. Still, how the hell hadn't she noticed someone taking it? She'd scanned the café and the bookshop a few times, but – she had to admit – she'd been too engrossed in Archie's revelations and intrigued by the promise of more to follow later on, that she'd let her guard down.

A band constricted across her chest as she thought back to her meeting with Archie not twenty minutes ago and a new concern formed in her mind. *What if Lisa Kane had overheard their conversation?* She scrutinised the image, looking for clues as to where it had been taken from. The only logical place was from beneath them in the bookshop itself. She and Archie had sat at the tables overlooking the activity below and anyone could have taken a quick shot of her. What remained to be determined was who had taken it and why? Nikki was convinced that the photographer hadn't been Lisa Kane. She'd sure as hell have noticed if she'd been browsing through the books below her. With a sigh Nikki scrolled down and the headline of the online edition screamed at Nikki.

Bradford's "WOKE" policing inadequate
to investigate multiple deaths

Underneath the provocative headline the article started with:

Bradford CID rate the "Woke" team of detectives headed up by DI Nikki Parekh who, according to an unnamed source close to the investigation, is "not up to the job". Worse than that though is that since the discovery of four bodies, believed to be the entire Salinger family: dad, George; mum, Patricia;

and their two teenage children Jason and Karen on Sunday night, there has been no progress in the investigation. Another reliable source confirms that Parekh and her motley gang of inefficient officers are scrambling about looking for clues that more experienced officers, relegated to the side-lines by Bradford policing's unofficial policy of "Wokeness", would not have missed. Bradford deserves better than this. The Salinger family deserves better than this.

Jaw clenched, Nikki clicked off the article and glared out the window, shutting down any attempts that the taxi driver made to engage her in conversation. As they approached Trafalgar House, she looked down at her red swollen wrist and realised that for the short ride to the station she'd been forcefully twanging her elastic band against her wrist. *Bloody Kane!*

Nikki paid the driver and got out, dreading whatever repercussions were about to land on her head inside Trafalgar House. The last thing they needed right then was to be distracted by unsubstantiated and inaccurate news reporting. At the back of her mind, she cursed herself though. If she hadn't been so abrasive with her nemesis, Lisa bloody Kane, perhaps the reporter wouldn't have outed Sajid and maybe she'd have been less inclined to set her sights on discrediting Nikki with her toxic headlines. Head down, she marched into the building, trying not to feel like a lamb to the slaughter as she made her way up to the incident room.

Chapter 17

Then: Marnie

I don't know how long I've been here; it doesn't really matter. All the days blur into each other and where my heart used to be is a hole. A hole big enough to hold all the pain, all the hurt and all the embarrassments. It's a crater of numbness, because once I put the bad stuff in there, I don't have to think about it. Every day, I say my real name inside my head. Marnie, Marnie, Marnie, but every day, it sounds stranger and stranger. I'm not Marnie anymore. Marnie was the girl with attitude. Marnie caused her parents grief. Marnie yelled at her sister. Marnie played hooky from school. Marnie had loads of friends and Marnie wasn't here in this hellish place. Marnie was free.

Maybe I am Lily. Maybe she's who I've become. Silent Lily who cries, but makes no noise. Voiceless Lily who never smiles, but also never fights back anymore. Quiet Lily who endures and doesn't complain. Mute Lily who is still alive when others have died. Even Jilly's **'Don't let the Beep Beeps get you down, Marn. Don't ever let the Beep Beeps win'** *is all tattered and faded in my mind. Like a scrap of paper blowing in the wind and rain with the writing all smudged.*

Sometimes Scarface comes and is nice to me; gives me sweets or warm water to wash or hot food. But sometimes he says I'm bad; that the man didn't like it when I struggled and then he throws freezing cold water over me and he leaves me shivering and scared down in this hole with no dry clothes and a bed that's sodden. After the third time, I stopped struggling. But then he says the other men don't like when I cry, so he pinched me hard and left me with no food. I won't cry anymore. I'll pretend to be with Jilly, that's what I'll do – if I can. Thing is, it's been a long time since she visited me. A long time since I smelled her strawberry shampoo and I worry I'll never see her again.

There's nothing else for me to do down here, so I close my eyes and let sleep take me. That's what I do most of the time when I'm not upstairs with the men.

At least when I'm asleep, I feel no pain.

But then he's there. Scarface!

He drags me from my room and marches me up four flights of stairs, the last set. I hadn't realised there was a fourth floor. Instead of the damp dusty stench of my cell, here there's perfume and carpets and furniture and the faint murmur of music. Not like the shiny stuff on the third floor, but still there were chairs and coffee tables and a dining table with more chairs. After prodding me in the shoulder he yells at me, to **"be a fucking good girl, bitch, or you'll end up back down there or worse"**, then he leaves me there and for the first time since I'd been in this awful place, my chest loosens and I can breathe a little easier.

A door scrapes open and a head pokes out, followed by a skinny girl, not much older than me, with short black hair framing rosy cheeks. She gestures for me to come closer, and dragging my feet I edge towards her, hoping this isn't some horrid trick. Her smile is small and tight, as if she has to force it, but her eyes never leave me as I approach and when I stand in front of her, her shoulders relax a little. 'What's your name?'

I want to tell her my name. I really do. Not the one Scarface gave me, but my real name. The one Jilly called me by. When I

125

open my mouth, that scratchy thing lodges in my throat and I can't budge it. Wide-eyed, with my fingers plucking at the stupid dress Scarface had given me, I stare at her. She frowns and her dark eyes crawl over me. She's going to hit me or push me over or worse still spin round and slam the door in my face. I know she is. But she doesn't. Instead, she links her arm through mine and pulls me inside the room. 'I'm Rose.'

She hesitates, glances round and lowers her voice. 'My real name's Gwendoline, but they won't let me use that – you can call me Gwen.' She turns and slides the door shut, watching as my eyes drift round the room. There are two beds – not quite the size of my bed at home, but at least they aren't mattresses dropped on a concrete floor. The bedding is mismatched, but it looks clean.

'Your bed is that one.' She points to the one on the right of the small window. 'This one's mine.' And as if to demonstrate her ownership over the bed she strolls over and bounces on it a couple of times. All the while her eyes don't leave my face.

'Can't you speak?' Her tone's one of interest rather than the scathing, nasty tones sometimes used by the Beep Beeps Scarface takes me to meet. Sometimes they got so frustrated by my silence that they beat me, but that didn't help. Instead of opening up my throat, each whip, each punch, each jibe sealed it tighter.

I wonder if **she'll** tease me too, or hit me. I bite my lip and glance towards the window. After so long, it feels strange to have only glass separating me from the outside world rather than a brick wall – like I'm free. I know I'm not free though and as my eyes wander over the delicious square framing outdoors, I realise that even with the soft beds and the girl called Rose and the nice smell, I'm still in jail. There are metal bars behind the glass panes, but at least I can see clouds strut across an angry grey sky. Tears gather in my eyes, but I blink them away. Who'd ever have thought that seeing clouds would make me want to cry. When I move closer the sight of trees, lush and green swaying in the breeze, makes my tummy flutter. It's been **so** long since I've seen the outside world.

So long since I've seen anything other than the Beep Beeps and my cell in the dungeon.

I lean my brow on the cold glass and exhale. My breath steams the window and I realise I **can** talk to Gwen/Rose. With my finger, I write Marnie on the steamed-up window pane and turn towards her. She looks from me to the word on the glass and then a smile flashes over her lips, before being replaced by the same tight half-smile I'd seen earlier. She jumps to her feet and joins me by the glass. Using her sleeve, she rubs out my words and then breathes heavily, creating her own steam bubble. She grins at me and writes, "Flower name?"

Now it's my turn to rub out her words and replace them with the name Scarface gave me. "Lily," I write. Then, almost as an afterthought, I add: "Hate it!"

Outside our small room, footsteps walk along the corridor and all at once, Gwen grabs my arm and after obliterating the first real conversation I've had in weeks, she drags me over and pushes me onto my bed. She then poses, cross-legged on her own bed, pretending to read a book she snatches, last second, from the rickety table beside her bed.

When the door opens, I expect to see Scarface, but instead a tall woman with the biggest boobs I've ever seen marches in. Her hair puffs out around her head like a lion's mane and a frown mars her forehead as she glares first at Gwen and then at me. 'Rose, have you told Lily our rules?'

Whilst I sit, transfixed by the woman, Gwen jumps to her feet, head bowed, and shakes her head. 'No, Auntie Lee-Lee. Not had time.'

Auntie Lee-Lee rolls her eyes and her massive breasts heave upwards as she exhales. 'You need to take responsibility for the other children now, Rose. You're our eldest and we need you to keep them in line.'

Children? There are more of us than just me and Rose. My thoughts drift from the long line of dark closed doors in the dungeons to the line of painted doors along this corridor. **How many more flowers are trapped in here?**

Although the words are uttered in a calm tone, the flash of panic that drew Rose's eyebrows downwards and the way she jostles from one foot to the other tells me that Lee-Lee isn't always as mild-mannered as she appears and I store that nugget away for future reference. Jilly would be so proud of me, planning and trying to think ahead. Inside my head I hear her sweet voice: **Don't let the Beep Beeps get you down, Marn. Don't ever let the Beep Beeps win,** and I smile – not on my face, but inside. Even with Auntie Lee-Lee to contend with, things have got better for me. I have a nice, clean bed and a new friend. **I'm winning, Jilly,** I think, **I'm winning.** I switch back to Gwen, who's still talking with Auntie Lee-Lee.

'Sorry, Auntie Lee-Lee. I'll keep them in check. I promise.'

With a waft of her hand, Aunt Lee-Lee dismisses Gwen's promises and turns to me. She tugs at her necklace as her dark eyes rake over me, from top to toe. For a second, I imagine she can see into my soul and my heart contracts, but when she speaks, her voice, although not gentle, isn't as nasty as Scarface's. 'So, you're Lily, are you? The one who doesn't speak?'

She gestures for me to stand and I jump to my feet, heart pounding as she approaches. 'You're popular with our clients. Maybe the selective mute act makes them feel powerful. Whatever the appeal, it's got you this promotion.' She glares at me. 'Well, that and the way your behaviour has improved. Your job is to make sure you don't piss them off. You got me? **No pissing off the clients.** They ask you to do something, you do it. That's rule number one.'

She smiles and turns to Gwen. 'And rule number two is . . . ?'

Gwen, hands behind her back, standing straight as a soldier on parade, says, 'Bathe yourself before and after an interaction with a client.' She speaks the words like she's reciting a times table at primary school.

'Rule three . . . ?

'Take care of your costumes – if they need mending get it done. If they need washing get them washed.'

Lee-Lee smirks, her dark eyes lightening as if each rule was something to celebrate. 'And the last one . . .'

'Accept that this is your life from now on and you will survive. Be disobedient and you will suffer.'

The word **survive** echoes in my head like a klaxon and my earlier bravado about planning and escaping fades. I'm not sure I'll survive this. How can I? This is a monstrous life, and as Lee-Lee turns and leaves the room, I realise that I'd give anything to be at the school my parents chose for me rather than here, in hell.

We stand by our beds for a long time, not moving. I'm trying to process the rules and what they mean. I'm in no doubt that I'll still have to go to the third floor, but if I stick to the rules then I'll get to come back here, to this room with its nice bed and my new friend. I wonder what would happen if I disobey – if I struggle when they take me to the third floor. Then, I remember the dungeon – the cold water being thrown over me, the light being put out leaving me in the dark, the stench of shit and piss from my bucket, the gnawing in my stomach when Scarface forgets to feed me – that's what the punishment would be.

Gwen takes my hand and pulls me onto her bed. 'Listen, Lily, I know your real name, but I can't risk using it in case it slips out when Auntie Lee-Lee's there. That's a punishable offence, you know? We have to forget our real names. Forget our lives before.'

As her words with their echo of permanence shake me, she squeezes my hand. 'It's not all bad. Yes, we're locked in and we have to work but, when we're not working, we've got food and books and DVDs and TV. It's not as bad as being in the dungeon. It's okay. You'll get used to it and you've got us.'

A light knock on the door has me jumping to my feet in case Auntie Lee-Lee has come back. But when the door opens, instead of the formidable woman, eight figures walk in. Three boys and five girls, all of them under the age of fourteen. They study me in silence as if I'm an exotic plant in a greenhouse. Then one, a boy, steps forward and thrusts his hand out. 'Hi, I'm Gold. What's your name?'

I look at his hand but don't take it.

Gwen moves forward. 'She's Lily. This is Lily, everyone, and she's replaced Honeysuckle. She doesn't talk.'

Replaced Honeysuckle? What does that mean? I look at Rose willing her to tell me, but when she catches my eye, I see the tears lurking there and I know what happened to Honeysuckle. Rose moves on. 'Lily, the boys are named after metal so this is Gold, Silver and Bronze.'

The boys' lips twitch into a semblance of a smile, but their smiles are forced – just like the one I'd seen on Rose's mouth earlier. Nobody here smiles for joy. No one. As Gwen continues the introductions – 'This is Daisy, Bluebell, Sunflower, Peony and Crocus.' The same forced half-smiles appear on each of the children's lips, but none of them look happy. Who could blame them? It seems I've only replaced one prison cell for another and it remains to be seen how much of an improvement this set-up will be. But at least I'm not alone. At least I have friends. At least I'm not downstairs in the dungeon – or on the third floor – not right now anyway.

As I extend my hand to each of the kids, Jilly's words ring in my mind. **Don't let the Beep Beeps get you down, Marn. Don't ever let the Beep Beeps win.**

Chapter 18

Nikki hesitated by the door of the subdued incident room, taking in the scene and gauging the atmosphere. It felt like anger mingled with frustration and helplessness filled the office. She had to do something to dispel that and damn quick too. Experience had taught her that allowing unhealthy emotions to fester would be detrimental to the overall performance of her team. But how could she dispel it? It already seemed that the officers under her command were sending sideways accusatory glances at each other and she didn't think her paltry offering of chocolate-covered M&S snacks would cut it. Shit, being a DI was hard sometimes, and it was particularly hard for Nikki who was often so focused on the task in hand that she couldn't assess how others were feeling. Thank God she had Saj to help with that. They complemented each other. He smoothed her prickly side and she made him more incisive.

The few uniformed officers, dotted at tables around the room, lowered their gazes and hammered away on their keyboards when they noticed Nikki by the door. In different circumstances Nikki would have found the Mexican wave of quiet that rippled over the room funny. Today though, she wondered if one of these officers was Lisa Kane's "reliable source close to the investigation". Just as quickly she dismissed the thought. She'd worked with these officers for years and was sure that she'd gained the respect of most of them. Okay, sometimes she was a tad – or maybe a lot – abrasive, but she was efficient and dedicated and that went a long way. Or did it? She exhaled and thrust the creeping maggot of doubt from her mind. She couldn't allow herself to be engulfed by paranoia. There was too much at stake and she had to focus. No time for outside distractions. Besides which, she wouldn't put it past Lisa Kane to have made the entire article up just to discredit Nikki and her team and get herself a few hours in the spotlight. *Bitch!*

She stepped forward, her eyes scanning the desks as she strode towards her own desk. DCs Williams and Anwar sat, bodies angled away from each other, their gazes focused on the reports they were typing up, unaware that she'd entered. Nikki frowned. Was there some tension between the two DCs? Shit. Last thing she needed was for her core team to start doubting each other. She relied too heavily on them for any dissent to take hold.

Sajid spotted her first, jumped to his feet and rushed towards her. 'You read the damn article?'

Nikki shook her head, and kept her voice low as she replied. 'Only the first couple of paragraphs. Made me too angry, so I thought I'd wait till I got back. What's Ahad saying about it all?'

'Ahad,' said a voice from behind her, 'is spitting mad. How could you *not* have seen that photo being taken?'

Nikki flushed but raised her chin. She'd been thinking the same thing herself, but that didn't mean she'd let DCI Zain Ahad run roughshod over her. Her voice dripped with sarcasm as she replied, 'Funnily enough, I was too busy focusing on obtaining essential information from my source to be scrutinising the Waterstones café for stray reporters.'

Ahad's lips curled, but his tone became milder. 'Well, maybe you should have. That journalist, what's her name?' He clicked his fingers in the air as if expecting her name to appear in neon lights before him.

Sajid took pity on him. 'Lisa Kane.'

'Hmph, yes this Kane person has it in for you. What's all that about?'

Nikki wafted her hand in the air and shook her head. 'Long story, but no time to go into it now.'

She paused and studied Ahad. Tall and handsome, he'd taken over the DCI job only recently when Archie had retired. But even in that short space of time, the effect of the job was already taking its toll on him. His suit, normally almost as perfectly fitted as Sajid's, hung off his shoulders and Nikki reckoned that work pressures had stolen his regular gym time. Permanent lines fanned out from the sides of his mouth and his scowl had scored a line over his brow. Ahad was knackered. He'd been flung in at the deep end at a moment's notice and all too soon they'd landed a big case. The entire team was still reeling from their previous investigation yet, up until now, they'd operated like a perfectly synchronised orchestra. She'd no intention of losing that. 'What's the fallout from the big bosses on this?'

Ahad exhaled a long breath and cracked his neck. 'Breathing down our necks. Questioning whether left-wing affirmative action earned us our places in CID, suggesting that *I've* been promoted too quickly and, of course, following that up with their doubts about *your* promotion to DI. The buggers dragged up your mental health record, which has, in their eyes, made it a questionable appointment.'

Nikki started to speak, but Ahad tutted and flopped into a chair. 'I know, I know. You don't have to tell me about your track record, Parekh. I made a point of highlighting every bastard you'd arrested, every case you'd solved, but all they can see is their precious bloody optics. And, after that article, let's face it the optics look bad.'

Nikki slid into a seat next to her boss and got her phone out. 'Better read the whole thing then, hadn't I?'

As she scrolled down the article, which described Williams as the "token white cop" on her team and a "pity" appointment, Nikki's shoulders tensed. With each additional barbed jibe from Lisa Kane's poisoned pen, Nikki's leg jiggled faster and faster and a pulse began to throb at her temple. Anwar was characterised as being "blinded by her religion" whilst Sajid was dismissed as a "dandy of no substance". The article was a complete character annihilation of a team who had earned their stripes by sound investigative strategies over a series of difficult cases, which had resulted in a higher than average arrest rate. Their dedication to their job was above reproach and to have their credibility questioned so openly was too much to bear, particularly when it appeared that they were getting no backup from the top. She could take the slurs against herself but those against her team were unacceptable. Eyes flashing, she glared at Ahad. 'I take it from your reaction that we can't rely on the bureaucrats to defend us?'

Ahad rubbed his fingers over his stubble and sighed. 'They want to issue a statement at a live press conference about the Salinger murders later this afternoon and they want . . .' He paused, and met Nikki's eyes, with a shrug that Nikki took to be sympathetic.

For a moment she looked at him slack-jawed, waiting for him to end his sentence, but Ahad nipped the bridge of his nose between two fingers and exhaled. 'You to give the report.'

A laugh caught in the back of Nikki's throat. Surely, he was yanking her chain. It was rare for a DI to lead the press conference for such a high-profile case and in the past Archie had done them as and when required. Public speaking wasn't one of her strengths, so why would they want her to do it? Especially given the very personal newspaper article.

Sajid, his voice high and wobbly, moved to Nikki's side. 'Hell no, not Nikki. Are they *insane*?'

With Sajid's words hanging in the air, Nikki jumped up, palms held out before her, her head swivelling from side to side as she backed away from Ahad. 'No! No way. No damn way, Zain.'

But Ahad shrugged. 'It's decided. Three p.m., Nik.'

His belated 'Sorry' did nothing to mollify Nikki as she looked round, noticing for the first time since Ahad had entered the incident room that all eyes were on her.

'They're hanging me out to dry.' The words were less question than statement. Her lips curled and her eyes flashed. 'They'd rather waste *my* time attending a fucking press conference than let me do my job. They should have my back. They should have my team's backs, not sacrifice me to the baying hounds.'

She lifted her foot and kicked the nearest chair, sending it skidding over the floor till it hit a desk. The pile of folders on top wobbled for long seconds before toppling. Williams jumped up, dived over and caught the pile before it landed on the floor.

Frustration spent, Nikki exhaled long and slow – out for three, in for three – and then turned to her team. 'I'm sorry. That was unacceptable. I want you all to know, each and every one of you, that you got on this team through merit, hard work, skill and dedication. The powers that be might not have our backs, but be reassured that I have yours.'

She marched to the front of the room, her cheeks warm, her legs quivering as she tried to thrust the thought of what awaited her at the press conference later on in the day. 'Right, we've got four murders to solve. Where are we?'

Waiting whilst everyone gathered round, tablets in hand, eyes focused on the incident boards that were filling rapidly, Nikki turned to Sajid and lowered her tone so only he could hear. 'As for you, what the hell do you mean, "are they insane"?' She delivered the last three words in a parody of Sajid's earlier panicked tones and prodded his arm with a bony finger. 'I'll have you know I'm more than up to the task of defending my team.'

'Eh, yeah, we get that, Nik. That's what we're afraid of. You need to tone it down. Look professional, sound professional, you know?' His eyes raked over her T-shirt and jeans. 'Maybe you could lose the tomato-sauce-stained T-shirt, eh?'

Nikki's snorting laugh released some of the tension in her gut. 'Now there's a thought. A topless press conference.' She glanced at her top and scrunched up her nose. 'But I take your point. I'll find the time to run home and grab a blouse. Shit!' Her shoulders slumped.

'What?'

'I don't have any ironed and Marcus is working today.'

Quirking his eyebrow, Sajid shook his head. 'You're not telling me you don't know how to iron, are you?'

Eyes narrowed, Nikki tutted. 'And what if I am?' Conscious of the thick, solid-concrete-slab-sized wedge jammed in her throat, Nikki grabbed a bottle of water from her desk and took two large gulps. Although furious that Lisa Kane's irresponsible reporting had hijacked the investigation, she was more irate that her big bosses were prepared to let her sink or swim. Whilst the water flowed down her throat with ease, it didn't do a single thing to remove the obstacle so, playing for time, Nikki took a moment to scan the more recent notes that had been added to the incident boards. It was a paltry amount of information and Nikki wished, not for the first time, that she could clone herself and everyone on her team and work at double speed. Now, especially with the press nipping at her arse, it was even more important to make inroads.

Langley had already started the first post-mortem with a young DC drafted in to be in attendance. He'd elected to start with George Salinger and, to date, the only confirmation was that cause of death was due to exsanguination or blood loss from the knife wound to his jugular. Time of death, toxicity reports and a catalogue of wounds along with any likely inferences to be made from their findings would filter in over the coming hours and days. Langley had admitted to Nikki at the crime scene that he thought George Salinger was the likely first victim, but wasn't prepared to be any more definite than that till after the post-mortems had been carried out and the findings from his on-site 3D tests had been finalised.

Nikki had thought it prudent to divide the post-mortem attendance between the team – spread the misery – and she and Sajid were due to attend the next one. She didn't know how Langley coped with it, but he'd insisted that for continuity and consistency it was best that he conduct each of the four PMs, and although there was a time lapse because of that, Nikki agreed. Langley was the best – even though he must be exhausted from working overnight at the scene.

Close-up images of the bodies from the scene had been stuck on the boards alongside close-ups of the most visible wounds. Nikki didn't need images to remember the scene though. During her few hours' sleep earlier that day, she'd woken up multiple times, breathing heavily, her heart hammering against her sternum and her mind at the scene. It would be a while before she would forget the way the Salingers had died.

Turning, she faced the room of expectant officers. Whilst not the largest team she'd ever worked with – budget cuts had seen to that – she was happy with the uniformed officers designated to work the case. Although some were out and about, tracking down CCTV, questioning school friends and teachers and neighbours, those who sat before her, tablets at the ready, were au fait with the information in the shared files. 'So, any more details I need to know about?'

One of the officers, a skinny ginger lad, who reminded her of Williams a few years earlier, stood up. 'They found a smudged footprint – probably from a trainer – near the back bi-fold doors. They were unlocked and the working hypothesis is that someone left the house that way. The print is only partial and so they can't confirm a size, but there is a nick out of it, which makes it distinctive.' He shrugged. There was no need to elaborate on that. Should they find the actual trainer and its owner then this was valuable evidence. He cleared his throat. 'The paving by the doors leads down to the lawn and from there to a high fence that encloses the entire back garden. The gate was unlocked, so again a likely egress point for our assailant, who may or may not be the missing fifth person.'

He flushed, glanced round at the room of attentive officers and promptly focused back on his tablet before continuing. 'The CSIs are still working the area, but the rain has washed away the likelihood of finding any blood trail across the patio and lawn. Best hope is maybe a few prints outside the fence, but the neighbours say all four Salingers came and went that way frequently as it led to the paddock and stable where they kept two horses. The kids often parked up near there and entered the house that way rather than driving round to the main entrance that was used by the emergency services. It's a shortcut. They're keeping at it though.'

Nikki nodded. Although the information indicated a likely escape route for their killer, the lack of tangible evidence was frustrating. 'What about CCTV around the paddock and stable area?'

But before she'd finished her question, the officer was shaking his head. 'The CCTV for the stable and paddock area is activated from the house and for some reason all three of the cameras in that area were switched off.'

'Damn, damn, damn.' What was it with these people who had top-notch security, yet didn't bloody utilise it? Annoyed and frustrated, Nikki loosened her ponytail then grabbed her hair in a handful, folding the bobble round it and yanking it tight so it stood right on top of her head. 'We're just not catching the breaks on this one, are we?'

Sajid threw a pen on his desk and tutted. 'Makes you wonder why the hell the Salingers turned off all their security, though. That's a bit dodgy to me. Like they were expecting their visitor but didn't want to leave any evidence of their visit?' He shook his head. 'No idea what the hell that means though, do you?'

The officers one by one shook their heads. And Nikki decided it was time to change tack a little. 'No idea how relevant this is, but bearing in mind the lack of anything more concrete, it is something we need to bear in mind. DCI – or ex-DCI Hegley – shared his concerns that the investigation into the eldest Salinger child's abduction was closed down prematurely. I want one of you to go over the official investigation more closely. I know DC Dosanjh started last night, but we need to either close down that line of inquiry or else find a strand to run with. Any other information on the family?'

'Yep.' Farah flicked through her tablet. 'Got the family medical records through from their GP. Nothing particularly notable – a few childhood injuries for the kids, mainly as a result of falling off their horses – a broken arm for Jason and an ACL injury for Karen. Then of course Mrs Salinger's horse-riding injury, which we already knew about. George Salinger, however, was taking, quite a high dosage of Venlafaxine and has been seeing a psychiatrist privately, for depression and anxiety issues since last September. Might be worth seeing what she can tell us.'

'Yeah, you get on that, Farah. With him being deceased, I see no reason for the psychiatrist not to comply. As you know, Sajid and I visited Ashleigh Kholi this morning. Now, the woman is clearly angry and distraught about the breakdown of her marriage. There's no love lost between her and her husband, and she displayed little sorrow about the deaths of the Salingers – not even the two kids. She was drunk and therefore unable to provide a foolproof alibi for the presumed time of the attacks. We need to probe deeper on her and her relationship with both her husband and Trish Salinger, with whom she was in a well-documented acrimonious battle for chair of the Yorkshire Children's Cancer Trust.'

Lips pursed, Nikki glared at the list of suspects, which seemed to be getting unmanageably long. 'It would have been good to cross someone off our suspect list, but we can't exclude her yet – if at all.' She looked at Liam. 'What did you and Farah discover from Kholi about that whole debacle. Does he have an airtight alibi?'

'Dick.'

Williams spat the word into the room and then flushed as Nikki frowned. 'Eh, I thought his name was Sukhjit.' She peered at the board, casting her eyes down the list as if looking for confirmation of Mr Kholi's name.

'No, no. You're right, boss. It is Sukhjit – sorry, my mistake.' Liam's flush darkened as Nikki's gaze rested on him.

'Daft mistake to make, Williams, don't you think?' Although her gaze was penetrating, she had trouble stopping her lips from twitching. Williams had clearly formed an opinion on Mr Sukhjit Kholi and she was keen to hear it.

As Williams bowed his head, she glanced at Sajid, and winked. Saj rolled his eyes, but he too grinned. Williams was so easy to wind up.

'Kholi is a bit of a show-off – you know? A bit of a big talker, but according to him he couldn't have done it because he had only just returned to his very posh, highly secure Leeds flat after a business trip abroad and didn't leave again till after he'd heard about the murders. Farah and I swung by his building and secured the security footage, which does seem to confirm his story, still . . .' With his head tipped to one side, Liam rubbed the palm of his hand up his nose and glared at the room in general, but left his sentence hanging.

Sajid leaned forward. 'You're not convinced?'

'He's a bit of a di . . .'

'He means a smarmy git,' said Farah. 'Kholi thought he was all that and despite the circumstances, we both felt he was obstructive. The only time he showed any real concern was when we mentioned the kids, but even then, that was a bit strange.' She exchanged a quick glance with Liam and when he inclined his head, continued. 'He seemed more concerned with Karen Salinger, the daughter, than with any of the others. Nothing too icky, but still . . .'

But still. Those two words had an ominous ring to them and a shiver rippled up Nikki's spine. 'Right, get a deep dive done on Kholi – social media. You know the drill. I want his movements verified and . . .' She scratched her head and looked at Sajid. 'Remember that case a few years ago when that drug lord, Baxter, nearly got away with a stabbing? The one when the security cameras on his building showed him entering the building before the attack and not leaving again till afterwards?'

Saj snapped his fingers. 'Yep, I remember that one. It wasn't till we caught him on CCTV two streets away from the crime scene that we realised the footage from his gaff was misleading. When we went back and double-checked we discovered the scrote had dodged out a window and avoided the security cameras . . .'

'Doubt Kholi would be dodging out windows and suchlike, boss. He's up three flights and he's not really your batman type . . .' Williams's voice trailed away.

Nikki waited a moment, enjoying the transformation that played out across his face.

He shook his head and exhaled. 'Aw, I get it. You mean there might be other exits – maybe tradespersons' exits? Don't know where my mind's at today. I'll check it out.'

Nikki didn't know either. Williams was thorough, pedantic sometimes, and he was nearly always one step ahead of them. She studied him and Anwar for a moment. Their body language was off – she'd noticed it in passing earlier when she'd first arrived back in Trafalgar House – but now it seemed really obvious. As if they'd had a tiff or something. She hoped there wasn't a problem in their partnership because they normally worked so well together. She'd let it pass for now, but she'd be sure to keep an eye on them moving forward. She couldn't risk their team dynamics affecting this investigation – they had more than enough crap to contend with already.

Williams, flicking through his notes, continued. 'He wasn't keen to hand over the details of his business dealings with George Salinger. Insisted they'd put a line under the affair and now had a perfectly amicable business relationship.'

Williams flipped his finger across his tablet and tapped the screen. 'The financial reports are coming in from the Salinger business, and at first glance it seems to me that although the two companies still do business together, the amount of business has been tailing off in recent months. Of course, this is only an initial trawl through their accounts and the forensic team will find more detailed information with time, but it tells us that things weren't as hunky-dory as Sukhjit Kholi is trying to make out.'

'Yes, we'll keep an eye on that. What about Bland's financials?'

Williams face lit up as he scrolled. 'Now, that's intriguing. Going back at least twelve years, Derek Bland has been receiving a sizeable bonus of nearly 250K from the business. The thing I noticed is . . .' Williams face gleamed in anticipation as if awaiting a drum roll. 'The date of the bonus. It's paid one week before Winnie Salinger was abducted and has continued all these years. But what makes it more notable is that all other bonuses are paid at the *end* of the firm's financial year in April. Bland receives one then and then this additional one a couple of months later. Strange eh?'

It was strange. Why was Bland in receipt of two separate bonuses? The date of the second one was undoubtably suspicious. Looks like she and Saj would have to squeeze in a meeting with Derek Bland before attending the PM. She looked forward to seeing him in his offices. Keen to round off the briefing she changed tack. 'What about information from Jason's school or from Karen's university?'

The two constables Nikki had tasked earlier with interviewing Jason's schoolmates and teachers stood up. The older one, an experienced male officer who Nikki had worked with on many occasions, jumped right in. 'According to Jason's form tutor he was a nice enough kid – a few detentions for minor pranks and not the best scholar in the world, but popular with the other kids and teachers too. Spent a lot of time in the PE department, but nobody had a bad word to say about him. We talked with the PE teachers who seemed to know him best and they could only sing his praises – said he had a rare competitive spirit that made him a natural sportsperson.' He snorted. 'Your guess is as good as mine as to what that means. His friends were devastated, so I've arranged with their parents to pop in later on tonight when they've had a chance to process what's gone on. On the whole though, they couldn't shed any light on what Jason was doing yesterday or who he was doing it with.'

The officer rocked on his heels, a frown spreading slowly over his forehead. 'Thought it might save time if I asked a bit about the daughter, Karen, whilst I was there, like.'

Nikki's heart skipped a beat. He clearly had something worth sharing and right now she'd welcome any small strand of information that could pull them out of the quagmire of information they were currently struggling through.

'Well, unlike her brother, Karen Salinger was a pain in the arse.' He flushed. 'That's my words, like, not the teachers', but still that's what they meant. She was a handful – caught smoking on the premises, weed found in her schoolbag, flouting uniform rules, skipping school, bullying. Some of the teachers expressed disgust that she appeared to get away with bad behaviour on account of her father's money. Still, she was a bright kid, but the general consensus was that the school was glad to see her leave.'

Now that *was* interesting. Derek Bland had given the impression that both Salinger children were perfect. She turned to Liam Williams. 'Liam, let's pull that strand a little more, eh? Exert pressure on the techies to scrutinise both kids' devices more quickly and liaise with the Cambridge police. Maybe Karen Salinger is the key to these murders.'

She glanced at her watch, ignored the jolt of disquiet that thumped against her chest when she saw how quickly time was passing. 'You three, come with me. We need to iron out a strategy for this damn press conference before Saj and I ruffle Bland's feathers – and we're due at the morgue too.'

When they entered the DCI's office, Zain got down to business straight away. 'Right, how are we going to play this press conference?'

Nikki edged forward and glared at him. 'What do you mean *we*? There is no *we* in this. It's *me* – on my own – who's going to face the crap.'

Williams stepped forward, tablet open and a smile on his face. 'You're not on your own, boss. I think—' he cast a sideways look at Farah that didn't quite reach her face '—and Farah agrees with me that we've got a strategy that will work.'

Farah nodded and stepped closer to Liam. 'Yes, we've got this. I'll sort out your wardrobe. All you have to do is turn up by two-thirty so we can run it by you.'

Nikki looked from Williams's serious face to Farah's slightly less serious one. If these two said they had it in hand then she believed them. She spun on her heel and strode back towards the door. 'Come on Saj. Liam and Farah will sort this. We've got a CEO to hassle and a date with your beau afterwards.'

Chapter 19

With each passing moment, Nikki's shoulders tightened and the snarling ache behind her eyes intensified. She was used to working under stress – but the looming press conference was a different kind of pressure and now she had to get her head in the game if she was going to get anything worthwhile from Derek Bland. She'd opted not to phone ahead so as to maintain the element of surprise when speaking with Bland. Of course, by now he'd know that they had access to the firm's financial records. She was hoping that he'd assume they hadn't had time to peruse that in detail yet.

The first thing that struck Nikki when entering the Salinger offices was the contrast between the blindingly white walls, which hosted replicas of the photography that had been in the Salinger home, was the aura of subdued panic. The receptionist at the front desk looked up when they entered, her eyes widening when she clocked that they were police. Her hand fluttered to her necklace and her eyes flicked towards a corridor to the right, as if wishing for someone to miraculously appear from there and rescue her. When she spoke the tremor in her voice was pronounced. 'How can I help?'

On her best behaviour, Nikki smiled. 'I know you must all be in shock and it's a credit to you that you've managed to come into work today. Don't worry, we're not here to ask you any questions – uniformed officers will get round to that in due course. We just want to have a quick chat with Mr Bland.' Nikki stepped towards the corridor that the receptionist had looked at earlier. 'This way, is it?'

'No, I mean yes, I mean . . .' The woman lifted both hands to her face and used her fingers to wipe away tears that sprung from her eyes and had already began to make her mascara smudge. 'Look, I'm really sorry . . .' She gulped and took Sajid's handkerchief to wipe her eyes. 'He's not here. Mr Bland hasn't come in today and it's all hell let loose.' Her lips quivered. 'We're trying our best to field contractors and reassure clients, but . . .'

Nikki's heart thudded in her chest. Where the hell was Bland? She nodded to Sajid who walked away to make a call for uniforms to visit Bland's flat. Nikki was torn between teasing out as much information as she could from the distraught receptionist, barging down the corridor to Bland's office, and turning on her heel and speeding over to his flat herself.

Dammit, dammit, dammit. She should have expected something like this. She should have told the PC she'd placed outside his flat to stick to him like glue. She twanged her wristband a few times to ground herself before turning back to the receptionist. 'I'm going to have to access Mr Bland's office and I need to speak with his PA.'

The receptionist responded to the authority in Nikki's voice and picked up the phone. In less than a minute a tall woman in her fifties appeared, introducing herself as Bland's PA and escorting Nikki with no further ado to his office. Once inside, Nikki stood at the door and studied the room. The desk was filled with the sort of annoying executive toys Nikki had got Ahad as a joke when he became DCI. To her, the room looked untouched. No half-open drawers, no signs of a hasty withdrawal. Nikki turned to the PA for confirmation. 'Can you tell if he's been here since Friday?'

Despite her pallor, the PA – Betty – was efficient and able to push any feelings to the side. A small smile played on her lips as her eyes swung round the room. 'If Derek had been in this office for more than two seconds his desk would have been littered with Post-its, coffee cups would be everywhere and half the drawers would be open as well as the filing cabinet.' Her smile faded. 'I don't think he's been here. Not since I cleaned up after he left on Friday.'

'Have you spoken to him since you heard about the Salinger family's death?'

Her eyes clouded and she inhaled. 'Yes, we spoke last night. He said he'd be in today, but wasn't sure when because he'd have to ID the . . . ID . . .' her hand fluttered in the air '. . . everyone. You don't think . . .'

Nikki interrupted her. 'We don't know anything yet. But I do need to ask you some questions. Will that be okay?'

When the woman nodded, Nikki guided her out of Derek Bland's office and into the one she indicated belonged to her. 'What was the relationship between Mr Salinger and Mr Bland like?'

Betty frowned as if that was the last question she was expecting. 'You can't think that Derek had owt to do with . . .' again with the hand flutter '. . . no that's just senseless. They were best friends – the three of them – and he doted on those kids. Whoever hurt them, it wasn't Derek. No, I'm certain of that.'

Nikki changed tack. 'You've been with the firm for how long?'

'Fifteen years come summer.'

'So, you know everything there is to know about the business.' Betty preened and nodded. 'Almost as much as Derek and George, I'd think.'

'So, you know about the bonuses paid to shareholders.'

'Of course. Derek was responsible for issuing those and very generous they are too.'

Nikki nodded. 'And they were paid, when . . . ?'

'End of our financial year, regular as clockwork.'

Gotcha. Nikki leaned forward and kept her voice low. 'So what about the yearly bonus of £250K paid into Mr Bland's account every year for the past twelve in July?'

Betty frowned, her mouth fell open and she shook her head. 'No, I think you must have that wrong. Mr Bland got his bonus with all the other shareholders in April . . .'

An alert from Saj had Nikki drawing out her phone. She stood up. 'You'll have to close up the business for the foreseeable future. My partners confirmed that we have a warrant to seize all electronic devices and have full access to all the accounts. A team of officers will come to take statements from everyone before they leave the building. I'm really sorry, but we've been unable to locate Mr Bland at his flat. Do you have any other addresses for him?'

Betty blinked and shook her head. 'No, no . . . I'm afraid . . .'

Nikki smiled at her. 'This is a shock for you, but the sooner we can do our job, the sooner you can go home.'

As she left a stunned Betty's office, Nikki saw Sajid waiting by the door. 'Got a BOLO issued?'

He nodded. 'What next? His flat?'

But Nikki shook her head. 'No, send a team to support the CSIs there and another one for here. Looks like our budget is fried and we've only just bloody started.'

Chapter 20

Present Day: Marnie

I pace the room and for now my distaste with my surroundings is of secondary concern. So much so that I barely notice the worn carpet or the yellowing damp stain crawling down the wall from the ceiling above, like an ever-growing centipede. Even the persistent stink that, no matter how many times I spray the air freshener, dominates the room. It's so bad that it seems to have made its way into the bedding and even my clothes.

My mind's all over the place. Where the *hell* is Gwen? I plonk myself down on the edge of the double bed that we share and think about her. We've been together for years now. Not sure how many – maybe eight or nine? A smile twitches my lips as I remember her thrusting her arm through mine, her eyes dancing as she said. 'Even if you don't speak, Marn, we're besties now, you and me. I'll always look after you. I promise I will.'

And she had. Well, as best as a scrawny kid could under the circumstances. Even when she couldn't protect me from the really bad stuff, she was always there afterwards, holding me, whispering reassurances and stroking my hair whilst I heaved silent sobs. She taught me how to make things easier for myself. How to take myself away to other worlds when the bad things happen. Most importantly she taught me that giving in was easier in the long run. Even now, all these years later, I shudder as I remember the punishments for not giving in. Gwen, as usual, had been right. Giving in to whatever they wanted me to do was easier once I'd learned to take my mind out of my head and focus on the good times with my sister and pretend it was all happening to someone else. By learning to do that, I kept myself safe. Safe and alive so that one day I could find Jilly.

I smile, remembering, even after all this time, the smell of her hair and her serious little face when she looked at me and told me, "*Don't let the Beep Beeps get you down, Marn. Don't ever let the Beep Beeps win.*" And in the end, I hadn't. They didn't win, for now I was free.

Thoughts of Jilly and Gwen's friendship were the things that kept me going. Other kids came and went, but Gwen and I didn't – *we* survived – we outlasted them all . . . until we were rewarded and they released us.

Before we were freed, I thought I knew everything there was to know about Gwen. We'd spent so much time together, so many long hours. She talked all the time. For years all she did was talk and me? – well I listened. I listened to her tales of princesses and ballerinas. Of huge mansions and castles. Of picnics and friends and sunshine and laughter. For all those years *I* listened to her, soaking up *her* stories, letting them give me hope, believing that someday we'd be free to be princesses and ballerinas living in mansions or castles and going on picnics in the sunshine.

For all those years, my only communication was written down on scraps of paper, or – in the early days at least – on misted-up windows. Gwen was as much of a sister to me as Jilly was. Gwen was my best friend *and* my sister, yet still, I kept my silence in for Jilly. I'd made her a promise – one she knew nothing about, but a promise nonetheless – that I wouldn't speak until we were reunited.

Aw, Jilly? Thinking about her makes that machine inside my chest slam together, squeezing the air from my body. It always happens when I think of her. My little sister. The one I left behind. No, that's not right. I didn't leave her behind; I was taken. I slam my hand on my forehead, welcoming the pain. *Stop* thinking about that. Stop thinking about what happened that day. Gwen told me it only makes things worse. She told me to focus on what we had. Whatever food we fancied, whatever clothes we wanted, no bedtimes . . . as long as we were good, we had it all . . . but then they released us and we ended up here in a one-room flat with a bed and a manky kitchen with a tiny bathroom sectioned off in the corner with only a loo and a slimy shower curtain that hid the scurrying cockroaches in the shower tray. I don't understand why. I don't understand any of it and now Gwen's gone out and she's been gone ages.

To distract myself I wonder about Jilly. She would have grown loads since I last saw her. Is she taller than me now? How old will she be? I frown. I should know that, but I'm not even sure how old I am. How long I've been away. I could be fourteen or I could be thirty. I just don't know. There's a little lump in my chest, right under my sternum. It only comes when I think about Jilly. I've spent so long wishing I could see her again, and now that it might be possible I wonder if she'll even remember me. Will my mum and dad have forgotten me? Will my mum hate me for being taken? For being such a cow-bag about secondary school? That lump hurts so bad, so I force myself to get up and walk about.

I'd almost prefer to be in the dungeon – that's what all the kids called the cellar – rather than here. At least then I'd know where Gwen was and that, eventually, when I'd been punished enough, I'd be returned to her. I thrust the memories of the dungeon from my mind. It had been so long since I'd been punished, so long since I'd been locked in the dungeon, made to piss and shit in a bucket – so long that I could almost forget it . . . almost, but not quite.

But what if Gwen doesn't come back? *Where the hell are you, Gwen?* I want to yell the words out loud, but I don't know how anymore. I take a slug of water and swallow hard, clearing my throat. Maybe if I forced myself the words would come out. Maybe if I tried my hardest, I'd be able to make a sound. I open my mouth, but my throat closes over and my heart starts to hammer in my chest. I can't do it and I won't. I won't break my promise to Jilly. The one I made that very first night, in the dungeon: I won't speak till I see her again. I can't break that promise – not to my little sister. Not to her, because, somewhere in my mind, I think that if I break that promise, then she'll end up here with me and that's not I want for her.

Come on, Gwen. You said you wouldn't be long. I can't survive without you. Can't survive on my own. I need you with me. I need you to be my voice. I need you to help me find Jilly. I know we're not supposed to. That was the condition, but I don't care. They can't hurt us now. Not now we're free. *Please come back, Gwen. Please hurry back.* I fling myself back down on the mouldy mattress. *Come on, Gwen, what are you doing? Please be safe.*

I know she'll come back. I know it. But still in the back of my mind I wonder what would happen if she didn't. What would happen to me?

I'm still not sure why they let us go. Scarface turned up one day and told us we could go. Said we were too old to be kept like kids. That we'd done our duty and as a reward, we could leave. They gave us money and passports and stuff like that – not in our names, but in some other girls' names. They're still there, safe in Gwen's backpack with most of the money. He told us we'd earned it, but I don't know what to do with money or passports or stuff.

Scarface – looking older and, now I'm not a kid anymore, not quite so scary – sneered at me as he thrust the bag of cash into Gwen's hands. '*You* know how to keep schtum, don't you, Lily?'

I nodded, but he gripped my upper arms and made me look right into his evil eyes and shook me. 'You don't look back or bad things will happen. *Really* bad things. You keep it zipped and you stay away from your old home, got it? You don't go back there, right?'

I nodded, but that wasn't enough for Scarface. He yanked my hair, till tears sprung into my eyes and held tight till Gwen pulled him away. 'Leave her alone. We'll keep quiet. We won't go back, I promise.'

He snorted and let me go, looking at Gwen now. 'I know that creepy quite bitch won't speak. It's *you* I'll be keeping an eye on. You've been paid now and we've set you free. You've got a life to live, so do it. But . . .' he leaned closer, his eyes boring a hole into first Gwen then me '. . . you never open your mouths. Never!'

He flung Gwen away from him and turned to me, his sneer widening. 'Course you can't say owt, can you, bitch?'

It's been so long that I suspect he forgets that I'm not dumb, that I do have a voice – I've just chosen not to use it for all these years. I saw no point in reminding him, so I shook my head.

Now, as I look out the window, I wonder if maybe I should try to speak. If Gwen doesn't come back I might have to. But no. I can't do that. I have to find Jilly and make sure she's safe. That they didn't get to her. Maybe then, I'll find my voice again. For now, though my worry is for Gwen. She's been weird since we got here. Instead of her usual stream of stories and chatter, she's been sullen. Almost as silent as me and that worries me. It's like she knows something that I don't. As if, now we no longer live locked up in that house, she's given up. Even her eyes look different. The sparkle's gone and they look like dark rolling thunderclouds before a storm. That thought makes me shudder. This isn't the Gwen I know. I get up again and move over to the window and, after breathing onto the glass, I use my pinkie to write my name on the pane. I smile, remembering the first time I did that to communicate with Gwen. But the happiness of the memory is short-lived as I realise something I haven't till then . . . I know nothing about Gwen. Not a thing!

She knows all about Jilly and the stupid argument with my parents about my school and how I loved to play football. Over the months and years, I wrote it all down. Shared everything with her, from my address to my favourite colour to the crush I had on Billy Grieg. No, surely I've got that wrong. Gwen spoke all the time. She never shut up. A constant stream of chatter rolled off her tongue, lulling me into sleep and greeting me first thing in the morning, when I awoke. I lean my brow on the cool glass and think, really hard, probing deep in my memory for a glimmer of information. Does she have a sister? A brother? A dog? I screw up my face, really searching my memory for a snatched piece of information – anything that Gwen has actually shared with me about her past. Anything that could help me find her or her family if she doesn't come back for me.

It's only when I realise that tears are rolling down my cheeks and soaking into the thin T-shirt I wear that it sinks in. I know nothing about her. Maybe she didn't even give me her real name. It's then that I realise I'm on my own. Gwen isn't coming back. She's left me here in this filthy flat and I'm completely alone. Me a voiceless girl who hasn't spoken in years and who has only the money Gwen left behind and a passport I don't know how to use, in a name I don't recognise and I've no idea where I am.

A strong wave of yearning makes me shiver. As my legs wobble, I stumble away from the window and fall back onto the bed. I want to be back there, back in the dungeon. Back with the other kids. Back where I know what to expect. Back with Scarface and the nasty men. Back in the room I share with Gwen. Safe and secure.

Chapter 21

The threat of the press conference preying on her mind, Nikki left Derek Bland's office with Sajid. Each caught up in their own thoughts, they made their way in silence to Sajid's car. With Nikki trying to control her breathing and to force the thought of the demise of her career at the enforced press conference from her mind, flashes of the bloody crime scene, the press headlines, Ashleigh Kholi's alcohol-induced desperation and Archie's face as he told her about Winnie Salinger's abduction zoomed in and out of her head as if ridden on neon surfers, vying with conjecture regarding the whereabouts of Derek Bland. It was disconcerting and made it hard to gather her thoughts together, so she decided to hold on to something neutral. Something that didn't instil such a plethora of raw emotions – Sajid.

Sajid with his back ramrod straight and a persistent pulse beating at his temple. Nikki was attuned enough to his emotions to realise that whilst his mind was focused mostly on the ongoing investigation, a tiny part of it would also be wondering if Langley was going to throw some other curve ball about their wedding arrangements at him when they saw him at the PM. Of course, Nikki knew Langley wouldn't do that, as did Sajid deep down, but her partner was in a quandary and his upcoming nuptials were making him think slightly irrational thoughts. She suspected that he and Langley had argued before work this morning, which was the root of Sajid's emotional upset. Nikki for her part wished she only had wedding preparations and the post-mortem to worry about. Not that she took PMs lightly. She hated them – perhaps not as much as Sajid did, but they still weren't the most pleasant of activities in her top-ten list of things she loved about her job. In fact, they didn't even make her top twenty. Yet, they were a very necessary part of her responsibilities and so, with stoic respect for the deceased, she attended them.

By the time they arrived at the morgue, the sun was breaking through the earlier thunder clouds and Langley had already completed two of the four post-mortems. As they entered the observation suite and relieved the constable who'd been in attendance for both of the previous post-mortems, Langley – masked and haloed in the bright forensic light cast over the table – greeted them with a slight nod. Karen Salinger, her skin a bluish white except where the knife wounds had been inflicted on her body, lay naked on the steel table before him. From the viewing platform, Nikki looked down on the young girl, a turmoil of anger knotting in her chest as she saw the waste of a young life snuffed out so violently. How must she have felt when the frenzied attack on her family began? Had she had no inkling of it as she sat with her family to play a board game? Or had she sensed something was out of sync around that dining room table? – that something evil was about to descend on them? Had her last thoughts been filled with love, or fear or anger?

She looked so young, so innocent with her long auburn hair haloing her head and her young body so skinny it looked almost malnourished. How dare anyone think they had the right to snuff out this precious life and those of her family in such an abrupt and violent manner.

Langley placed his scalpel back on the steel tray, stepped away from the table and moved closer to the window that separated the viewers from those conducting the PM. On closer inspection, Nikki noted the trail of lines radiating from the corners of his eyes. Even with his mask in place, his pallor was evident. His eyes were red-rimmed from concentrating for so long under the bright lights and his shoulders slumped as if he could scarcely hold his head up. Away from the table, he rolled them, wincing as he did so, and when Nikki's gaze drifted to his assistant she saw a corresponding slump in her shoulders. The ruthless and violent annihilation of four family members was hard to come to terms with – even for trained pathologists who dealt with this sort of depravity on a regular basis.

Nikki felt Sajid tense beside her and a quick glance told her he'd placed his hand, fingers splayed against the glass in a silent show of support for his partner. Something fluttered in Langley's eyes and he raised his gloved hand, palm forward towards Sajid. The kinetic energy between them was almost palpable and although when he spoke, Langley's tone was laden with weariness, each word slow and textured with grief, his eyes seemed brighter. 'Hey, Nik, Saj. Before I start on young Karen here, I'll run through what the other two PMs threw up, shall I?'

Taking a moment, he gathered his thoughts before beginning. 'Basically, both George Salinger and Jason Salinger had eaten pizza, chips and drunk fizzy pop very shortly before their deaths – their food was completely undigested, indicating that they were killed soon after eating. This tallies with the five glasses on the table which had Coke, Tango and Lilt in them and the five plates stacked in the kitchen sink. Looks like our missing person joined them for dinner.'

Nikki's mind flashed back to the scene she'd witnessed only hours earlier as she tried to replace the destruction with an image of five people chomping though pizzas before setting up and beginning to play a game of Monopoly. It just all seemed so incongruous to her. Had they had some sort of disagreement during the game? But as usual the most important piece of information they were missing was the identity of the fifth and missing Monopoly player. Nobody they'd spoken to thus far had been able to suggest who it might have been. 'What about order of death, Langley?'

Langley nodded as if he'd been about to move on to that. 'Well, as we discussed at the crime scene, I brought in a 3D laser technology operator and a blood spatter analyst. It took us hours, but working together has given us quite a clear reconstruction of how the attack went down. We basically isolated the various blood spatters from each attack, then correlated that information with other information deduced from the scene itself, like the positioning of each knife wound, heights of the victims, positions of each victim when found in relation to their position, as derived through blood spatter when first attacked. We're certain that George Salinger was the first victim. He was struck from behind and had half turned towards his attacker, which gave the killer the chance to catch his jugular with the knife. This means that . . .' Langley moved over to a computer and pressed a few buttons '. . . that the attack would have gone down something like this.'

Nikki watched as a 3D animation appeared on the large screen at the back of the post-mortem room. Four featureless simulated figures, each one representing one of the Salingers, were positioned around the dining room table. When Langley started the programme, trajectory lines, measurements and points of movement appeared on the screen beside the figures, each of which moved in slow motion. A figure entered the room by the door behind George Salinger – the one that led to the kitchen and subsequently to the door leading out onto the patio at the rear of the property where the bloody footprint had been found.

Langley paused the recording. 'This scenario has been re-created by inputting all the pertinent data garnered at the crime scene. We had no real way of knowing the precise movements of the attacker prior to the point when they took their first swing. Because we know now that someone – possibly the attacker – left the house via the kitchen, we've used the door as both a point of egress and a possible entry point. It's worth bearing in mind, though, that although it's *impossible* that any of the other three victims *could* have been in a position to start the attack *and* end up where they were found, the *fifth* person in the room could have moved from their place at the table and round to the attacker's position here or could have left the room earlier and re-entered from the kitchen, or indeed could have been an intended victim who somehow managed to escape or evade the killer.' Langley used his finger to demonstrate the movement.

That was something Nikki hadn't considered. The way the fifth person's chair had been pushed back from the table had made her assume that the player had done that either as a prelude to attacking the Salingers or in response to an intruder appearing and attacking George Salinger. She stored that thought away to consider in more detail later and focused on the scenario playing out on the screen.

'The first thing we are certain of is that the attacker struck George Salinger, the first victim, from this position, with Salinger half turning in his chair, like so—'

The figure moved swiftly holding a knife in their hand, raised above their head towards George who began to stand, his body turned towards the unidentified person, his right arm raised and bent in a protective action. Langley paused the recording and, using a laser pointer, indicated the point of impact around three inches beneath the elbow. 'This was the first wound George received and as you can see, it was a defensive wound. However, after his arm was hit, George lowered his arm and the killer slashed twice across his neck, slicing both the carotid artery and the jugular vein. He would have bled out in less than thirty seconds.' He pressed play and the scene played out exactly as Langley had described. With Jason, who was sitting next to his father on the right, hesitating for a few seconds before jumping up.'

When Langley paused the recording, Nikki asked, 'So what can you tell us about the knife?'

'Well, clearly it was very sharp because those double swipes cut at least an inch and a half deep and examination of the wounds show it was unserrated. If we knew the precise height of the attacker we'd have more of an idea of the length of the blade. But, judging from the depth of the stab wounds found on the two bodies I've already post-mortemed, the blade length was no less than six inches long and it would have been no more than two inches wide.'

He inhaled, causing the blue of his mask to flutter against his mouth. 'So, although not a hundred per cent accurate, we can estimate that – judging by the position of George Salinger when first attacked, his height and the parameters for blade length and the trajectory and angle of the first wound – his attacker was between five foot ten and six foot one.'

They were getting closer to this attacker. Nikki was beginning to get a picture of the attacker in her mind – a tallish, right-handed person carrying a whole load of rage – enough rage to annihilate an entire family. Okay, it wasn't much and it still didn't clarify the role of the mysterious fifth player in the attack, but it was more than they'd had when she first came into work that morning, which felt like a lifetime ago. *Watch your back, because we're coming for you!*

Langley pressed some buttons on his keyboard and an image from the crime scene appeared on the screen. 'The images taken at the scene showed that Jason's foot had become entangled in the chair leg, which was substantiated by a visual assessment of his foot that on arrival in the morgue showed a faint bruise and scraping on his inner right forefoot consistent with a sudden wrenching movement against a solid surface.'

Another image came on the screen of a pale foot, with the merest indication of a bruise, which Nikki would have missed if Langley hadn't used an arrow to show his findings. Langley continued. 'The lad had bare feet at the crime scene, which meant there was no protective cover to cushion his foot. I suspect he was sitting with both feet hooked round the chair legs with his inner foot resting against the leg, and that this caused him to stumble as he attempted to reach his father. That would have cost him precious seconds and his life as he was unable to even raise his arm in a defensive movement.'

Langley jumped back to the 3D reconstruction, which showed Jason trying to extricate himself from his chair whilst his father slumped half off his chair and the attacker in two steps sliced Jason twice with swift economy, aiming once more for the boy's neck and continuing round the table to despatch the rest of the family in order.

As the scene continued to play out in horrible slow motion, the featureless figures succumbed one after the other to their death yet failed to shield the watchers from the violence. Nikki, although she knew what to expect and had thought herself prepared, held her breath as she witnessed Karen push her chair back. Beside her Sajid's gasp was audible as Karen, instead of jumping to her feet, remained seated. What thoughts had gone through the girl's head in those short seconds as she met her death? Did she recognise her assailant? Was it someone she'd introduced to her family? An old family friend? A colleague of one or other of her parents?

Having killed her brother and father, the unnamed assailant, skimmed the table, brutally sliced her throat and, barely breaking stride continued, round the table to her mother who appeared to have bent over grappling to find her crutch, which had fallen to the floor when her throat was cut.

'Wow.' Sajid was the first to respond when the recording ended. 'That's chilling. Really fucking chilling.'

Langley shrugged. 'It's only one scenario that the computer has generated using the criteria I've inputted from the crime scene. There is an alternate, but very similar scenario that would fit all our findings so far. Watch.'

This time, the scene played out in almost exactly the same way, except that the fifth place at the table was empty. The inference was all too clear – the fifth guest had left the room, leaving the Salinger family completely at ease, and returned with the murder weapon and killed all four of them.

'According to that second scenario the fifth guest is the killer? Which of the two seems more likely to you?'

Langley shrugged. 'Look, this computer-generated scene shows how and the order in which the Salingers died. Whether it was the guest or a sixth person, we don't know. Either way, I wonder if one possibility for the sluggish responses from the Salingers was the fact that they were trying to reason with the killer *or* buying time for the fifth player to get help for them or escape. Either would work, but it's still conjecture. Who knows how any of us would react in those circumstances? All we know for certain is that the guest wasn't killed in that room, but there is evidence that they were there at some point – not necessarily during the attack. Hopefully, we'll get DNA and possibly a match for that person. In the meantime, here's what I can tell you about the killer based on the evidence collected. They began their attack from behind George Salinger near the door leading into the dining room.'

Sajid stood and moved closer to the window, and studied the now-still screen. 'I get that, Lang, but the Salingers' response times still worry me. I mean no matter how you try to spin it, I'd expect some level of activity? Their reactions seem delayed like they're on half speed or something and I don't understand that.'

Langley nodded. 'I think you're basing that assumption on your own reactions, Saj. I think many things could come into play to skew your assumptions.'

Saj scowled at him, his bottom lip sticking out as if Langley had poked him with a red-hot poker. The tension in the room was palpable and Nikki wanted to bang their heads together. This wasn't how these two got on. This was like two strangers who'd taken an instant dislike to each other.

Nikki bumped into Sajid and threw him an exasperated look before addressing Langley. 'You'll let us know what the tox screen says?'

Avoiding looking at Saj, Langley nodded. 'Sure. The stomach contents so far show no indication of alcohol consumption. I've asked for an extensive screen, so if they had anything in their system it will show up. On the other hand, they may just have been in shock or alternatively some sort of threat was used to subdue them. I mean, Trish Salinger obviously was still in a lot of pain and her movements were severely restricted by her injury and George was taken down before he had a chance to fully defend himself. Jason's reactions, if you allow no more than a stunned pause of a second or one and a half secs tops, was more than enough for a violent attacker to inflict those wounds. This leaves possibly only Karen and the mystery guest who could have jumped up and challenged the attacker, but fear often leaves us acting inconsistently. As you know I've only completed two of the four PMs, but anything additional that I find will be added to the programme and maybe will offer some specifics.'

Whilst Sajid and Langley had been talking, Nikki had been running through her first impressions of the crime scene and she was puzzled. 'What about the wounds? These scenarios only show the kill wounds – which seem to be quick and effective, but what about all the other wounds? I saw the scene. I saw the state of the bodies. There was definite overkill there.'

Langley sighed. 'Yes, you're right. It seems that our killer went back after killing the entire family and stabbed them randomly and brutally. There was no need for the additional wounds. The Salingers were already dead. This was rage; pure and simple rage.' He clicked the screen off.

He moved back to where Karen Salinger's body lay and said in a low voice intended only for her. 'I'll do everything I can to discover who did this to you and your family, Karen.'

He raised his head, rolled his shoulders a couple of times and nodded to Nikki and Sajid. 'Let's get this show on the road.'

Langley paused for long seconds and studied the naked body of Karin Salinger. From the observation suite Nikki followed his gaze as it started at her toes and moved up over every inch of flesh, pausing for long moments on each of the wounds on her torso and arms, before coming to rest on her face. With Saj standing beside her, Nikki waited for him to select the instruments he needed to begin the Y incision. She'd seen him do it count- less times before and couldn't work out why he was hesitating this time. He stepped back from the trolley and said something Nikki couldn't hear to his assistant. Then, eyes pulled together in a frown looked up at the two observers. 'We've got a problem.'

Nikki watched as his assistant worked around him to take Karen Salinger's fingerprints. Langley stepped closer to the window that separated them. When he spoke, his voice sounded tinny in the quiet of the room and Nikki felt a slow chill worm its way into her gut. Langley pulled his mask down so they could see his face and what Nikki saw there, apart from the obvious signs of tiredness, was worry, possibly confusion and something else – annoyance most likely. 'I don't think this is Karen Salinger, Nikki. We've made a mistake. I'll . . .'

Nikki shook her head. 'No, No you're wrong. You've got to be wrong. We compared them to the photos; we got Derek Bland to confirm via photo this morning. Of course it's Karen Salinger.'

As her voice rose and she began plucking at her elastic band, Sajid rested a hand on her arm. 'Langley's not made a mistake, Nik. You know that. If he says it's not Karen Salinger then it isn't.'

Nikki pulled her arm away from Sajid and glared first at her partner then at Langley as she fought to compose her thoughts. 'This isn't what you said last night. Last night you said family annihilation. Last night you . . .'

Langley, unlike his usual calm self, threw a staccato 'Stop' into the room causing three sets of eyes to widen and focus on him.

His eyes flashed when he looked at Nikki. 'I gave a preliminary examination last night focusing on the information you gave me. You told me this was a family of four and I proceeded on that basis.' He inhaled long and deep, filling his lungs and then smiled. 'It was an obvious conclusion to arrive at, Nik. Amid the destruction of that room we used what clues we had to ID the victims and you also had her ID confirmed by the person we thought was her godfather. Look at her – she looks very like the girl in the family photos. So similar in fact that they . . .'

Nikki slumped back into one of the chairs that lined the observation suite window and with her fists resting on her thighs she clenched and unclenched them. '. . . could be sisters?'

Pulling his mask back over his mouth, Langley nodded. 'Precisely. But as you can see, this girl is older. Maybe around five or six years older – early twenties, I'd say. She's also missing the appendectomy scar that I have on record as being one of Karen Salinger's identifying marks. I suspect I'll find that, although she's not exactly undernourished, that she's had periods of her life where she's been underfed. Perhaps she's been bulimic. A dental examination will confirm that and, I have no doubt, it will also confirm that she is not Karen Salinger. Her pallor is unnatural, which indicates to me someone who perhaps didn't go outside much and her musculature indicates a lack of exercise. Certainly not the muscle structure of an active young woman and definitely not the muscle tone of someone who regularly rode horses.'

'Shit, this just got a whole lot more complicated didn't it?'

Chapter 22

Peggy Marks flicked through the TV programmes – channel surfing the other women called it. She'd give anything to go surfing right now. To walk through this grim grey building and out into the sunshine. To feel its warmth on her face and to know she could stay outdoors as long as she wanted to. To keep walking – take a train or a bus to the seaside – Whitby or Robin Hood's Bay perhaps where she could enjoy an ice cream and surf if she wanted to, like they did when they were kids. Or she'd do a bit of kayaking in Ruswarp near the Riverside Café – even that would be brilliant. The thoughts conjured up images of happier times and made her smile.

Then, the sounds of the two women nicknamed Thelma and Lou – for obvious reasons – arguing intruded and her smile faded. She'd never be free of these four walls. Of sharing fart space with women she barely knew and some she wished she'd never met. Of eating on schedule, crapping to order and showering when told. Of gulping her food down with her arm curved protectively round her plate and with her eyes in perpetual motion, circling the room on high alert. Of lying alone at night, the sounds of others' masturbating echoing in stereo through the dark, yet never quite silent night. Everyone did what they could to survive the

166

repetitiveness of their days, the loneliness of their nights and the inevitability of losing a little bit more of themselves every day.

Peggy continued to flick, delaying the inescapable purgatory that awaited her when she chose a programme to watch. Channel Four news. She smiled. Krishnan Guru-Murthy – she liked him. He had a kind smile. Maybe she'd let his words flow over her for a while? Not that any news impacted her – not really. Then the headlines came on and it was like a sledgehammer to her brain. Her eyes widened and her lungs closed. She couldn't breathe. Surely this wasn't happening, not again. As dizziness swamped her, the TV control slipped from her hand and the headlines behind Guru-Murthy seemed to enlarge until they were all she could see on the screen. *Family annihilation in Bradford. Police accused of floundering.*

No! No! No! Not again. Not again! As her eyes fluttered back in her head, her caught breath released, flooding her lungs and making her gasp. She jumped from her seat and paced her small room, hearing only odd words from the newsreader: family of four, stabbed, murdered, annihilation. Words that pierced her with icicles making her blood freeze. It was happening again and she could do nothing to stop it. Could do nothing to help! White lightning flashes clouded her peripheral vision and she only just made it back to her cot before the darkness took hold and she fainted.

Chapter 23

'What the hell is this all about, Saj? No sooner do we think we're making a little progress on the investigation and something else gets thrown in the mix.' Nikki slammed her palm against the dashboard of Sajid's precious Jaguar.

Oblivious to Sajid's scowl and tut as he muttered something under his breath about charging her for damages, she followed up by tapping an agitated rhythm on her thigh with her fingers. 'It's got to be Winnie. Don't you think she has to be Winnie? I mean who else could it be? She looks so much like Karen and as far as we know there are no other female family members in that age bracket. It's got to be her.'

Sajid turned the key in the ignition. 'Don't think we should jump to conclusions on this one. Not yet anyway. That's what we did before and look where that landed us – up excrement creek with no paddle and with the tide pulling us further into the middle of the crap.'

'You're right. Langley will expedite the DNA results and before long, we'll know for certain who she is and if she's related to the Salingers or not.' She thrust her chin up and pursed her lips. 'My bets on it being the abducted sister. But . . .'

She lifted her hand to slam the dashboard again, but Saj caught her sleeve. 'No, if you've got excess energy to expel we'll take a trot in the rain round the car park. I'm not letting you vent your frustration on my baby.'

Nikki slumped back in the sumptuous leather, allowing the heat from the heated seats to warm her back and, as it did so, her muscles loosened a bit. She shrugged. 'Sorry, Saj. You're right. Taking it out on this old rust heap is unnecessary. I'm frustrated and pissed off, which, of course, is no excuse. Talking of excuses, you do know you were a dick to Langley in there, don't you?'

Saj averted his gaze but gave a small nod. 'Not talking about it, Nik. Not now.'

Glad that Sajid was aware of his behaviour and wanting to focus on the investigation, Nikki watched the steady stream of rain hit the windscreen and roll down in an unrelenting trickle as she mulled over the shock that Langley had just delivered. Then, after playing back her reaction to Langley's bombshell in the post-mortem suite, she took out her phone and fired off a text. Seeing Sajid's raised eyebrow she shrugged. 'Langley – an apology. I'll apologise to him properly in person, but I was a cow in there and I can't let that lie.'

'Think we all got a shock in there. Definitely not how we expected that PM to go.' He paused, his fingers tapping against the steering wheel and shook his head. 'What do you . . .'

Nikki caught his train of thought. 'You mean what do I think has happened to Karen Salinger, if that's not her lying in the morgue? Is she with Bland and if she is what does that mean for the investigation?'

'Yeah, something along those lines. Where is she? Is she the killer? Are her and Bland in this together? Where the fuck did Winnie Salinger appear from if that's who the poor sod in there is, but mostly . . .' He turned so he could look Nikki in the eye. 'Mostly, I'm wondering what you're going to say at your press conference about this. Will you come clean and put out a Be On the Look-Out for Karen Salinger, or . . .'

In all the confusion, Nikki had lost track of time and had momentarily forgotten about the press conference. Now as she glanced at her watch, her stomach flipped and the enormity of how the rest of her day might pan out sent tsunamis of unease hurtling through her body. 'Shit, Saj. We need to get back to Trafalgar House. Farah's going to make me presentable for the press conference and I need to consult with Ahad about this. My gut instinct is that we keep it on a need-to-know basis for now, but Ahad will take the heat if it goes wrong so it'll be his final decision.'

Saj engaged the clutch and smoothly guided the Jaguar from its parking place and made his way back to the office, with each of them absorbed in their own muddled thoughts regarding the investigation and the upcoming press conference. They'd almost reached Trafalgar House when Nikki broke the silence.

'By the way, Malik . . .' Although her tone was mild and a trace of a smile hovered at the corner of her lips, neither were a disguise for the worry lines across her brow. Still, an overwhelming need to break the tension that seemed to have pinned her to the car seat took over. 'I saw that look on your face when I told you Farah was going to make me look presentable.'

Sajid's laugh, full-bodied and melodic, filled the car and teased a wider smile from her lips as he reached over and squeezed her arm, yet kept the joke going. 'She using a body double with more dress sense than you, is she?'

Nikki folded her arms across her chest. 'I'm not rising to your insubordination, Malik, but be aware that your card is marked.'

With Sajid's laughter still filling the car, Nikki looked out the window, wishing with all her heart that Farah had indeed found a body double to stand in for her at the press conference. No way would this go well. Not with Superintendent Geoffrey Rawdon and the Chief Super Nathanial Lyons there – both were supposedly on her side, yet the underlying message had been clear – Nikki was on her own and if she faltered then they'd allow the press hyenas to destroy her before washing their hands of her completely. It was called plausible deniability. Either or both of the two men would be happy to feed her liver with some chianti to Hannibal Lecter if it kept their hands pristine.

Chapter 24

I spy with my little eye, something beginning with B . . . Bottles

Bottles in a row. I form two fingers into a gun motion, twirl round in my desk chair and pretend to fire at the imaginary bottles I see lined up in my mind's eye. Each of the six bottles has a cardboard head attached to it:

Ex-DCI Archie Hegley – *Pow!* – Gone!

DCI Zain Ahad – *Pow!* – Gone!

DS Sajid Malik – *Pow!* – Gone!

DC Farah Anwar – *Pow!* – Gone!

DC Liam Williams – *Pow!* – Gone!

Each of the heads explodes before me in a spatter of blood and brains and it's oh so satisfying. But now for the last one.

DI Nikita Parekh – I hesitate. I want to savour this one. Savour her destruction, because she's always been a cocky cow.

Her comeuppance to be delivered so publicly later on today hasn't come a moment too soon. This has been long deserved. Her card was marked the moment she poked her nose into my friend's business two years ago. But today is the day of Operation Annihilation Nikki bloody Parekh.

I take aim, savouring the imaginary moment, using it to bolster my anger, making it work for me. Two more hours and the little cow will no longer pose a threat, nor will any of her idiotic sycophants. My thumb cocks the gun, I squint at the bottle wearing Nikki Parekh's smirking head and I fire, inhaling the non-existent cordite and welcoming the resonating gunshot to reverberate in my ears.

DI Nikki Parekh – *Pow!* – Gone!

Chapter 25

'What the hell do you mean, the fourth body isn't Karen Salinger?' Ahad jumped up from behind his desk and strode round to the front of it, his movements staccato with barely concealed annoyance.

Nikki risked a quick glance at Saj and then shrugged as both of them sank onto the chairs positioned in front of the desk in almost exactly the same place that Archie had left them when he resigned. Taking a moment to order her thoughts, Nikki paused before replying. 'The post-mortem threw up some questions regarding the identity of the younger female victim. First appearances at the scene of crime spoke of a family annihilation and amid the destruction of the scene we used a visual comparison with photographs around the home to ID the victims. We then had confirmed visual ID of a photograph taken at the scene from Karen Salinger's godfather, Derek Bland. Bear in mind that, at this juncture, none of the team had a full family history, nor were we aware of the existence of Winnie Salinger, who we consider the victim is most likely to be.'

Shit, did I really just use the term juncture? Nikki paused and held Ahad's accusing glare. 'It was an honest mistake and one that has been rectified quickly. There has been no official statement from us regarding the identity of the victims and it is beyond our control that the press has published unconfirmed IDs of the victims, so . . .'

'It's a pile of crap, Nikki, and you know it. Stop trying to dress it up as something it's not. We made a mistake and it couldn't have come at a worse time with the brass scrutinising us even more than normal after your friend's hatchet job on us in *The Chronicle* earlier. Someone – presumably someone involved in the investigation – leaked the victim IDs to the press. The press – and the public for that matter – won't give a rat's arse that the information was leaked. All they'll take from this is that we fucked up – the "woke" police team that your mate Lisa Kane is banging on about at every sodding opportunity. This is a massive fucking clusterfuck.'

Ahad's "mate" jibe cut deep, but Nikki swallowed her anger. He was allowed to vent. Hadn't she and Saj spent the drive back to Trafalgar House doing just that? So, she remained silent whilst Ahad paced back and forth before them, his eyes flashing as he tried to digest the information he'd just been fed. Instead, to block out his reaction, Nikki's eyes wandered round the room. Gone were all of Archie's photos from the walls and the room, rather than holding the faint scent of Archie's Old Spice mingled with strong coffee, was now filled with the smell of freshly painted walls and an undernote of citrus.

As the colour drained from her face, Nikki wanted to say something in her defence, but no words would come. Finally, with Ahad still pacing back and forth in front of them like a lion in a safari park, Sajid spoke up, his tone calm and measured. 'I agree that it's a . . .' he hesitated, bit his lip and then continued '. . . problem. But it's not Nikki's fault. We're not even twenty-four hours into this investigation, boss. And we're running ourselves ragged. Nobody on the team has drawn breath since we got the call last night. Every one of us is committed to finding this killer. However, we're being pressured from all sides – from the higher-ups at the top, the press and—' he glared at Ahad '—you too.

It's not on. We need someone on our side. Nikki needs someone on her side. She's about to go into the arena like a female gladiator facing down all sorts of hate and believe me, she doesn't need you making things worse.'

Ahad paused, glowered at Sajid, his entire demeanour more Dark Knight than it had ever been and for a second Nikki wondered if he was going to fry Sajid. Instead, Ahad exhaled. His shoulders slumped and he stretched his neck, bones cracking as he did so. He moved back behind his desk and slumped into his chair, his arms resting on the surface atop a pile of paperwork. 'Shit. You're right, Saj. I'm sorry, Nik, it's been chaotic here and I've let it get to me.'

Unable to speak in case her voice wobbled, Nikki just nodded. Ahad's apology was heartfelt and she knew he too was getting flak from everywhere. However, his apology went nowhere near stilling the hammering in her chest or making her think she'd be able to formulate a coherent sentence anytime soon. Thankfully, she didn't have to as Ahad continued.

'We've had the phones ringing off the walls with complaints about "woke" policing and the paper's online comments section is filled with jibes about getting decent white police on the job. It's crap. Bloody crap.'

As Ahad went on and on, Nikki thought about her ex-boss. It was before he'd become DCI that Archie had headed the investigation into Winnie Salinger's disappearance, yet from her earlier discussion with him it had still preyed heavily on his mind. She'd have to speak to him about this before the press caught wind of it. However, the important thing was to work out a strategy with Ahad about how she should deal with this piece of information at the upcoming press conference.

Shoulders slumped, Ahad – breaking Nikki from her reverie – jumped up again, dragged a chair from the corner next to the hideous potted plant Nikki had given him as an "office warming" gift, and set it in front of Nikki and Sajid, creating a more intimate discussion. He cleared his throat and dragged his fingers through his hair, eliciting a smile from Nikki. Despite the differences in their stature and attitude, in that second, Sajid and Ahad bore a marked similarity with their hair spiked up and their frowns determined and focused. 'So, you reckon the so-far-unidentified victim is the abducted sister?'

Sajid leaned forward. 'That's the working theory at present – her similarity in looks to Karen Salinger, the fact that nobody, including the kids' godfather George Bland, knew about this gathering seems to hint that she reached out to her family recently. We're checking the family's devices to ascertain how they were contacted and obviously we need DNA confirmation; however, because we have Winnie Salinger's DNA on file from when she was abducted, that should be easy to get.'

The trio sat in silence for a moment then Nikki, finding her voice, said: 'Whether this victim is or isn't Winnie Salinger, it throws up lots of questions that need answering.'

She glanced at Ahad and saw she had his full attention. 'If it is Winnie, then where the hell has she been all these years and why has she returned to the family home now? Langley said the body showed signs of periods of malnourishment and that she was significantly underweight for her height. Also, why wouldn't the family involve the police or confide in their closest family friend?'

'Also,' Saj continued, 'where is Karen Salinger now? Is she another victim or is she the killer or involved with the killer in some way? But, whatever we think about it, we can't ignore the possible link to Winnie Salinger's murder. It's all just too coincidental and we seem to have a missing person's case on our hands as well as a multiple murder.'

After a nod in Sajid's direction, Ahad pierced Nikki with his eyes. 'You'll have to tell Archie about this. Get his take on things. Go through everything he thought, felt, smelled, intuited – every fucking thing he remembers from that investigation. If this dead girl is Winnie Salinger things just got a whole lot more complicated. And you'll need to rope in officers from Missing Persons to help with that angle.'

Nikki – arms folded cross her chest, lips curled and eyes flashing – felt anger replace her earlier trepidation and she couldn't quite contain her derisive snort. *Like I don't know how to investigate. Like I need telling how to move inquiries forward.*

Ahad's lips twitched and a slow flush spread over his cheeks. 'Sorry, Nik – Granny and eggs and all that.'

Nikki – halfway through a nod that accepted his apology – paused. Her eyes flicked to Saj who just a tad too slowly wiped the smirk from his lips and then back to Ahad whose grin was wide. 'What the hell? Granny? Who the hell do you think you are . . . ?' She hesitated then added: 'Boss.'

The brief interlude defused the tension and Nikki leaned forward. 'I'll speak to Archie tonight. He's coming for tea. You're more than welcome to come too if you want, but Saj and I are on this. However, my most pressing worry is this press conference. We know it's been designed to discredit you and me and this team.' She waved her hands to encompass Sajid and the rest of her absent team. 'I would like your permission to delay sharing this new information with the press yet and continue with reference to "a family of four" but with no additional specifics. It'll take the heat off us for a short time, but that delay might be crucial in allowing us to garner additional information to propel the investigation forward.'

Ahad thought for a moment, then nodded. He looked at Nikki. 'I'm sorry you have to go through this, Nik. I don't know what Rawdon and Lyons's agenda is, but you're not going to have an easy ride. I wish there was something more I could do, but there isn't. So in answer to your question – yes, I'm happy for us to delay releasing this information for now. I suspect they'd weaponise it to discredit you rather than to move the investigation forward, so I'll give you until the DNA results hit my desk before taking that information to them. In the meantime, do you have a strategy? I'd recommend . . .'

Nikki held her hand up, her tone staccato. 'No, don't recommend anything. I've got a strategy in place. I know what I'm doing. It'll be fine.'

The worried look didn't leave Ahad's eyes, but Nikki refused to say any more about her intention at the press conference. She knew Ahad was concerned she'd lose it and go off on one, but in the interests of deniability for him, she had to leave him in the dark on this one. She and her team – well mainly her team – had come up with a game plan and although she'd no idea whether it would work or not, she hoped it might at the very least move the press focus from her and her team, to the investigation itself.'

She glanced at her watch and, seeing the time, her heart fluttered. Not long now till feeding time with the jackals.

Chapter 26

It had been a long time since Nikki had last felt so completely out of her depth. Well perhaps not that long – not really. Nikki regularly felt dissociated from those around her and had grown accustomed to the slight off-kilter sensation of not quite connecting. However, her prevailing desire to reach the truth mostly overrode that feeling. Not this time though. This time, she was to be paraded in front of a gaggle of journalists and as if that wasn't bad enough, she was to be the sacrificial goat.

Again, the knowledge that, as far as the brass were concerned she was disposable, rankled. Every day, she and her team, in increasingly difficult circumstances, put their lives on the line. Public opinion of the police throughout the country was at an all-time low, with the people's perception of them tainted by the racism and sexism and double standards displayed by the Met police over the past few years. The fact that Nikki's team was the very antithesis of that sort of abhorrent policing was, to those needing police protection, often irrelevant. How could you trust any coppers when some of them were bent, racist, violent or whose best interests weren't those of the very people who paid their salaries? Nikki saw that regularly on the ground. The disconnect between community policing and what the media portrayed when

180

creating headlines snatched by a few aberrant officers, as well as the perceived culture of cronyism and serving those with more than those without, made building trust harder. People were less inclined to get involved and help the police.

Nikki saw this daily and yet, here she was being dragged before reporters baying for blood because it served the interests of those at the top. Why that was the case, Nikki had no idea. It seemed completely counterproductive, especially in a city like Bradford where diverse communities necessitated inclusive policing. However, once she'd got through the ordeal in front of her, Nikki was determined to get to the bottom of it. No way would she stand idly by whilst the dedicated officers she worked with were slandered. Especially not since she could list an entire breed of officer insidiously spreading their racist and sexist crap through Police Bradford. No, when this investigation was complete and she and her team had brought to justice those responsible for the deaths of the Salinger family, then Nikki would spend time – her own time, no doubt – exposing those officers who needed exposing.

When her desk phone rang, she scowled at it, throwing the pen she'd been twiddling between her fingers across the desk before lifting the receiver. Her snarled 'Yeah?' made no attempt to hide the fact that she was in no mood for useless time-consuming conversations. Had the call been from anyone on her team, they'd have rung on her mobile, so this was no doubt some bureaucratic call about a form she'd forgotten to fill in.

'DI Nikki Parekh?' The voice on the other end of the line was male and carried just the sort of authoritative tone that set Nikki bristling.

In response her tone was clipped. 'Yes, who's speaking and how did you get this number?'

There was a nanosecond pause, during which Nikki hoped her tone had made the caller reconsider wasting her time, but she was disappointed. When her caller finally spoke, amusement laced every word, causing Nikki's lips to tighten in response. 'I'm Colin Hewes. I'm solicitor to Peggy Marks. You may have heard of her?'

Nikki sighed. It was going to be one of those guessing game sort of conversations – the sort where the caller asked stupid, not quite hypothetical questions rather than just get right to the point. Still, she cast around in her mind and came up empty. She'd no idea who Marks was and, to be honest, didn't really care. 'Look, I've no idea who your client is and have no idea how I can help you. I'm in the middle of an investigation at the . . .'

'That's just it, Detective. My client, Peggy Marks, is innocent of the crime she has been imprisoned for, yet still she has important information for you that might help you in your current investigation. She would like to meet you.'

Nikki rolled her eyes. She didn't need this sort of crap right now. The prisons were chock-full of convicted people proclaiming their innocence and the last thing Nikki needed right now was to be embroiled with some prisoner who wanted to use the Salinger murders as the key to their cell door. 'Look, Mr Howes . . .'

'Hewes.'

'Eh?'

'Hewes. My name's Hewes not Howes.'

Nikki's eyes flashed. Hewes, Howes, who the hell cared? She just wanted to be done with this conversation and move on. 'Okay, Mr Hewes. I'll give you the hotline number for the Salinger investigation and you can give your client's information there where it will be logged and acted upon in due . . .'

'Ex-DCI Hegley gave me this number . . .'

Nikki's mouth snapped shut. That Archie would supply this solicitor with her direct line was astounding, particularly as it seemed he must have done so in the few hours since they'd met up earlier. She paused and ran the name Peggy Marks through her memory bank once more. Still no luck. As far as she knew she hadn't come across this woman before. Unable to keep the annoyance from her voice, Nikki said, 'And you didn't think to start with that? Might have saved a bit of time. Time that, as I'm sure you are aware, is very precious in an ongoing investigation.'

'Archie mentioned you were prickly, DI Parekh . . .'

Prickly? Bloody traitor. I'll tie Archie's proverbials in a knot when I see him next!

'. . . but in the interests of expediency, I've arranged for you to meet with myself and my client tomorrow at 10 a.m. in New Hall prison, Flockton. Archie tells me he is meeting with you tonight, so this will all become clearer then. I look forward to meeting you tomorrow.'

Before Nikki could reply, the line went dead. *Bloody Archie!* Couldn't he have just phoned her and made the appointment himself if he thought it was urgent enough to divert her time away from the Salinger case? She sighed, aware that most of her annoyance was down to her nerves over the press conference. Another glance at her watch told Nikki she had twenty minutes before her team would do their final briefing her for the press conference, after which Farah was going to make her "camera ready" – whatever the hell that was. She had two choices. She could use the twenty minutes to transport herself to a Zen-like calm – but that was never going to happen – *or* she could find out what she could about Peggy Marks using the police databases.

Within minutes, Nikki had learned quite a bit about Peggy Marks. Aged twenty-six now, Peggy Marks had been convicted of murdering her brother and parents by stabbing four years previously in the sleepy North Yorkshire village of Hutton-le-Hole. She had consistently proclaimed her innocence, but the prosecution had put forward a good case that, in the absence of any evidence of intruders at the property and the mainly superficial wounds suffered by Peggy – barring one deep wound to her left breast area – which the prosecution maintained had been self-inflicted and had provided many expert witnesses to support their position – Peggy had been sentenced to life at New Hall prison in Flockton near Wakefield. Lack of time made it impossible for

Nikki to come to any decision on Colin Hewes's claims of his client's innocence, so Nikki sent the file to print and thrust all thoughts of Peggy Marks to the back of her mind for now.

She'd learn more from Archie later and although still peeved that he'd allowed Hewes to ambush her, Nikki knew her ex-boss well enough to realise that he wouldn't have done so had he not felt it was important. So, he got a pass – for now. She'd just got to her feet to go to the private room Williams had arranged for her briefing when Liam appeared before her, his face flushed but the wide smile on his lips giving Nikki hope that maybe, just maybe she'd survive the press grilling.

Chapter 27

Not only had Anwar insisted she wear the flowing silky blouse instead of the less girly jade green T-shirt she'd preferred, she'd also insisted on slapping some make-up on Nikki's face.

Now, alone for the first time since the "makeover" session, Nikki glared at her reflection in the mirror in the women's loos. Not quite convinced that the elegant, albeit frowning woman staring back was her, she pulled at the hem of the pink floral blouse she'd borrowed from Farah. Still pondering the conundrum of why anyone would keep more than one spare set of clothes at work, Nikki tried not to think too much about what her kids would say about her transformation on TV. No doubt Sunni and Isaac would agree she looked "lovely" – but that in itself caused problems for Nikki. She wasn't a "lovely" person. She was a kick-ass good detective, not a "lovely" one. "Lovely" implied weak and fluffy and Nikki Parekh was definitely *not* that.

Charlie, she reckoned, would cast a critical eye over the entire ensemble and tell her, with a Charlie shrug, that she looked okay "for a change". Whilst Ruby – her fashionista killer kid would study each item of clothing, each piece of make-up, the borrowed jewellery and her demeanour before dissecting each with forensic precision and offering suggested improvements for next time.

Nikki's heart hammered like a rogue clapperboard in her chest – *next time*? No damn way would there be a *next* time. This was a one and only. A first and a last. A never again. An "I'll die before I repeat it" occasion. Her vision blurred, making her reflection all shimmery and fuzzy. *Shit, Nikki, get a grip. Get a fucking grip.* She pulled her shoulders back, closed her eyes and focused on her breathing. When after a couple of minutes that hadn't worked, she resorted to Sajid's suggestion and imagined herself sticking pins into a realistic Lisa Kane effigy – that felt good, she had to admit. However, it didn't settle her nerves and there was no way Nikki was going to use Williams's "picture them in the nude" suggestion, which only left one option. She'd have to go out there and, knowing she didn't have the support of the senior officers on the podium with her, push through it and do what she always did – her job.

As she pulled her shoulders back and glared for a last time at her reflection she gave the elastic band round her wrist three hard twangs, then exhaled, before striding out of the bathroom. Outside, Sajid and Ahad waited, both casting anxious eyes in her direction as she exited. Nikki could feel the warm flush on her cheeks and although she welcomed their support, she was reluctant to acknowledge it. *Show no weakness, Nik,* she told herself as, with a quick nod, she passed by them leaving them to trail in her wake towards the room where the press conference was due to take place.

The sounds of mumbled voices from inside the room rose and fell as she approached the side door where she and the super – Geoffrey Rawdon – and the chief super – Nathanial Lyons – were due to make their entrance. Both men were already present and wearing their dress uniforms. Their eyes raked over her as she approached them and Nikki was certain their lips curled in disdain when they saw her apparel. Lyons glanced at his watch and made a clicking noise behind his teeth. 'Glad you finally made it, Inspector.'

Despite her hammering heart Nikki smiled. 'I didn't realise it was optional, sir.'

The pause between "optional" and "sir" was intentional and Nikki was pleased to note the narrowing of the chief super's eyes, even as she felt Sajid's warning prod in the base of her back.

'You're cutting it fine, aren't you, Parekh?' The brusque interruption came from Rawdon as he stepped up next to the chief super, the two Goliaths showing their solidarity against Nikki's diminutive David. She was glad she'd packed her catapult, for she'd no doubt need it. 'Well, sir, you know how it is when you're working a major incident involving the deaths of a family of four, don't you?'

Ahad behind her cleared his throat and stepped forward, indicating they should enter the room and face the baying hounds.

With a last steadying breath Nikki followed the two men into the room, feeling like an inconsequential maid following at her masters' behest. Flashes went off all around as the photographers vied with each other for the best shot and there was a momentary increase in volume as the reporters surged to their feet and began yelling questions.

Nikki took her seat behind the desk and, clasping her hands firmly in her lap, she sat upright waiting to see how her denouement would unfold. The chief superintendent got to his feet and moved to the front. He tapped the microphone a few times and the room returned to some semblance of order. Nikki's gaze raked the faces lined before her. She was looking for Lisa Kane and she soon saw her smirking face beaming at her from the third row back. As her gaze rested on the woman, Nikki's expression remained neutral, as she thought *I'll get you for this* before moving on to scan the rest of the room – but not before noting the uncertainty flicker in the reporter's eyes at getting no apparent reaction from her nemesis.

Lyons's voice droned on and on, harping on about the value of transparency in Bradford policing and the importance of employing only the highest trained and the best detectives the region had to offer. He moved on to voicing his dismay at the lack of developments in the Salinger investigation thus far and ended by placing his hand on his heart. 'I hereby promise the people of Bradford that I, personally, will weed out inefficient officers regardless of their ethnicity and that "woke" politics will no longer have a place in West Yorkshire police employment policy.'

Amid a burst of camera flashes that blinded Nikki, he turned an insincere smile in her direction. 'I'm sure you all know Detective Inspector Nikita Parekh. She's here to attempt to reassure you of the progress made in the Salinger investigation.'

The use of the word "attempt" wasn't lost on Nikki as she nodded at Lyons, holding his gaze a fraction longer than necessary. She took her time moving to the podium, hoping that her shaking legs weren't noticeable to her audience. Hopefully if things went to plan, she'd get through this ordeal in one piece. Moments before she reached the microphone, the babble of voices from the audience of reporters faded away and Nikki snuck a glance at the screen that was situated behind the podium, but in plain sight of her audience of journalists.

When she saw the screen, a smile played across her lips as she saw that everything was under control. Her team had done what they'd planned and never before had she been so grateful to them or so in awe of their talents. It had been Williams's suggestion to take the wind out of everybody's sails by putting on a slide show documenting the successes of Nikki and her team over the past few years and the subsequent news articles that had praised the work done by Nikki's team – articles written by the very journalists sitting in the audience now.

Nikki had initially been sceptical about it, but Sajid and Farah had convinced her that letting it run in the background whilst she spoke about the Salingers' case was more effective than going on the defensive. By the expressions on the faces of the reporters with their eyes glued to the screen as headline after headline documenting every case Nikki's team had been involved in flashed soundlessly over the screen. A single glance behind her showed Rawdon with a smile on his face as he met her gaze and gave a surreptitious wink, whilst Lyons, arms crossed over his substantial chest, looked about to erupt from his uniform like a toxic boil.

Nikki licked her lips and tapped the microphone to get the attention of the journalists. She smiled and took her time, as Sajid had suggested, to move her gaze across the faces of each of the audience members to connect with each and every one of them. 'Well, after this morning's whipping, I thought I better bring my bodyguards.' Nikki turned and gestured to Rawdon and Lyons and a ripple of laughter went round the room. 'But I'm hoping I won't need them.'

She paused and lifted her chin up. 'I'd be in dereliction of my duty to the Salingers, their family, friends *and* the wider community if I spent my time here justifying myself. I'll let my track record speak for itself, shall I? After all, each and every one of you . . .' she homed in on Lisa Kane whose pursed lips and flashing eyes showed her annoyance all too clearly, and paused '. . . well most of you, have reported on the cases my team have brought to a satisfactory resolution. So, this press conference is going to be about the Salingers and how you, as responsible news reporters, can help us to identify the perpetrator of this horrible act by sharing facts with the public and not sensationalising a situation that must be horrific for those connected with the family.'

She paused again. 'So, here's what we know. I can now confirm that we have discounted murder-suicide as a motive for the family's deaths and are treating these deaths as murder. We ask the public for any help in identifying anyone seen around the Salingers' property in Oxenhope at any time over the weekend. We also request the public's assistance in sharing any information, no matter how small or seemingly inconsequential, with us. Often the smallest pieces of information can be the starting point for a valid investigative strategy. We want to garner as much information about the family as possible and welcome any information the public has at its disposal.

'With that end in mind, we will give a regular media conference here on a daily basis until the murders have been resolved. Now because time is of the essence, I'm going to head back to my team as we'll be working through the night. But any questions may be directed to Superintendent Rawdon or Chief Superintendent Lyon.'

As Nikki left the stage a plethora of questions assaulted the two senior officers.

'Is the Salingers' murder connected with the disappearance of their daughter Winne twelve years ago?'

'Are we to believe that DI Parekh and her team have your full confidence?'

As Nikki, head held high, turned the tables on her bosses and left them to respond to the journalists, Sajid and Ahad swept her up and transported her away from the reporters and back into the incident room before high-fiving and hugging her. 'You bloody smashed it, Nik. Good for you,' said Saj, looking ready to hug her again, if she hadn't sidestepped his advances.

Still flushed by her success on the stage, and also shaky from the adrenaline rush, Nikki allowed a momentary pang of doubt to seep through. Lyons and Rawdon – well perhaps not Rawdon – after all he'd winked at her and seemed amused by the turn of events, but definitely Lyons would seek revenge. Of that she was one hundred per cent certain. But for now, who cared. They had an investigation to crack on with and hopefully her team's ingenuity had bought them a small reprieve from the press.

Chapter 28

After extricating herself from her exuberant team, Nikki rushed to the loos, locked herself in a cubicle and vomited. As she sat on the closed toilet seat, a film of icy sweat formed across her forehead, which she knew was a direct downside of the earlier adrenaline rush that had got her through the press conference. Taking a moment to steady herself, she closed her eyes and replayed the events in her head. It had started off tricky with Rawdon and Lyons strategically placing themselves apart from her, but overall, she felt that her strategy, with the help of her team, had been enough to bring most of the journalists back on side.

The memory of Lisa Kane's angry expression and heightened colour as she'd elbowed herself through the crowds of fellow journalists flashed into her mind. God. Nikki was pleased she'd drawn the wind out from under the other woman's sails – she deserved it – but even as she thought that, the smile faded from her lips. Actually, she may just have cemented the animosity between herself and Kane a little more deeply. Kane had a long memory, little moral fibre and a vicious streak that was dangerous as well as hurtful.

She got to her feet and flushed the loo, wiped her sweaty

hands down her trouser legs and straightened her shoulders before leaving the cubicle. She needed fresh air. Needed to get away from the citrusy scent that pervaded Trafalgar House. Thankful that none of her team were waiting in ambush to make sure she was okay, Nikki headed down the back stairs and with relief burst through the deactivated fire doors into the smokers' yard at the back of the building. The drizzle of rain and fresh coolness of the breeze on her warm cheeks was welcome, so she stood just outside the door, her face turned up to the sky.

The sound of someone clearing their throat alerted her to the fact that she wasn't alone. Schooling her face into a neutral expression, she spun round on her heel to acknowledge her companion. When she saw that her companion was Superintendent Rawdon, she cursed her decision to sneak around out the back of the building to avoid bumping into anyone she knew rather than go out the front.

'Didn't have you down for a smoker, Parekh.' Rawdon looked ruefully at the remains of his cigarette and then dropped it on the concrete before grinding it out beneath his heel.

Nikki forced a semblance of a smile to her lips and shook her head. 'You're right, I'm not a smoker, sir. Just needed a bit of fresh air, that's all.'

Watching him littering, Nikki visualised herself stepping up to him and challenging him to pick up his discarded fag end. A smile quirked her lips when her thoughts went further to him refusing and her in a *Sweeney*-type move, spinning him round, in an arm lock up his spine, cuffing him and saying: "You're nicked".

Instead, sanity prevailed and she turned away from his grinning face, angling her head upwards so the mist of rain landed soothingly on her cheeks. Was he challenging her in some way? *Is that what the sarky grin is all about?*

'Handled yourself quite well in there, Parekh.' He laughed, a throaty smoker's sort of chortle that grated on Nikki. 'Old Lyons was fuming. You've set the cat among the pigeons there, lass.'

Nikki felt his gaze on her and risked a glance in his direction. His attempt at a Yorkshire accent annoyed her, but she wasn't about to let him know she thought he was a dick. A smile flitted around his lips, but the expression in his eyes, whilst revealing nothing of his true thoughts, left Nikki feeling as if he was playing her in some way. She shrugged. 'Not my intention, sir. Just reminding the press that we're all in this together, that's all.'

'Hmm. If you say so.'

His tone indicated the exact opposite of his words and Nikki was pleased that her message appeared to have hit home. Nevertheless, she released a small breath of relief when he stepped towards the door. Yanking it open, he paused before re-entering the building. 'He's a tough cookie is Lyons. Watch your back, eh, Parekh.'

His words brought a prickle of unease to Nikki's gut. She'd known she was playing with fire when she decided to fight her corner at the press conference, yet somehow the coldness of his words, accompanied by that half-smile of his made her shoulders tense and her face flush. She gave an abrupt nod, but didn't meet his eyes as she willed him to step inside and let the door slide shut between them, but he wasn't done.

'For what it's worth, Parekh, I think you handled that well and I think you were right to do it that way. We need to show a united front. We've worked for years to create more diverse, more relatable policing here in Bradford and we can't risk losing that. I won't have that. Not on my watch.'

With the sound of the doors sliding shut behind him, Nikki relaxed her shoulders and leaned back against the wall. *What the hell had that been about?* She couldn't make out what Rawdon's game was and it made her feel vulnerable. He seemed to be offering her his support, yet something in the way he observed her, the slight touch of sarcasm in his tone, the way his smile never quite reached his eyes left lingering doubt.

Shivering against the coolness of the drizzle as it soaked into her – no Farah's – shirt, she forced herself to wait a full five minutes longer outside before making her way back to her desk.

Chapter 29

Present Day: Marnie

Come on, Gwen. This is getting beyond a joke. Where the hell are you? I want to scream. The tension in my chest is so tight, I think I'm going to snap in half. Round and round I've paced. All day long I've worn a weary path between the bed, the window and the filthy bathroom. *I've counted to a hundred, then a thousand and then five and then ten thousand and still you're not back – will you ever come back for me, Gwen?* If I'm honest that's the thought that gnaws chunks from my peace of mind. What if she's left me? What if Gwen's finally got fed up with me not talking?

As darkness draws in, the only light comes from cars passing by the window, casting up flurries of rain with a hissing sound, and the streetlight on the pavement outside. The temperature in the flat has plummeted over the last few hours, so I wrap the smelly old duvet round my shoulders and pull one of the rickety chairs from the cramped kitchen space to the window and settle down for my lonely vigil.

All day long, the persistent thought that I don't know Gwen at all has been my constant companion. Like a bad devil sitting on my shoulder, mocking me for my stupidity. For my persistent silence. For my naiveté and neediness. I want to hate her for leaving me here like this, all alone. I want to despise her for not sharing more with me, but I can't. Gwen saved my life – I'm sure of it. A whisper comes on the chill from the window, fanning my brow. *Jilly.* I smile. *Yes, Jilly, you saved me too, of course you did, but it was the thought of you. My promise to find you when I escaped that saved me.*

With Gwen it was the real, physical stuff that saved me. The things she taught me, like how to take myself out of the bad place and onto a cloud where she and I could play or chat or laugh or eat popcorn. Or how to lock a bit of myself away so they could never touch it – a little bit of myself that was mine and only mine – Gwen taught me that. She held me when I cried, she tended me when they hurt me, she coaxed me back from the depths of despair – those are just some of the ways in which she saved me and I miss not having her here right now to save me again.

Hunched up in the blanket, eyes glued to the darkness outside, straining my eyes in the hope that I see Gwen's figure scurrying along the road, dodging puddles, I rack my brains for what to do. It takes a few hours, but then, I get it. Maybe it's my turn to save Gwen. This thought reassures me. I have no idea how to save her, but if she hasn't come back by tomorrow, then, I'll think of a plan.

With the tantalising smell of strawberries teasing my nostrils and Jilly's "Don't let the Beep Beeps win" on repeat in my mind, I fall into a hopeful sleep.

Chapter 30

I spy with my little eye . . . something that boils my piss

Rage encompasses me, envelops me like a shroud of sharpened nails. It prickles at my skin, before opening its jaws, spreading its claws and gauging and snaffling huge chunks of flesh from me. I'm so cross. I welcome this imaginary pain, embrace it, wallow in its savagery. It grounds me when all around seems filled with chaos. More importantly though, it fuels me. Energises me and makes me focus.

She made a fool of me! That Parekh bitch made a public laughing stock of me, but I'll make her pay for that. Before too long, I'll have her grovelling at my feet wishing she'd never started this.

I'm panting so hard and so fast that little multi-coloured flecks dart back and forth in front of my eyes and a wave of vertigo swamps me. I press two fingers to my neck and find my pulse is racing. This won't do. It won't do at all. I need to calm down and focus. I can't allow her antics to affect my decision-making. Slowing my breathing right down, I stumble across to my desk, flop onto my ergonomic office chair and swing it round so I can look out the window. It's still pissing it down, but the rhythmic pitter-patter of the rain hitting the glass and then gathering in droplets before trickling down the pane is surprisingly calming.

I focus on one globule of water, mesmerised as other smaller ones trickle down and merge with it, making it fatter and fatter, till it too trails its way down the pane before gathering where the pane meets the sill. Although my breathing is slower and the flecks have receded from my peripheral vision, an ache radiates from the base of my spine, up my back and across my shoulders, before sending shooting pains up my neck and into my jaw. Until this problem is dealt with, I can't relax. But what should I do about her? This Nikki Parekh – the one I'd chosen as the perfect scapegoat has proved herself to be a pain in the arse. Not only that, though, the woman is clever. She played me – played us – and now instead of being tarnished by the focus of the media, she's their bloody darling. This wasn't how things were supposed to go down and now, that bloody journalist is on my case.

The others are rattled by the events – and so they should be. They are, at the very least, partly to blame for what has unfolded, after all. However, I've always been able to use my rage to propel me forward. Adrenaline fuelled by anger, yet tempered by sheer willpower, surges through me and makes my focus razor sharp.

I have two options available to me: double down and baton the hatches or misdirection.

I smile. I've never been one for hunkering down, hiding my light under a bushel. I've always ploughed through difficulties, forcing my agenda by stealth or by blunt-force attack and this time will be no different. Our business model has operated successfully and covertly for a number of years and this one minor – all right, major – blip will not be allowed to affect it. I'm savvy enough to see the way the winds of change are blowing and so through misdirection and oblique posturing I'll save the day – my way!

My phone vibrates across the desk, and I sigh. It's her again – Lisa Kane. I hesitate, conscious that the pain in my jaw has radiated up to my ears, and then I snatch my phone up. No point in putting her off. She's persistent.

'Yes?' I keep my tone snippy. Give her an in and she inserts herself into your head, like an unmelodic earworm wriggling towards your brain.

'What are you going to do about Parekh?' Although her words are tight and delivered like machine-gun fire, the tension down the line is palpable in every husky breath that reaches my ears.

'I think that's my job, don't you, Lisa?'

Her voice fades in and out now as if she's marching back and forth and for a moment I visualise her beautiful face ravished by anger, her manicured fingers gripping the phone so hard it may well break. 'You owe me, though. I've been loyal to you for years now. I've had your back, done your bidding and all for old time's sake.'

Her insolence irks me but I don't let it show. Instead I thread my words with a sliver of humour. That really pisses her off. She's never been happy at not having a hand in the big stakes. 'Don't kid yourself, doll. You did it for the cash.'

Her voice rises on a hiss of fury. 'I risked my reputation to bring her down. I did that for *you*. I did that because you promised me she'd be broken, but look at her. She's risen to the top like a floating turd disguised as a rose. You need to sort this. You need to make her go away.'

My blurry reflection in the window pane stares back at me. My eyes narrowed, my mouth twisted at the audacity of the woman. How dare she tell me what to do? One somewhat unmemorable night in the sack and she thinks she owns me? We'll see about that. I mould my lips into a smile and inject chill into my voice. 'I don't take orders from you – or anyone else for that matter.'

She pauses, her fingers tapping against the phone as she considers what her next move should be. Sugar laces her tone as she backtracks. 'I'm sorry. You're right. Who am I to tell you what to do?'

Her tinkling laugh reverberates against my ear, sending more electric shocks up and down my neck and into my brain. For a moment I want to throw the phone at the window – anything to stop her ingratiating whining. Then as I visualise throwing Lisa Kane against the window instead of my phone, seeing the glass with all its rivulets of rain water shatter and her body fly through the abyss, ending with a firm but wet thump as her bones crash to the concrete beneath, I smile. I have a plan. 'Don't worry, my dear. I'll sort it.'

Still smiling, I hang up. Then I unlock the bottom drawer of my desk, extract a burner phone and dial. When Scarface answers, I issue my orders.

Chapter 31

Throughout the meal that Marcus had prepared for them, Nikki toyed with the pasta on her plate and nibbled half-heartedly on a piece of garlic bread. Her entire body buzzed and she had trouble containing her need to pace the house, slamming doors and twanging her elastic band with ever-increasing intensity as she went.

She kept casting glances in Archie's direction, wondering how she was going to tell him that the child he'd been unable to find ten years ago was now in a freezer in the morgue. It would hit him hard – really hard and yet, underlying her sympathy a vein of annoyance at him passing her work extension number to that lawyer niggled. If he'd texted her and given her a heads up, she'd have been fine with it. Well, maybe fine was too strong a word, but out of loyalty to him, she'd have made time for a conversation with the damn lawyer. But, all the cryptic hints and crap irked her. She'd no time for guessing games and wanted nothing more than to just get on with the investigation, which was becoming trickier by the moment.

She and DCI Ahad had agreed not to issue a BOLO for Karen Salinger until they'd had the DNA from the body they had initially presumed to be Karen confirmed. It wasn't ideal, but it was all they could do at this stage. Sajid was as anxious as she to get the results in, and he kept checking his phone to see if Langley had contacted him.

After what seemed like an eternity, with only the kids and Archie doing any justice to the meal, Nikki, Archie and Sajid migrated into the living room, leaving the kids to help Marcus clean up the remnants of their dinner. Before she closed the door behind her, she poked her head out and looked at Marcus. At the sight of him – tea towel slung over one shoulder, directing the kids with a light touch here and a murmured request there – the tension drained a little from her body. She was so lucky to have him. The entire family were. He was the ballast to her unpredictable life. It was because of his solidity that she could do her job. As if sensing her eyes on him, he turned, saw her in the doorway and his lips curved into a wide smile as he connected with her. His nod told her all she needed to know – he was there for her and their chaotic, sometimes off-the-scale hectic family.

Her shoulders relaxed as his gaze soothed her, grounded her. She mouthed "I love you" to him and then grinned when Sunni who'd chosen that precise moment to pop his head out from behind his dad and interrupt their private moment pretended to stick two fingers down his throat as he made mock-sick noises, which Isaac quickly joined in with.

Marcus rolled his eyes at her, then grabbing the tea towel from his shoulder, flicked it at the boys before chasing them round the table. Nikki, still smiling, clicked the door shut and turned to see that both Saj and Archie were grinning at her in a grown-up version of Sunni and Isaac's antics. The flush that spread across her cheeks brought a frown to her brow as she strode over and flung herself onto the couch next to Sajid and glared at them. 'So? You two got something to say?'

Both men exchanged glances then wiping the silly, juvenile grins off their faces settled down for the long discussion ahead. Archie handed them each a copy of his "unofficial" file on Winnie

Salinger's disappearance and Nikki took a deep breath. There was no way out of it, she had to tell him. 'Archie, before we discuss Winnie's disappearance, there's something you really need to know.'

Archie paused and peered at her over the top of his specs, looking like a wise old and very bald owl. His mildly interested look morphed into a frown, as he correctly assessed the severity of the information Nikki had to share. 'Spit it out then, lassie. You've got mah proverbials intrigued now, so just spit it oot.'

'We think we made a mistake when we ID'd the younger female Salinger body. During the PM Langley discovered some discrepancies in identifying marks on the body that we had initially and, as it turns out, incorrectly presumed to be Karen Salinger. Although the victim did look very similar to Karen, we realised that it's not . . .' Her voice trailed away.

Archie's frown deepened and as he pursed his lips, he drummed his fingers on the arm of the chair. Nikki glanced at Sajid, opened her mouth to continue, but then closed it again. This was the exact opposite of what they'd been trained to do at a death notification. She shouldn't be fannying about letting him come to the ultimate conclusion on his own. Okay, so Archie wasn't related to either Karen or Winnie Salinger, but he was heavily invested in the family. She took a deep breath and as she saw the flash of realisation dart across Archie's eyes she stuttered the words out in a rush. 'We think, I mean Langley, me and Saj, think that it's possibly . . .'

'Winnie Salinger. You think it's Winnie, don't you?' He snatched his reading glasses off his nose and launched them onto the coffee table that stood between his armchair and the sofa where Saj and Nikki sat. His eyes lasered first Nikki and then Saj, his lips a thin strip in his flushed face.

'We're still waiting on the DNA for confirmation, boss. Langley's expedited it and it should come through soon, but . . .' Saj shrugged and left the rest of the sentence unsaid.

'Aye, I get it, laddie. There's no' much doubt, is there?' His shoulders collapsed and he shrunk in on himself like a deflated balloon attached to a rose bush, biding its time till it was buffeted against a thorn and extinguished with barely a pop to mark its demise. For the first time in ages, Nikki feared for Archie's well-being as his breathing accelerated, each breath shuddering from his frame like a thundering tube approaching the station. His complexion alternated between deadly pallor and sweaty flush within a matter of seconds.

As she watched helplessly, he pinched the bridge of his nose between thumb and index finger, and moaned in low guttural tones that made Nikki wince as she jumped up, took the two steps over to him and fell to her knees by his side, gripping his arm and squeezing hard. 'No, no, no. Not after all this time. That wee lassie survived till now and then this.'

With tears gathering in her eyes too, Nikki wanted to say so much to her mentor and friend. He'd been there for her through the dips in her career, her personal crises, the death of her mother and now, she would be there for him, but right now, all she could do was share his grief and will him to overcome this. *Come on, Archie, Come on. We'll see you through this. You can't leave me too!*

The Winnie Salinger investigation had clearly been the one that haunted him and now . . . ? Well now, it seemed that there was a link of some sort between the death of Winnie, her brother and her parents and her abduction or disappearance twelve years previously. Nikki just couldn't fathom what Karen Salinger had to do with any of it. However, the fact that she'd not been seen since before the deaths of her family and that there had been a fifth player at the crime scene meant finding her was a priority – as soon as they had official ID on Winnie Salinger.

But for now, she could see the effect this news had had on Archie. He may not have expected to ever find Winnie Salinger alive, but to realise she'd been alive all these years and had died so recently was a real punch in the gut. All the guilt from not having found her in the first place would resurface and Nikki knew how that felt. When her own husband Khalid had turned up dead years after he'd deserted her and Charlie and supposedly returned to Palestine, the guilt had almost broken Nikki. She would make sure it didn't break Archie. 'I'm sorry, Archie. So sorry.'

Archie sniffed, exhaled and then turned to her, a weak smile on his lips as he patted her arm. 'It's no' your fault, hen. The only one tae blame for this is the bastard that killed her. Noo, let's see what the hell I missed first time round.'

With an inner strength that Archie had displayed on numerous occasions during their working relationship, he straightened his shoulders, ran his splayed fingers through his balding pate and swallowed hard. With a final nod as if to underscore his resolve, Archie lifted one of his files, flicked it open and focused on its contents, ignoring the concerned glances shared by Nikki and Sajid. Taking their cue from Archie, they likewise lifted their files and began to learn Archie's thoughts on the long-closed Winnie Salinger disappearance.

Half an hour later, Nikki slammed her file closed in her lap and, from where she sat on the couch between her and Sajid, she glared at Archie. 'You didn't mention that Rawdon and Lyons were involved in the investigation.'

'Aye, they were the bee's knees back then, but we'll come tae that in a minute.'

A smile that didn't reach his eyes twitched Archie's lips as Saj discarded his file and took up where Nikki had left off. 'Nor does your file adequately explain *why* the allocated resources for the investigation were so sparse or why the investigation was shut down prematurely.'

'Aye, it was shut down too early for my liking. We didnae hae time to get things into gear after the first twenty-four hours where we focused on sandblasting the area with officers, with dogs, taking statements, getting the local and national media on side, involving local communities in organised search parties through the woods, scrutinising the family and those at the picnic. Soon as the crucial twenty-four hours had passed without a body being discovered or the wee lassie being found alive, and with no viable sightings, and no ransom, it seemed that the powers that be sort of . . .' He grimaced and rolled one shoulder as he tried to find an appropriate way to describe it. 'Well, it was like they sort of lost interest or something – the high heid yins, that is – the big bosses.'

His eyes drifted between the detectives before resting on a point somewhere between the two. 'Like they knew something the rest of us didn't?'

Nikki stared at him, waiting for him to continue, but when he didn't she undid her ponytail, gathered her hair up and reattached the band as she considered what she was missing. What wasn't Archie putting into words? As he lowered his gaze to his hands, annoyance combined with impatience vied within Nikki. Impatience she could master . . . annoyance not so much. Now she had to consider which to allow dominance. But before she'd opted for annoyance, which would have had her demanding Archie stop pratting about, Sajid jumped in. His face was flushed, his brown eyes – normally so liquid and soothing – were filled with dark sparks, so Nikki settled back and let him take the lead. From experience when Sajid was so annoyed, he didn't hold back – and right now, Nikki was happy to play "good cop" to his "bad cop".

'Fuck's sake, Archie. We've no time for this. I could be out there chasing up leads on Karen Salinger's whereabouts; instead, I'm here with you on the understanding that *you'd* give us something to go on, but all I've read is the same sanitised crap that I read from the official files. Either you bloody tell us what the big mystery is or I'm outta here.'

Archie blinked a couple of times, his mouth half open as he looked at Sajid. He cast a glance at Nikki who shrugged in a "you're on your own, mate" sort of gesture before swallowing hard. 'It's not easy for me, Saj. I don't want to influence you and Nikki. I just want . . .' He blinked a few times and his voice trailed away.

The annoyance Nikki had felt earlier when she'd realised he'd given her extension number to Peggy Marks's solicitor trailed away. *When did Archie begin to look so lost?* It wasn't like him. He was always larger than life, gruff and opinionated. Where had that Archie gone? Nikki really didn't like seeing this one, nor could she quash the pang of worry that gnawed at the edge of her mind. 'Look, just tell us what you think – the things not in the official files – your gut feelings, impressions – just anything that might tell us whether Winnie Salinger's abduction years ago is in any way related to her murder now. I mean, going on the assumption that the body in the morgue is her, then where the hell has she been all this time? She must have been somewhere. Was she abducted and held captive or did she run away?'

At her last words, Archie shook his head, his lips curled into an angry snarl. 'Course she didn't run away. She was a kid. Them parents of hers and the others at the picnic should have been looking out for her. She didn't leave them woods of her own volition. Someone took her and God only knows what's happened to her over the years.'

He slammed his palm onto the coffee table, making it wobble so much Nikki feared that it might collapse completely. It had already had its fair share of run-ins with Isaac and Sunni's boisterous games, and it wouldn't be a tragedy if it collapsed. However, she didn't want Archie getting his proverbials in a twist if he broke it. She jumped up. Moved and replaced the table with another, more stable one. 'I tend to agree with you, Arch, but we've got to look at all the angles.'

She looked down at him, her brow pulled into a stern frown. With a slow nod, Archie exhaled, then bundled up the papers and slotted them back into their folder. 'Sit down, Nikki hen. Let me tell you what happened.'

He waited till Nikki had resumed her seat beside Sajid and, eyes focused on Nikki's carpet, which she was aware needed hoovering – a job she was supposed to have done – he began. 'It was such a lovely day. The sort of day where nothing bad should ever happen and yet, as soon as I arrived in those woods, I knew that we wouldn't find her. There was something off about the way the parents spoke about her. Like she was some sort of Lolita-type character when she was in fact just a wee lassie – a wean. They seemed more interested in their younger kids' wellbeing than in their older daughter's whereabouts. Their responses chilled me to the marrow. They looked . . .' he glanced from Saj to Nikki, his eyes daring them to disagree with his assessment of the Salinger parents '. . . shifty. Like they knew something yet weren't prepared to share it with us. Something felt "off". At first, I wondered if they'd had a ransom note from whoever took Winnie and were told not to involve us, so I got their bank accounts scrutinised and we were damned if we could find any notable movement of money that could have been a ransom . . .'

Settling back in the chair, fingers linked in his lap, Archie continued. 'It was almost like they knew something bad had happened to her, yet they couldn't tell us what it was. Derek Bland, the lassie's godfather seemed more distressed than they did, but even that felt off to me.' He wafted his hands in the air. 'Don't get me wrong, I wasn't judging them. God knows how I'd have reacted if it had been my bairn who'd gone missing. Maybe they were just trying to hold it together for the younger kids. But, no matter how hard I tried, I couldn't shake the feeling that I was missing something. All those years have passed and I can still feel it. Here in mah craw. I can still feel it even now. Like a wedge o' tattie that won't go doon mah gullet.' He prodded his chest.

'We were barely two weeks into the investigation and those at the top were making noises about us scaling things down. I mean what the hell?' Archie scraped his fingers over his near bald head again, this time sending straggly bits of hair standing up on end at either side of his head like horns. 'That wee lassie was out there and Lyons and Rawdon – they were both DCIs at that point – were talking about maximising resources and redirecting spending to investigations that they considered more likely to bring dividends. I wanted to smash their supercilious heids together. A wee lassie was oot there and they didn't think she was worth spending money on?' A sigh shuddered from him. 'Maybe if we'd kept looking we would have found her. Maybe she wouldn't be lying cold in your fella's morgue right now, if Rawdon and Lyons had just done their jobs all those years ago . . . and let me do mine.'

Archie's words hovered like an unexploded bomb in the room until at last, Sajid leaned forward. 'I saw from your original file that Rawdon was your DCI, but I hadn't realised Lyons was involved in the investigation too.'

'Ttt. He wasn't. *That*'s my point. Rawdon was my DCI yet it felt like it was Lyons pulling the strings. Like he and Rawdon had some agenda or other going on and to be frank I couldn't quite get to grips with it. None of us could.' He paused, head to one side. 'Apart from one of the DS's – bloke by the name of Ged Geraghty. He was a vicious git. Got admonished several times for being too physical with the prisoners he brought into the station. He was right up their arses. Bloody tosser couldn't hack it anyway and he left policing not long after the Salinger abduction.'

Nikki studied her file, looking for the DS whose name she was unfamiliar with. 'You ever come across this Geraghty again?'

'Nah. He wasn't one you'd forget. Ugly-looking fucker with a BO problem that was almost as bad as his attitude. He was no loss. Wasn't up to the job, but he was right good at smarming with the hoi polloi.'

'What happened to him?'

Archie shook his head. 'No idea. Probably went into security – that's what a lot of them that couldn't hack it did in those days.'

Archie met Nikki's eyes. 'Not finding that wee lassie tainted my proverbials ye ken, Nikki. Made me question myself, my abilities. That's why I decided I'd stop when I got to DCI. My heart wasn't in the idea of working too closely with the likes of Rawdon and Lyons. They played the game and got the stripes. Me? All I wanted was to catch the toe rags and scumbags.' He sniffed. 'Might have left myself not long after that, but a cocky wee prickly thing with no manners and the ability to rile everybody was assigned to my team and I knew right then and there that she was worth nurturing. That she had an honesty about her that would make her a good copper.'

The unfamiliar sensation of having her chest being filled with bubbles, whilst simultaneously being grounded, hit Nikki. Something tingled behind her eyes, making her nose twitch. She snorted. 'Get a grip, boss. Just cause you've retired doesn't mean you can go all soppy on me.'

Archie grinned. 'See, prickly as a haggis on a thistle.'

He leaned over and patted Nikki's knee. 'The reason I put you in touch with Peggy Marks's solicitor is that her case never sat right with me either. Peggy Marks was an abductee who supposedly escaped her abductors after years of abuse and made her way home to her family, only to kill them. It wasn't my case, but I watched it play out with interest. It always struck me as strange and her talk of being abducted made me request that we reassess Winnie's disappearance, in light of the Marks case. However, her conviction put the kybosh on that. Exert witnesses deemed her testimony about her abduction unbelievable and a figment of her over-fertile imagination. I believe that because she was convicted of killing her family, the evidence she gave regarding the years of her "alleged" abduction wasn't investigated fully enough. The jury seemed to buy allegations of drug dependence and prostitution as motive for her actions and not enough was made of the fact that she was a child when she went missing. Nobody seemed to want to dwell too much on how an eleven-year-old had survived for so long on her own. It was a farce.

The powers that be – namely our friends Superintendent Rawdon and Chief Superintendent Lyons – dismissed my concerns faster than a streaker in a snowstorm.'

Nikki exchanged a glance with Sajid, to see if he too was missing a link. His slight shrug told her that he was as confused as she. Why would Archie see a link between the disappearance of Winnie Salinger ten years ago and the murder of the Marks family by their daughter, four years later? Okay, it looked like Winnie Salinger had reappeared on the scene and had killed her own family eight years after going missing, but Nikki couldn't see how that could relate to a woman who'd committed a similar crime four years earlier and was now in prison. 'Eh . . . Not sure I get what you're driving at, Archie.'

Archie threw his arms up in the air and released a whoosh of air. 'I think we missed a trick, hen. I think something's off. Can't you see it?'

When Nikki shook her head, he turned to Sajid. 'You get it, don't you, laddie?'

But Sajid also shook his head.

'For all the proverbials . . .' Archie slowed his voice down as if he was addressing a couple of imbeciles. 'When the common denominator between two cases is the abduction of two pre-pubescent girls in a nearby locality and under similar circumstances, followed years later by the reappearance of one of the girls, Peggy Marks, and the subsequent murder of her entire family, it's a smoking proverbial, don't you agree?'

Before Nikki or Saj could respond he prodded his finger in the air to punctuate his point. 'Especially now it's happened again . . .'

Nikki took a moment to get her head round it. The files she'd scrutinised at work were all about the Marks family murder investigation and because she'd been pressed for time, she'd skim-read them. She hadn't thought to look any further than the most recent updates. Now, she realised that she'd also missed a trick. '*Two* abducted girls? You mean, Peggy Marks was abducted and then reappeared, just like we think Winnie did, therefore the two cases must be connected?'

'Now, you've got it. Didn't Hewes tell you?'

A slow flush spread over her Nikki's cheeks as she recalled her impatience with Archie for passing her number on and with Colin Hewes for disturbing her.

Archie, head to one side, tapped his fingers on the chair arm. 'Peggy Marks was abducted four years prior to Winnie and, like Winnie, was portrayed as some precocious kid – like a bloody Lolita. Can you believe it? The press all but bloody victim-blamed a twelve-year-old. Of course, nobody believed Peggy's account of what happened to her – that she'd been abducted – kept in a mansion with a whole load of other children, boys and girls, and then when she'd paid back what she owed them, they let her go with a bag full of money. The investigation was a farce. It was on the back of that conviction that both Lyons and Rawdon moved up the ranks. Nobody listened to me and, until yesterday, I'd put it to the back of my mind.'

Nikki looked at Sajid. 'Well, now we know where we're going tomorrow.'

Saj's phone vibrated across the couch and when he grabbed it up and read the text, his lips tightened. 'The DNA's back. Definitely Winnie Salinger, not Karen.'

'Fuck!' Although they'd been expecting this, having it confirmed meant decisions had to be made. At some point they'd have to release that information to the press, but that could wait till the scheduled press update at lunchtime tomorrow. Before that, she'd have to inform the chief super – maybe Ahad would tell Lyons for her. Not likely. *She* was SIO and it was her responsibility to keep senior officers informed of developments and both the chief super and Superintendent Rawdon had instructed her that they wanted to be informed of all developments.

Whilst Saj waited for her to expand on her expletive, Nikki looked at Archie. His expression told her all she needed to know.

She turned to Saj. 'We speak with Peggy Marks first thing as planned – get that sorted for me, will you?'

When Saj nodded she continued. 'Then, we'll share the DNA information with Rawdon and Lyons, prior to the next press briefing. I don't want to risk anyone leaking the information or putting a spin on it. After we hear what Marks has to share, we'll decide on how to proceed with that. Meanwhile, I'll bring Farah and Liam up to speed.'

Chapter 32

Peggy Marks looked nothing like Nikki had expected her to look. She'd seen the pictures of an emaciated, fragile-looking woman being escorted to and from court proceedings during her trial, but the person waiting in the interview room at New Hall prison looked very different. Instead of the bemused, childlike expression she'd carried during the trial she had a hardness to her eyes, a coldness that spoke of a lifetime of difficulties and traumas. It didn't escape Nikki that, if Peggy Marks's account was true, this young woman had spent more of her life incarcerated in one place or another, than she had as a free person. If her story was true, if there had been a huge miscarriage of justice, then this woman had been abducted at twelve, suffered ten years of abuse and exploitation only to be released at the age of twenty-two never having been outside the confines of the "mansion" she claimed to have been held captive in.

Hoping that fresh eyes might shed some light on the strange direction Marks's trial and the investigation into her family's murder had taken, Nikki had tasked Anwar and Williams with going over the files again. However, this time instead of considering the evidence in isolation, her officers would be scrutinising it for links or similarities with Winnie Salinger's disappearance and of course, the Salingers' murders. It would be time-consuming work, but Nikki trusted that if there was anything to be found, Liam and Farah would discover it.

The thought of how traumatic it would have been for Marks to re-enter a society that had changed so dramatically over her captive years, had Nikki itching to punch a wall. She'd met men like those who'd abducted Peggy Marks and Winnie Salinger – fuck's sake, her own father had been one – a predator of the worst sort. They existed, like shape-shifting monsters who could fit into normal society with ease whilst hiding their perversions beneath a cloak of respectability. Nikki was determined to snatch that cloak from Winnie Salinger and Peggy Marks's abductors and expose them for the animals they were.

Peggy's chin jutted towards Nikki and Sajid as they walked across the room and took their seats on the opposite side of the table. Her shoulders were pulled back, her entire body tensed as if bracing herself against whatever blow was about to befall her. Thin lines trailed across her brow and from the sides of her mouth. Scars etched far deeper than any twenty-six-year-old should have. But beneath the outward signs of her suffering, Nikki detected a strength born of necessity. It was there in the muscles that now bulged from her upper arms and the contours of her body. A fleeting image of Nikki herself hammering her punchbag flitted into her mind, but the face she saw, mouth stretched to a thin line, eyes flashing with hate and anger and frustration, wasn't her own. She'd overlaid her features with Peggy's and, as she met the other woman's unflinching stare, she recognised a fellow survivor. Like her, Peggy Marks found solace and redemption in bashing a punchbag to within an inch of its life.

Colin Hewes sat beside Peggy. He was younger than Nikki had expected – late twenties tops – and Nikki understood how Peggy's plight might have captured the interest of a young fresh-faced solicitor four years ago – one who had yet to harden himself against the cut and thrust of a murder trial. One who had been out of his depth and who felt he'd let his client down. The fact that he was still her solicitor told Nikki that he was committed to Peggy – that he believed her story. His gentle, hopeful smile reinforced that thought as he stretched over the table and shook first hers and then Sajid's hands.

Out of courtesy, Nikki introduced herself and Sajid to Peggy, but other than a slight nod of acknowledgement, Peggy Marks remained impassive – no smile, no flicker of emotion in her eye, no noticeable increase in breathing – a statue waiting for the blow that would shatter her.

Nikki not only understood the younger woman's reaction, but she admired it too. It was a coping strategy she herself adopted on occasion. By holding herself tightly in check, Peggy Marks would be better equipped to deal with whatever would come her way. When very little was within her control, maintaining a neutral façade allowed her to regulate herself – it was her way of harnessing some power. Nobody could snatch her interior thoughts and emotions away from her, and they certainly couldn't when she didn't allow anyone access to them.

Before they arrived, Nikki and Sajid had decided that they would be led by Peggy. Neither she nor Sajid had read the files on Peggy's disappearance, preferring to hear her account first. Nor had they delved any deeper into the files on the murder of her family and the subsequent court case that had found her guilty of their murders. If Peggy was actually innocent of the crimes she'd been convicted of, then Nikki could only imagine how difficult it had been for her to grieve for the family she'd been taken from years earlier and whom she'd only just reconnected with.

On the other hand, Peggy Marks could be a hard-faced liar. Despite Archie's conviction that Peggy had been wrongly convicted, Nikki and Sajid would keep an open mind. After all, an intensive police inquiry and subsequent trial had found this woman guilty of three murders. Over the course of her career, Nikki had encountered the evillest people who had managed to fool the general public for years. Her dead husband Khalid had been killed by two of them and, in all the years until their crimes were uncovered, Nikki hadn't once questioned their friendship to her or their goodness. This time she would be on high alert.

'Well, Peggy. You asked Mr Hewes here to contact me and . . .' she splayed her hands before her, palms up '. . . here I am. I'm here to listen if you want to talk. But . . .' Nikki met Peggy's dark gaze '. . . this is a one-time only deal. If you don't convince me you've got something that will help my current investigation, then we're gone. If I get the sense that you're lying – we're gone. You try to play me . . .' Nikki's lips twitched, her head to one side as she wafted her hand before her. 'You get my drift?'

Peggy maintained eye contact for a long time and it took all of Nikki's willpower not to blink. Finally, her voice croaky as if unused to speaking, Peggy replied. 'Yeah, I get it. I fuck with you and you're gone.'

She leaned forward, resting her arms on the table, revealing scars across her wrist and three prison tattoos that bore the names of her brother – Jamie – and Mum and Dad, each with a crude love heart encircling them. Nikki's eyes fell to the scars and the tattoos. The cynic in her wondered if the tattoos were a sort of trophy, but something about the way Peggy stroked the fingers of her opposite hand over them told Nikki that they served the same purpose as her elastic band. Their presence on her wrist was Peggy's stress buster. Of course, that didn't necessarily mean that she was innocent of killing her family, or that they weren't a reminder of her crimes. They could be a stress buster *and* a memory of a euphoric violent experience. As Sajid set his phone to record, Nikki leaned back and waited.

Before she began, Peggy exchanged a glance with her solicitor. His smile and the way he placed a hand on her tattooed arm for a moment before nodding made Nikki wonder if it there was something more personal in their relationship. But when Peggy started to speak, she shelved that thought as irrelevant.

'Saw the news, 'bout the Salingers.' Peggy tugged her sleeve down, covering her tattoos and the scars, then nodded once as if giving herself a silent pep talk. 'I recognised that kid – the one they say was taken years ago.' She frowned and her leg began bouncing up and down, sending a shudder over the table each time it hit the table leg. 'She was still there when he let me go – Rose, her name was.'

She exhaled and then bowed her head, her voice reduced to a husky murmur. 'Course that weren't her real name. None of us were allowed to use our real names.' She rubbed the palm of her hand up and over her nose before continuing. 'Best friends with a girl called Lily, she were. Poor cow couldn't speak – Lily that is – never made a noise.'

Peggy head jerked up, her juddering knee increasing in intensity, her eyes focused on something beyond Nikki's shoulder. Something beyond the walls of the prison, something in the far reaches of her memory. At that point, observing Peggy, Nikki knew in her gut that every word this tortured woman spoke was true. Now, all she had to do was prove it. Prove Peggy's innocence, find Karen Salinger, whose innocence was still in doubt, and bring down every one of the bastards responsible for what she was beginning to suspect had far wider ramifications than the fate of these two women.

Peggy's voice lowered to barely a whisper and Nikki leaned closer to catch her words. 'I hope she's all right. Rose, I mean. She were a nice kid. And the quiet one – her too.'

Nikki's heart contracted. Although she'd have to tell Peggy that Rose/Winnie was dead before the press leaked it, she took a deep breath and said, 'They gave you new names? Flower names?'

'Only the girls. Mine was Violet.' Head bowed, she added, 'The boys were named after metals.'

It didn't surprise Nikki that both boys and girls had been abducted and kept in this mansion, but it did chill her. The way Peggy was talking made it seem that there were many more victims than they'd originally suspected and as Peggy had been abducted fourteen years ago, then that meant this had been going on for over a decade. The hairs on Nikki's arms stood on end as the enormity of what she was hearing sunk in and a rage as dark as hell itself almost robbed her of breath.

How many children had been taken? How could no one have noticed that so many kids were being abducted? How could her colleagues not have put all these missing children together? She swallowed hard, avoiding looking at Sajid, because she knew he'd be thinking of what her father had tried to do to her and Anika and the extent of his depravity. She couldn't bear to see the sympathy in his eyes. Not right now, because this wasn't about her. It was about Peggy Marks and all the little flower girls and metal boys whose innocence had been stolen. In a quiet voice, she asked, 'How many children were there with you, Peggy?'

Peggy rolled her shoulders and glanced at Hewes who cleared his throat, opened his briefcase and extracted a file, which he pushed across the table to Nikki. 'We've worked together on this since the trial. This is everything Peggy can remember about the children she lived with.' He paused, looked down at his hands. 'They came and went over the years. It seemed some couldn't adapt to . . .' he frowned and bit his lip '. . . their new living arrangements.'

New living arrangements? Such a sanitised way to describe how these children lived, yet Nikki got it. Even that phrase had made Peggy flinch. She wasn't ready to hear it spoken of in any other way. Nikki looked at the file on the table, then raised her eyes to meet those of the pair sitting opposite. She didn't want to reach out and take the file. Didn't want to open it and see the suffering of these children in black and white. 'You gave this file to the officers investigating Peggy's family's murder?'

His lips lifted in a smile that didn't meet his eyes. 'It's been added to over the years, but yes, of course we gave them as much as Peggy could remember. They said it was fantasy. Got "experts" to discredit everything she said. We got our own, but the police chose to believe the witnesses they'd paid for and refused to sanction they investigate further.'

Peggy scraped her chair back from the table, stood up and began pacing the room. 'They said there was nothing that could be substantiated in here. I didn't know the kids' real names or anything about them.'

Peggy turned and stood facing the wall. From the tension radiating across the other woman's shoulders, Nikki knew she was struggling to regain control. When she eventually turned back to face them, her face was flushed. 'I couldn't tell them where the mansion was. Couldn't describe it from the outside. The description of the man who took me – Scarface, we called him – wasn't accurate enough.' She strode over, flopped into the chair, her legs splayed at an angle as if she couldn't hold herself upright for a second longer. Her hands trembled in her lap as she whispered. 'I was just a kid myself.'

This was hard, so hard, but Nikki couldn't allow Peggy to hear of Rose or Winnie's death on the media. She cleared her throat and looked directly into Peggy's eyes, her face schooled to display none of the squirming flutters that filled her chest. The easiest, most humane way to deliver this sort of news was straight out, with no faffing about. Yet despite knowing this, the temptation to be oblique and allow them to work it out for themselves was almost overpowering. Nikki positioned her hands under her thighs to avoid the temptation to twang her band and straightened her shoulders. 'Peggy, I've got some bad news for you. I'm afraid Winnie, or Rose as you knew her by, is dead. The younger woman, who we initially thought was Karen Salinger, has been identified positively as Winnie Salinger, her sister. I'm sorry.'

For long seconds, Peggy remained immobile, then her eye twitched and her brow furrowed. 'They let her go and then killed her . . . Scarface killed her. You've got to put a stop to this. You've got to.'

Her fingers found her scarred wrist and she began plucking at the scars, her eyes empty, like she was the one who was dead. There was nothing Nikki could do and as Hewes reached across and gently removed Peggy's fingers from her wounds, Nikki nodded. 'I will. I promise, I will.'

She lifted the file from the table. She gave an abrupt nod to first the solicitor and then Peggy. In a trembling voice, rough with emotion, she said, 'We'll be in touch if we need anything else from you.'

And without a backward glance she strode to the door, Sajid trailing behind. She hammered on the door and when it opened marched out.

Chapter 33

Present Day: Marnie

I must have been exhausted because I wake up disorientated and in a sweat with my heart pounding. At first, I think I'm back in the dungeon, that they'd come and taken Gwen and me back – that we'd done something wrong, but then I realise that the smell is different, that I'm in the cramp crummy flat Gwen got for us.

As I try to catch my breath the sky growls and flashes of lightning streak through the room, revealing it in all its dismal splendour, and I see that Gwen's still not back. *Oh, Gwen, where are you?* It's been over two days now – forty-eight hours at least since she left and every part of my skin itches with worry for her. I know all too well that a lot can happen in a couple of days – a lot can go wrong.

I haven't forgotten my pledge from the previous night. If Gwen doesn't come back today then I'll have to do something. I just don't know what yet. My stomach rumbles, so I force myself to my feet. Gwen bought in some shopping for us, but I can't be bothered cooking eggs or bacon. Instead, I open a box of Cheerios and fill a bowl and add a splash of milk. Cross-legged on the bed, I try to force them down my gullet, but even with the milk they scratch my throat and I can barely swallow even a couple of mouthfuls, so I place the bowl on the threadbare carpet and stroll over to the window.

Outside, rain pounds onto the street throwing sprays of water in its wake as people scurry about under cover of umbrellas, trying to dodge puddles as they make their way through the storm. Thunderclouds cast a strange grey shadow on the proceedings and for a moment I imagine I'm watching one of the old black and white films Gwen and I sometimes watched when we weren't required elsewhere. Gwen told me they were called silent movies and were made specially for me. I didn't believe her, yet it was nice to think of them as mine – ours. We'd smiled, holding hands, cuddled close as the images and old-fashioned humour flickered across the screen. Those were some of the rare moments when Gwen seemed truly relaxed. Like she wasn't acting at being all tough and in charge, for once. Like we were in a bubble where the only things that existed was us. A bubble that made up for all the bad stuff.

I peer through the gloom, willing Gwen to appear, drenched and cold, but with a smile on her face. But no matter how hard I try to conjure her image up in the rain's mist, she's not there. *Oh, Gwen, where are you?* A slimy cold sensation spreads slowly up my spine, like acid burning my flesh away – it's piercingly cold, yet caustic and I can't pretend to myself anymore. Something has happened to Gwen. There's no other explanation for her continued absence. What should I do? What can I do?

I whirl back from the window, stumbling in my haste and heedless of the tears blurring my vision. I release a silent roar into the room – my chest explodes as no sound accompanies my anguish. After what might have been ages, but may equally have been only seconds, I come back to myself. My tears begin to dry on my cheeks and I'm aware that the sound of the storm outside is less aggressive. The mellow splashing of rain on my window echoes my heart and I throw back my shoulders and it's then that Jilly's voice sounds in my mind and this time it's not her usual mantra about the Beep Beeps. This time, her voice seems sort of three-dimensional – like she's within reach and, this time, I *know* I need to act when she tells me, *You can do this, Marnie. You can do this on your own. You're strong enough. You've survived this long. You can do it.*

I sniff a last sniff, brush the last of my tears away and smile. 'I'll try, Jilly.'

The words are still only in my head – in my thoughts, but they're made of iron and bronze and silver and all the metals my still-captive brothers are named after and they grow, strong and firm and fragrant like my captive flower sisters Daisy and Bluebell and Peony. For the first time, I realise that this isn't only about us – about me and Gwen – this is about those others. The ones we left behind. The ones we're expected to forget, the ones who are still suffering. It's not even only for them though. It's also for all the ones like Honeysuckle who were taken away. The flowers discarded like weeds somewhere they'd never be found.

Anger at Gwen for leaving me and not helping me to see this before slices though me, but I don't give it space. Without Gwen, I *have* to do something. I have to be strong. My frantic gaze flutters round the room and comes to rest on Gwen's rucksack. What a fool I am. In an instant I'm over the room grabbing the backpack and throwing it on the bed. My fingers pulling at the buckles, yanking it open. On top is the wad of cash Scarface gave us. I toss it to the side. It'll be useful, but it's not essential. Underneath that are the passports – I've seen those before – another name they've given us, another lie they want me to live, so I toss those aside too. What I want is something – *anything* that might tell me where Gwen has gone, because I'm convinced now that she's broken Scarface's last rule and she's gone back home.

Of course, she has. That was *always* what she would do. If only I'd been smart enough to see that. Smart enough to realise that although Gwen pretended to comply all these years, she never did – not really. She only ever gave them enough to keep herself and us safe. That's why she's gone off on her own, leaving me behind with the money and a new identity – in case something happened to her.

I'm so angry with her that right now if she walked through the door, I'd scratch her eyes out – well after hugging her, I would. She'd no right to take control away from me – no right at all. That's not what we do. It's then as I'm fumbling through her meagre supply of clothes that it strikes me again – harder this time. Although I'm the one who doesn't speak, Gwen's the one whose silence is more pronounced. She's left me with nothing – no clue to where she might have gone or who she was before all of this. Even now, her silence yells at me in this quiet dismal room and I feel let down.

At the very bottom of the rucksack wrapped in a vest top, there's a very thin pile of pages – scraps of paper ripped from magazines and books, folded over to make a different book. She's used an elastic band round the middle to keep the pages together. At first, I think it's something she's smuggled in from her previous existence – a book she's made as a kid and kept with her all this time, then I open it and see handwriting that I recognise as easily as my own. Gwen's rounded letters and stubby scrawl.

I will make you pay.

I will make you pay.

I will make you pay.

I will make you pay.

I will make you pay.

I will make you pay.

Like lines given as a punishment – I know who the "you" is. It's got to be Scarface or maybe at a push Auntie Lee-Lee – or maybe both of them. The lines go over both pages, so I turn to the next page and it's the same again. I flick through another three of Gwen's makeshift pages before I find something different – a note addressed to me.

> Dear Marnie,
> If you've found this note it's because they've found me.
> No matter what they told us, you have to be brave. You **have** to go out into the world and you **have** to find Jilly. You have to go to the police and tell them what's happened. You have to. You can do this. You have to use your voice.
> Love always, your Gwennie xxx

Then tucked behind the letter to me are the final pieces of paper. I unfold them. They're not scrappy bits like the others; these are proper pieces of good paper. I frown as my eyes scan down the sheets, then I fold them up and tuck them down my bra.

Chapter 34

'Well?' Nikki moved so fast that Sajid had to scurry to keep up with her, yet she couldn't slow down. Not with all those jumbled thoughts crowding her brain, making her want to clutch her pounding head and scream. Peggy Marks's story rang too true to be dismissed. Nikki could see it, Archie could see it, Colin Hewes could see it and she was sure her partner, Sajid, could see it too. Yet still no one had properly investigated her account. Everyone had been too focused on putting her away for killing her family and they'd let her account of her abduction and abuse slide.

True, Peggy Marks, regardless of whether she'd been abducted as a child, might still be guilty of murdering her family. However, that didn't mean her disappearance shouldn't be investigated to the fullest extent of the law. Which drove Nikki to consider why the young woman would kill her entire family. Had she blamed them for her abduction? Had she thought that neglect on their part had resulted in her being taken? Perhaps she thought they should have rescued her or maybe a jealous rage had overcome her and she'd lashed out with a knife to hurt those who'd lived their lives without her. Who knew? Nikki didn't – nobody could.

However, none of that mattered, right now. What was important was corroborating Peggy's story and going from there. For, if what she'd told them was true, and if the information in the files Peggy and Hewes had compiled during her incarceration proved accurate, then they had to investigate and investigate fast. Who knew how many children were suffering? How many families of missing children were needlessly grieving?

'Wait up, Nik.'

Sajid's strangled voice made her pause and glance at him. His skin was pale and his hands trembled as they reached out to rest on her arm. She wasn't the only one affected by what they'd just heard, but she was the boss and she needed to lead by example. She placed her hand over Saj's and squeezed. 'Sorry. Just . . .'

He smiled and shook his head. 'No . . . no apology. I'm shaken. You're shaken. Let's take a moment and then swallow up our rage before driving back to Bradford.'

He was right. Nikki forcibly relaxed her shoulders and felt some of the tension drain away. Not all of it – she was too angry for that – but enough to calm her. She could use the drive to look at the file Hewes had given her. 'Come on then. Let's get cracking.'

The first page of the file gave a list of flower names – each a stolen girl according to Peggy. Rose was on there with a brief description of how she'd looked last time Peggy had seen her. A description that matched the images held on file of Winnie Salinger when she'd gone missing. Ones that matched the woman now confirmed as Winnie Salinger and who now lay in Langley's morgue.

Pansy. Crocus. Bluebell . . . Nikki's throat clogged up with unshed tears as she read more and more flower names. Never again would she be able to appreciate flowers in the same way. Flowers should be free – in gardens, in forests, in the wild. Not viciously plucked from the hearts of their families and trapped in a life of hell.

So many of them – at least fifteen – yet, according to the scrawled handwritten note at the bottom, this list was not exhaustive because Peggy had suffered from long periods of being on "automatic pilot" where she couldn't remember things very clearly. How could these children not have been missed? Of course, Peggy didn't know their real names, which made it harder to find them. However, using the approximate ages and descriptions provided by Peggy, Nikki and her team would have a damn good shot at trying to identify these girls from the missing persons' lists. She flipped a page and was confronted by a shorter list of seven names – Zinc, Iron, Cobalt, Silver, Bronze, Gold, Copper – the abducted boys, named after metals. Again, Peggy had provided an approximate age and as detailed a description as she could of each of the boys.

Taking a deep breath, Nikki closed the file and looked out the side window without seeing a thing.

'Nik?' When she didn't respond, Sajid raised his voice. 'Nik, Nik. You okay?'

As if surprised to find herself in the car beside Sajid, Nikki turned to him, blinking rapidly. A smile fluttered across her face. She could tell by the sideways glances and the criss-crossing frowns on his forehead that Saj was concerned for her. He was worried that this was too much for her to handle. That she'd succumb to the dark destruction of depression that she'd had before.

Would she?

She considered the possibility for a moment and then discarded it. No, she wasn't in *that* place anymore. Nowadays, she was better equipped to take care of her mental health. Besides, she was angry and that anger propelled her forward.

Of course, the contents of the file, the meeting with Peggy, the crime scene of the Salinger murders and the attitude of her senior officers bothered her, but she'd deal with it. She reached over and squeezed his arm. 'This is one of the worse cases we've been on.'

She tilted her head to one side. 'And we've been on a few nasty ones together, but we'll do this. Together we'll solve this.'

She released his arm and then prodded his shoulder. 'I'm not *losing* it, Malik. Not yet anyway.'

'Ouch, Nik. You need to bloody stop that prodding business. It's hurting.'

Nikki grinned, aware that Sajid was hamming it up, to keep their spirits raised. 'If you think that hurt, just wait till you see what I've got planned for your stag do.'

The car veered slightly, then Saj mumbled under his breath, 'Knew I should've gone for Liam as my best man.'

Chapter 35

I spy with my little eye something beginning with D . . .
Dispensable.

Weeding out the rot is always such a satisfying feeling. Pruning the dead wood away, leaving room for future growth, amputating infected branches – it's all a necessary part of business management. Perhaps not the *most* satisfying, but for me at least it's up there with directing funds to offshore bank accounts. Being in control engenders a feeling of being cocooned and safe yet the edginess of my risk-taking keeps me alert and focused. Having dispensed with a problem, I feel alive – like every synapse is on fire. So much so that I almost bounce into my office, smiling and greeting people with an affability they don't quite know what to do with.

Despite the perpetual downpour, I have a good feeling about things. Especially now that Scarface has carried out my instructions. Such a feeling of satisfaction when your orders are carried out to the T. The day has started off so well. Particularly in light of yesterday's fiasco. My mind flicks to it and some of my good humour is doused, so I shut those thoughts down. No point on dwelling on yesterday's troubles when you have today's delights to look forward to. Now all I have to do is wait for the inevitable commotion to kick off and I'll be able to kick back and watch it all from a distance.

Still, I mustn't be complacent. I have to keep on top of things, so I pick up the burner phone and double-check that Scarface is in position. 'Eyes on?'

When he replies, his voice is tinged with amusement which, on another day, I might interpret as verging on insolence. But today, I'm omnipotent and gracious, so I let it go – for now as he says. 'Eyes on.'

I hang up, toss the phone back in my drawer and lock it, humming The Black Eyed Peas' "I Gotta Feeling" as I settle down to work.

Chapter 36

Crowded into DCI Ahad's office, Nikki had elected to bring her team up to speed away from the rest of the officers involved in Operation Chalice. Although she had known most of the uniformed officers for years, she couldn't shake the feeling that she had to watch her back because she still wasn't sure who was leaking information to Lisa Kane. Besides, she wanted to keep this side of the investigation under her belt until she'd spoken about it with Superintendent Rawdon and Chief Super Lyons. She wanted to look into their eyes when she told them that she'd visited Peggy Marks in prison and that she wanted to link Peggy's abduction allegations with the abduction and subsequent murder of Winnie Salinger and the rest of her family. She had a strong case – the fact that two missing girls had reappeared years later and had links to a crime scene where their entire families had been killed was a strong argument.

However, no one on Nikki's team thought she'd have an easy ride. Rawdon and Lyons had shown all too clearly that they were happy to sacrifice Nikki if it furthered their agenda – whatever that was. Archie's suspicions regarding Rawdon and Lyons's honesty worried her. Would they be prepared to ignore Peggy's evidence in order to save face? For that matter, Nikki couldn't fathom why they hadn't immediately drawn a link between the Marks case and Operation Chalice. It was almost as if they knew they were linked and had decided to insert themselves closely into the investigation to thwart progress. Of course, they were entitled to any and all information on ongoing investigations, yet they'd never indicated any desire to be so hands-on before.

They'd closed the office blinds and DCI Ahad had cleared his desk by piling all his files and paperwork into a huge box and depositing it by the wall next to the plant Nikki had gifted him. Sajid, Zain, Farah and Liam sat round the desk, hot drinks in front of them and a pack of ginger nuts beside Farah, whilst Nikki, still agitated after their meeting with Peggy, paced back and forth at the end of the table, trying to get her thoughts in order before she began the briefing.

'Before we start, any updates on Derek Bland or Karen Salinger's whereabouts?' Nikki would have been notified immediately if there were any credible sightings of them, but she couldn't resist asking. After being met with headshakes, she put the thought of those two out of her mind for the time being. Everything that could done to locate them was being done. Bland, however, had been smart. He'd left his phone and his vehicle behind. Unless they got a witness ID, they were stumped.

Now, with Peggy's files copied and distributed to her team, Nikki took a deep breath and set about issuing instructions. 'The dilemma we have right now, is that we have to juggle various elements that may or may not be linked. Our task today is threefold. One, we need to find Karen Salinger, who at the moment is either a suspect in the murders of her family or a key witness. Two, now we have confirmed that victim number four is Winnie Salinger, we need to revisit her initial disappearance with fresh eyes; re-interview the other people at the picnic that day – the kids will be grown up now, so perhaps they can offer some insight based on hindsight or stuff they might have picked up over the years. Thirdly, we need to match every name in this file with children reported missing, over the past . . .' she paused and gave a one-shouldered shrug '. . . say thirteen years and up to five years ago when Peggy Marks says she was returned to society, having passed her expiry date. We can extend the search parameters if necessary, but that gives us a solid starting point. Thoughts?'

Williams looked up. 'If it's okay with you, boss, I'll light a firework under the techies. They should have reported back on Karen's devices by now and I'd say that's imperative at this point. They've requested information from her phone service provider so I'm hoping that might also point us to her regular haunts. As you know her phone has been inactive since Sunday evening. I've also arranged Zoom meetings with her friends from Cambridge—' he looked at his watch '—in an hour's time. After that I've set up meetings with some of her school friends.'

Nikki was about to respond when he lifted his hand in the air. 'Oh, and if I've got time, I'm going to follow up on the CCTV at Sukhi Kholi's flat.'

Nikki grinned. She was pleased that Williams was showing so much initiative and that he was juggling various balls in the air. 'Good for you, Liam. Looks like you and Farah will be busy today.'

As the two exchanged a look that Nikki couldn't quite define, Farah spoke up. 'Actually, Liam can handle this on his own. I'm going to focus on these files, if that's all right?'

Nikki scowled and took a moment to study each of them in turn. Williams, his lips turned down, was angled away from Farah, whilst Farah, who looked a tad clammy, was nibbling on one of her infernal biscuits. Nikki's gaze went from the younger woman's pallid face to the biscuit and back again. *Oh crap!* With a mental note to speak to Farah later in private, Nikki smiled. 'Yes, Farah, that's a good use of your skill set. Just keep me in the loop. Now, about Winnie Salinger's abduction? Any thoughts?'

Deliberately directing his gaze away from the Dark Knight, Sajid looked at Nikki. 'Look, I know this might not be popular, but bearing in mind the nature of the investigation and the restrictions of feet on the ground so to speak, I reckon we should . . .'

Ahad chipped in, nodding. 'Yes, I think Sajid's right, I think we . . .'

Sajid was shaking his head. 'No, no, you don't know what I was going to say. You won't think I'm right. We're not on the same wavelength here – not at all.'

Ahad's smirk was fleeting as a pucker flickered across his brow. 'Really? Not on the same wavelength? You and me?' A huff of air left his lips as he shook his head from side to side, hands clutched to his chest like he was mortally wounded. 'I thought you were Robin to my Batman, Saj.'

A bloom of red blossomed across Saj's cheeks as he glared at Nikki before getting back to his point. 'What I'm suggesting is that we . . .'

'Enlist Archie to re-interview the witnesses from the Winnie Salinger investigation.'

'No, that's . . .' Saj's lips tightened and a frown creased his forehead.

'No . . . ?' Ahad's lips pursed.

'Well, I mean yes. That's what I was going to suggest, but . . .'

Nikki's voice cut across them, as Liam and Farah attempted to cover up their amusement by becoming engrossed in their tablets. 'If you two are quite finished clowning about . . . I agree. Exceptional circumstances call for exceptional measures. We'll get Archie in on the QT and I was thinking PCs Harry Dosanjh and Gemma Gregson would work well with him. Agreed?'

As everyone nodded, Nikki pulled a chair out and sat down. For the first time since meeting Peggy Marks earlier, she felt her mood shift. These people – her team – were phenomenal. 'So, Sajid and Farah will work Peggy's files whilst DCI Ahad and I brave the Lyons's den . . .' She paused, grinning, and looked expectantly round the table. When nobody responded she rolled her eyes. 'For God's sake, don't you get it – Lyons – lions?'

When she was still met with blank looks she tutted and scowled at them. 'L.y.o.n.s's den not l.i.o.n's den. Get it now?'

Sajid grinned and slapped his thigh, insincerity lacing every word as he said, 'Good one, Nik!'

Chapter 37

'You ready for this, Nik?' DCI Ahad's tone was light, yet tension radiated off him in spades. His shoulders were pulled just a little too far back, his chin jutted up at an almost pugnacious angle and a pulse played at his temple.

Nikki, seeing all this, inhaled right to the pit of her gut, filling her entire upper body with air, which she released in a slow measured breath. She wasn't going to let Ahad's trepidation affect her mood. *Dark Knight indeed.* If Sajid could see him now, he'd have a different name for him. It was only as this thought passed through her mind that she realised: Zain's tension wasn't for himself – it was on her behalf. He was fearful of how she'd be treated and wanted to protect her.

Aw sweet!

However, if there was one thing set to get her gander up, it was feeling like she was being pitied. It brought out her inner Rottweiler and, in response, her own chin jutted out, her shoulders swung back, and her eyes darkened like glittering coal. *Now, I'm ready!*

She nodded once, then stepped forward and rapped her knuckles against the door bearing a gold plaque with the title *Detective Chief Superintendent Nathanial Lyons* in gold cursive script.

It wasn't often that Nikki was called up to the upper echelons of Trafalgar House, but on the rare occasions she visited, she was always struck by the plush carpets, the artworks displayed in matching frames along smoothly painted satin sheen walls and the over-sweet fruit scent that lingered in the corridors. It was as if she was in another world where the assorted aromas that pervaded her nostrils as she journeyed through the lower corridors of the police station were a distant memory: no vomit, no chemical scent of junkies high on synthetic drugs, no sweat, no bleach, no artificial lemon smell.

Regardless, Nikki knew where she preferred to work. Downstairs was real and honest and meant something. Up here were the pen pushers, policymakers and those wooed by the buzz that having authority gave them. Of course, there were a few exceptions to this rule. The previous superintendent had earned her stripes and made it her job to keep herself attuned to what was going on both above *and* below her. Nikki wasn't sure that either the current chief super or super had those skills at their disposal.

'Come!'

Nikki glanced at Zain and pretended to stick two fingers down her throat, but even her childish behaviour wasn't enough to tease a smile from his lips. This was bad. Zain was expecting the worst. So, Nikki stepped forward, thrust the door open and marched into the Lyons's den, stopping only when she reached the huge mahogany-coloured desk behind which he sat. Behind him the glare from the sun that was penetrating the grey clouds flitting across the sky haloed him, and Nikki had the feeling that Lyons knew all too well the image this provoked.

Three chairs were positioned in front of the desk, but Nikki ignored Lyons's indication that she and Zain should join Superintendent Rawdon who already sat on one of them, which was angled slightly away from the other two chairs. Instead, she jumped straight in. 'We don't have a lot of time to brief you, sir, as we're following many crucial leads at the moment and our attention must be on those. However, bearing in mind this afternoon's press briefing, we thought it wise to keep you updated, so . . .'

Lyons's smile mutated into a frown that pulled his brow tight. As his chin lifted, his jowls swung pendulously beneath it and his lips tightened. 'I'm afraid you seem to be under the impression that *you* can dictate the agenda, but I'm afraid you are mistaken, Detective Inspector Parekh. Perhaps your inability to manage your time and your staff has resulted in this—' he wafted his hand in the air between them '—desire to escape your responsibilities of feeding back to your senior officers.'

Nikki opened her mouth to refute his assertion, but behind her Superintendent Rawdon cleared his throat. 'Come on, Nat. Give the lass a chance, eh? Let's hear what she has to say; after all she requested the meeting. Then we'll decide whether she needs to hotfoot it back to the dungeons below or whether we should grill her a bit more.'

Beside her, Nikki was aware that Zain's shoulders had tensed further and a downward glance revealed that he'd tightened his hand into a fist and then just as quickly released it. Even if Zain was rattled by Rawdon's sarcastic put-downs, she couldn't afford to be. So, pulling every bit of diplomacy she'd ever learned from Sajid, she pasted a smile on her face and nodded at Rawdon before turning back to Lyons. 'Something has come to light as part of the ongoing investigation into the Salinger family murder and we need to decide how to proceed.'

Lyons held her gaze for a moment and then once more nodded to the empty chairs positioned just behind Nikki and Zain. 'Sit.'

Whilst turning and taking her seat, Nikki swallowed the anger that tightened her chest. There was no call to be so over-bearing. Being a dick didn't make Lyons a better boss – it just confirmed his dickiness. She quirked an eyebrow at him and waited for his nod before beginning. 'DNA analysis conducted during the post-mortem of the body originally believed to have been Karen Salinger has revealed that it is in fact that of her sister Winnie Salinger, who was abducted twelve years ago when she was eleven years old.'

Without intending to, Nikki found herself holding her breath, bracing herself for Lyons's and Rawdon's reactions. Outside the office, the sound of a muted conversation and phones ringing in the distance were the only discernible sounds for interminable moments. During this time Nikki focused on analysing the fleeting emotions that flicked over Lyons's face. Was that an anxious frown or an angry one? A surprised eye flicker or a calculating one? A worried lip twitch or a puzzled one? The man before her was a cipher, his emotions almost impossible to interpret. It was a shame she hadn't thought to angle her chair so she could assess Rawdon's response to the news.

Tapping his fingers on the desk, Lyons finally spoke. 'You mean Gwendoline Salinger. The Salingers' oldest child? The one everyone called Winnie?'

Nikki's nod was brief.

'Are they . . . ?'

Rawdon's voice had an edge to it when he interrupted. 'Of course, they're sure. They wouldn't be here now if they weren't, would they, Nat?'

'Quite, quite.' Lyons frowned, his eyes narrowing in on Nikki. 'When did you find out?'

Nikki held his gaze. 'The DNA report was emailed to me this morning just before briefing.'

Whilst this was true, it wasn't the whole truth, but Nikki wasn't about to reveal that she'd had confirmation of Winnie's identity since the previous night. She didn't trust either Lyons or Rawdon enough for that. 'Thing is, whilst this clearly opens up new lines of inquiry for us, which in my capacity as SIO, I have actioned this morning, it leaves the question of the press conference to consider.'

Lyons stood and moved round his desk to rest his frame on

241

the edge of his desk. Arms folded over his middle, he eyed first Nikki and then Zain. 'I suppose you have a suggestion on how the press should be handled?'

For the first time since entering the Lyons's den, Nikki felt that things were going her way. If Lyons wanted her opinion then perhaps she could make this work to her advantage. 'Our belief, sir, is that it is in the investigation's best interests for us to not reveal the true identity of the fourth victim. This will give us more of a chance to locate Karen Salinger and ascertain her possible involvement as either a suspect or a witness in the deaths of her family. To that effect, we have many strands of investigation ongoing at this present time.'

The smile that crawled slug-like over Lyons's face sent a shiver up Nikki's spine. 'Phaw! I don't think so, Parekh. I think you've assessed this all wrong.' He extended both hands and used his right index finger to count off his points one by one on his left hand. 'One, there were five places at that table – FIVE! That means Karen Salinger is a suspect – a *key* suspect, not a witness. Two, I won't allow you to cover up your incompetence over IDing a dead girl by not sharing the information with the press. Three, you know as well as I do that public assistance in locating Karen Salinger is essential.'

Nikki felt her blood boil and fizz through her veins. The man was an insufferable gorilla. He had no interest in hearing her reasons and when she opened her mouth to expand on her reasoning he shut her down with a shouted 'No! We're going public with the mistaken ID at the press briefing. That's my final word. Now go and find that girl. Last thing you need is her killing someone else on your watch.'

The use of the pronouns "you" and "your" weren't lost on Nikki. The mistake over IDing Winnie Salinger would lie at her door. That was fine. Nikki was prepared to explain the circumstances, but the spin Lyons and Rawdon would put on, that would discredit her.

Their insistence on releasing their new findings could put Karen Salinger at risk. If she hadn't killed her family – like she suspected Peggy Marks hadn't killed hers – then the real killer was still out there and Nikki really wanted to find Karen before he or she did.

Chapter 38

Present Day: Marnie

I tried. I really tried to leave the flat, Jilly. I got dressed. Even braved the poxy shower with the cockroaches and woodlice. I put my coat on, left Gwen a note in case she came back and shoved fifty quid in my jeans pocket. But, I couldn't do it.

I got as far as the door and I just stood there. Trying to psych myself up to unlock it. I even reached out and touched the lock, but I couldn't turn it. I just couldn't.

Then I heard voices outside, people walking along the corridor. A man's voice all loud and arguing with a girl – effing and blinding. He slammed his hand or his fist into the wall, shouting and yelling at her. It was so loud it shook the door and I thought he might smash his way into our flat. And then I was right back in the dungeon with Scarface looming over me; yelling at me, frightening me and then grabbing me by the hair and dragging me across the floor.

All I could do was stumble back from the door and into the little room. I shut the inside door but I could still hear them outside in the corridor, screeching at each other, and I knew I couldn't leave – not without Gwen. Not on my own. So, I curled in a ball on the bed and sobbed and sobbed and sobbed, till I had no tears left.

When I come round, it's raining again. I like the sound of it on the window. It seems normal somehow. Normal and soothing. I wrap the duvet round me and stumble across the room to the window. Maybe Gwen will be walking along the road now. Maybe this time I'll see her striding through the rain. She'll stop and wave up at me and I don't care how angry I've been, I'll be sooo happy to see her. So happy!

But, she's not there and it's all grey and drab outside. The rain isn't my friend. It's just something else hammering on the window trying to get in. I flop onto the chair and stare through the glass. My reflection is all distorted. I want to be brave like Gwen. I really do. Instead, I'm a snivelling useless cow. I've not escaped Scarface or Auntie Lee-Lee or the groping sordid men. All I've done is replace one prison with another. *The worst thing is, Jilly, this time I have the key to the door. I could escape – if I was brave enough – but I'm not. Maybe I never have been, for I know I've let the Beep Beeps win, Jilly.*

I huddle over myself. My stomach is aching, my throat's raw, my head thumps in protest as I try to conjure up Jilly's strawberry smell – her diaphanous image, just a sense of her. But there's nothing. Only blackness and cold. That's all that's left for me.

245

Chapter 39

On her return to Ahad's office, Nikki took a moment to observe the quiet industry of the room. The contrast between this haven of tranquillity and the testosterone-fuelled environment she and Zain had just left was striking, so she took a moment by the door to savour it.

When she finally entered, Sajid – his hair mussed and his jacket hooked round the back of his chair – glanced up from the pile of papers scattered around his laptop. 'How'd it go?'

Zain sliced his finger across his throat and Nikki shrugged. 'About as well as expected. Lyons wouldn't listen to reason and went all Rambo, insisting we inform the press of the fourth victim's identity and issue a BOLO for Karen Salinger immediately afterwards. Which means we need to crack on with finding her. Has Liam been back?'

Farah, nibbling on another biscuit, flushed but met Nikki's gaze. 'No, not yet. But he's only been gone an hour.'

'What about Archie? You brief him on what we want?'

Sajid nodded. 'Archie, Dosanjh and Gregson are on it. I've got the rest of the team busy scrutinising Kholi's and Salinger's business accounts, interviewing Salinger's clients and employees and doing background checks on Ashleigh Kholi, Derek Bland and the rest of the key players.'

Whilst Zain grabbed a file and dashed off, murmuring some-thing about a budget and resources meeting under his breath, Nikki moved over and drew out a seat between Farah and Sajid. 'How are you two doing? This must be grim work?'

Farah, looked up from her laptop. 'It is, but it needs doing.'

Nikki wondered if Farah realised her hand had moved to cup her belly as she spoke, but the thought was lost when she continued.

'We've split Peggy's files in half. Sajid is taking the boys and I'm taking the girls. It's easier to filter out kids of the opposite sex, those who have since been found, those who went missing outside the parameters we set and those not in the correct age bracket – which of course is dependent on Peggy's assessment of their ages being accurate. We've each just established a core group of missing UK children to work with. Over the time period my core group of missing children fitting our parameters stands at three hundred and fifty-nine. We'll narrow that down by filtering by age and hair or eye colour – hopefully we'll be able to ID some of these children.'

Although the words "before it's too late" were left unspoken, they filled the room, making it hard not to hear them echoing in every rustle of paper, chair creak and pebbledash of rain on the window.

Sighing, Sajid flung a sheet of paper onto the desk with more force than was necessary. 'Mine stands at two hundred and thirty-two. Can you believe it? Between us over a fifteen-year period we've got nearly six hundred kids who've disappeared without trace. It's fucking sick!'

He was right. It *was* fucking sick that so many children could go missing, but they needed to control their emotions for now. That was the only way they could do this. The only way they could perhaps save some of those kids. 'Look, you two keep narrowing it down. I'll get the map up and we can colour-code any kids who fall within our parameters by their abduction sites. Maybe we'll see some sort of pattern, which might help.'

Whilst Sajid and Farah worked on narrowing Peggy's list down, Nikki pinned up a map on the whiteboard and kicked it off by pinning in two green pins. One to mark the woods they knew Winnie Salinger had been abducted from and one marking the street that Peggy Marks said she'd been snatched from on her way home from school. Although Winnie's abduction from Fogarty Woods was on the outskirts of Bradford and Peggy's was in North Yorkshire, the distance between the two sites was only about eighty miles. Barely an hour's drive between the two locations. Nikki wondered whether when they added other pegs to the map, it would help them find a location.

'Got one.' Sajid's voice brought Nikki from her reverie.

'Bronze. I think Bronze – around thirteen years old six years ago, brown hair brown eyes, of dual heritage—' Saj turned his laptop round so Nikki and Farah could see the missing person's image of Kai Green.

Both women took a moment to look at the face of the boy in a green school uniform smiling from the screen. Then Nikki picked up a red pin. 'Place of abduction?'

'Children's park off Burnley Road in Padiham near Burnley.'

Nikki found it on the map and stuck the pin in. 'Only about thirty miles from Bradford – less than an hour's drive. Get his file out and start a photo pack. When we've ID'd these kids, I'll get Peggy to confirm their identities.'

As if finding one of the children had injected them with caffeine straight to their bloodstream, Farah came up with another two identities within the next fifteen minutes.

'Crocus! Peggy reckons she was around ten years old and had just arrived when Peggy left, so she'd be around fourteen years old now. Didn't get a definite hit, but this girl – Amy Cuthbert – is a little bit older but has black hair and green eyes and she has a mole just below her lip – just like Peggy mentioned.'

Green pin at the ready, Nikki pushed it into a small village called Market Weighton. She paused with her fingers still on the pin head. 'That's a stone's throw from the Kholis' residence in Holme-on-Spalding-Moor and again isn't more than an hour's drive from Bradford.'

Before she had time to pursue that thought, Farah yelled out again. 'Lily. Peggy reckoned she was about sixteen when she left and that she'd been there for four or five years. Says she was a close friend of Winnie's.'

Farah turned her screen so they could see the girl. 'This is Marnie Ford – matches Peggy's description from the long blonde hair and blue eyes, down to the scar on her right elbow that's listed as an identifying mark. Only thing that doesn't add up is that Peggy says Lily doesn't speak, but there's no mention of that in her MP report. What do you reckon?'

Nikki and Sajid looked at the image of Marnie, then Sajid said, 'Any other kids thrown up when you inputted Peggy's information?'

'No.'

Nikki shrugged. 'We'll include her for now. That scar on her elbow is compelling. We can always remove her if Peggy doesn't ID her. Where was she abducted from?'

'Her back garden in Ripponden near Halifax.'

As Nikki pushed the pin in, adrenaline surged through her. So far, they had five locations within an easily commutable distance of each other where five children had been abducted. She was just about to suggest they narrow their location parameters from England to the north of the country to speed things up – they could always widen them later – when her phone rang.

Ahad! Nikki answered and, at the sound of his laboured breathing and staccato tones as he spoke, she tensed. 'Nik. Need you and Sajid ASAP. Dead body on Baildon Moor.'

Nikki's heart lurched. 'A child?'

'No. Just get here, Nik. Just fucking get here and bring Malik with you, too.'

Nikki cut off the call and turned to her colleagues, her actions slow as she tried to process what Ahad had just told her. She twanged her wristband a few times and then exhaled. 'We've got to go, Saj. You okay here on your own, Farah?'

As Anwar nodded, a slight frown spreading across her forehead, Nikki continued. 'Get on the phone to Liam and direct him to meet us at a crime scene. A body has just been found murdered on Baildon Moor.'

Chapter 40

I spy with my little eye, something beginning with B . . . Bitch!

I'm furious with her. Everything about her oozes insolence and disrespect.

I'm on my own, in my sanctuary, but it doesn't feel like safety. It's like I'm trapped with nowhere to go. All the intel that Scarface gets from his source tells me things are going awry. It's like I've got a target on my back and I hate being unable to mould the narrative. Talk of prison visits and secret meetings – things are not going to plan. Holding one of the shiny metal balls on my Newton's cradle as high as I can, I release it with force. For a nanosecond, the sound of them crashing together, setting off a chain reaction of clanking and shimmering light on the steel, gives the illusion that I am in control. Then, I realise that no matter how much force I exert, those fucking balls in the middle just sit there like faceless wallies, mocking me.

A wave of anger sweeps like a tidal wave from the soles of my feet right up to my head. The pores above my lip spew out globules of sweat and the hammering between my ears is so intense that the only way to release it is to destroy something. I reach out and sweep the entire contraption to the floor, angered even more by the way the carpet absorbs its landing and it just lies there inert and unremorseful.

Panting, I fling myself back in my chair, grip the arms and force myself to exhale. When my breath is back to normal, I take the burner from my locked drawer and ring the only contact stored on the phone. 'One more job.'

'Who?'

'Parekh.'

Scarface takes his time replying. 'So soon after the last one?'

My tone is clipped. I'm taking no prisoners and his delayed reaction has me tightening my grip on the phone. 'Last time I looked, *I'm* the one making the plans.'

With barely disguised humour Scarface replies. 'Yeah, so you are. I almost forgot. However, we've been creating a lot of activity recently and I'm still working on locating our other asset. Plus, there's that kid – when do you want me to snatch him?'

He paused, letting his words sink in, then in a softer tone says, 'We don't want to draw too much attention to ourselves right now. Maybe hold back a bit? See how things settle? No point at this juncture, in endangering everything we've worked so hard for. Some of the clients are expressing concern. Lee-Lee told me she's had cancellations from some of our most loyal buyers. We've been doing all right – operating under the radar, making big bucks. It'd be a shame to risk exposing our business venture by sticking our heads over the parapet, yeah?'

Despite the parapet cliché, I have to accept that Scarface has a point. There has been a lot of activity and this situation with Winnie Salinger, and all the stuff that's dragged up is worrying. We'll need to review our policy on disposing of those assets that have exceeded their best-by date. No doubt about that. It's a shame really, of the six that we've released into the wild over the years, three of them followed our directive to the letter. Until recently we'd had a seventy-five per cent success rate with this strategy, but with the Salinger fiasco that has dropped to fifty per cent.

No way I can tolerate those sorts of odds. However, we can put a review of that policy on hold, for a while. For now, two things are on my agenda: Nikki fucking Parekh and our lost asset. 'Okay. Point well made. We'll reduce our activity. Delay procuring the new target for now. A few months won't have a negative impact on his worth, anyway. On the contrary, Lee-Lee can hype him up to the clients in the interim, so we'll get our money's worth in the end.'

It sticks in my craw to issue my next directive, but needs must. 'You're right about Parekh. In light of recent events, she's too visible to be disposed of at the moment. However, her comings and goings need to be monitored. I have a sneaky suspicion that the cow is happy to work outside the constraints of her job. And I need to know what she's up to at all times. Any time she's not on the job, I expect you to know where she is, who's she's meeting with and what she's up to.'

'Copy that, boss! I'll split that task with one of my operatives and divide my time between Parekh and locating the missing slag.'

The slight exhalation of held breath gives away the fact that Scarface is relieved by my instructions. Had he expected me to take a more militant approach? As I hang up, I tap a jaunty rhythm on the desktop. I always feel so much better when I take control. That's *my* special skill set – being in control.

Chapter 41

The persistent drizzle didn't show Baildon Moor in its best light. To be honest, as she got out of Sajid's car, Nikki was too busy yanking her hood up and fastening her coat to be concerned with the scenery. Thankful that she'd had the foresight to grab her wellies from the boot of her Touran before leaving, Nikki sat sideways on, in the passenger seat, and replaced her new DMs with the colourful floral wellies the kids had given her at Christmas. Though she'd secretly been horrified by their brightness at the time, today she was grateful for them.

With both she and Sajid suitably attired against the weather, Nikki glanced round. The entrance to the road that led from Bingley Road to Dobrudden Caravan Park had been blocked by two constables standing between two patrol cars. With the weather being what it was, very few vehicles seemed inclined to head down that way – nobody seemed keen to brave the elements to traipse across the moor today, which of course made their job easier. Sajid and Nikki had been waved through and had parked behind the CSI vans, two other patrol cars and DCI Ahad's Mercedes, just short of the inner cordon, which was marked off by crime scene tape strung between two posts spanning the narrow road.

An area around twenty metres or so off to the right of the track was populated by around a dozen white-clad figures, spread out from the crime scene tent where the body lay, protected in death from the elements. If Nikki had been in a better mood she might have likened them to a bland version of the Teletubbies. However, her mood was still tainted by Ahad's abrupt instructions for her and Sajid to get to the scene pronto, without giving her any indication of who the victim was. She'd grumbled most of the twenty-minute drive over and all through the process of donning her protective crime scene clothes and had no intention of stopping now. 'Better be related to our investigation, Saj. Not like ours isn't complex enough as it is without adding in some other unrelated murder.'

She sloshed over the shrubland, her feet squelching into the moss, her shoulders hunched against the rain that had become heavier as they trudged onward. 'He better not have pulled us . . .'

Sajid gave an exaggerated sigh and nudged her, causing her to lose her footing and momentarily wobble, before righting herself. 'What'd you do that for?'

'Stop your bloody moaning, Nik. You know as well as I do that Ahad wouldn't drag us away from ID'ing those kids if it wasn't important. You're just using him as an excuse to vent because you can't process your emotions about all those kids.'

As she stopped abruptly in her tracks, Saj bashed into her again. This time he grabbed the back of her anorak before she landed face first in the gorse. Her eyes were wide as she turned to look intently at her partner. When she spoke, there was no accusation in her tone – just wonder. 'And you can? After seeing *all* those kids, reading Peggy's files – all of that – you can process your emotions?'

With a slight shrug, Sajid shook his head. 'No. Course I bloody can't. But we need to at least be aware of them. How they affect us and our behaviour.'

Nikki bit her lip, nodded once, then linked her arm through Sajid's. 'Yeah. You're right, for once. I'm being a dick about Zain because it's easier than thinking about those kids.'

Saj squeezed her arm. 'That's fine. It's fine to vent. Just be aware of it, eh? Don't want you landing one on the Dark Knight, do I?' He paused and grinned, ignoring the persistent drip that fell from his chin, landing in the gap between his neck and his anorak, soaking into the designer suit underneath. 'Actually, I wouldn't mind seeing that. But now's not the time.'

As they moved forward one of the taller figures peeled away from the others and approached. 'At last. Where the hell have you been?'

One look at the tension radiating from her boss's narrowed eyes stopped Nikki from responding in kind. Instead, she ignored his comment and nodded towards the tent. 'Who is it, Zain?'

With a peremptory waft of his gloved hand, Zain indicated they should follow him and marched across the moorland, his designer shoes slushing through the sodden grass until he reached the metal plates laid down by the crime scene investigators. At the entrance, he hesitated. 'It's Lisa Kane, Nik.'

For a moment, Nikki could make no sense of his words. *Lisa Kane?* No! She'd heard wrong. In her mind, the woman was destructive yet indestructible. Vibrantly venomous was another descriptor Nikki had often used about the reporter. Salaciously sordid had been another. As the list of adjectives flew through her mind, she took a step forward, thrusting the door flap to the side. Only years of training reminded her to stick to the plates and not just barge in. *Lisa Kane?*

But two steps inside the tent was all it took for Nikki to realise that Ahad was telling the truth. Kane lay like a discarded doll, her arms extended at different angles, one leg bent back on itself and her pale pink clothes drenched. It took a moment for Nikki to realise that Kane's blouse was actually white and that the rain had diluted the blood from her wounds.

Crouched beside the dead woman, Langley angled his head to greet Nikki and Sajid, who stood in silence looking down at the woman who had made such an impact on the direction of

256

their current investigation. 'I'd put time of death provisionally at late last night. Of course, the post-mortem will tighten that estimate. However, what I think might interest you two more is the cause of death.'

He beckoned them closer and as they squatted beside him, he angled his torch to a wound at her neck. 'Cause of death is a sliced jugular.'

Nikki inhaled and then wished she hadn't as the metallic taste of blood invaded the back of her throat via her olfactory system. She swallowed hard, and then followed Langley's torch beam as it guided them down Kane's body, stopping momentarily at each wound as he did so. 'Look familiar?'

Although his question had been rhetorical, Nikki nodded. 'Yes.'

'Again, I can't be a hundred per cent sure of this until the PM, but the wounds are very similar to those found on the Salinger family's bodies. Unserrated, sharp blade of roughly the same length and width.'

'She was dead before all those wounds were inflicted, wasn't she?' Disgust laced Sajid's tone. 'The bastard slit her throat, and as she bled out, he stabbed and slashed her repeatedly.'

'I've isolated at least twenty knife wounds so far, but what's interesting is this.'

He lifted the journalist's right arm and pointed at the skin, which was punctured in a few places.

'More knife wounds,' Nikki offered.

'Yes, defensive wounds, but what's more interesting is the lack of hypostasis.' He smiled at Nikki. 'Livor mortis to you, Nik.'

'Ah, but, shouldn't she . . . ?'

'Exactly. If she'd been killed and or moved here soon after death this arm would have shown evidence of livor mortis, but . . .'

'There is none, so the killer killed her elsewhere and then moved her here?'

Langley nodded at her like she was his favourite student.

257

'Exactly. The presence of livor mortis on her back, buttocks and the soles of her feet, along with the absence of any on the back of her thighs and arms, indicates she sat in a seated position for some time after death – certainly long enough for lividity to settle, which is between two and four hours post-mortem.'

'Thanks, Langley.' Nikki stood up and turned to Ahad. 'Who found her?'

'Would you believe, a dog walker?'

'A masochistic one if you ask me,' said Sajid, following his two bosses from the tent.

'The bloke and his wife are staying at the campsite and he drew the short straw when the pup needed a wee. I've had uniforms take his statement and also got them chasing up CCTV from Bingley Road in either direction from eight o'clock last night till eight this morning. Not that I'm optimistic we'll catch anything, but . . .' He shrugged.

Nikki knew what he meant. *They had to try.*

'You told Rawdon and Lyons yet?' she asked and was pleased when Ahad nodded.

'Well, I reported to the chief super. He said he'll update Rawdon. Also—' a glimmer of a smile flickered across his lips '—seems for some reason that the focus of the press conference later will be on Lisa Kane's death and, for some reason, you're not required for that.'

Although she had mixed feelings about the chief super's motivations for excluding her from the press conference, Nikki was relieved that she'd be able to focus on the investigation rather than answering pointless questions about the it. So what if Lyons and Rawdon put a negative spin on her absence – despite her dislike of Kane, her focus was on finding who had killed her.

As she and Sajid started to make the short trek back to his car, a thought struck Nikki. She spun on her heel and began marching back towards the tent, yelling over her shoulder, 'I'll catch up with you at the car.'

Langley was just packing his things away when Nikki re-entered the tent. 'Lang, can I ask a favour?'

'Course you can. What is it?'

'Can you access the post-mortem reports for Peggy Marks's family? They should be in the system from about four years ago?'

'Yes, I can do that, but what am I looking for?'

'I want you to compare the wounds from Lisa Kane's body, the Salinger family's bodies and Peggy Marks's family's bodies. Can you do that for me?' She looked around. 'On the quiet, if you don't mind.'

Despite the cloak-and-dagger stuff, Langley – to his credit – just nodded and said, 'Okay. I'll be in touch.'

Still reeling from Lisa Kane's murder, Nikki was trudging back towards the car when her mobile rang. 'What have you got, Liam?'

DC Williams's overexcited voice crackled down the line. 'You know I mentioned double-checking the CCTV around Sukhjit Kholi's flat?'

'Yeah.' Nikki paused, wishing he would just blurt it out. He had clearly found something important, but she wasn't in the mood to coax it from him. 'Spit it out, eh.'

'I bloody found it, boss. Sukhjit Kholi was caught on CCTV from the pub behind his flat, just near the maintenance entrance. He was out and about on Sunday night from around six-thirty. His alibi's shot.'

'You following his route?'

'I've got a couple of PCs on it. Shall I bring him in?'

'Too bloody right you will. Good work, Liam.' If she hadn't been so knackered she'd have punched the air. As it was she settled for a slight smile as she got into the car beside Saj.

Chapter 42

The last thing Nikki had expected to find when she finally returned to DCI Ahad's office at almost seven in the evening was DC Farah Anwar in floods of tears and DC Liam Williams hovering over her with a packet of ginger nuts in one hand and a tissue in the other. Sajid, pushing past her into the office, looked from one of the young detectives to the other and then said, 'Thank fuck for that. I was beginning to wonder if you two would ever talk to each other about this rather than me.'

Nikki gawped and, taking a step further into the room, glared at Farah. 'You confided in him? You told Sajid before you told me?'

Face flushed, Williams cleared his throat, a grin spreading over his lips. 'Well, boss, in all fairness, I think I've more of a right to be pissed off about it than you?' His eyes opened wider and he moved closer to Farah, placing his arm round her shoulder and tipping ginger nut crumbs all over her in the process. 'I don't mean about . . . you know – the bump. I mean . . .'

Now it was Farah's turn to go all wide-eyed. 'The bump? Let's get this straight, Liam. You are never to refer to our embryonic child as "the bump" ever again. Got it?'

'Really? Really? You want me to call my unborn baby an embryonic child?'

Just when Nikki thought the conversation couldn't get any more ridiculous, Zain walked in, glanced at the trio of officers gathered round Farah and said, 'Well thank Christ for that. Now I don't have to go about pretending I don't know about you two being in a relationship or about Farah being pregnant. Makes things a whole lot easier, don't you think? Now, are you all up to date on Lisa Kane's murder?'

Amid the nods and mumbled comments, Nikki had no time to work out if she felt more miffed that she'd been the last one to work out that Williams and Anwar were dating or that neither Sajid nor Ahad had given her a heads up about it. Thrusting that aside she allowed her mind to drift to the press briefing that she'd caught on her phone as she and Sajid had been driving back to Trafalgar House. To be fair, Chief Superintendent Lyons had struck the right note of outrage laced with determination when speaking of the journalist's death and to give him his due, he'd excused her absence from the briefing by insisting that she was doing her job and investigating the journalist's murder. However, that hadn't prevented the flurry of online opinion pieces on Nikki's suitability to investigate Kane's murder in light of her acrimonious relationship with the reporter.

But she couldn't focus on that right now. Everything was in order and there was little more she could do until information began to flow into the main briefing room. Before returning to their clandestine work in the DCI's office, she and Sajid had set up an incident board in the main incident room alongside those of the Salinger family's and had ensured that all actions were covered. Now though it was time to push forward with the work her smaller team were doing.

'Liam, what you got for us? Other than the stupendously wonderful news that you and Farah are going to be parents, that is, and that Sukhjit Kholi is wallowing in a cess pit of "no comment" in our most uncomfortable cell.'

For a moment the lad looked bemused, then he straightened

his shoulders and rearranged his features into what Nikki thought of as his "reporting back" pose. 'I was just about to phone you, before you and Saj walked in, boss. Erm well, we don't have Kholi yet, but the tech team just sent over the phone transcripts provided by Karen Salinger's mobile provider. They make for interesting reading.'

Rolling her shoulders to loosen them, Nikki closed her eyes for a second. God she was tired. This day had seemed interminable. What with the emotional meeting with Peggy Marks – had that been only this morning? Her subsequent battle of wills with the chief super. The traumatic trawling through of missing kids' files and finally, topped off with Lisa Kane's murder. Stifling a yawn, she exhaled and refocused on the room. 'Liam.'

Still with his arm round Farah, who had grabbed his proffered tissue and was scrubbing her cheeks, he said, 'Looks like Karen Salinger and Sukhjit Kholi were in a relationship. Quite a torrid one by the number of sexts sent between them, complete with images.'

'Shit! Any idea how long that was going on for?'

'Seems like it was since just before she headed off to Cambridge – so last September – around eight months.'

Sajid, in place behind his laptop again, groaned. 'Eww, that's just gross. That means he was shagging mum and daughter at the same time. What sort of sick bastard does that?'

But Nikki wasn't interested in the morals of the situation. 'So, that means that she could be at Kholi's, yeah? It also gives both of them quite a compelling motive for murdering the rest of Karen's family. Have we located him? Is he at home?'

Williams grimaced. 'He's in the wind. Nobody has seen him since yesterday. He's not at his penthouse and his car's in the garage. Looks like they've skipped town. However, I've put in for a warrant to search the property to be sure. Two uniforms are going over the footage as we speak. If we can just plot his movements we'll know if he went anywhere near the Salingers' home.

Nikki groaned. 'Get a BOLO out for him too, then.'

He paused and inhaled deeply as if desperate for a second wind to see him through the rest of his report. 'The police in Cambridge are keeping a look-out for Karen Salinger – they've stationed officers outside the flat she owns, but so far there have been no sightings of her, and her friends insist she hasn't been in touch. Mind you with all of Kholi's and or Bland's money at their disposal, why would she return to Cambridge? Her friends from school – three of them – were more eager to pump me for information than to offer any useful insights into where Karen might be. However, they were keen to throw up every perceived character flaw and every bitchy comment or deed the girl ever committed. All in all, they were bitches and if their behaviour is indicative of Karen Salinger's personality, then I'd hazard a guess that she's a bitch too. Which is basically what her teachers said. Spoilt rich kids, eh?'

'Good work, Liam, that's a huge step forward for us. Well done.' Nikki looked at Farah. 'How did you get on with the missing persons?'

Farah gestured to the map, which had more green pins distributed within a one-and-a-half- to two-hour drive from Bradford. 'I'll be honest, boss, I'm knackered. Can hardly see straight and I've still got three kids to match with Peggy's file.'

'You've done a grand job, Farah, especially with the morning or in your case all-day sickness to cope with. You and Williams can head off when we've finished here, okay. You'll have a lot to talk about, but be sure to rest up, for I suspect tomorrow's going to be a long day too.'

Unlike Nikki, Sajid didn't bother to hide his yawn as he sprawled in his chair. He thumbed through his tablet, his tie awry and his pristine suit crumpled. He was less than the Mr Sartorial Elegance Nikki was used to seeing, but after the day they'd had, who could blame him? 'Archie doesn't seem to have come up with anything worth reporting. He paid a visit to some of the families at the picnic, but was mostly given the cold shoulder. Understandably, they want to put it behind them. One kid, now grown up, has agreed to speak with him tomorrow. Hopefully that'll throw up something.'

Nikki glanced at her watch. Nearly eight o'clock. Time none of them were here. 'Right, you lot. Piss off home. I'll see you all at seven sharp tomorrow. I've got a meeting arranged with Peggy and her lawyer at nine. Let's hope she gives us positive IDs on the kids we've matched. At least then, some families will have some sort of closure.'

Chapter 43

Present Day: Marnie

When had it got so dark? I must have dozed off, but I've no recollection of doing so. I remember doing that a lot when they put me in the dungeon. It was like I was too scared to think, too scared to move, almost too scared to breathe, so instead I forced my body to shut down. Gwen had once told me that was a coping mechanism. Maybe she's right. Maybe I'm just shutting my body down little by little because I can't cope anymore.

The only light is that coming from the streetlight outside, but I can't be bothered to get up to put the lamp on. Instead I breath onto the cold, rain-spattered window pane and when I've made a large enough steamy patch I shuffle along and make another steam balloon on the glass. In the first one I draw a love heart and inside it, I write, *I Love You, Jilly*. I repeat the process in the second one, but this time I write, *I Love You, Gwen*.

As my steam love hearts fade against the dark night, leaving my messages unread and unreadable, I begin to sob. There's nothing else for me to do.

Chapter 44

Seeing her living room lit up behind the drawn curtains and imagining her loud, affectionate family inside brought a smile to Nikki's lips as she drew into the space opposite her terraced house in Listerhills. Both attic bedroom lights were on, telling her that Charlie was home, probably doing homework. She'd be lying on her belly on top of the bed, her duvet drawn round her head, like a weird horizontal ghost. Her headphones would be on, the interminable bass throb audible despite both Nikki and Marcus's warnings about sensible volume limits and premonitions of hearing loss. How she could concentrate with that level of racket was beyond Nikki – but judging by Charlie's consistently good grades, her study method worked for her.

By contrast, Ruby – in the next room – would be at her desk, sketching and humming along to some boy band or other, also played at a level that Nikki thought was too loud. Earlier Sajid had messaged Ruby asking for her assistance with his wedding table decoration and colour scheme. As Nikki had known she would, Ruby had jumped at the chance to flex her artistic muscles. Nikki only hoped Saj knew what he was getting into, for Ruby could be tenacious in her defence of her work – in fact sometimes Nikki preferred to go head to head with a killer triple her size than her middle daughter. She could picture Ruby, huddled over an A3 sheet of paper, pencil in hand, her tongue just visible at the side of her mouth, her focus on the task in hand complete. She got her artistic talent from her dad. Marcus's artistry played out in his landscaping and cooking the family meals, whilst Ruby's was definitely fashion and décor centred.

Both Sunni and Isaac's bedroom lights were off, which told Nikki she'd find them in front of the telly in the living room – probably watching *Dr Who* and definitely, in between replaying scenes – sometimes three or four times – and imitating Dalek voices, debating why David Tennant's Doctor didn't have a Scottish accent.

Marcus would be either in the kitchen tidying up after dinner or with the boys, checking that Sunni had indeed done his homework and indulging them in their shared joy of *Doctor Who*, whilst telling Sunni that he had only five more minutes before bedtime because it was a school night. Next door, her sister Anika's lights were also on and, recognising her boss Ahad's car parked two spaces down, Nikki knew that, even if Haqib was out, Anika had company. That thought pleased her. For too long, Anika had been on her own – Haqib's dad had been a washout and was now in prison, and it had taken Anika a while to think about beginning another relationship. Although she would prefer that her sister's new boyfriend wasn't also her boss, Nikki didn't begrudge Anika some happiness. She deserved it. They'd had a tough few years and it was time now for the extended Parekh family to hold its happiness with both hands and not let go.

With the tension of the day heavy on her shoulders, Nikki stretched her arms out and, gripping the steering wheel lightly, inhaled a deep breath. Closing her eyes, she imagined herself by the seaside at one of the many beaches along the North Yorkshire Coast. As she exhaled slowly, she imagined the ebb and flow of a gentle time. Each time the tide receded, Nikki imagined the stresses of the day receding with it. For months now, she had employed this method of offloading at least some

267

of the baggage of her day before she went indoors. And it usually worked for her.

Tonight was different. No matter how hard she tried, she couldn't entirely shift her worried thoughts from the day. Worry intruded over the whereabouts of Karin Salinger and whether she was guilty of murdering her entire family, including the sister who had been abducted when she herself had been a kid. *Where was the girl?* Then her run-in with Chief Super Lyons had set her on edge and that was after the poignant, emotionally draining meeting with Peggy Marks. It was Lisa Kane's murder that had almost gutted her though. It had come out of left field and although she'd disliked the woman, the evidence indicated that her death might be connected to the Salinger murders. Though Nikki had no idea how.

Persevering with her sandy beach imagery, Nikki tried to shut down her concerns over issues within Trafalgar House. The niggling feeling that Superintendent Rawdon and the chief super had it in for her persisted. To Nikki it felt like a which came first – the chicken or the egg scenario. And for the life of her she couldn't work out whether their reactions to her were the result of the press allegations against her team or if the press allegations were somehow orchestrated by them. She and Sajid had gone around in circles, trying to work out where the accusations of "woke" incompetence had originated from and had been unable to rule out that, rather than Lisa Kane's virulent brand of revenge journalism being at the heart of it, the flames were being fanned from within Bradford police. Now, with Kane dead, she wondered if she'd ever find out.

She released the steering wheel, rolled her shoulders a few times and decided that tonight her meditation techniques weren't going to cut it. Glancing in her side mirror before opening the car door, Nikki paused. Had she seen movement in the car parked further down the street behind her? Releasing her hold on the door handle, she moved her gaze to the rear-view mirror. It was dark and the car in question was parked in shadow, yet Nikki could see someone in the driver's seat. All the hyper-alertness that had been part of her being whilst her family were being stalked by her father kicked right back in. Her heart hammered and she sat stock still, trying not to let the blackness flood her mind and rob her of the ability to think out a strategy.

As her brain fog cleared, common sense prevailed. There was no doubt that someone was sitting in a car she didn't recognise, in the dark, in her street. It was probably a man, judging from his height and stature, but not necessarily so. It could have been a tall woman. Regardless of that, the presence of someone in a car in her street didn't necessarily mean he was watching her. There were any number of reasons for his presence here. He could be visiting one of her neighbours and had arrived too early. Hell, he might even be doing exactly what she was – releasing the day's tensions, before going home.

Despite these thoughts, Nikki remained unconvinced. It was odd and oddness was something she looked out for in her job. Out of the ordinary things were often an alert. With small movements, hoping not to alert the man, she reached over to the passenger seat and grabbed her phone. Using her handbag to shield the light from the screen when she unlocked it, she flicked it to speaker phone and keeping her mobile out of sight in her lap, she dialled Marcus's number.

'Hey, gorgeous. You coming home soon? Two boys here have got David Tennant ad nauseum lined up for you to watch.'

Despite her coiled stomach and hammering heart, Nikki's lips twitched at this little slice of normality. Marcus, her rock, was with her. If not right beside her in the car, his warm soothing voice was there, calming her and he was only a few yards away. She had no doubt that he'd react to her request without asking a load of questions, so she jumped right in. 'Marcus, go upstairs to our room, no lights. Check out the car further down the road behind mine. See if you can get a reg number.'

His hesitation was brief and then Nikki heard him moving, mumbling something to Isaac and Sunni, as he left the room and headed upstairs as she requested. 'I'm on it. Stay on the line.'

With both hands repositioned on the steering wheel, Nikki attempted to appear like she was still meditating, whilst casting surreptitious glances in the mirror. The man was still there and, like her, was hardly moving.

'Nik, I got eyes on the car. Definitely someone in there, but I can't see the reg from this angle. I'm going to go out the kitchen door and circle round as if I'm out for a walk or coming home. Give me thirty seconds and keep an eye for me at the top end of the street. When you spot me, get out of the car, so that if he's watching you, he'll be focused on you and not me. Then walk slowly up to the house. I'll approach from the front with my phone on video and angled at him so hopefully we'll get the reg and be able to identify him.'

The tension that had crept along Nikki's shoulders as she observed the man in the car behind loosened. She could always rely on Marcus. 'Good plan. I'm probably just being paranoid, but . . . You know?'

Marcus dismissed her doubt. 'Yeah, I know, Nik. No harm done if he's innocent and no harm in making sure you're safe. Love you.'

When he hung up the sense of being on her own made her stomach churn. Then, within seconds she saw him in his bulky coat with the collar pulled up. He'd wrapped Isaac's scarf round his neck and had his woolly bobble hat pulled down over his forehead. As he strolled towards her car, his phone held in front of him as if he was FaceTiming someone, his deep tones reached her. He was simulating an argument with a fictional partner.

As agreed, Nikki got out of her car and, taking her time, pulled her coat closed, zipped it up and wrapped her scarf round her neck, before walking over to her gate and pushing it open. As Marcus passed her, she glanced his way, but didn't interact and then continued along the path, up the stairs and with relief pushed open the door to step inside. That was when she heard it.

The shot rang out like a car backfiring but *so* much louder, *so* much closer. Nikki swung round, dropping her bag, keys and phone at her feet. She stumbled back down the stairs towards the gate, her heart pounding, her vision blurred as she ran, her eyes probing the darkness, seeking Marcus. Her strong beautiful, reliable Marcus. With no concern for her own safety, she reached the gate, her blood chilled and her hands shaking. Where was he? A strangled 'Marcus!' left her lips as she yanked open the gate and stepped onto the pavement.

The roar of a car engine starting up, followed by the screech of tyres as the car that had been parked behind her tore along the road to the junction at the end. With only a momentary flash of its brake lights, it turned onto the main flow of traffic and disappeared from view.

Alerted by her screams, Sunni and Isaac huddled in the doorway, and then, as Nikki stood in the pavement, her head turning this way and that, tears pouring down her cheeks, Marcus appeared behind the boys, still wearing his outdoor clothes.

As Nikki saw him haloed in the light from inside the house, she fell to her knees, gulping in relieved breaths of cold night air as her sobs intensified. He'd circled the block and re-entered the house by the back door. She hadn't heard a gunshot. Marcus was safe. When he reached her and gathered her up in his arms, she gripped him tightly, only half hearing his mumbled reassurances. Then, her tears turned to laughter and as her hands curled into fists, she pummelled his back. 'What the fuck, Marccy? What the actual fuck? I thought I'd lost you. I thought . . .'

Marcus pushed her away from him, kissed her forehead and smiled, that steady dependable smile of his and in his best Jack Reacher voice said, 'It'll take more than a car backfiring in the next street to take me out, Parekh.'

Chapter 45

'Chances are he was watching her. Why else would he have taken off like that?' Marcus addressed the people gathered in his and Nikki's living room. After he'd got Nikki inside, Marcus had calmed Sunni and Isaac with ice cream and checked the older girls were okay. They were. Neither of them had heard any of the excitement outside – probably because of their damn music and neither seemed particularly fazed when Marcus told them what had happened. After settling his family, he'd alerted Sajid who, as expected, had hotfooted it straight over from his flat in Manningham.

DCI Zain Ahad, alerted by the racket outside Anika's house, had arrived as Marcus was helping Nikki into the house, and now everyone was sitting in Nikki's front room, waiting to watch the video recording Marcus had managed to take as he ambled past the car.

Nikki had initially regained enough control to phone the incident into Trafalgar House with a description of the car – a navy or dark-coloured Ford Galaxy – and a request that traffic cameras try to follow his route from when he exited her street. She'd promised to supply the reg number when they had it.

Whilst Marcus knelt next to the coffee table and connected his mobile to Nikki's work laptop, Nikki sat wedged into the corner of the sofa, with her legs curled up beside her, hugging a cushion. Anika sat beside her with Zain on her other side. Sajid sat on a cushion on the floor where he had a good view of the laptop. Although her heart rate was back to normal, her legs still felt wobbly and her stomach still churned. What was worse though were those persistent "What if?" thoughts that wouldn't leave her alone. What if it had been a gunshot? What if Marcus had been killed? What if they'd both been killed and the kids were left on their own?

Knowing it was the result of the adrenaline surge she'd experienced at the thought of Marcus being shot didn't make her shakiness any easier to deal with. She hated feeling weak, but even worse than that, she hated others witnessing her weakness. The worst thing of all, though, was their pity. When she'd visited the loo a short while ago, she'd been appalled by her pallor and the ugly mascara-tinged tear streaks on her face. All of the people in this room had seen it and although she'd quickly washed her face and retied her ponytail, nothing seemed to bring the colour back to her face, or cover the anguish that showed in her eyes. She wasn't a victim and she loathed feeling like one.

Thrusting the cushion to the floor at the side of the couch, Nikki swung her legs round and sat up straight. 'Right, let's see who this fucker who was watching me is.'

Marcus pressed play and muted the sound so that their full attention was focused on the recording and not on his fictional FaceTime argument. As he walked closer, angling the camera in the direction of the car parked in the shadow beyond where Nikki had parked, the car came into focus. There was definitely someone sitting in the driver's seat, but no one in the passenger side. Marcus swung the camera downwards, trying to catch the number plate.

'Stop. Stop right there.' Nikki leaned closer, eyes straining so as not to miss any of the recording.

Marcus rewound the recording, pausing it at the point where he had homed in on the car registration number. He edged the recording forward, paused when he had the clearest viewpoint and zoomed in. Everyone leaned in, then Zain slammed his hand on his thigh. 'Bastard's muddied the plate, hasn't he?'

Jaw clenched so hard it hurt, Nikki glared at the paused image. 'Well, I think that confirms it, doesn't it? Taking off after—' rather than mention the car backfiring incident she circled her hand in the air, trying to ignore the flush of heat that spread from the back of her neck up to her ears and onto her cheeks '—and the obstructed reg number pretty much shows that he was watching me. So, two questions, who the hell is he? And *why* was he watching me?'

Sajid looked at Marcus. 'Did you manage to get a clear view of his face?'

With a shrug Marcus pressed play. 'Not sure. It was dark and he'd parked in the shadows, well away from the nearest streetlight, so we'll just have to watch it and see if we can grab a screenshot of his face.'

Anika, who was sitting next to her sister, moved closer and took Nikki's hand in hers. Nikki tensed ready to pull away, then, noticing the frown that marred Anika's brow, she smiled and squeezed her sister's hand, leaving their fingers linked as they watched the replay.

Marcus had clearly learned a few tricks over the short period of time since he'd been working with Archie, for the footage wasn't too wobbly and he'd managed to zoom in quite close to the driver, who, as Marcus had predicted, seemed more focused on Nikki exiting her car further along the street than in the man in the bobble hat having a loud argument with his girlfriend walking towards him.

Before Nikki could direct him to pause the recording, Marcus halted it and zoomed in. 'Recognise him, Nik?'

Nikki took her time, studying the shadowy face, then shook her head. 'No. Anybody else?'

Zain and Sajid shook their heads too, so Marcus hit play, allowing the recording to edge forward slowly in the hope of finding a better, clearer image of the mystery man. On screen, Marcus had almost drawn level with the car and their chances of catching a better glimpse of him were reducing by the second. They were all caught off guard when Anika yelled, making Nikki jump. 'There. There. Look. Rewind, Marcus.'

Whatever Anika had seen, none of the others had, but nonetheless Marcus rewound to the first image of the man in the car and, slowing the speed right down, inched forward, snippet by snippet. Everyone held their breath and Nikki found herself physically crossing her fingers, hoping that Anika had spotted something they had missed.

'Nearly there . . . go slow, Marcus. Really slow.' Anika's voice was a whisper as if worried that if she spoke too loudly, the unidentified man would hear her and cover his face.

One more click and: 'Stop!'

All four of them yelled it at the same time, but Marcus was on it. Before they could say any more, he'd zoomed in on the fraction of a second when the man in the car had momentarily moved his focus from Nikki and directed his gaze to the man in the bobble hat passing his car. His head was angled upwards, and he peered right into Marcus's camera through the windscreen for a mere nanosecond. It was enough, though.

Marcus zoomed in closer. The man was probably in his late forties or early fifties and wore a peaked baseball cap. Despite pulling his collar right up around his neck and the hat, when he'd angled forward close to the steering wheel, his face became haloed in a glimmer of moonlight that flickered through the rear passenger-side window.

'Is that . . .' Nikki frowned, edging closer to the screen '. . . a scar on his cheek?'

'Yep, it definitely is,' said Saj with a grin. '*Just* the sort of feature that'll make identifying him easier. Anybody recognise him now?'

Nikki and Zain shook their heads, but Anika bit her lip, her frown deepening.

'Anika?' Nikki's tone was gentle as she stepped back into big-sister mode with ease. 'You know this man?'

Wide-eyed Anika looked up at her sister. 'I'm not sure, Nik. He seems familiar, but . . .' She tutted, her gaze resting on the man's scarred face. 'I've seen him before, I just can't think where. I'm sorry.'

Zain put his arm round her and pulled her to him. 'It'll come to you, Anika. Just put it out of your mind for now and it'll come back to you.'

As Anika cuddled into his chest, Zain met Nikki's eye. Nikki gave a slight nod, realising they were thinking the same thing. If Anika had come across the scar-faced man before, then perhaps it wasn't *Nikki* he'd been following. Perhaps Anika was his target and, if that was the case, now Freddie Downey was out of the picture, Nikki could think of only one person who might wish her sister harm. Which, of course, meant a trip to another prison tomorrow. Two prison visits on the one day wasn't something to look forward to. The only upside was that both prisons were near to each other.

Struggling to keep her voice steady, Nikki went into police mode. 'Sajid, get a copy of that recording to the tech team. I want that recording cleaned up and that man's face isolated and run through every database we have access to. Also, check out if they had any luck tracking his route after he left here.'

Nikki knew it was unlikely they'd be able to confirm his route without the benefit of the car registration number; still, they might be lucky.

Chapter 46

I spy with my little eye someone beginning with I . . . Idiot!

Can you believe it? Not only has he interrupted me when I'm reviewing footage of our most recent procurements, but – even after all his banging on earlier about being careful and not taking chances – he's put our entire operation at risk by nearly being caught red-handed outside that bitch's home. Aching spasms grip my gut as the rage works its way up through my body, lacerating every damn organ en route. My fingers tingle – itchy little worms niggling their way up my arms like scarification tattooists working from the inside out. I slam the phone on the desk and flick it to speaker mode, and then flex my digits trying to coax the pins and needles into submission.

I'm not in the mood for any more viewing now. He's spoilt it for me – tainted my joy at seeing another one of our assets succumb to the programme. Willing my body back under control, I allow the silence between us to weigh down on him. *Hope it suffocates him – pulverises him to within an inch of his life.* He clears his throat, ready with some more meaningless apologies. More pointless excuses. But I beat him to it. 'No apology can make up for this, you know? You're totally out of order. Call yourself a professional?'

I inject as much venom as I can muster into the accompanying "Humph" and wait till my blood stops thumping through my veins like a tsunami on speed. He doesn't reply and that cheers me. The memory of his earlier, barely concealed insolence hasn't quite faded yet, so I'm going to savour his discomfort. 'I think you're getting past *your* sell-by date, Scarface.' I issue his moniker like a slap to the face – a gauntlet thrown at his feet. Let's see how he responds.

The sound of him swallowing drifts from the phone. True, it's faint – but still, it's an indication that I've rattled him. Before he can speak, I pounce. 'Where are you? Right now, this instant, where are you?'

The swallow increases in volume and I roll my eyes. The fucking idiot has compounded his earlier error by rushing home to the comforting arms of his mistress. Fool! Idiot! Hasn't he realised that she's still under observation? That now is not the time for any physical contact between the players in my game?

The chill in my voice sends a shiver up my spine, never mind his. 'You're with her, aren't you?'

Silence.

'*Answer!*'

The silence is tinged with something that I can almost smell over the line – the stench of fear.

'No, no. I'm not with her. No way I'd be with . . .'

'LIAR!'

I wait till the word stops resonating through my living room before issuing my coup de grâce. 'You are *finished*. You understand? From this point on you and your whorish bitch are on your own. Come near me and my operation and I will annihilate you. Got it?'

'But . . . but.'

I cut him off and sit staring into space, my fingers at my neck checking my pulse is under control. I'd always had a contingency plan in mind. Just hadn't expected to ever have to use it and I certainly hadn't expected to lose my two most useful contacts in one fell swoop. A flutter in my chest makes pause. Have I been too hasty? No. I can't go back on my decisions. Therein lies weakness and I'm nothing if not strong. I'll have to pull in a favour. One I'd wanted to keep as a last resort, but hey. Maybe this is a last resort.

I get up and, ignoring the slight tremor in my knees, move to the abstract painting of a garden filled with strikingly vibrant flowers of various species. It's my favourite painting – the inspiration behind my whole venture. I click the secret catch on the bronze frame and it swings out into the room. Inside lie the various elements of my contingency plan. Burner phones, false passports, bank account details held on encrypted on USB sticks, cash and the other USB. The one that hosts details of where the bodies are buried – both literally and figuratively. Not that I'll be here when these files are leaked. No. I'll be long gone, smoothly slipping into my alter ego in the Bahamas and, by sleight of hand and misdirection, everyone will be more focused on rounding up my clients than finding me.

Chapter 47

The improvised incident room in DCI Ahad's office was upbeat when Nikki entered. Farah and Liam had come in early and between them had provisionally identified the last few children from Peggy's files. Nikki gratefully accepted the mug of coffee Liam offered and with a slight smile said, 'So, things are okay, are they? Between you two?'

Whilst Liam flushed and shuffled on his feet, Farah grinned. 'Course it's not going to be plain sailing.' Her lips tuned downwards as she sipped on a glass of slightly steaming water with a slice of lemon floating on top. 'Neither of our families are ready to embrace grandkids of dual heritage. But, we'll make it work.' She paused and, reaching for Liam's hand, squeezed so hard his fingers turned white. 'With or without them, eh?'

Liam's nod was firm. 'Damn right we will. Their loss if they can't embrace it. I mean, it's not like we're living in the 1990s, is it?'

Sajid grimaced. His own experiences of bucking the family trend hadn't been good. 'No, we're not, but some arseholes don't get that. Never mind, that sprog will have three uncles and an auntie at its disposal from the start. That right, Nik?'

Nikki frowned and stared at him until he rolled his eyes and opened his mouth to clarify, before turning to Liam and Farah with a grin. 'Yep, he's right. Just as well Aunty Nikki will be on hand because that kid's three uncles – Marcus, Langley and Sajid – won't be any bloody use.'

With Liam and Farah sniggering and before Sajid could work out a reply, Nikki stepped over to the map with its green and red pins. 'You matched them all, Farah? Well done. There's been a bit of a change of plan this morning. Sajid's going to take the photo pack to Peggy on his own this morning. Something weird went down last night and the boss and I are going to visit the male prison in Wakefield.'

She explained briefly what had happened the previous evening, leaving out her mistaking a car backfiring for a gunshot – she'd leave Sajid to wax lyrical about that when she wasn't there. 'The techies are trying to clean up the footage, but don't hold out much hope. The databases haven't thrown out any likenesses yet, but bearing in mind the quality of the image, that's not really surprising. Hence, mine and Ahad's trip to New Hall prison.'

'So, updates?' She looked at Sajid, who brushed his hands down his almost but not quite turquoise jacket before speaking.

'Langley has scheduled in Lisa Kane's post-mortem for first thing this morning. However, he did a preliminary examination of the wounds last night.' He inclined his head towards Nikki. 'At your request, I believe.'

Nikki nodded and Saj continued. 'Seems he was able to match the knife wounds inflicted on Lisa Kane with those found on the Salinger family.'

Liam punched the air with one fist. 'Result. Get in!'

Choosing to cut him some slack on account of him just discovering he was going to be a dad, Nikki contented herself with a slight headshake and a soft sigh as Sajid continued.

'He also found a positive match with a cold case . . .'

'Peggy Marks's family?' When Sajid nodded, she winked at Liam before raising her fist and punching the air 'Result! Get in.'

This piece of intel from Langley confirmed that Nikki and her team were right to tie the Marks's family's murders with their current investigation. However, until they had positive ID from Peggy of the children they'd managed to match to her descriptions, the families couldn't be alerted. More than that, though, it indicated that Peggy Marks may have been wrongly convicted. If nothing else it added weight to the evidence her lawyer, Colin Hewes, was compiling to have her case reopened. 'Saj, be sure to pass that information on to Peggy's solicitor when you see him.'

She turned to the two detective constables. 'In the meantime, can you two keep trying to locate Karen Salinger and Sukhjit Kholi? Give his ex-wife a ring. See if he's been in contact or if she has any idea where he may have gone.'

Just then, DCI Ahad thrust the door open so abruptly that it clattered against the wall, releasing tiny shards of painted plaster onto the carpet and reverberating there as he strode in before slamming it shut behind him.

'Shit, what's up? You look like someone pissed in your breakfast.'

Barely taking the time to glower in Nikki's direction, Ahad strode over to his desk, spun round and addressed the room at large. 'Bloody incompetent idiots!'

'Okaay.' Nikki looked at his flashing eyes and flushed cheeks. 'Care to tell us what's up?'

Ahad's chest rose, as he took in a sharp breath. 'Bloody Rawdon and Lyons up to their power games again. Pair of them have buggered off somewhere – probably to the nearest golf course – and left me to do the press briefing.' He puffed out his cheeks, which sent the red flowing upward to his forehead. 'Not that I object to doing it. It's just after all the fuss they made about them leading it and *you* being present and then on a whim, they just bog off at a moment's notice.'

He raked his fingers through his hair and forced a smile onto his lips. 'Forget it, I'm more interested in this map that you've been working on and if we can corroborate Peggy Marks's assertions. What have you got?'

Nikki gathered her thoughts. 'Well, Langley was able to match the knife wounds found on both the Salinger family's bodies and Lisa Kane's with those found on Peggy Marks's family, which . . .'

'. . . is a pretty fair indication that she's telling the truth. So, in that case . . .' Ahad gestured to the map.

Nikki nodded. 'The green pins – representing the possible matches to the children Peggy Marks described – show the spread of localities where those kids were last seen. As you can see, all of them are within a ninety-minute drive from Bradford with the majority being to the north-east of Bradford heading towards York.'

'Which helps how?'

'Well, Sajid and I were talking about this and we want to collate the information Peggy has given us about the building she was kept prisoner in and see if we can locate buildings that fit that criteria?'

Ahad frowned. 'That's a long shot don't you think? That's quite a substantial area with countless buildings to rule out.'

'Yes, it is a long shot, boss. But . . .' Nikki paused '. . . if any of those missing kids were mine, and were possibly still alive, then I'd take the long shot.' She paused, softened her tone and, refusing to feel guilty for it, played her trump card. 'Wouldn't you?'

Ahad's cheek pulsed for a moment and Nikki knew she'd made her mark. Zain had tragically lost his own child and that made these sorts of investigations harder for him. Keen to push home her advantage, Nikki continued. 'From Peggy's account, we know quite a bit about the building. We know it has a really sizeable cellar with room for twelve rooms on either side of a corridor. We know that it has at least four floors above ground level and we know that it has massive sweeping staircases. From the upstairs bedroom windows, Peggy was unable to see any main roads, although she could hear and see helicopters flying in and out frequently. She said there was a large square of grass with a white "H" painted on it, where the helicopters landed. All this information makes the house quite distinctive, which could narrow it down to only a few properties. I suggest we focus on the area with the largest proliferation of pins first.' She paused and circled her hand round a glut of pins in between Bradford and York. 'Then if we have no luck, we'll spread out.'

She looked at Ahad, whose gaze was fixated on the map and waited. He clicked his teeth, spun round and spoke to Farah and Liam. 'Get on it, now.' Then he turned to Nikki and Saj. 'Come on, we've got a couple of prison visits to make. You're driving, Nik, and we'll drop Sajid off en route.'

Chapter 48

Present Day: Marnie

The dream startles me awake. It takes me a moment to realise I'm cramped and cold and still huddled in the creaky chair by the window. The contrast between that and the warm touch on my hair and the smell of strawberries makes me gasp. For a second there I'd thought she was with me. I'd thought Jilly was right beside me, stroking my hair and whispering my mantra. *Don't let the Beep Beeps get you down, Marn. Don't ever let the Beep Beeps win.*

But that's not all she said. This time her whispers, like wisps of breath in the air, are more insistent. *Don't you dare give up. Not now. You're nearly there. You're so close to home.*

I can see her too – she's a bit flickery – almost translucent – like a ghost and she's crying. Sobbing loud and ugly tears like she's never going to stop and then she says: *It's getting harder to remember what you look like, Marn. Come back to me before I forget you completely.*

I sit up, forcing my creaking bones to move, and then I lean over and breathe on the window pane, making it steam up. And there it is, the love heart with the words *I love you, Jilly* in the middle. I move over and steam up the other side of the love heart and *I love you, Gwen* appears. I look at both messages written by my hand and I take a deep breath. If what I've written is true then I need to move. I need to fight for my freedom. I need to fight to find Jilly again before she forgets who I am.

I stink and I'm hungry, but I don't care. That's not important. Not now. Not when I know that even if there's a man in the hallway outside shouting and swearing at his girlfriend, I have to leave the flat. Even if I can't speak, I need to get out of here and get help – for me and for Gwen.

I grab Gwen's rucksack and snatch the paper and the pen from the bottom. I'll need these. I'll need everything I have – all my strength, all the tools, my money – everything.

My heart's hammering as I approach the thin door. I press my ear to it, straining for sounds of anyone outside, and when I'm content that no one's there, I grab the lock with my shaking fingers, turn it and yank the door open.

Cold air gusts up from the stairs, bringing with it a whiff of weed mixed with urine and damp. I shrug the rucksack on my shoulders, shove the paper and pen into my pocket, and head down head for the stairs. Once outside the flats, I look round. It's not raining anymore but the ground is wet and the people scurrying past are wearing raincoats.

Don't know if it's the noise or the light, or the overpowering closeness of the people elbowing past me, but I can't breathe. When we arrived at the flat, it had been by taxi, in the dark with hardly anyone about. Now everything seems a threat – looming shop doorway, reflections in the glass, tooting car horns. I want to go back inside, I want to not be here on the pavement. I bite my lip when the thought *I'd rather be back in the dungeon* hits. Then, I grasp just a hint of strawberry in the air. It's gone before I can be sure I didn't imagine it, but it's enough to root me to my spot on the pavement. Enough to loosen my chest and allow me to look both ways up and down the street.

I can't decide which way to go. To the right the street seems never-ending and to the left it seems even longer. I don't even know where I am – which city I'm in. A group of women pushing prams pass by me heading up the road to my right. They seem friendly – unthreatening, so I fall in behind them, keeping pace with them but two steps behind. Their chatter is reassuring and I find myself glancing around, checking out the shop names, looking at the buses.

I know what I'll do. I'll walk until I see a police officer or a police station and then I'll write down my name and tell them what's happened. I feel better now I have a plan in mind. It's easy. All I have to do is walk and use my eyes. No need to try to speak to anyone – not till I see Jilly.

Chapter 49

Sitting in her Touran, in the driving rain outside His Majesty's Prison Wakefield, took Nikki back to a time over a year earlier, when she'd sat outside Armley Prison in Leeds waiting to visit the same prisoner. It had been pissing it down that day too; however, then although the prisoner she'd come to visit was the same, her companion had been different. Then she'd sat with her sister, contemplating visiting the man who had been Anika's off-again on-again partner for years and who was Haqib's dad. Today, she sat with her boss, Zain Ahad, who was also her sister's new partner. Yousaf Mirza had been transferred to Wakefield prison – known as Monster Mansion – soon after his trial and Nikki had been happy to think of him housed in one of the country's highest security prisons with the other low-life sex offenders and murderers.

Neither of them spoke. Neither of them wanted to be here, yet they both – out of love and respect for Anika – were compelled to be there. Yousaf Mirza was scum if the earth as far as Nikki was concerned. Unbeknownst to them, he'd headed up a heinous trafficking organisation that sent ripples through the very fabric of Bradford's society and nearly broke Anika when the extent of his depravity had been revealed. Haqib, on the other hand, had disliked the man who had lent his DNA to him, yet had never been a father, preferring to focus his affections on his "legitimate" family and had removed all thoughts of him from his life with scalpel-like precision. Nikki had been the one to bring him down and that had fractured her relationship with Anika for a while. Now, Nikki feared that this visit might once more cause tension between the two sisters.

Although the tech team were working on cleaning up the recording Marcus had made of the man parked up outside their home, they were backed up with digital stuff from the Salinger investigation, which had to take priority. Which meant Nikki didn't know when they'd get an ID on the unidentified man. Already she'd had word that the Galaxy had merged into traffic and had all but disappeared on the Bradford streets. Her only chance at a shortcut to this man was to approach Yousaf Mirza, for he was the only threat against Anika that Nikki could identify. The fact that Anika recognised the scar-faced man indicated that she may have crossed paths with him during her time with Yousaf and, rather than wait for what might be days to get an ID from the system, Nikki was prepared to ask Mirza for a favour.

Nikki swallowed hard and looked at Zain. His jaw was clenched and a pulse throbbed at his temple. Once more Nikki wondered if she should have brought Sajid with her rather than Zain. She dismissed the thought. She'd chosen to bring Zain for a very good reason; he was totally invested in Anika and when Mirza clammed up for Nikki, Zain had the darkness to intimidate him. Her main concern was that he might lose it and end up thumping Mirza. Not that the thought of Mirza in pain caused Nikki any grief – she'd welcome the scumbag feeling even a splinter of the pain he'd inflicted on his victims, but she liked Ahad and didn't want him in trouble over a piece of crap like Yousaf Mirza. 'You ready?'

Zain nodded once and the pair of them exited the car and walked towards the entrance, each focused on the job in hand. As they neared the doors, Nikki's step faltered. She'd give anything never to have to see Mirza again, but for Anika she'd do it. After the necessary security checks, Nikki and Zain were escorted to a private room, where they could speak with Yousaf Mirza.

They sat with their backs to the door awaiting Mirza's arrival. Twanging her wristband didn't settle her nerves, yet Nikki still twanged it, again and again as they waited. On hearing footsteps approach, Nikki straightened her shoulders, pushed her hands under her thighs so she wouldn't be tempted to show weakness by twanging her band in Mirza's presence and waited for him to enter.

As soon as he recognised Nikki, Mirza's face broke into a huge smirk as he slouched across to take the chair opposite his visitors. 'Well, well, well, if it isn't the great and wonderful DS Nikki Parekh – and who have you brought with you?'

Prison had not been kind to Mirza. Carb-heavy prison food and lack of exercise had taken its toll on his waistline and his double chin wobbled as he spoke. Apart from that, his hair was receding and turning grey. Nikki quirked an eyebrow and, holding eye contact with him, ignored his question. She had no desire to tell him Ahad's rank or name. 'DI actually – I got promoted. How are your career prospects?'

Mirza slapped his palm on his thigh. 'Always the joker, eh, Nikki?' He studied her for a long time, and it took all of Nikki's resolve not to flinch when his eyes raked over her body and then back up to her face.

'How's the whore?'

Beside her, Nikki sensed Zain tense, but she forced her lips into a smile. 'Far as I know, your wife and your daughters are fine – although I had heard the younger one offers blow jobs in Kirkgate to finance her crack habit and the older one's joined the police, so she can lock up dicks like her old man.'

Mirza's eyes narrowed and his hands, on top of the table, clenched into fists. 'Fuck off, Parekh. Fuck right off and leave my family out of it. Nobody believes the crap you lot pulled on me.

The way you framed me up. No way would any of my family taint themselves by joining your lot. No fucking way!'

Neither of Mirza's daughters had joined the police, but his response was telling. It seemed that, much as he'd like to give them the impression that he was all happy families with his wife and kids, he knew nothing about their day-to-day lives. Nikki, the smile still on her lips, inclined her head. 'Gladly, we're not here to talk family stuff.' She turned over a printout of the image of the scar-faced man captured from Marcus's amateur video. 'Recognise him?'

Without even glancing at the image, Mirza pursed his lips and leaned back on the plastic chair. 'Nope.'

Nikki nodded and pushed it closer to him, then turned to Zain. 'Your turn.'

Zain's impenetrable face broke into a wide smile, which was belied by the flashing anger in his eyes as he leaned closer to Mirza. 'Look at the photo.'

Mirza's eyes moved to Zain's and stayed there for long seconds. Then, he shook his head. 'Nope, don't recognise him.'

Zain leaned over, covered Mirza's hand with one of his own and squeezed until the other man's knuckles ground together and his fingers blanched of colour. 'I'd look again, if I were you.'

Mirza tugged his hand from under Zain's and glanced at the image. 'Nope. Don't know him.'

But Nikki saw his eyes widening and his shoulder twitch. She was sure he recognised the man in the photo. Zain, clearly agreeing with Nikki, lowered his voice. 'Thing is, I know your wife's claiming benefits that she's not entitled to. That sort of fraudulent activity can lead to months in prison. Hell, maybe she'll end up next door in New Hall.'

Mirza shrugged, but didn't look at the photo again, so Zain continued, his tone conversational. 'Also, I've heard that there's a load of the big H gone missing from the drugs lock-up. It'd be hilarious if it ended up in your daughter's car, wouldn't it? Especially as she's due to get married next month.'

The surprise in his eyes was momentary, confirming Nikki's earlier suspicions that the Mirza family were estranged from their dad, but the flush that suffused his cheeks was not. Mirza inhaled and closed his eyes, clearly weighing up his options. Then he placed a chubby finger in the middle of the photo. 'I want your word you'll leave my family alone . . .'

'We just want the name, that's all,' Nikki confirmed.

He laughed. 'Well, I'm surprised that Scottish twat of a boss of yours didn't recognise him. That bastard Hegley sure knows who he is. After all he was one of yours.'

One of ours? This man was a police officer? Nikki refused to respond to his taunting, but inside she was cursing herself for not consulting with Archie before hotfooting it over here. Mirza leaned his chair backwards, lifting the front legs from the floor, and with an insolent sneer on his pasty face looked first at Nikki, then at Zain. 'That fucker's Ged Geraghty.'

That the man in the car had been a police officer, threw up an entirely different set of possibilities. Perhaps, Nikki's first assumption when she'd potted him in the car behind her the previous night was correct. Perhaps, as she'd thought, it had been Nikki he was observing. Which meant it was more than likely something to do with the Salingers. Nikki racked her brain. The name sounded familiar, yet she couldn't quite place it. Mirza's use of the past tense told her that Ged Geraghty was probably not an active police officer anymore and the fact that both Anika and Mirza recognised him more than likely meant he was a bent copper.

Nikki glanced at Zain. Where had she heard that name before? 'In your pocket was he, this Ged Geraghty? One of the bent coppers you bribed to ignore your disgusting trafficking business?'

Mirza released a halitosis-filled belly laugh into the room and raised one finger to tap the side of his nose. 'That's for *me* to know and you to find out, innit?'

Still laughing, he clattered the chair back onto four legs, and propelled his upper body across the table so he was almost within grabbing reach of Nikki. 'Tell that fucking whore of a sister of yours that she owes me and I aim to collect. Tell her not to sleep too lightly in case I send a visitor to keep her warm, if you get my drift.'

Nikki allowed her mouth to curl, but other than that gave no outward reaction to his proximity. She'd beat bigger men than him before now; but not through violence. Still, the desire to grab his balding head with both hands and smash it into the table surged through her, making her fingers twitch. The thought of stabbing her fingers through his mocking eyes and making him squeal in pain fizzled like an extreme sugar rush through her entire body.

Over her lifetime, Nikki had experienced first-hand the sort of damage animals like Mirza could do. Yet, although making him hurt would give her momentary satisfaction, she knew he wasn't worth losing her career over. Still holding his gaze, she stood up and without another word, Nikki, with Zain close behind her, strode to the door.

Mirza's sneering voice filled the room, but this time when he spoke it was laced with just a hint of desperation – high and jarring – a child unused to not being the centre of attention. 'Hey you, Ahad? That little whore any better a lay for you than she was for me?'

Nikki sensed the tension radiating from her boss, and for a second, she thought he was going to spin round and land one on Mirza. Instead, without even turning back he said, his tone lazy, unconcerned – mocking even. 'I'll tell you who *is* a good lay, Mirza. Your eldest daughter, Shazia, that's who. Pants underneath me, she does, begging for more whilst Daddy's locked up in here and can do fuck all about it.'

The door swung open and they left to the sounds of Mirza's chair scraping over the floor and the man yelling obscenities into the now-empty room.

Desperate to clear her lungs of the fetid air created by Yousaf Mirza, Nikki heaved in great breaths of bleach-filled air as the door swung shut behind them. Her last sight of Mirza was him on his feet, bulbous face tomato red, and rabid eyes flashing as he clenched and unclenched his fists ineffectually by his sides. Nikki fluttered her fingers at him in a sarcastic bye-bye action and smiled when his response was to lunge towards the closing door.

She turned to Zain, a shaky smile tugging her lips. 'You're good, boss. Bloody good.'

Chapter 50

As Sajid slipped into the back seat behind Zain and Nikki, his wide grin told them all they needed to know.

'She ID'd the kids, didn't she?' Until she heard the words coming from Sajid's lips, Nikki didn't dare get her hopes up.

'Damn right she did. She was in bits, but she did it. ID'd and named every one of them by their flower names without prompting.' He bit his lip. 'That woman is one of the bravest I've ever met. She's been through so much and yet, despite the tremors in her hand and the tears streaming down her cheeks, she looked at image after image and ID'd them.'

'And you told Hewes about the knife wounds?'

'Yeah, I did. I waited till Peggy had been taken away before telling him. Didn't want her getting her hopes up till everything was more certain, you know?'

He exhaled so loudly that Nikki felt his breath on the back of her neck. 'What about you? Get a name from Mirza?'

'Yes, sure did. Ged Geraghty. He was one of ours apparently. Name sounds familiar, but I can't place him. I've called it in and Liam's getting his file up. Mirza said Archie knew him so I've texted him, but he's not re . . .'

'. . . Geraghty? Geraghty? That was the name of the officer

that Archie mentioned. The one who was on the Winnie Salinger abduction. The one Archie said was right up Rawdon and Lyons's arses.'

Ahad's phone began to ring. 'Williams, what you got? Saj says this Ged Geraghty was on the Winnie Salinger investing . . .'

When Ahad stopped mid-sentence, Nikki frowned. 'What's up?'

But Ahad wafted his hand to tell her to be quiet, before saying, 'Hold on, Liam. I'm putting you on speakerphone.'

Liam's voice echoed into the car. 'Just had an alert from the officers stationed near Ashleigh Kholi's house. Sukhjit Kholi turned up ten minutes ago followed soon after by Derek Bland. The officers report shots fired and have requested backup. Should Farah and I head there?'

Shit! She hadn't been expecting that. She'd expected Kholi and Bland to have fled the country, one or other of them taking Karen Salinger with him, but instead he'd turned up out of the blue at his ex-wife's house and now there were reports of gunfire. Who the hell had fired them and what was Derek Bland doing visiting Ashleigh Kholi? After finding Ashleigh in such a state the other day, Nikki couldn't dismiss the idea that she might be the one responsible for the shots. She'd been mad enough with her husband, hadn't she? On the other hand, Kholi himself, according to Liam and Farah, had no love lost for his wife. As for Derek Bland, had he got wind of his goddaughter's affair with Kholi and come to have it out with him? But then why go to the York address rather than Kholi's penthouse in Leeds? None of this made sense.

Nikki started the engine. 'Is it only the three of them in the house?'

'The uniforms say a bloke arrived about tennish last night and, unless he left via the back of the house he's still there?

'A bloke? What bloke? Did they ID him?'

'They're sending an image through as we speak hold on . . .' Sounds of Liam clicking keyboard keys drifted down the line as Nikki set off.

'Fuuuuck!'

Pulling into the traffic and heading towards Holme-on-Spalding-Moor, Nikki exchanged a glance with Sajid in the rear-view mirror. Liam wasn't a swearer and the word on his lips set Nikki's nerves on edge.

'You're not gonna believe it, boss. The other guy at Ashleigh Kholi's house is Ged Geraghty. The same . . .'

'. . . bastard who was outside my house last night. The same fucker who was on Archie's team when Winnie Salinger was abducted. The ex-police officer who was all over Rawdon and Lyons?'

'The very same.' Shock had made Liam's tone husky. 'What do you want me to do, Nik?'

'You and Farah have got three jobs and now isn't the time to be bothered about press leaks. We've reached crisis point in this case. Call every available officer into the incident room. I want to establish a link between Ashleigh Kholi and Geraghty or Sukhjit Kholi and Geraghty or both. Have Farah locate the family of each of the children Peggy identified and . . .'

She glanced at Ahad, wondering if he'd object to what she was about to suggest. 'Get Archie and his team to locate Rawdon and Lyons. Tell them I don't care how they do it, I want them both found as a matter of urgency.'

As she uttered the instructions she squinted at Ahad, hoping he'd not put obstacles in her way, but to his credit he smiled a grim smile and said, 'Let's move.'

Chapter 51

I spy with my little eye something beginning with T . . .
Transformation.

I look at my reflection in the bathroom mirror of the Travelodge
and smirk. Okay, the red hair dye job wouldn't fool anyone I know
well for long, but at first glance it's enough of a distraction. The
real transformation though is the clothes. A hoodie and joggers. I
grin at how ridiculous I look. I'm like an extra on a *Little Britain*
sketch, but it does the job and that's all that matters.

In an attempt to maintain a low profile, I'd signed in to this
dive after leaving my home last night – paid with one of my many
credit cards in a different name. I'd travelled here to York via a
combination of train and bus, hoping it would make tracking me
more difficult. Last night had been busy. I'd had a lot to do and
making sure that Ged Geraghty was in the spotlight for everything
was a big part of my diversion strategy. I knew I wouldn't be able
to cover up my involvement indefinitely, but that had never been
the plan. As long as I left British soil on schedule, then I could
put up with a bit of hardship for now.

I wander back through to the bedroom and throw myself on the
bed. Ouch – no give on the bloody mattress. This budget hotel was

truly abysmal – scratchy sheets, noisy neighbours and a lingering smell of Chinese takeaway – definitely one for the proles, not for the likes of me. At least it wasn't for much longer. I'd made my plans and by this time tomorrow I'd be drinking piña colada by the beach, not a care in the world – unlike Geraghty and "Auntie" Lee-Lee and all those clients whose disgusting perversions have lined my pockets well over the years. No, every one of them will be exposed, when the bitch Parekh receives the recorded delivery with the USB stick inside.

I thought twice about letting her have the information. Didn't really want her career to benefit from exposing all my hard work and all those clients with their sordid little secrets. In the end though, who else was worthy? Zain Ahad who'd only been in his job two minutes? I don't think so. Thus, by default, Parekh won the prize. I can't wait to see what she does with it.

Chapter 52

Nikki's Touran was a lifesaver, getting them from Wakefield to the Kholis' mansion in Holme-on-Spalding-Moor in record time. When she drew up at the end of a long line of police cars, armed police unit vans and ambulances, Nikki barely turned the engine off and wrenched the handbrake on before she, Sajid and Zain spilled from the vehicle and hared towards the front of the mansion where the firearms squad with a hostage negotiator were in control.

Spotting a familiar figure, she barged through the milling uniformed officers and detectives from York and approached him. 'Marty, can you give an update?'

Marty turned, his slender frame bulked out by his Kevlar bulletproof vest, his visor pulled back for now and his Heckler and Koch MP5SF swung over his shoulder, ready should he need to use it. 'Hey, Parekh. This your case?'

Eyes raking the front of the mansion for any signs of activity, Nikki nodded. 'Yep. All four of those inside are involved in my current investigation. Any word of injuries or fatalities?'

'No. We only arrived ten minutes ago and are still trying to open lines of communication. So far, we've been unable to establish which one of the three men has the gun. Greenie, our boss, brought a negotiator in and we're trying to ascertain if anyone's been injured. Only one shot has been fired so far and we want to keep it that way.'

Nikki edged her way closer to the firearms unit leader. Nikki didn't recognise her, but she wanted Greenie to be aware that she might be able to provide information on the four people inside. This was her job and, until she and her team had secured the scene and liberated the hostages, Nikki and her team had only observational roles.

Greenie glowered at her and opened her mouth, presumably to tell Nikki to back off. However, she was interrupted by a voice from the speakerphone that the negotiator was using to communicate with whoever held the gun inside the Kholi house. The voice was male and his words were accompanied by heavy breathing. 'You lot need to get the fuck away from here. This is private business and you lot are trespassing.'

Nikki leaned toward Greenie. 'I'm DI Nikki Parekh and that's Sukhjit Kholi. His wife is the female hostage and also inside are a business associate of his – Derek Bland – and an ex-police officer Ged Geraghty, who we suspect of being involved in multiple murders and possible child trafficking. I've no idea why Bland is here, but my team are working on establishing links between the four of them.'

Greenie's nod was curt, but she relayed the information to the negotiator who gave Nikki a thumbs up. 'Mr Kholi, a gunshot was heard. Could you at least let us know if there are any casualties inside?'

The negotiator's request was met by silence. Nikki, still scanning the front façade of the Kholi home, thought she saw movement at an upstairs window. 'First floor far right window.'

Greenie's smile was taut. 'Our snipers have eyes on that, thanks. Now, can you head over there where your colleagues are or put a stab vest and helmet on and keep your head down. What's it to be?'

Nikki looked behind her and saw that Sajid and Zain had been

301

stopped by two of Greenie's team and now stood behind a police car out of range of any potential gunfire. 'I'll vest up,' said Nikki grabbing the body armour from Marty and quickly putting it on.

A crackle from the speakerphone focused their attention once more on the house as Kholi spoke.' I want to speak to whoever's in charge of the Salinger family murder investigation.'

The negotiator raised an eyebrow to Greenie who hesitated briefly before speaking to Marty. 'Can you vouch for her?'

Marty winked at Nikki. 'Yep. She won't lose her head, boss. She's a Trojan.'

'Don't need a Trojan – just a sensible low-key negotiation that gets those four out here in one piece, right?' Her scowl intensified as she turned to Nikki. 'You take guidance from the negotiator – he's the expert, okay? He tells you to clam up – you clam up. He tells you to flirt – you flirt. He tells you to do ten burpees with your bare arse in the air and what do you do?'

Nikki held Greenie's gaze and replied – deadpan, 'I do ten burpees with my bare arse in the air.'

Resting a hand on Nikki's shoulder the other woman squeezed. 'Sometimes the personal touch works. If you've got insight that we don't, it might play in our favour . . . just don't rush things. Take your time before replying, okay?' She nodded to the negotiator, who unmuted the speaker. 'DI Parekh is here. You can talk to her, Mr Kholi. She wants to work out what happened to the Salinger family. Here she is now.'

Nikki stepped forward, sweat making the bulletproof vest seem heavier. 'Hi, Mr Kholi. Before we talk, I need you to confirm *who* is in the house with you and if any of them are injured.'

The pause before he replied was interminable. 'Bullshit. You're not calling the shots. You had your chance to sort this out, but you fucked up. This time, *I'm* going to sort things out. These people are animals. Fucking animals. Can't believe I didn't see the lying bitch for what she was. All those years married to her and I'd no idea what she and her fucking boyfriend were up to.'

That was interesting. Who was Ashleigh Kholi's boyfriend? Bland? That didn't sit quite right with Nikki, so was Geraghty Ashleigh Kholi's boyfriend? If so, that made Kholi's outrage more understandable. From what Williams and Anwar had reported back, Kholi was a snob. He'd hate the very thought that someone like Geraghty was cuckolding him. As for his disclaimer – well that could work two ways. Either he was trying to squirm out of it by laying the blame at his wife's door or he genuinely had nothing to do with the trafficking operation and the Salingers' deaths. The easy way to find out for sure was to extricate all four of them in one piece.

Nikki's tongue flicked out, moistening her dry lips. 'There's no need for anyone else to get injured, Mr Kholi. No need at all.' Grasping for something that might spark a connection with the man, Nikki landed on something. 'What about Karen? You don't want to leave her on her own to clear all of this up, do you? I mean you know that if you fire . . .'

Whatever she'd been going to say next was drowned out by the sound of a gunshot; sharp and loud. All around Nikki the air seemed to move of its own volition as another retort rent the air and a cry from inside the house rung out.

Greenie, speaking into her chest-mounted walkie-talkie swung her gun into her hands and, with her team flanking her, headed for the entrance. 'All units to the house. Suspect has been neutralised. Be on guard to clear the house.'

Nikki glared after them. She'd been played. They'd used her to lull Kholi into a false sense of security and then when he'd reared his head, they'd taken him out. Anger flooded her body as she took to her heels after them. This was her investigation. Her case and Greenie had killed off one of her main suspects.

She made it as far as the edge of the grass before Sajid launched at her in a full-out rugby tackle that landed her flat on her face with his arms wrapped round her knees as he wheezed like a fifty-a-day smoker into the grass. She struggled to extricate herself. 'Get off me.'

But Sajid held on limpet-like till Ahad appeared and dragged her to her feet with a 'Get a grip, Parekh. What the hell do you think you can do in there now? You're not the bloody cavalry, you know?'

Meanwhile Saj looked down at his once-pristine white shirt, which was now covered in mud and grass stains. His gaze travelled down further to his almost turquoise trousers and a low groan left his lips. 'Look what you made me do, Nik.'

If she hadn't been so angry she may have been amused by his huffy little hard-done-by look, but she could barely see straight, through the red haze that floated in front of her eyes.

A shrill whistle splintered the air and shouts from the doorway made Nikki turn just in time to see paramedics with a stretcher jogging over. Within a couple of seconds Marty appeared and another piercing whistle followed by his waving hand beckoned her inside. Followed by Zain and Saj – who was still moaning about his clothes – Nikki, ignored the chill of her wet clothes and marched over. On reaching the door, she glowered at Marty, who responded with a wide grin as she barged past him, jogging upstairs to the room on the far right.

As she wended her way through the house Greenie's team, having cleared the premises, allowed her access. The door of the room was open, the breeze from the shattered window chilling the air. Nikki stepped in and glanced around. In one corner a tear-stricken Ashleigh Kholi cradled the dead body of Ged Geraghty in her lap. Geraghty's blood smudged her face and hands as she rocked him back and forth, the gaping hole in his chest bloody testament to how he'd died. Sajid peeled away from Nikki, approached Ashleigh Kholi and read her rights. The woman continued rocking the body of her dead lover, her eyes staring unseeing ahead.

'She's in shock, sir. We'll take her to hospital and you can interview her later.'

There was nothing Saj could do as he watched the paramedic coax Ashleigh to her feet, so he turned to a constable who hovered by the door. 'You go with her. I want to know the second she's given the all clear to be interviewed, okay?'

Supported by the paramedic and the police officer, Ashleigh paused before shuffling from the room and with a glint in her eye that belied the paramedics' earlier assessment of her condition and said, 'You'll never catch the smarmy bastard. You know that, right? He's long since gone. Now I want a lawyer.'

Fists clenched, Nikki – who'd witnessed the interaction – glowered at the woman for a second before turning her attention to Derek Bland who was slumped against the back wall. When he saw Nikki, he tried to get to his feet, but stumbled and had to lean against the wall to remain upright. Her eyes bounced past him to the figure huddled on the floor under the shattered window. Two paramedics were tending a wound on Sukhjit Kholi's upper arm whilst as he stared straight ahead, tears trickling down his cheeks, his eyes glazed. Heart hammering against her chest, Nikki exhaled slowly. She'd been convinced the sniper had killed Kholi and in the process denied her the chance to interview him. She wasn't concerned that he was injured. He was a key suspect and at the very least he had information on the whereabouts of Karen Salinger.

In two strides she was looming over him. 'Where's Karen Salinger, Kholi?'

His eyes flickered up to her, then as he registered who she was, a thin smile twitched his lips. 'She's safe. Safe from that murdering paedo Geraghty and that whore of a wife of mine who helped him.'

The paramedics tried to obstruct Nikki, but she pushed past them. 'Are you saying Geraghty killed her family? Did he have something to do with Winnie's abduction?'

Kholi's lips turned into a sneer. 'The two of them planned it together – that bitch over there and Geraghty and one of your lot. One of your bosses. We heard them arguing about it before we came in. Something about a house nearby.' Kholi lifted a shaking hand to sweep his sweat-drenched hair from his forehead. 'They're sick. So sick.' But Nikki had no intention of going easy on him. 'Is that why you shot him?'

Kholi's eyebrows flew upwards, his face paling. 'I didn't . . .'

'He didn't shoot him.' Bland, having mastered the ability to hold his own weight, walked over. '*She* did that. Ashleigh shot Geraghty because he was going to leave without her. He's always been her bit of rough, has Geraghty. Always had her wrapped around his finger. That's why she got involved with the whole trafficking thing in the first place. Let her take the fall for everything.'

A wave of exhaustion made Nikki's shoulders slump. This was a nightmare and they still hadn't located Karen Salinger or any other abducted children. She'd no time for distractions. 'What are you even doing here, Derek?'

'Karen made me come. She was worried about that piece of shit's safety.' He jerked his chin towards Kholi. 'Made me promise to stop him doing anything rash. Personally, I wanted to kill the bastard myself, but she begged me not to. Said they're in love.' He all but spat the last word at Kholi.

Nikki took a moment to digest the information, only half conscious of Greenie, Sajid and Ahad waiting by the door.

'So Geraghty was going to leave Ashleigh to take the fall for the murders and Winnie's abduction?'

Bland's laugh was hoarse and filled with venom. 'And the rest. That's only the tip of the iceberg. They've been up to this stuff for years. That bitch couldn't talk enough before you lot arrived. She was boasting about what they'd put those kids through. Can you believe it? Boasting.' He gripped his cheeks with both hands, his fingers leaving red marks as they scrawled down his face. 'They're monsters. Both of them fucking perverted monsters.'

He took a deep breath. 'After she shot him, she sort of collapsed into hysteria, so we overpowered her and took the gun. Sukhjit held it to her head and made her confess. Here . . .'

306

Bland thrust his phone to Nikki. 'I recorded her confession. I got it all down on here. It'll tell you all you need to know.'

Nikki's eyes narrowed. 'The only thing I need to know right now is where the fuck is Karen Salinger?'

Chapter 53

Leaving DCI Ahad to supervise the Kholi house crime scene and arrange for the transportation of Ashleigh Kholi and Derek Bland back to Trafalgar House for interview, followed by Sukhjit Kholi when he was cleared by the paramedics, Nikki flew out of the house with Sajid, still bemoaning his spoiled clothing, and dove into her car.

'Can you believe this? What a bloody fiasco.' As she waited for Sajid to belt up, she slammed her hand against the steering wheel. If that little madam had come straight to us instead of swanning off to Kholi, then Lisa Kane would still be alive and we'd have located the children still held captive by now.'

Soon as he was strapped in, she screeched past the ambulance that had Kholi inside and tore back towards Leeds. The only reason she wasn't still inside the house tearing a strip off both Kholi and Bland was because she wanted to get to Karen Salinger before any harm befell her. When Bland admitted that he'd smuggled her into a room at the Midland Hotel at Kholi's behest, Nikki had wanted to throttle him. Instead she'd diverted her energy into getting to Leeds as quickly as possible.

With Liam and Ahad on the line with constant real-time updates, Nikki had requested radio blackout on Karen Salinger's whereabouts.

With so many questions churning in her mind, plus the continued absence of both Rawdon and Lyons and the uncertainty surrounding the location of the children identified by Peggy, Nikki was taking no chances. She and Sajid would collect Karen Salinger themselves. Her only concession had been to request that Archie stake out Bland's apartment from a distance until they arrived, to make sure nothing happened to the girl. Of course, Karen would be in shock. If Bland was to be believed, she'd barely been reunited with her long-lost abducted sister Winnie, when she'd witnessed her entire family being annihilated and had only just managed to escape with her life. But that didn't excuse the irresponsible behaviour of her much older lover and her godfather in not encouraging her to share her information with the police. Under her breath she mumbled vows of prosecuting both of them on obstruction charges.

Pulling into Forster Square car park behind the Midland Hotel, Nikki waved to Archie as she passed his car and parked a few spaces down from him. Not wasting time with unnecessary conversations, she and Sajid ran straight to the entrance and pulled their warrant cards to ensure speedy access to the hotel suite. Bland had given Nikki his keycard in case Karen was too frightened to open the door for them. Nikki didn't bother knocking; instead she marched straight in, leaving Sajid to sort out the alarm and strode through to the living area where she found Karen Salinger, huddled on a couch, TV remote in hand, flicking through the channels.

As soon as she saw them, Karen was on her feet, fleece blanket gripped in her clenched hands under her chin as if that would be enough to protect her should they wish to do her harm.

Her hair hung in greasy rats' tails around her face and her cheeks were sunken.

Nikki stretched a hand out in a soothing gesture and edged closer as if the girl was a frightened horse. 'It's okay, Karen. It's okay. I'm DI Nikki Parekh and that's DS Sajid Malik. We're here to help you. Geraghty, the man with the scar, is dead and your uncle Derek and Sukhjit Kholi are helping us with our inquiries. You don't need to be scared anymore. You're safe.'

The girl closed her eyes and gulped in huge breaths of air as if she'd been holding her breath since the night her family was killed. 'He's dead?'

Her eyes, wide and blinking, looked so much like those of her sister that Nikki was momentarily struck dumb. Winnie and Karen were mirror images of each other and the tragedy of Winnie escaping her abductor and reuniting with her family, only to be brutally killed, pierced Nikki's heart. However, she had a job to do and so much time had already been wasted. 'Yes, he's dead and you're safe, Karen, but we need your help. Will you help us?'

Sajid, so as not to startle the traumatised girl, had remained by the door, but as Karen's eyes met his, he smiled and did his Sajid thing. 'DI Parekh is right, Karen. We need your help to find some other kids who have been taken from their families, like Winnie was taken from yours.'

Sajid's soothing tones had the desired effect and as the tension left the girl's shoulders, Karen nodded and plonked herself back down on the couch, still clutching her comfort blanket close to her chin. Nikki sat next to her, leaving a little space between them. 'Karen, we need to ask you lots of questions, but we won't do all of that right now. What we most want to know about, right now, is Winnie and what she told you. Can you do that?'

A single tear trickled down the girl's cheek, but she nodded.

'How did Winnie come to be there in your home on Sunday night?'

'She phoned the house phone and Dad answered. They'd never changed the number. In all those years they'd never changed it. Just in case she phoned. At first, he couldn't believe it was her so he asked her why we all called her Winnie and . . .' a wistful smile tugged fleetingly at her lips '. . . she told him it was because instead of calling her Gwennie when I first started to talk, I called her Winnie. It stuck. We all called her Winnie and she loved it. So, you see, he knew it was her.'

Nikki smiled, and let the girl talk.

'We didn't know what to do at first, so Dad said he'd come and collect her and bring her home. She was in York near the train station, so Dad went and brought her. That was in the afternoon. She'd made him promise that only we would be there – nobody else, so Mum and Dad didn't tell anyone and they cancelled Uncle Derek coming. We thought we were getting her back.'

Sajid approached and handed her a glass of water, which Karen took and sipped from a few times before placing it on the coffee table. 'At first all we did was cry. Then she said she wanted pizza and then she wanted to play Monopoly. We had our own simple rules for the game and she said she'd never forgotten them. We'd barely set up the game round the dining room table when she began to cry. It was like she'd never stop. Then my dad put his arms round her and said, "Tell us about it, Winnie. Tell us what happened to you."'

Karen chewed on her chapped lips until she'd regained control. 'She told us a man with a scar on his face had grabbed her from Fogarty Woods when she was playing hide-and-seek with her friends. She said he took her to a massive house and kept her in a dungeon for ages and told her to forget her old name; she was to be called Rose from then on. Eventually, she said, he took her upstairs and she was allowed to live with the other kids as long as she . . .' She looked straight at Nikki. 'As long as she let the men do what they wanted to her.'

Nikki reached over and squeezed Karen's knee. 'You're doing fine, Karen. Really good. Did Winnie have any idea where this big house was?'

'No, she said they blindfolded her when they let her go.'

'Did she know why they let her go after so long?'

Karen shrugged. 'Winnie said they told her and Lily that they were too old to please the men now. She was supposed to stay away from us – that was the deal – but she didn't. She came to us and now she's dead, *and* Mum *and* Dad *and* Jason. They're all dead.'

With each successive name that left her lips, Karen's voice became higher and more agitated. Nikki wanted to gather her in her arms and rock her to sleep, like she would if it was Charlie or Ruby, but she didn't have that luxury. 'Karen, I wish we didn't have to ask you this, but we do. We need to be clear about what happened to your family. How they came to be killed. Can you be brave and tell us?'

Karen closed her eyes, her leg jiggling under the fleece, her fists clenched by her sides. It was a long time before she spoke and when she did it was in a whisper that Sajid's phone was only just able to record. 'I needed the loo. Can you believe that?' She glared at Nikki. 'I'm alive because I needed a fucking piss and they're all dead because they didn't want to give away that I was upstairs. That's why they stayed quiet. That's why they didn't bloody move or try to overpower him. They were hoping I'd escape or phone for help or something.'

Tears fell from her eyes, but it was as if the girl didn't even notice them. 'It was all a bit too much for me, you know? Winnie coming back. The things that had happened to her. The board game. Playing happy families like nothing had happened – all of it, was too much for me, so I escaped to the loo. Don't know how long I was gone, but it must have a while. Then I heard noises from downstairs. It sounded like a scream, but I thought that couldn't be right so I waited. Then I heard more noises – Dad yelling, Mum crying and I crept to the top of the stairs where I could look over the banister. The dining room door was open and a big man was there. His hand was . . .' Her eyes snapped open.

'He went for them one at a time and they just let him. Nobody moved, except Dad – don't know if they were stunned or what. Then when they were all dead, he went around the table stabbing and slashing them and there was so much blood. He was laughing like it was the most fun he'd ever had. Like he was enjoying it.

I sat on the steps with my fist stuffed in my mouth, then I realised he'd come for me next, so I crept down and snuck into the kitchen, but he heard me and yelled. I shoved on Dad's old wellies and dashed out the back door and down to the stables. He followed. I could hear him behind me, but I snuck in beside Jet, my horse, and covered myself in the straw from his stall. I was there for hours. Then, when I thought it would be safe to leave, I snuck down the back lanes and over the fields and then I phoned Sukhi and he snuck out of his flat and came for me.'

Nikki gave the girl a moment to recalibrate then gently touched her knee. 'We're almost done, Karen, but this is really important. Did you say Winnie was released with another girl?'

Karen dragged the back of her hand over her face and sniffed. 'Yes, Lily. She was waiting for Winnie back in the little flat Winnie had got for them in York.' Almost as an afterthought she added, 'Lily doesn't speak.'

Nikki glanced at Sajid, but he already had his phone out and was stepping out of the room to phone that information in to Liam who was still coordinating things from Bradford.

Nikki reached over and gestured for the family liaison officer who Sajid had requested to sit next to Karen. 'This is Sal. She's going to look after you. She'll take you to the police station and you'll be able to see your godfather, okay?'

Chapter 54

Present Day: Marnie

It gets easier being outside with all the people. Now it's like they're protecting me. Offering me cover. The ladies with the buggies had gone into Costa and for a moment I watch them settle themselves in the soft seats by the window. As two of them head over to the counter, I wonder if I'll ever have kids. But then the thought of what that entails grips me and I shudder. I'll never ever do that "thing" again. Never – even if it means I can't have kids.

I move on down the road and enter an area that's filled with little shops and loads of people but no cars. It's all cobbly, like the little path behind our house. That makes me think of Jilly and I start looking round wondering if she's nearby and if I'd even recognise her. The name of the street catches my eye: Little Shambles. That makes me smile, but then as I walk on, I see something else. Something that makes my heart flutter – and I pick up my pace. It's a green sign pointing in all different directions and I recognise one of the words on it: Jorvik. I know where I am now. York. Then I see a policeman up ahead and he's looking at me – staring – and I begin to panic. I back away down the street, but he follows, speeding up. So I go faster and then he raises his hand and shouts, 'Marnie? Marnie? Is that you? I want to help.'

I stop and turn round. *How does he know my name?*

He's slowed right down now, smiling at me, not moving any closer and I realise he's giving me a choice. It's a long time since I've had a choice, so my eyes dart back the way I've come and then back to his smiling face and I make my decision.

Chapter 55

Adrenaline helped Nikki bench the emotions her conversation with Karen Salinger evoked. Plenty of time to dissect those later. She followed Sajid back out to the car and tossed her keys to him. 'I'm done in. Can you drive?'

Sajid grimaced. 'Me, drive that thing?'

Despite his joking response, his eyes betrayed how much the meeting with Karen had affected him. Whilst Nikki's go-to coping strategy was to mull over things whilst Sajid drove, his was the opposite. He liked to have something to focus on and driving was his thing – even if the vehicle in question wasn't his own Jag.

Nikki, in the passenger seat, glanced at her phone which she'd had on silent whilst interviewing Karen Salinger and realised she'd had five missed calls from Liam and two from Zain in the past five minutes. 'Your phone on silent too, Saj?'

He grimaced and checked his iPhone. 'Shit, yeah. I've got a load of missed . . .'

But Nikki was already speaking to Liam with the phone set to speaker. 'What you got?'

'Thanks to that tip-off about Lily, or Marnie as she's known, I put out a BOLO as per Sajid's instructions and we got a hit. A super-vigilant constable spotted her from the age progression image and brought her in. She's being transported from York to Bradford Royal Infirmary as we speak so she can be checked over. Although – she's not actually speaking. Not yet anyway. But Farah's contacted her family and by luck they still live at the same address. They're heading direct to BRI. Farah's going to interview the girl in the presence of her parents after she's been given the all clear at the hospital.'

York? Too many connections with that city and its surrounding district. She rolled her shoulders, anticipating another journey in that direction, but still, the fact that Marnie Ford had been found alive and well was cause for celebration. Hopefully, if she wasn't too traumatised, she'd be able to provide some valuable information for them. 'That's brilliant. Bloody brilliant, Liam. Any progress on the manor house Peggy described?'

'Well, nothing specific yet. I've been watching DCI Ahad interview her and she's blaming Geraghty for everything, However, she let slip that the house wasn't far from her house. I've alerted the firearms unit to be on standby and York police too.'

'Sajid and I will head that way now. Maybe by the time we get there, you'll have narrowed the search parameters a bit more. Any luck locating Rawdon or Lyons?'

'Not a bloody thing. Uniforms went to both their homes, but they were locked up tight. We've managed to link Geraghty to both Rawdon and Lyons, but purely professionally so far. We'll keep at it.'

'What about boltholes for either Rawdon or Lyons. Or significant others – can they shed light on their whereabouts?'

'Neither are married and we're having difficulty finding any recent significant other for either of them.'

Nikki exhaled. 'Figures, really. Nobody would put up with those dicks. Keep me informed, Liam.'

Chapter 56

I spy with my little eye something beginning with F . . . Freedom!

I drive down the long drive to Blossom Top Manor in the beaten-up Mini I bought for cash from a scrappie on the outskirts of Bradford. It juddered and hiccupped all the way here and at times I wondered if it would make it, but here we are.

As the house comes into sight, I veer to the right. I'm not heading up there. No need. Yet I pause and peer through the light drizzle to the windows on the fourth floor. A crowd of little flowerheads and a huddle of metals are gathered at one of the windows. They'll be expecting Auntie Lee-Lee to come, or Scarface, but I don't care. I drive on, not letting myself dwell on the fate of my assets should they not be discovered for days. Not my problem. I drive right past the helipad and nose the Mini into the underground garage, before grabbing my bag and getting out. Not long to wait now. Minutes, I should think. Humming George Michael's "Freedom" to myself, I scan the air for signs of the helicopter I've ordered. It's not taking me far. Just up to Inverness, where I'll catch my chartered flight to Amsterdam under the prestigious name of Karl Merriweather. From there it's a commercial flight to the Bahamas.

Chapter 57

The mid-afternoon sun cast its rays through the scurrying white clouds and a rainbow appears, as Nikki and Sajid pull off the M62 at Junction thirty-six. The only pot of gold Nikki wanted to find right now was the missing children, but she found herself taking hope from the delicacy of its colours and the perfection of its arch. They'd find the kids and when they did they'd know who was in the trafficking ring with Ged Geraghty and what role Ashleigh Kholi had played.

Her phone rang, rousing her from her reverie. As she leaned forward in the passenger seat she answered on speakerphone. 'Tell me you've narrowed it down, Liam.'

Matching his boss's clipped tones and with tension vibrating through every word, Liam said, 'Five possibilities: *The Shambles, Orchard House, Hill Crest, Flower Top, The Stables.* I've texted you the codes. What do you reckon?'

Nikki looked at the list for a moment and then caught Sajid's eye. He nodded and together they said, 'Flower Top. It's got to be Flower Top.'

Even with her decision made, a tight band of tension circled her chest. *What if we're wrong? What if we got this wrong?* Exhaling, she blocked the thought. They had five choices and only one stood out. They had to make the choice. 'Get armed officers and paramedics there. Sajid and I are on our way.' And without further ado, she typed the GPS coordinates for Flower Top into the sat nav and almost collapsed with relief when she realised the property was only five minutes' drive away.

Without another word, Saj swung the car round and headed towards their destination. This would be one of the longest short drives of their lives.

On the edge of her seat, seatbelt stretched behind her, Nikki peered through the windscreen, determined not to miss the opening into the long swirling drive. She dreaded to think what might await her when they arrived, but at least the rainbow was still there – almost as if it was leading them to that pot of gold she so craved.

With a screech, Sajid swung off the road, through gates that obligingly stood open and sped up a serviceable narrow lane that led to the sprawling mansion in the distance. The gates being ajar was ominous. Nikki's jaw clenched even tighter, making her teeth ache. What if she'd made the wrong call? What if Flower Top wasn't the headquarters?

'Come on, Saj, go faster.'

A whirring noise overhead distracted her. It was getting ever louder. *A helicopter. A fucking helicopter.* Why hadn't she thought of that? She stretched even closer to the windscreen, peering into the sky trying to get eyes on the aircraft. Behind her, the sound of sirens and squealing wheels joined the fray and Nikki cast a glance behind her. Backup had arrived but would they be in time? 'Come on, Saj. Come on!'

In silence he put his foot down and her Touran pressed forward. Ignoring the ever-looming helicopter that was circling a patch of land to their right, Nikki scanned the fascia of the enormous house. Were those faces in the windows upstairs? Then movement near the helipad made her grab Sajid's arm. 'That way.'

But Saj had already seen the abandoned van, driver's door

open and a large man, tie flapping behind him running full pelt towards another man – an equally huge man with red hair carrying a large bag of some sort who was approaching the helipad from the opposite direction.

'What the fuck? Is that . . . ?'

But Nikki batted Sajid's words aside. 'Just drive onto that helipad. If we're on it the helicopter can't land. Move it!'

Changing direction to comply with Nikki's instructions, Sajid screeched towards the marked-off area with the large H, the line of blues and twos, the armed response vehicle and three ambulances following at speed. Nikki, bouncing on her seat, suddenly slipped off her seatbelt and as they grew level with the two men who had fought one another – like two enormous mountains battling for the valley beneath, she swung open her door and flung herself sideways out of the car, rolling onto the grass verge and without a moment's hesitation she ran full tilt towards the fighting men. Saj's anguished 'NIKKI! Noooooo!' ringing in her ears.

A quick glance behind her told her the armed response unit had mounted the verge and were overtaking police cars to get to her, but she didn't even have time to process that thought properly. The two men were on the ground punching each other, blood flying, the thwack of fist meeting bone rending the air. Now she was right there, Nikki recognised them both, and a wave of anger so powerful surged through her stealing all logical thought from her as she launched herself at them. The one with the red hair was on top so she focused her attention on him. All her weeks of pummelling that inanimate punchbag radiated from her bare fists as she went in – a fireball half the size of the behemoths on the ground beneath her. The skin on her knuckles split as her fist landed on the side of his head, knocking it to the side and giving the man beneath him a lifeline. But Nikki couldn't have that. They were a threat to her and no way did she want either of them getting into that helicopter, which now hovered a few feet off the ground near where Sajid had left the car.

'Nikki, stop it.'

His voice came to her as if through cotton wool, and she continued pummelling – first the guy in the suit, then the red-haired guy – *left, right, left. Left, right, left. Left, right, left.*

'Parekh, I'm the good guy. Stop it. He's getting away.'

Nikki looked down into the blood-spattered face of Superintendent Rawdon. His hands were cupped together defensively over his face and she realised she had straddled his chest and with her hand raised. She was ready to drive her fist into his face. She glanced to the side and saw the red-haired man, limping and dragging his bag towards the helicopter as Saj tried to cut him off. She rolled off Rawdon, and darted towards Sajid, as he launched himself at their quarry. A warning shot rang out and for a second everyone stopped.

Then, the helicopter pulled upwards and disappeared off into the sky, while a battered and broken Chief Superintendent Lyons fell to his knees, hands raised to the retreating copter. 'NNNNooooooo!'

Nikki, bent over, bleeding hands resting on her knees as she barked out orders to the various officers now storming the area. 'Get both these two men secured, then get up to the main house.'

Greenie and Marty from the firearms unit approached, Marty trying unsuccessfully to cover his smirk, whilst his boss's face was as dark and dangerous as the thunder they'd had the other night. 'What the actual fuck was that? Who do you think you are, fucking Mel Gibson?'

Nikki closed her eyes and studied the blood pooling from her wounded knuckles and tried to catch her breath. Without warning, she leaned over and vomited . . . then vomited again.

Chapter 58

'You won't tell him, will you, Saj?' Nikki was sitting at the back of an ambulance having her hands dressed by a paramedic.

Greenie had insisted on taking over the Flower Top crime scene and because of Nikki's involvement in the fight between Rawdon and Lyons, had arranged for both men to be escorted back to Trafalgar House where DCI Ahad would interview them. With remarkable efficiency and sensitivity, Greenie's team had cleared the house and escorted the children who were captive inside out to waiting ambulances.

Refusing to have her hands looked at till the children – eight girls and six boys – had been assessed by the paramedics and were en route to be reunited with their families at the nearest hospital, Nikki watched as they blinked and held hands, their slight frames fragile, their expressions uncertain. Whilst the residue of her earlier rage still churned her stomach, it was overtaken by worry for what the future would hold for these kids. Whilst rescuing them was a huge achievement, Nikki knew the road ahead for them and their families would be hard.

'You're kidding, right? You really think Marcus isn't going to notice when you roll up home with two massive balloon bandages on your hands?'

Nikki looked down at them. The paramedic had wrapped them tight and now, although her fingers peeked out the top, Nikki knew she was in for an uncomfortable few days till they began to heal. Not only that, but Marcus would also be furious. 'You think I could kip on your couch for a few days? Just, you know, till . . .'

But Sajid was already shaking his head. 'No bloody way, Nik. You're on your own on this one.'

He was right – she couldn't avoid Marcus. That wasn't how they did things. But how could she explain the rage that had made her act so irresponsibly? The after effects of her diving from the car and doing a kamikaze roll over the ground were beginning to make themselves felt. Her shoulders ached – her thigh too – and she was sure her knees were scraped and her nose felt swollen. All she could tell him was that seeing two senior officers – officers who should be above reproach – had loosened an anger like never before. Everything she'd stood for in all her years as a police officer meant nothing in the face of this level of corruption.

Okay, she'd heard Rawdon was saying he'd grown suspicious of Lyons, which was why he'd been tailing him, but that didn't wash with her. By not sharing his suspicions with her and her team he had compromised the investigation, risked the lives of those children, protected the abusers and was indirectly responsible for Lisa Kane's death. The police force she'd joined was all about cooperation and keeping the streets clean. The bosses were supposed to exemplify the honesty and integrity of the entire organisation and now one senior officer had used his position as a cover in order to run, without detection, a perverted child trafficking ring, whilst a second had thwarted an ongoing investigation.

Nikki vowed to make sure both paid for their actions in the harshest ways possible.

With the CSIs in place now, Nikki knew Flower Top would be an active crime scene for many weeks. Bearing in mind Peggy's assertion that some of the children had just vanished, never to be seen again, Nikki had suggested that Greenie bring in cadaver dogs.

They'd made a beeline for the gardens at the rear of the house and a team of specialist forensic anthropologists had been called in to exhume the area. At the thought of how many children's bodies would be discovered there and how many families would be affected, a lump formed in Nikki's throat.

The sense of satisfaction she felt at putting an end to this perverted business was tinged by an overpowering sense of helplessness. She got to her feet, thanked the paramedic and, stifling a groan as her muscles protested, she shuffled towards her car. 'Come on, Saj. Back to the office. This case isn't over till we've unveiled the name of every sick bastard who acted out their perverted fantasies here in this house. She glanced at the sky and saw that the rainbow – or was it a different one? – was still there.

Maybe it was telling her that doing her job was enough. Making sure Peggy Marks's wrongful conviction was squashed, that the rescued children were now free, that those buried under the flowerbeds would be found and returned to their families, that Marnie Ford was reunited with her family, that those responsible were prosecuted and those who used these children were exposed, that Karen Salinger saw justice for her family – maybe that would have to be enough.

Chapter 59

Present Day: Marnie

I try so hard to tell them everything they need to know. I write it all down. The nice officer – Farah – sits nearby smiling at me, offering encouragement and eating ginger nut biscuits and my mum, older and with grey in her hair and sad eyes, sits beside me. She tells me Jilly will be there soon – that she's on her way from uni just to see me. That none of them, not her, not Dad – who sits in the corner, trying not weep – not Jilly, none of them have ever forgotten me. I want to tell her I would have been happy at the school she chose for me, but I can't speak. Even now the words won't come out.

When they first saw me, Mum and Dad hugged me so tight and after we'd stopped crying, she told Farah that her questions would have to wait. But I pulled away from them and took the scraps of paper Gwen had left for me and wrote NO in big letters.

So, I write down all about Scarface and how he stole me from my garden a long time ago. I tell them about the dungeon and being dressed like a doll. About the cold water, about being hungry and about all the other kids, about Auntie Lee-Lee and the rules and, although it's hard and I cry the whole time I'm doing it, I tell them about the men too.

Page after page, and Farah reads them all, her face growing paler and paler with each leaf of paper. But still she smiles at me. Tells me I'm safe. Tells me I'm doing a good job. Tells me I'll feel better for getting it all out.

After I've told her about the men, she bites her lip, pushes another can of pop towards me and says, 'Can you describe them, these men? Distinguishing marks? Scars, moles, age, hair colour – anything?'

But I can do better than that – I can tell her their names. I grab the sheets of paper from my bra and hand it to Farah. As she reads down the list of typed names, she frowns. 'Where did you get this, Marnie?'

I write: *Gwen.* Then add, *She stole it from Scarface before we left.* I gesture for her to turn the page and as she reads it her mouth makes an "o" shape. When she looks at me, her eyes are sad and I know what she's going to say. I've known from the moment that police officer with the nice eyes said my name in York. I shake my head. I don't want to hear the words.

I write: *I know she's gone. I know Gwen didn't make it, but don't say it – not out loud, not yet.*

As I bow my head and try not to cry, she reaches out and squeezes my hand. Then the door opens and all at once I can smell strawberries and my head jerks up as I look into a familiar face – older, slimmer – but still familiar to me.

'Jilly' I say – the one word croaky and alien to me. I swallow again as Jilly moves closer, her smile wide, tears in her eyes and I say out loud, 'I didn't let the Beep Beeps get me down, Jilly. I didn't ever let the Beep Beeps win.'

Chapter 60

Eight Weeks Later

Nikki, dressed in her best "going out" rags, slouched with her feet up on her desk and massaged her temples with her eyes closed. Evidence was still coming in from Flower Top house and it had taken its toll on the entire team. Although no longer in the throes of morning sickness, Farah carried a gaunt look with her. Liam had lost some of his bounciness and Sajid veered between slamming his hand on the table and taking himself off for walks round the block to cope with the horrific details that were emerging on a regular basis.

Although Superintendent Rawdon had been cleared of any involvement in the child trafficking ring operated from Flower Top, he had been censured for his actions and had opted to retire before he was forced out. At first it had annoyed Nikki that he'd been allowed to sidestep the bullet, but other things preoccupied her. Despite Chief Superintendent Lyons's attempts to pass all blame for the organisation on to the deceased Ged Geraghty and Ashleigh Kholi, otherwise known as Auntie Lee-Lee, forensic technology experts had been able to link him conclusively with the ring. Besides which, the list of "clients" provided by Marnie Ford – courtesy of Winnie Salinger – had made it easier to find chinks in his armour. He was going to go down for a lengthy prison sentence.

As for the clients named on Gwen's paper – it hadn't been an exhaustive list. However, the ongoing evidence gathering at the site was providing more details and upwards of forty men and thirteen women had been arrested for abuse of the children and participating in child trafficking. Eight men with conclusive evidence documenting their abuse of the children had died in the interim and one had taken his own life, presumably aware that he would be exposed. The list would grow, Nikki was convinced, and she would see that every one of them was exposed, prosecuted and imprisoned. Of the twelve children's remains found so far in the Flower Top gardens, eleven had been identified. There was still so much work to do, but Nikki was persistent and her team were committed. Everyone involved would have their comeuppance.

Little glimmers of light emerged from the darkness. Peggy Marks had been released and had been spending a lot of time with Marnie Ford, their shared experiences uniting them in their determination to be strong for the other victims – some of whom were struggling to cope. Marnie had refound her voice, and although she had told Farah she had her dark days, her sister Jilly was a constant source of comfort, whilst Jilly proclaimed that Marnie's bravery was her inspiration as she entered her final year of law. Karen Salinger had emigrated to be with her aunt's family in Canada, although she was determined to come back for the various trials.

Footsteps alerted Nikki to the fact she had company and, when Marcus's arms went around her, hugging her tight to his chest, she felt some of the tension leave her body. With Marcus by her side she could do this and, more importantly, she could guide her team through this.

'We're going to be late, if we don't leave now.'

Nikki opened one eye. 'I organised the damn thing, surely I don't have to be there too, do I?'

Marcus laughed. 'Actually, Ruby and Charlie organised most of it and yes, you do need to be there. You're the best woman.'

Nikki grinned and got to her feet. 'Okay, okay, but he better bloody like it.'

Marcus just rolled his eyes and taking her hand led her out of Trafalgar House and down to his car, where the rest of the Parekh clan waited.

Chapter 61

'I'm not sure about this, you know. Not sure at all. I mean did any of you even think to ask if he got seasick? I mean, I reckon Langley will be all right, but Saj? He's a bit of a wuss.'

'Muum, we're not even on the sea.' Sunni rolled his eyes at Isaac who responded in kind.

'All, I'm saying is, it feels a bit wobbly to me.'

Marcus nudged her forwards with his hips. 'Just get on the damn barge, Nik. We're the last to arrive and I need to let Liam know he can blindfold them and bring them in.'

Nikki boarded the barge – which was one of the biggest she'd seen. It had been specifically refitted as a "party" barge and now she was inside, she saw just how spacious it was. The curries – brought in from the Aagrah, in heated containers – lined a table at one end, whilst another table was filled with a variety of alcoholic and non-alcoholic drinks. Around the edges of an adequately sized dance floor were tables filled with forty or so smiling faces. Archie was there, Ali and Jane, Langley's parents and his siblings, Sajid's cousins, Zain and Anika with Haqib, and many of their work friends.

When Nikki had overheard a whispered discussion between Langley and Sajid agreeing to just get married at Bradford Town

Hall on the quiet, an idea had formed in her mind. The Salinger case had got to Saj and all he wanted to do was marry Langley. It was as if he realised life was too short for faffing about with inconsequential details and that the most important person in his life was Langley. So, they'd gone ahead with their plans and Nikki, despite knowing that she'd been given a get-out clause from organising the stag do, had gone ahead with hers – with the help of her family, of course.

Clapping her hands together, Nikki absorbed the beautifully understated yet perfectly designed party decor. She turned to Ruby. 'Bloody hell, Ruby, this is brilliant. You are a genius.' And she grabbed her daughter and kissed her on both cheeks before she could object. 'And you're sure they don't suspect anything?'

Scrubbing her cheeks, to get rid of her mum's lipstick, Ruby shook her head and, reassured, Nikki turned again to marvel at her daughter's skill. She'd opted for Sajid's favourite colour – turquoise – for the main theme. The delicate colour was echoed in the napkins – silk she noted – the flowers in the centre of each table, the heart-shaped balloons that read *Congratulations Langley & Sajid*, the streamers that hung from the ceilings and the icing on the wedding cake that sat next to the food. Twinkling lights that changed between gold and turquoise flashed from glass jars that stood behind each flower posy. Sajid would love it!

'Right, they're coming. Lights out, poppers in hand and complete quiet.' Charlie's voice brooked no argument.

Seconds later, Sajid – wearing his favourite turquoise suit with matching tie and moaning at being waylaid so unceremoniously from the registry office – stumbled into the barge, hand in hand with Langley. As Liam and Farah whipped their masks off, poppers popped and "White Wedding" played from the concealed speakers, and Sajid and Langley looked round in wonderment.

Well – Sajid did – Langley winked at Nikki and mouthed "Thank you" through the chaos of all the guests crowding the happy couple.

Later, curry eaten, first dance complete and cake cut and scoffed – mainly by Sunni and Isaac – Marcus clapped his hands and called for order. 'Speech time. Can the best woman come up?'

Nikki flashed Marcus a horrified glance. Nobody had warned her about doing a speech and ow, here she was being landed in it by her own damn partner. As the resounding chant of *speech, speech, speech* built up momentum, Nikki knew she had no choice. So, she grabbed her champagne glass, walked to the DJ and stood and whispered in his ear, before turning to the happy couple. Raising her glass, she blinked away a tear from her eye – must be dusty in here – and smiled at them. 'Sajid and Langley, you are my friends, my confidants and a huge inspiration to me. Sajid, you make me a better person, but I'm sorry to say, I just haven't got a speech for you. All I can say is I love you both and this is my hope for your future.'

She nodded to the DJ who grinned and as the first strains of Dire Straits "Walk of Life" filtered into the room, she lifted her glass and said, 'To Sajid and Langley.'

A Letter from Liz Mistry

Thank you so much for choosing to read *End Game*. I hope you enjoyed it! If you did and would like to be the first to know about my new releases, you can sign up to my mailing list here: https://signup.harpercollins.co.uk/join/signup-hq-lizmistry

End Game is one of those novels that came about because of a discussion I had with author Ayisha Malik at Bradford Literature Festival about the power of silence as a form of protest, self-preservation and more.

This idea struck a chord with me, particularly in current times when so many people seem to feel their voices remain unheard and, as a crime writer, I developed a storyline where silence for one character became their form of protest and their coping mechanism through the darkest of days.

But *End Game* was about much more than silence. It's also about how people of all ages can support and help each other and how the term 'family' has such a wider meaning than mere genetics. The strength my characters, and Nikki in particular, find from their friends even when their families fall short of the mark is formidable. In *End Game* Nikki's close relationship with her work, her friends and her own family comes into play and I think shows Nikki in her best light. Over the six books in the series, Nikki has grown and developed as a character and has given me so much enjoyment. I hope you, the reader, feels the same.

If you enjoyed *End Game*, why not delve into one of my other books.

Also, one of the best gifts a reader can give an author is a review on Good reads or Amazon and I would appreciate it greatly if you'd consider doing this. Alternatively recommend my books to friends and family, or talk about them on social media. As you can imagine, writing can be a lonely profession and to receive feedback on my work truly makes my heart sing.

I appreciate you taking the time to read End Game and hope you enjoyed reading it as much as I enjoyed writing it.

Thanks,

Liz Mistry
x

Twitter: @LizMistryAuthor
Website: lizmistry.com
Facebook: https://www.facebook.com/LizMistrybooks

Last Request

When human remains are discovered under Bradford's
derelict Odeon car park, DS Nikita Parekh and her team
are immediately called to the scene.
Distracted by keeping her young nephew out of trouble,
Nikki is relieved when the investigation is transferred to the
Cold Case Unit, and she can finally focus on her family.

But after the identity of the victim is revealed,
she's soon drawn back into the case. The dead man
is a direct link to her painful past.

As the body count begins to rise, Nikki must do
everything she can to stop the killer in their tracks
before anyone else gets hurt – even if it means digging
up secrets she had long kept hidden . . .

Broken Silence

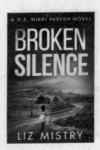

**When Detective Felicity Springer is reported missing,
the countdown to find her begins . . .**

On her way home from a police training conference, Felicity
notices something odd about the white van in front of her.
A hand has punched through the car's rear light and is
frantically waving, trying to catch her attention.
Felicity dials 999 and calls it in. But whilst on the phone,
she loses control of the car on the icy road, crashing
straight into the vehicle ahead.
Pinned in the seat and unable to move, cold air suddenly
hits her face. Someone has opened the passenger door . . .
and they have a gun.
With Felicity missing and no knowledge of whether
she is dead or alive, DS Nikki Parekh and DC Sajid Malik
race to find their friend and colleague.
But Felicity was harbouring a terrible secret, and with
her life now hanging in the balance, Nikki can only hope
that someone will come forward and break the silence . . .

Dark Memories

THREE LETTERS. THREE MURDERS.
THE CLOCK IS TICKING . . .

When the body of a homeless woman is found under
Bradford's railway arches, DS Nikki Parekh and her trusty
partner DC Sajid Malik are on the case.
With little evidence, it's impossible to make a breakthrough,
and when Nikki receives a newspaper clipping taunting her
about her lack of progress in catching the killer, she wonders if
she has a personal link to the case.
When another seemingly unrelated body is discovered, Nikki
receives another note. Someone is clearly trying to send her
clues . . . but who?
And then a third body is found.
This time on Nikki's old street, opposite the house she used to
live in as a child. And there's another message . . . underneath
the victim's body.
With nothing but the notes to connect the murders, Nikki
must revisit the traumatic events of her childhood to work out
her connection to the investigation.
But some memories are best left forgotten, and it's going to
take all Nikki's inner strength to catch the killer . . .
Before they strike again.

Acknowledgements

Progressing that germ of an idea that starts off a book right through all the stages which ultimately result in the end project of a finished novel, complete with amazing cover, carefully edited prose, publicity and more is the work of a family all working towards a singular end goal; to get the book out to you the reader. HQ has an amazing family of supportive colleagues, most of whom I haven't met in person, yet they work so very hard behind the scenes to make the process as smooth and painless as possible. Thanks to everyone at HQ!

My first thanks must go to the amazing Belinda Toor who saw something in Nikki right from the get go and has backed her through these six books. Belinda is a dream to work with – so supportive, so skilled at getting the best from me (and Nikki) and whipping my initial efforts into tip top shape. She is moving on in a secondment for a year and already I miss her.

Besides Belinda though there is a huge team at HQ who work avidly and I'd like to take this opportunity to give them a shout out. Audrey Linton makes the entire process, from the edits to proof copies, to interfacing with ARC readers and so much more effortless – thanks Aud!

My copy-editor Helena Newton has a keen eye for detail and

keeps me on point when I go off on flights of fancy – thanks so much. My beautiful book cover is thanks to the wonderful Anna Sikorska, who never ceases to amaze me. Just when I think the covers can't get any better, they up the stakes.

I have a wonderful team of BETA readers whose excellent attention to detail and guidance really helps make the book be the best it possibly can. Thanks to Maureen Webb, Alyson Read, Lynda Checkley and Carrie Wakelin. My ARC readers are also brilliant but too many to mention here. The biggest thanks though, has to go to you, the reader who takes the time to read my books. There would be no point to my writing without you to entertain and I truly appreciate your support. Thanks so much!

Dear Reader,

We hope you enjoyed reading this book. If you did, we'd be so appreciative if you left a review. It really helps us and the author to bring more books like this to you.

Here at HQ Digital we are dedicated to publishing fiction that will keep you turning the pages into the early hours. Don't want to miss a thing? To find out more about our books, promotions, discover exclusive content and enter competitions you can keep in touch in the following ways:

JOIN OUR COMMUNITY:

Sign up to our new email newsletter:
http://smarturl.it/SignUpHQ

Read our new blog www.hqstories.co.uk

: https://twitter.com/HQStories

: www.facebook.com/HQStories

BUDDING WRITER?

We're also looking for authors to join the HQ Digital family!
Find out more here:

https://www.hqstories.co.uk/want-to-write-for-us/

Thanks for reading, from the HQ Digital team